THE IRISH TEMPEST

Elizabeth J. Sparrow

The Irish Tempest
Copyright 2016 by Elizabeth J. Sparrow
The Library of Congress Cataloging-in-Publication Data is available upon request
2016911683
ISBN 978-0-9976851-1-4
First Edition: November, 2016
Printed in the United States of America

158-18 Riverside Drive West #5N
New York, NY 10032
thewaxinggibbouspress@gmail.com

<u>Acknowledgements</u>

Copy Editor: Laura Lavington
Cover Art and Interior Images: Laura Duffy
Interior layout and design: Polgarus Studio

In beloved memory of
D.M., T.W. and P.D. -
ever tall in the saddle

"I see by my outfit what I am a cowboy.
I see by my outfit what I'm a cowboy, too
We see by our outfits that we are both cowboys;
If you had an outfit, you could be a cowboy, too."
—Peter S. Beagle

Contents

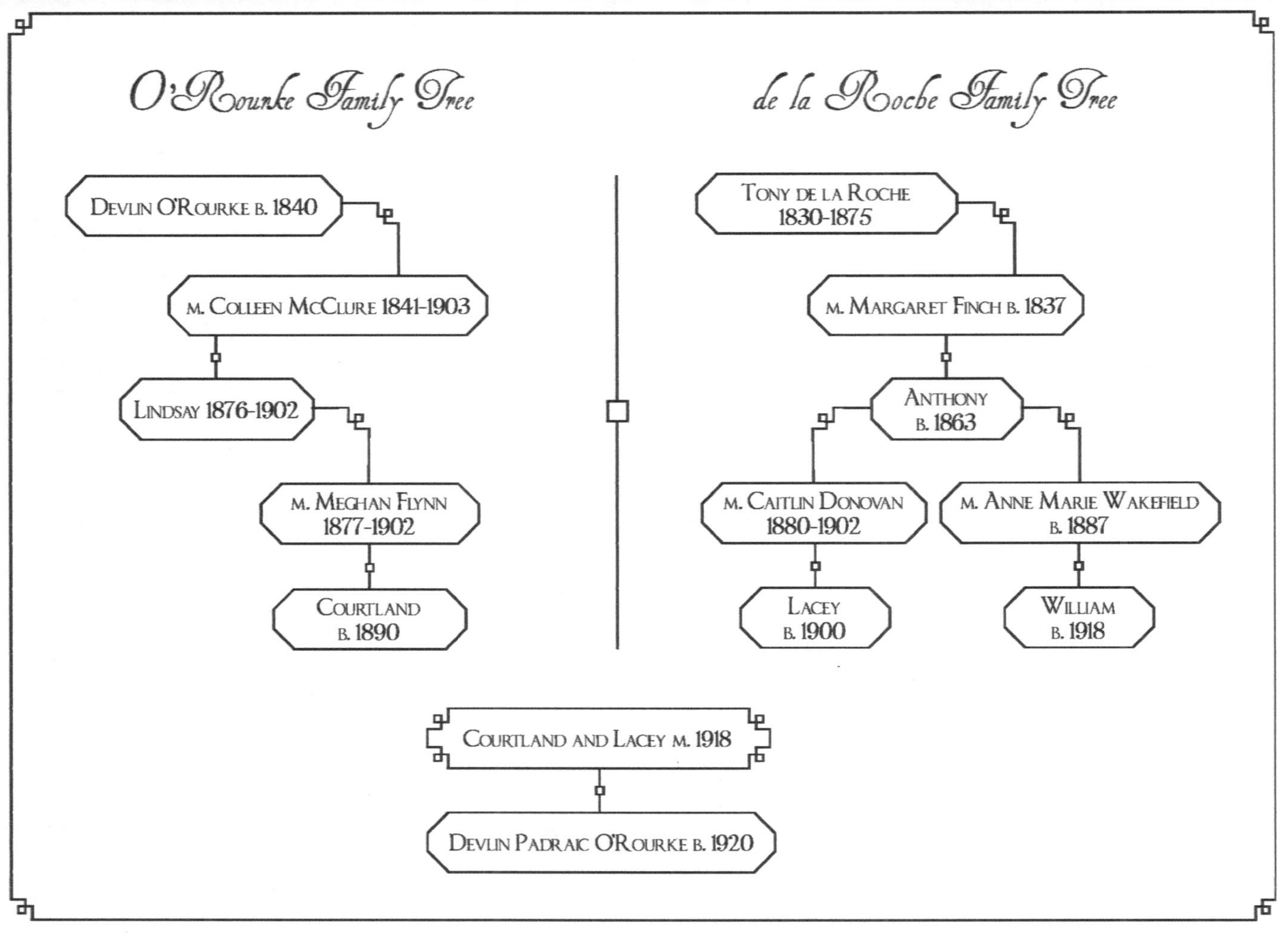

O'Rourke Family Tree

Devlin O'Rourke B. 1840
M. Colleen McClure 1841-1903
Lindsay 1876-1902
M. Meghan Flynn 1877-1902
Courtland B. 1890

de la Roche Family Tree

Tony de la Roche 1830-1875
M. Margaret Finch B. 1837
Anthony B. 1863
M. Caitlin Donovan 1880-1902
Lacey B. 1900
M. Anne Marie Wakefield B. 1887
William B. 1918

Courtland and Lacey M. 1918
Devlin Padraic O'Rourke B. 1920

Part I

"The Four Seasons"
1911-1912

Spring

There is an inevitable forgetfulness that comes with inheriting a privileged albeit circumscribed life. When there is wealth and abundant resources to pass on to the next generation, one may forget that those ancestral woes—the devastation of blight and famine, the theft of birthright and property, the debasement of language and culture—still may claim a person, in the here and now of one's very indulgent existence.

This particular life belongs to Courtland O'Rourke, a pretty young man of twenty-one, Irish Catholic in the truest sense with not a hint of Protestantism in his bloodline. The Norman and Scottish bits have been subsumed by the last one hundred years of vigorous Irish procreation. In the full bloom of youthful pomposity, he is returning to the provincialism of southern Ireland after a riotous month in London.

"Would you be good enough to leave them against the wall, out of harm's way?" Court directed the sweating porter with a flourish of his walking stick, a fashionable affectation acquired in London. "My man seems to be delayed." He offered this with a resigned shrug, for after all, this was Ireland.

"To be sure, sir," gasped the porter as the last trunk thudded against the peeling wall.

A few strides around the stationmaster's bungalow confirmed to Court that Lafferty was nowhere in sight and that he was quite alone among the bursting daffodils and dusty sparrows of Cloonsheelin. This first warm day of April had cast an enervating spell over the normally peripatetic townsfolk. What a sorry homecoming after the exuberant din and vulgar delights of city life. Spirits lagging well behind him, he set off for Sully's tavern, pausing to observe a panting mongrel have a go at McCarthy's prized Irish terrier bitch.

"They'll be a nice bit of fussing over this," he called out to the writhing dogs.

Such hasty coupling kindled a wistful recollection of the women he had frolicked with in London. These sirens of wit and charm were so unlike the feckless girls he readily sported with in Cloonsheelin. The country rake, with gray eyes and unfashionably long black curls, immediately became the object of bold intentions after a discreet introduction by a conspiring acquaintance. Lured into escorting them to the races, tea parties, and shopping forays, he learned that daytime was the ideal time for romantic adventuring.

Distracted by this memory of scented bosoms and velvet thighs, Court wandered into a pack of jeering children, two of whom wrestled furiously in the dirt. His dismay turned to alarm when he saw thirteen-year-old Padraic Knox leaping with idiotic glee around the combatants. One wave of his walking stick scattered most of them into the shelter of the woods. Court seized the apparent victor by the scruff while sneering down upon the loser.

"What a sight you are to behold, Sholto Gallagher! Flat on your back—kicking like a squalling babe in a wet nappy! Be off before I give you a few more lumps to blubber about."

The squirming victor attempted a final kick to Sholto's fleeing backside but was deterred by Court's grip.

"What's this set-to about? And mind, none of your lies or you'll be feeling the back of my hand." Court demanded of the now subdued Padraic.

"Don't be blaming Padraic! They started it!"

"Go on then." He released his captive. "And I want the truth first time round. None of your shillyshallying."

"We were off to Mrs. Conway's for tea when they began ragging on us, for no reason at all."

"You mean ragging on Paddy here! That godforsaken bunch doesn't have the brass to mix it up with you. They'd not be wanting the bloody US cavalry on their backs!"

"But Court," came the all-too-familiar whine, "they're always ragging on him."

"Don't you think it's a mighty queer thing to have this wisp of a girl do your fighting for you?" he asked Padraic with pitiless sarcasm.

"Oh, I don't mind at all, Master Court. Lacey's not afeared of anyone."

"Isn't she now? You know what I think, Padraic Knox? You've been smacked in the head a wee bit too often! As for you, miss…"

Both of her braids hung loose, and dirt and blood smeared her face, while the right sleeve of her shirt flapped in the breeze. It was Court's shirt, a hand-me-down, as most of her wardrobe seemed to be these days. She was even wearing a pair of his old riding breeches with a strip of burlap to keep them from falling to her knees!

"You shameless savages are coming with me!" Court snatched their hands and Lacey struggled to keep up with his long legs. "You'll be a lovely sight to greet your father with that black eye, my lamb!"

Perched on the table in Mrs. Conway's kitchen, Lacey twitched under her ministrations while Padraic slurped tea and nibbled on a potato pancake.

"To think, during my entire stay in London, I did not witness a single display of brawling! Only to return and find you hammering away at a brute of a boy, like you were born to the underclass! How many times must you be told? Young ladies of breeding do not engage in fisticuffs with common thugs!"

"Pish! I'm not a lady. I'm only eleven."

"Don't be impertinent!" Court hovered by Mrs. Conway's elbow. "Shouldn't she be getting a stitch or two for that?" His finger brushed away a lock of auburn hair from the jagged cut above her left eye.

"Ah, don't be fretting so, Master Court. This here looks worse than it 'tis. Not deep, just messy. Bridget, fetch me the iodine and a bit of plaster."

Eighteen-year-old Bridget Knox slunk away but not before cuffing her brother and inspiring Lacey to make some mischief. She was familiar with the rumors about Court and his sporting ways with Bridget and her ilk.

"What did you bring me?" Lacey asked as her prying hands fished through his pockets.

He bent close with a teasing smile. "Not that you're deserving of my consideration. But if you were, and I happened to remember, it would be a might too big for my pocket, lamb."

"Then who is this for?" She waved a gold necklace for all to see.

"You're a thieving brat in need of a good seat warming."

Court saw the rapt look of curiosity on both women's faces. "No mystery, ladies. Just a trinket for Aggie. She's been stuck with grandfather all this time, and you know what a bear he can be."

By six o'clock, Lafferty had collected Court's trunks and tracked him down at Mrs. Conway's.

"Will we be stopping at Durbin House, sir?"

"No. Go straight on to Torrey Castle. Miss Lacey is to be our guest."

When she began to protest, he hissed, "You're under lock and key till your father returns from Dublin."

"How do you know where he is?"

"I happened to have had supper with the captain night before last. He made a point of asking me to check on you—with good cause, I might add."

Lacey sank back, her despair and pain welling into a single sob.

"What's this?"

"I want to go home! I'll not get into any more trouble."

"If I thought you'd be properly looked after, I would! Old McTeague is too worn out to muster the strength to leash you. Indeed, you should be packed off to boarding school and taught to behave."

This was not what she wanted to hear, least of all from someone who had spent the better part of his adolescence in disgrace, thanks to a hefty number of transgressions. She moved to the opposite side of the carriage and curled into a tight ball of woe.

Court's left cheek began to pulse as he squinted at her in exasperation. Was it always to be this way between them? From the first day they had met—

she, a stalwart five-year-old eager to ride and he, the fifteen-year-old reluctant teacher—they had squabbled and sparred with precious few interludes of peace.

"Look here, if you behave yourself for the next few days, you may come with me to Queenstown and meet my latest investment."

"You bought a horse?"

"Aye, she's a lovely little thing. Blacker than the devil's brow with a sweet and steady gait. Grandfather will have a fit, but she was worth every shilling."

"When can I ride her?"

"We'll see," he said, lifting his arm as she eased into the curve of his side. There was something seductive about these rare moments of harmony that made him susceptible to her manipulations.

"Will you unpack my present first, please?" She yawned in his face.

Clasping her mouth closed, he murmured, "Greedy little lamb."

◆

In the rising mist, Torrey Castle appeared to float, a watchful wraith. Oil lamps glowed in a dozen windows strung across the three-bay façade, illuminating the finely etched Venetian glass and elegant corbelled arches. A maze of parks housed a collection of delicate sika deer and black-faced sheep along with cantankerous flocks of grouse and plover. None fared as well as the precious herd of thoroughbreds—allowed to graze at will, foraging in the herb garden and stomping around the rose bushes.

As the carriage passed through the castle's iron gates, the imposing front doors opened, and Court's grandfather, Devlin O'Rourke, limped down the steps. Aggie Knox, housekeeper and mother figure to Court and Lacey, chased after Devlin, threatening him with a wool shawl.

"Will you leave me be, woman! I'm no invalid." With a leonine head of white hair and a wiry body, he looked quite spry for seventy-one.

"Three whole days in bed with a nasty head cold and meself, waiting on your every pitiful need. I'll not go through that again, old man!"

"Hullo folks! I'm not alone, and this may give you a bit of a turn," said Court.

"Who did this to her?" Devlin roared, clasping his grandson's arm to steady himself, as a battered Lacey stood before them. "I'll whip the cur from now to Michaelmas."

"Settle down, Grandfather, and let me explain! And mind, no petting from you, Aggie. She's on punishment."

"Is that so? You ought to be ashamed of yourself, treating her like a brick-face criminal."

"By Judas, she took it upon herself to defend the cowardly carcass of your feeble-minded nephew!"

Court briskly herded them into the front hall, but Lacey, eager to ride this tide of sympathy, finally spoke. "Aggie, my head is thumping. May I have a tray in bed?"

"Of course, my angel. Cook made a lovely lamb roast with glazed yams and a nice tureen of creamed turnips—all for Court's homecoming. There's even a rhubarb cobbler!"

"Ah, there'll be none of that for her, thank you very much. She is being punished," Court reminded them with a wagging finger. "Bread and milk 'tis good enough."

Lacey lingered on the stairs. "But what am I to wear to bed?"

"Seeing you're so partial to my clothes, Aggie will give you one of my dress shirts. Off you go!"

"But what about my present? You promised."

"Don't be shining them doe eyes on me, all teary and supplicating! You'll get it when I decide and not a moment before."

Court turned away, only to run into Devlin's dark frown. "If I didn't know better, I'd be of the mind you were the blackguard who beat her."

By the time the brandy was poured and the cigars lit, Devlin's mood had improved and Aggie was back to fussing over Court.

Placing an ashtray by his glass, she kissed his cheek. "'Tis lovely to have you home, darlin' boy. I can't wait to wear the necklace to Mass. Them old hens will be speechless with jealousy."

Time had not diminished Aggie's inviolate sense of superiority over others.

Even at sixty, she attracted suitors who appeared with shuffling expectancy to woo the "green-eyed goddess"—so named, not only for her preternatural comeliness, but for the winsome cruelty with which she spurned all of them.

"Then I chose well," he laughed, feeling the sweet heat of the liquor relaxing his body into a sentimental stupor.

"Not another can compare with it!" She snatched the cigar from Devlin's mouth. "Enough! You know smoking bedevils your lungs."

"The only thing bedeviling me is an old biddy of a housekeeper who doesn't know her place!"

"As if there's another willing to put up with your vile habits and blistering tongue?"

"It's good to be home," Court sighed, floating away on a cloud of contentment before remembering his affliction. "Aggie, darling, when you have a moment to spare, give a look in on Lacey."

"I was intending to do that very thing, when himself, started up with me. And for your own good, young man, I had Katie unpack the music box. It would be a most pleasant way to start off the morning."

"You're right, as always," Court agreed.

As soon as she left, Devlin lit another cigar in defiance, puffing away and rubbing the gold signet ring on the middle finger of his right hand. His once shapely hands were plagued with arthritis, and the ring was welded in place.

"How did you find London, my boy?"

His grandfather may have delivered the first broadside, but Court was poised for the return volley. "I thank you for inquiring—quite delicious."

"So you wasted your time between a woman's legs?"

"Grandfather, you can hardly send me to such a place and not expect me to break one or two… well, a few of the commandments."

"Might I remind you, why the devil you were there? To learn something about managing money, you ungrateful wastrel! Your father went to university and matriculated with honors! In just a few years, you'll be coming into your inheritance not having an imbecile's notion what to do with it!"

"Thanks to the devious Mr. Boyle, I'll be getting a miserable quarter of it."

"Don't be blaming the solicitor for minding my instructions! 'Tis a Midas fortune compared to what I had when I married your grandmother. How dare you turn up your nose at what you have the insolence to think is just a pittance!"

Devlin gripped the table, wheezing from the effort of shouting. "You'll get another quarter when you marry and the rest when you have a child. Those are my terms!"

"I'm no better off than one of your prize studs! Only as good as my seed."

"Mind where you spill it! The only whelp that matters is the one baptized an O'Rourke."

"Then pick the mare, old man, and tell me when to show up!"

Devlin rose from the table, his blue eyes violet in the candlelight. "So we've come to this dismal reckoning, have we? Though you may think otherwise, I have but one wish for you! To be so blessed by a woman's love, she bears you a child: someone to cherish you in your old age."

Court helped himself to another brandy, rankled by Devlin's unwelcome sanctimony. So what if he never was anything more than a wastrel? Prospects for marriage were sparse: most of the good families had arranged their daughters' betrothals before their first communion.

Turning his thoughts to where he felt some measure of control, he decided to send for Dr. Seacord in the morning, just to make sure there was nothing truly amiss with Lacey. When her father, Captain de la Roche, returned, he intended to put forth his argument, yet again, for boarding school—or better yet, a convent! Any place that would contain her and prevent her from involving him in her little messes.

Summer

Social norms regarding children are prey to climate changes, industrial inventions, plagues, and parenting skills. What is considered precious and innocent in one century is another's cheap labor. What remains constant is this: an egocentric creature, standing small but powerful and almost always in the way. How that child is shaped into a socially agreeable being is the essence of civilization.

Less seismic in scope is the civilizing of Lacey de la Roche. She is a motherless child who knows not what she has lost, only what she has—a smitten father and little more than eleven years of blissful and pampered childhood. There is no doubt she will become a woman as beautiful and contrary as her dead mother, but for now, she is a child looking forward to a summer's day.

A pillow covered Lacey's face, sparing her from the early morning light and allowing her to slumber on. With a sudden jolt, she remembered it was Saturday at last, the day of the regatta on Lough Phair! She savored all the lovely things to look forward to. First and best of all, she would be with her father. Second, Padraic finally would have time to play with her, something that rarely happened during the summer months. As the only boy in the Knox family, he was sent off to tend cattle and a scraggly bunch of Norfolk sheep in the hills. And third, Mrs. McTeague promised to make her delicious salmon paste sandwiches and pink lemonade. The old hag was good for something.

Yet Lacey had to consider the following as well: she would have to wear a dress, a dreadful affliction, she was forbidden to swim with Padraic and the others, a silly social restriction, and Court was to be master of ceremonies, making him all the more insufferable.

She stretched her legs to see if she had grown lately. Her toes did look farther away, and her slender arms rose closer to the canopy. Did all her parts grow at the same time? That would be a good question to ask Father Ryan. He liked when she asked scientific-type questions during her lessons with him. Ever since Mrs. Donner took ill and returned to Mallow, Lacey had been tutored at the rectory, under the wavering attention and circumspect teaching skills of the parish priest.

It would be much more to her liking to attend Mrs. Tobin's cozy one room school, by St. Peter's Crossing, with Padraic and the other children, but her father had deemed this as "unsuitable." Lacey believed that if they learned together, she could help Padraic over the hard parts. Rather than pursue this with her usual tenacity, she relented, lest her father remember the boarding school idea, which others were so free to pester him about—filthy troublemakers, all of them!

Lacey bounced from her bed and crept across the hall to her father's bedroom. He lay in majestic disarray, snoring much too peacefully for her purposes. She stood on tiptoe, inhaling the masculine scent of lavender water and pipe tobacco. This was the one place where the two of them engaged in intimate conversations, whispering, so as not to provoke Mrs. McTeague's Calvinist sense of propriety.

Captain Anthony de la Roche, a forty-eight-year-old American cavalry officer, had married an Irish noblewoman, Caitlin Shannon. When she died in childbirth along with her son, the locals assumed the distraught widower would sell off Durbin House and return to the States with his four-year-old daughter. But he found Cloonsheelin conducive to raising a motherless child and Devlin O'Rourke quite congenial as a business partner.

Anthony snorted and rolled onto his side, one muscular arm draped over his eyes as Lacey watched him sleep, admiring the way his fine blonde hair, whitened by the sun, set off the humorous set of his mouth and the defiant thrust of his chin. She held her pale hand to his cheek, comparing how much darker he was from his years on the western plains. Surely, there was no one more handsome, smarter, or braver than her father?

The room faced west and despite the summer's warmth, held a chill and hint of dampness. As Lacey shivered in her light nightdress, he growled, "get under" and she gladly curled against his chest, matching her breathing to his. They laid together, his heart beating in her ear, his body warm and solid.

"Good Lord, your feet are like icicles! And where's my coffee? You come to wake me empty-handed, pet?"

"It's too early," she said, enraptured to have him all to herself. "Daddy, might we go fishing tomorrow? Court knows a place on Livvy's Pond where there are lovely, brown trout—really big ones!"

He pondered her request. "Can we not enjoy our today?"

"Pish! We know what we're doing today. We must prepare for tomorrow. Mrs. McTeague has to pack a picnic, you need to pay Padraic to dig worms, and the line on my reel needs mending."

"Stop! Today we sail, tomorrow we fish, and come Monday, you must practice the piano."

"For how long?" she asked, rubbing the stubble on his chin.

He brought her hand to his lips. "I think all morning will be satisfactory, in view of how poorly you play."

"Will you be home?"

"I have an appointment with Devlin, and he's staying for dinner. You may join us if you behave properly."

"Very well!"

"That was too bloodless a negotiation. What are you up to?"

Lacey wiggled closer and laughed, "My playing will drive you mad—you won't be able to stand it for more than an hour."

"You're too damn cunning for your own good, Lacey! We'll be conducting our business in the stables, so play as badly as you like, as long as you don't stop!"

Lacey's look of surprise greeted Mrs. McTeague as she lumbered into the room, dressed in her best black silk dress. Her doughy complexion bore the mark of the rouge pot on her cheeks and lips; her obstinately pious nature afforded her this touch of vanity on very special occasions.

"Good morning, Captain." Her usual hint of disapproval hung between them as she set down the breakfast tray. "You belong in your own bed, miss. Sophie's fetching your tray."

As the housekeeper bustled about the room, pulling open the thick gold drapes and retrieving articles of clothing, Lacey knelt up and stuck her tongue out.

"I'm having coffee with Daddy!"

Mrs. McTeague looked to Anthony for support, but he waffled. "It's rather a special day." He winced and then made his second bargain of the morning. "I promise, just a few sips and she's all yours."

Lacey intercepted his raised cup and drank half of it. "It needs more sugar." She smiled with malicious satisfaction as the defeated woman slammed the door behind her.

"You're to be more respectful, young lady! Do you know how hard it would be to replace her?"

"Daddy, I wonder if Allesandro the magician will be there? Remember those beautiful white doves he pulled from his hat? How does he fit all of them in there? How do they breathe?"

Sophie, another one of Padraic's sisters, was recruited to dress Lacey. The sixteen-year-old was the bearer of news, good, bad or scandalous, and the only one in the household who treated Lacey as a peer and confidant. It was from the perpetually shocked lips of Sophie that she heard of Court's many escapades—romantic, illegal, or sacrilegious.

"The captain certainly spares no expense for you," she noted wistfully, admiring the spread of fine cloth and French workmanship on the bed.

There were several petticoats, a pair of bloomers, a chemise and vest, stockings, and a hand-embroidered cambric and lace dress. A straw hat with periwinkle ribbons and a pair of crocheted gloves lay on a slipper chair. Lacey grimaced at the many layers of clothing she was forced to wear, simply because of her misfortune to be born female. She bargained with the easily distracted Sophie to wear but one petticoat and the chemise, without the vest.

"Old McTeague will have me hide if she finds out," Sophie fretted, brushing Lacey's mass of curls into temporary sleekness. She used a white satin ribbon to keep the hair off her face and stood back to admire the effect.

"Why, you're the very picture of perfection, Miss Lacey! Looking so much like your dearest ma. She was quite the beauty."

Except for the massive portrait of Caitlin in the drawing room, there was little to remind her of her mother. Once a year, father and daughter brought massive bouquets to the grave. It was a ritual she loathed, for it meant a resurgence of Anthony's grief. She couldn't bear the desolation in his eyes and the ragged quiver in his voice as he prayed. The dead were dead, she reasoned with childish callousness, and life was too glorious to squander on those beyond temporal moorings.

Between a limestone cliff and a string of heather brushed hills, a radiant Lough Phair shimmered in the cloying heat of July. As Anthony steered his Rolls Royce Silver Ghost, the only one of its kind in southern Ireland, the haunting sounds of bagpipes sharpened Lacey's anticipation. Soon the bold green and white stripes of the marquee came into view, and clusters of townsfolk thickened into a noisy wedge of revelers.

"I'm not about to fight this crowd," Anthony said, parking under a trio of silver birches. "Are you up to walking?"

"Oh yes! We'll see more."

He whistled at some boys lounging nearby and enlisted them to carry the hampers and blankets to the viewing stand. Lacey nearly swooned from the exhilarating chaos as she pointed out a fleet of colorful skiffs, bobbing on the west shore of the lake. Black-headed gulls and puffy coots swarmed along the route to the pavilion, fighting over scraps of food dropped by the harried vendors. Most of the stalls were in business for the day's events, with luscious displays of pies, cookies, and iced cakes, bushels of fresh-picked fruits and vegetables, tin pails of wild flowers, and hand-painted pots of geraniums. A few of the more enterprising women of Cloonsheelin sold fanciful quilts and whimsically embroidered table linens.

Lacey's favorites were the hand-carved figures of mythical creatures: the griffin, selkie, and best of all, the unicorn. She carried no pocket money but knew her father would buy anything she fancied, and for this reason, she rarely asked. It was better to wait and ask for really important things, like a new saddle or fishing reel. There was always Court, who could be so easily beguiled into indulging her with a trifle.

Anthony was the first to pick Devlin from the crowd as the old man hobbled toward them, his right hand on Padraic's shoulder, and a stout blackthorn cane in the other. With his mane of snowy hair and old-fashioned frock coat, he cut a rather eccentric figure.

"Devlin, you old faker! Since when do you need an extra pair of legs to get around?"

"I must confess, my dear captain, this rheumatism of mine is giving me a few twinges. I'm not as steady on my feet as I once was!"

He paused to take a deep breath, wiping the perspiration from his face with a yellowed handkerchief. "Has all the makings of a blazing day. I, for one, will be glad to leave the hosting duties to my rake of a grandson. My dear child, let me have a proper look at you. You're a vision of spun sugar and Devon crème!"

"Thank you," Lacey responded politely, giving Padraic their secret look. Her impatience was not lost on the old man, who accommodated her.

"Captain, I need a few minutes of your time. Our South African investments may be in jeopardy, if what I read in the London Times comes to pass."

Before Lacey could escape, Anthony steered her to the edge of the marquee. "Do you see where the sun is now?" He pointed to the eastern shore of the lake. "In one hour, it will be shining from behind the viewing stand, and I want you there—neat and tidy."

The two children lay on their stomachs, dangling wisteria vines from a ledge in one of several inlets along the lake. An indignant moorhen, hidden in the rushes, squawked at the intrusion.

"She's scaring them off," Padraic whined in frustration as another minnow slipped away.

"Pish! She's just protecting her babies. Damn, I almost got one." Lacey pulled up the vine and adjusted the dripping glove. It was her idea to put the crocheted gloves to better use as little nets.

Kingfishers and dragonflies hummed over the opaque surface, reflecting iridescent sparkles of blue and orange; the syrupy scent of honeysuckle mixed with the rank odor of stagnant water. Lacey's hat hung down her back, her face pink and freckled from the late-morning sun. She flattened herself against the rock, cheek pressed to the warm slate, and tried her luck again. Thus preoccupied, she failed to hear Court ride over on Drummer, his favorite hunter.

"So this is where you've been lurking about! Do you know the time?"

She shielded her eyes to see where the sun was; she had forgotten the time and her father's warning!

"Will you give me a ride to the viewing stand?"

"You'll get there by the power of your two good feet as a lesson in tardiness! And mind, keep that bloody hat on your head or you'll perish from sunstroke!"

Lacey endured her father's crude attempt to smooth her hair with his pocket comb, ears burning from the consequences that awaited her for such forgetfulness. As he fumbled with the ribbon, Mrs. Fitzgerald gracefully intervened with a gentle reproach.

"'Tis a woman's task, Captain de la Roche. Please allow me." She neatly knotted the bow as Lacey sighed a grateful thank you. "I imagine you may have other things in need of a womanly touch, eh?" But Anthony was out of hearing range, much to her consternation.

Mayor Sheehy vainly called for silence but was drowned out by Court's sworn declaration to Mrs. Fitzgerald's twin daughters that he could not bring himself to choose between them as an escort for the race.

"Alas, I must deny my own selfish desires, lest I break one beauty's heart for the other."

This pained Mrs. Fitzgerald, who had tried to engineer a match for the last two years, with no encouragement from Devlin, and less enthusiasm from Court. Lacey considered the twins frightfully stupid in their shared infatuation.

The first row filled with local dignitaries as well as the mayor and Court. Devlin, Anthony, and Lacey sat behind them, facing the throng of people clamoring for the start of the race. Each summer, the landowners sponsored a regatta for tenant farmers, fishermen, servants, tradesmen, and just about anyone who could man a boat, for a princely purse of ten gold sovereigns. It was a paid holiday for the staff of the castles and great houses of Cloonsheelin, and the prevailing mood was jovial, to the point of wantonness, abetted by Sully's beer wagon.

As this year's host, Devlin had donated a case of his best French champagne to toast the winner and to christen the launch of the new mail boat.

"Merciful heaven, I do hope they keep the speeches short," he said, waving an elaborate fan, "I'm too old to suffer the chatter of empty-headed clucks— me own grandson most particularly."

Lacey's attention was centered on Court and his long legs, tucked so tantalizingly under his chair. As she maneuvered to the edge of her seat to deliver a kick of retaliation, he stood up and she slid off. With a quelling look, Anthony raised her up by the collar of her dress and snapped, "You're making a damn spectacle of yourself!"

Padraic was a terrible card player, so Lacey let him win most of the hands, in the hope of lifting his spirits. It pained her to see the exhaustion cloaking him from long days of physical drudgery and constant abuse. His light green eyes ringed with purple shadows seemed too old for his face, and his bony physique was all the more transparent in his worn summer clothes. The two reclined under a lush chestnut tree with an almost empty hamper and the promise of lemon ices, if they stayed put for a few hours. Devlin and Anthony had gone off to Tinker's Hut, supposedly to discuss politics, but more likely to sample some of McCarthy's poitin.

"I thought for sure old Monahan was a goner when his boat turned over," Padraic muttered, trying to concentrate on his cards and not the near disaster. But the lure was irresistible. "It must be a frightful way of dying. Gasping for air like a pike on a hook. Lungs filling up with water."

"Well, you're a good swimmer, you'll never drown."

"Don't make a bit of difference if you get caught in one of them rip tides I heard about. One of Lafferty's cousins was swept away by a monster tide in Bantry Bay. Never found the body."

Lacey needed to change the subject so as not to have nightmares later on. "I haven't seen Bridget about. Did she come today?"

"Aye, likely dogging Master Court."

At that very moment, Court ambled over, somewhat disheveled from a game of road bowling and wearing a long frond of honeysuckle around his neck.

"Padraic, my lovely lad, I need you to run a holy errand for me. Are you up to it?" He threw his jacket over the hamper and poured a fistful of coins into the boy's cupped hands.

"Surely sir."

"I'm feeling dreadfully parched and nothing will do as a pail of Sully's fine beer. Fetch me some and you may have the change to spend on treats for the both of you."

Court stretched out on the blanket. "Be a dear and fan me for a bit," he asked, tossing his hat on her lap.

"You're drunk!"

"I'm not drunk but have drink taken. Now for pity's sake, fan me! I'm feverish from the heat."

"Fan yourself," she fired back and dropped the boater on his face.

"Now lamb," he reasoned from beneath it, "I may have treated you badly earlier, but if the Almighty were keeping score, you'd be way ahead of me in the tormenting game."

Lacey saw Bridget half crouched behind a scrub willow, and even at a distance, her jealousy could burn the shell off an egg. Perhaps, she could exact some revenge after all, and began to fan away.

"You're an angel to let bygones be bygones."

"If you're very thirsty, there's some lemonade left."

He roused himself, exclaiming "Why drink such humble brew when we have the nectar of the gods at our fingertips!"

She remembered the day when she was no more than six, and Court had shown her how to pinch the bottom of the honeysuckle, pull out the wispy filament, and lick the honey clinging to it. He readied the flower and commanded her to open her mouth. Drops fell on her tongue and trickled down her throat; he teased her with his aim, missing her mouth for her nose or cheek.

"Now it's your turn," she said, one eye on Bridget.

Court pillowed his head on her lap. "Fire away and mind you don't miss the target!"

Lacey carefully dribbled the honey on his tongue as he smacked his lips in exaggerated pleasure. Bridget was in full view, shredding strips of willow through her fingers. While he dozed, Lacey decorated his damp black curls with the blossoms. In repose, he resembled a Greek statue with its classic contours. Unlike her father, there were no creases around the mouth or eyes and barely the trace of a beard.

Padraic was intercepted by his infuriated sister who slapped him across the face to get his attention. The only way to break free of her pinching grasp was to nod in agreement.

"Master Court," he lisped, rushing over to deliver brew and missive. "I must tell you something!"

After hearing the whispered message, he clapped the boy on the shoulder and remarked, "How would I manage without you?"

Not looking in Bridget's direction, he shook the blossoms from his hair, caressed Lacey's cheek and chirped, "Good-bye my lamb, I must be off."

Padraic emptied his pockets to reveal a hoard of peppermint sticks, taffy, licorice, and ginger snaps. "And I even have a few pennies left," he said proudly.

Dusk brought a welcome coolness, inspiring the children to explore the outer reaches of the lakeshore. Their prowling found them at an abandoned boat house, and in the quickly fading light, they made their way through the high grass for a closer look. Several yards from its crumbling wall, they halted, as the murmur of voices floated toward them.

"Thems got to be banshees!" Padraic squeaked and crossed himself in protection.

Lacey signaled for silence to hear what was being said, but the voices were no more than a sigh lost on the breeze.

"Let's get closer."

Being a dutiful soldier, he inched along with her through the dusty weeds, until their eyes were level with the wall. Two figures swayed in a crush of desire under the kiss of the full moon. A pendulous breast was lifted to the man's mouth, his touch electrifying the woman who writhed under the probing caress.

"Why, that's Bridget!" Padraic's exclamation triggered panic between the voyeurs and the lovers.

"Run Padraic! Run for your life!" But Lacey did not know where to run, for the light had vanished, as a cloud swallowed the moon. She tripped over a knot of exposed willow roots and lay trembling in the moss and leaves.

"Damn your eyes, I should have known it was you!" Court pulled her up and squeezed her arms until she yelped.

"Spy on me, will you?" He pushed her back down, his face twisted in a venomous grimace that chilled her heart.

Breaking off a willow branch, he struck her arm with full force—once, twice, and a third time—halting when the first of the roman rockets ignited the evening sky.

He fell to his knees and began to cry. "Dear Lord, what have I done?"

Stunned more by his sobbing than his rage, Lacey cried, "It's all my fault—truly it is. It was wrong of me!"

The apology only deepened his remorse as he reached for her hand and saw the swelling red ribbons streaking her arm.

She had never witnessed her father, or any man, so drunk and so distraught. "It doesn't matter! You didn't mean to!"

"Don't be blaming yourself for my bad temper," he said, suddenly calm and steady. "I've had too much to drink and Bridget's been stalking me all the day. I'm ashamed to say, it's led to this. Let me tidy you up some before we find your father. Poor man's probably at his wits' end wondering where the devil you are."

Court brushed the leaves and dirt from her dress, wiped her face with his handkerchief and retied the sash around her waist.

"Dear me, you've lost your ribbon," he murmured, running his fingers through her thicket of curls. "This will have to do." He bent to kiss her forehead, his lips lingering. "You looked like a princess today, and I behaved like a beast. Can you forgive me, lamb?"

"Of course." She reached out to button his shirt but he flinched and pulled her hands away.

"Mind where you step," he cautioned, leading her through the woods and back to Anthony.

Autumn

It was nearing the end of October, and the heavy rains of the previous week had left the ground spongy to the touch, deepening the brilliant spectrum of the changing foliage. As master of the hunt, Court reveled in the virile mayhem, ordering Lafferty to stir up the dogs and cursing the stable boys when they failed to welcome guests dismounting for an outdoor breakfast.

Confined to the dog cart and well covered with blankets, Devlin contributed his share of criticism to the proceedings. "In all of County Cork, 'tis the best you could find?" He shook his fist as Seamus Knox revealed a fur-tattered fox clawing up the side of a cage.

Court, carelessly perched on Drummer, dodged the milling guests and shouted back, "A finer specimen you're not likely to find in all of Ireland. He'll give you a run for your money, old man!"

Devlin stood as he glimpsed Anthony with Lacey in tow. He waved them over, offering a flask of sherry to the captain while beaming at Lacey.

"Let me look at you, child."

It had taken the concerted efforts of Devlin, Aggie, and Lacey to convince Anthony that she was old enough to join the hunt. Devlin went so far as to enlist his tailor's assistance in altering a barely worn riding habit, which had belonged to his dead wife, Colleen.

"My darlin' wife wasn't much of a horsewoman," he had confided to Lacey, "but she turned many a head with her exquisite sense of style."

She dismounted to show off the black wool suit, its skirt altered for riding astride with a snug jacket accenting her developing bust. Sophie had tucked her curls tightly under a matching velvet bowler with a lace veil that gave her a mature allure. Anthony, so delighted with her appearance, had ordered a new pair of black kid boots to complete the ensemble.

The only one unmoved by popular opinion was Court, who thought the men hopelessly daft. "Grandfather, you're sadly besotted with this peacock of a child," he said while his mouth tilted in a grudging smile of admiration.

"You will admit, will you not, that she's the very image of your dearest grandmother?" Devlin leaned back for another sip.

Lacey continued her prancing, sweeping the hem of her skirt along the gravel and taunting Court with a puckish curl of her lip.

"You and the captain know my feelings about letting her ride." He nodded at Anthony, who faintly acknowledged his words as he conversed with Father Ryan. "And you, Miss Fancy Boots!" He aimed his riding crop at her, "Are to stay in the back—out of the way—and pay close attention to my commands. Or else!"

Lacey shrugged, stuck out her tongue, and accepted a plate of sausage and bread from an attentive stable boy.

A sudden blast of the horn signaled the riders to mount, and there was a rush of movement as the horses scrapped the ground with eager hooves. For a short while, Lacey docilely rode alongside Devlin, impressed with his determination to keep up. But the passion of the hunt intoxicated her, and soon she regretted her promise. The high-pitched cries of the hounds and the sight of a red streak heading for the orchards urged her forward.

Devlin's call was lost in the rush of wind in her ears as she pressed forward, heart thumping, eyes straining to see the exact path of the frenzied prey. Her tawny mare, a natural jumper, flew over hedgerows and fences. Anthony, devoting himself to a visiting Englishwoman with inviting eyes and a silken voice, assumed, as he so often did, that Devlin or Court was keeping close watch over his daughter.

Lacey galloped on, staying parallel to the front line of riders, away from

Court's peripheral vision. He was easy to spot with horn blasts and lively cursing when the dogs lost the scent. She caught a blur of moving russet in the copse ahead and recklessly charged straight on, but not before Court saw her detour away from the main party.

"Damnation! I'll throttle her." He tossed the horn to Lafferty, whipping poor Drummer to intercept her.

Lacey came out the other side, headed toward Calliope Creek. The rains had raised its level, and the current, which fed into Lough Phair, made it treacherous under flooded conditions.

The trusting mare plunged in before Lacey could pull her away, and the water rose up with biting ferocity, the unfamiliar long skirt dragging them down. Fearing for the horse, she dropped the reins and was left to swirl in the current, unable to maneuver her legs as the mare cried out in bewilderment.

The riderless horse made her way up the bank and was the first thing Court saw, followed by a dark shape thrashing in the water. Lacey struggled to float on her back, but the riding habit weighed her down like a suit of armor. She gasped for air, losing consciousness as the water rushed over her.

Court tore his coat off, gripping Drummer with his knees, and looked for a spot to jump in. The swift current smashed him about like a pinball, keeping Lacey out of reach, until a partly submerged tree limb stopped her long enough for him to grab a fistful of the skirt. His lungs throbbed from the exertion, and he feared there was no strength left to drag her to safety.

When he saw how deathly pale she was, he cried out, "Don't die on me— you can't die!"

She lay before him, not breathing, a bluish tint suffusing her throat. He administered a crude form of resuscitation and then rolled her over and pounded between her shoulder blades; she gagged and coughed, water gushing from her nose and mouth.

Court cradled her in his arms. "Easy now, relax and look at me, Lacey darlin'."

She took deeper breaths, her gaze never wavering from his. "Better now?" She nodded, shuddering from the cold, and he crowed with relief. "Thank you, God! I'll not ask for another thing in my life—this will do for me!"

He kissed her eyes and cheeks. "You'll live another day to cause me grief, my lamb."

Lacey's eyes fluttered in fatigue and shock, and he panicked anew. "What a dunce I am to keep you in these wet things! You'll catch your death."

Court carried her over two fields to Tansy Cottage, the home of one of Devlin's tenant farmers. Soon they were wrapped in thick quilts, and he was lighting up a pipe with the man, getting ready to recount his tale. Lacey, dozing by the fire, surrendered to the comforting lilt of his storytelling voice and a dreamless sleep.

It seemed only moments later she was being awakened, but it was now dark, and there was a great commotion outside the cottage.

"Dearest lamb," Court whispered, "can you slip your arms around my neck so we can be off?"

She obliged; content to stay in his arms forever, if always he would be this nice to her. Lanterns were lit and swaying in the stiff breeze. So many male voices speaking at once overwhelmed her, and she pressed her face into his neck. Through the din, she picked out Devlin's sonorous and somewhat imperious voice, but this was overshadowed by her father's commanding baritone.

"She is my daughter, you know," Anthony said possessively as he wrested her from Court's arms.

"That she is, captain," he answered with a whiff of truculence. "Were she mine—this never would have happened. I have the good sense to know a child has no place on a hunt!"

"If she were yours, she'd be the bastard of a scullery maid!"

Lacey's eyes popped open as the two men tensed for further sparring, and the crowd quieted in anticipation of a hearty row.

"Is it more honorable to keep a mistress in Dublin and a spare in London?"

A vise tightened around Lacey's heart as the two men who mattered most to her spouted vile accusations. Wasn't it enough she had nearly drowned? She yearned for her bed and broke into exhausted sobs, putting an end to the day's excitement.

⬥

Caitlin gazed down upon Anthony with the barest wisp of a smile. He imagined he smelled the sweet odor of wood violets as he remembered the day of the sitting. She had been adorably addlebrained that morning, imploring him to pass judgment as she wiggled in and out of several voluminous dresses. All had been purchased during their recent honeymoon in Paris, and he was hard-pressed to make a decision. His masculine sensibilities were dazed by a whoosh of flounces and ruffles with tempting glimpses of décolletage.

Caitlin's beauty, intelligence, and steady humor kept him in a state of arousal; the slightest gesture, the shyest sweep of lashes would kindle a passionate response.

In the bright morning light, her skin shimmered with the translucence of a thousand pearls as she perched on his knee in a pale yellow wrapper. With the scent of violets infusing her hair, he lifted an auburn coil to his cheek and listened to her dilemma.

"Anthony darlin'," her voice caressed him, "this is of historical importance. If I'm to be painted for posterity, I must know what you think."

"I think you look best this way" and he slipped the wrapper from her perfumed shoulders to reveal the lustrous silhouette of her breasts. "This is how I would paint you." His lips found the hollow of her throat, and her pulse quickened in abandon.

Anthony had convinced himself that this was the day Lacey had been conceived, and each time he was drawn to the painting, it struck him with bruising sorrow that Caitlin's smile held the secret of the life within her. A log's rustle on the fire roused him, and he tended to it, adding a scoop of coal to keep the chill away.

Caitlin had left such an emotional abyss within him that it had become his custom to avail himself of woman as it pleased him, though none sated a single desire. Now this was in jeopardy, thanks to the hot-headed Courtland O'Rourke. He would have much explaining to do; Lacey was at an age when her inquisitiveness could not be put off with oblique excuses or figurative myths. Just recently, dinner conversation had been brought to a mortifying halt when she asked what fornication was.

He reached for his pipe, berating himself for being indiscrete around Court.

What was he thinking when he invited the rascal to dine with him and his mistress, Katherine Piers? He had not expected to find the boy in Dublin, and when their paths crossed on Sackville Street, it seemed a harmless thing to do. He delighted in Court's salacious wit and fabulist gifts. Katherine had been at her provocative best, all bosom and lips, regaling them with spicy tales of the theater.

In a moment of indulgent bravado while Katherine was off powdering her nose, Anthony had said, "If you think this one's delectable—you should see the one in London!"

This rift would not mend with time, and a part of him rejoiced at the possibility. Perhaps now he could get his daughter back. He was not so self-absorbed as to be unaware of the tempestuous bond between Court and Lacey, and of Devlin's less than demure hinting at a match. This was not another business deal! It was his only daughter's future, and if any scheming was to be done, it would be by his hand and not that pirate's!

Lacey nearly died. He had failed to keep her safe. For too long, he had allowed others to bear the responsibility for her welfare. Today had been a dire warning, and it would not go unheeded. Anthony needed a subtle but resolute strategy to nudge Court aside so that he could reassert his primacy as the only man of consequence in Lacey's life.

A leather-bound book of poetry slipped from Devlin's grasp as he dozed. Such a sweet dream: Colleen playing hide-and-seek in the rose garden with a newly walking Lindsay. The baby waddled among the lavender and roses, stalking his mother with rapt determination when an enormous heath butterfly distracted him—alighting upon a rose, drawn to its hypnotic attar.

"Nish, nish," Lindsay lisped and grabbed for it, his tiny fingers curling around the stem.

When he bellowed in pain from the bite of the thorns, Colleen flew to him, prettily windblown from the game. "My poor, precious baby."

The images receded, and Devlin fought to bring them back. "No, no, don't go." His eyes opened in regret; Court was shaking him.

"Wasn't sleeping. Just resting me eyes waiting for you," he said, lapsing into his brogue and marking his place in the book.

"I've been walking about in a stupor. I daresay you must have a thing or two to say."

"Indeed I do but not till you've explained yourself!"

"By Judas, I don't know what possessed me! There I was—handing over his rescued daughter. And the man insults me!"

"Come and sit down," Devlin coaxed. "You're making me dizzy with this pacing. If you take your pleasure with such carelessness, you've no right at all to be insulted when another speaks of it."

"But to say it in front of Lacey?"

Devlin shook his head in admonishment. "Let me finish before you go spouting your rhetoric. You did a mighty fine and courageous thing saving our darlin' girl. Heed my words! When the captain settles down, he'll be coming round with a thank you and an apology."

"Has he ever thanked us? Just once—for looking after her while he's been off wheeling, dealing, and whoring?"

Devlin pounded the bed. "Don't be speaking of him with the bile rising in your throat! You forget how much we owe him! You'd have no inheritance. We would have lost this castle—your birthright—years ago!"

"I'm sick to death hearing about the bloody Land Act and how the brilliant Captain de la Roche outfoxed the commission." Court resumed his pacing.

"And I suppose you're sick to death living this blessed life of leisure and good fortune when you could be toiling in some field as a day laborer?"

"You're saying we must dance to his tune because he plays the pipe? Where's your pride old man—buried in your wallet? I say the slate is clean as of today! The price of his daughter's life has settled the debt!"

Unperturbed, Devlin adjusted his pillow, reopened the book, and asked, "And risking your life had something to do with evening this score? I may not have been there, but I imagine a good deal of praying and a wee bit of bargaining transpired between you and the Almighty. Thanks to you my boy—Lacey will get older."

Even in the candlelight, he could see his grandson color. Ah well, his scheming was done for now, and he returned to the poetry of Robbie Burns.

Winter

A row of amber flames warmed Lacey's cheeks as she lit a trio of candles at the feet of St. Joseph. Fresh-cut cedar boughs and baskets of poinsettias adorned the church in celebration of her favorite time of year. It looked to be a dismal Christmas, unless the power of prayer and ritual offerings could bring the two families back together. Anthony, too clever to forbid Lacey to visit Torrey Castle, steered her to other social acquaintances and took her on business trips to Limerick, Galway, and Dublin. She was stunned by his sudden rush of attention—until she saw through his paternal manipulations.

"Joseph, you know what's going on." She was on a first name basis with her favorite saint. "Christmas will be horrid without Court! And it's all Daddy's fault. He's being absolutely pigheaded! Can't you do something?"

The door to the sacristy opened, and Father Ryan appeared with his arm around a soulful Bridget. Prayer was replaced quickly by shameless curiosity.

"It's my heart's grief you must be making this decision my child. I'll hear your confession, but then you must hasten to pack. There's not much time."

As if she were Mercury himself, Lacey flew to the pew nearest the confessional and slithered along until she could hear their voices.

"Bless me Father, for I have sinned most grievously. Please forgive me for I have fornicated."

Lacey, now aware of what the word meant, thrilled to hear details and moved to press her ear to the door.

"I'm ashamed to say I let three men have sport with me."

Father Ryan droned on about sex and procreation outside the sacrament of marriage while Bridget wept, swearing repentance and begging for absolution. "I believe your remorse to be true, but you have drawn disgrace upon your family. Our good Lord blesses you and this child you have conceived in sin."

Too many thoughts tumbled about in Lacey's head: her father's scathing words, "bastard of a scullery maid," Court and Bridget by the boathouse, Sophie's relentless gossiping. Sophie! She would be the one to give her the answers she needed.

Lacey waited until bedtime, when Sophie was worn-out and more apt to ramble. The contents of Lacey's jewelry box were spread on the dressing table. Most of it came from her paternal grandmother, Margaret, who believed all little girls wanted to wear such things. Lacey thought jewelry to be a tremendous nuisance, easily lost or broken during rambunctious play. Her father had put aside the heirloom pieces as well as her mother's immense collection for the day when she would want to be so expensively encumbered.

At nine o'clock, a wan Sophie trudged in with a tray of hot chocolate and biscuits, oblivious to everything but her own fatigue, yawning without apology.

"Here you go, miss. I had cook sprinkle a dash of nutmeg in it. I know how you fancy the taste."

Lacey had been given the perfect opening. "How thoughtful of you, Sophie. You always take such good care of me!"

"'Tis me job." And with another hearty yawn, she began to brush out Lacey's braids.

"Do sit for a bit. You look all done in."

The thin veil of formality dropped like a stone as Sophie plopped down and said, "'Tis bedlam down there! All day long, I've been doing old McTeague's bidding without so much as a please or thank you leaving them lips. You know what a merciless tyrant she becomes this time of year."

Lacey nodded, pouring the chocolate, its steamy sweetness wafting between them.

Sophie took a breath and prattled on. "That day worker—what's her name? Duffy. She's good for little else than a lick and a promise. From the way that one smells, you know she's not on speaking terms with soap and water!"

"Let's share," Lacey suggested, "you're needing something to soothe your nerves."

"Heavens! If the captain saw this, I'd be out on me rump!"

"Pish! He doesn't know what it's like being an only child." She paused for calculated emphasis. "You know when I can't sleep, I pretend we're sisters, and then I can fall sleep. I may not always be showing it—but I do think of you that way."

She lay her head on the dumbfounded girl's shoulder.

"Lord, miss, I've two sisters and that good-for-nothing excuse of a brother. Many a time I've wished to be an only child."

"You wouldn't like it one bit. Why, with all those sisters, I can just imagine the lovely Christmas presents you get."

Sophie refilled the cup and said with considerable rancor, "T'would be easier sucking milk from a she-devil than get a drop of anything out of the likes of them."

"You have one sister who'll not forget you this year! Here's all my jewelry for you to pick something!"

There was a cautious glimmer of greed in Sophie's eyes as she expressed some misgiving. "Ain't proper, miss, but if your blessed heart is set on it."

"Choose something that matches your best dress and suits your complexion," Lacey advised, as if she knew about such things. "What color is your Sunday dress?"

"I've got a blue wool for now and a green cotton for the summer. But I'll be needing something new for Katie's wedding in the spring."

"Katie's getting married?" she asked with vigorous self-interest and then sprung her trap. "Why I thought Bridget would be next! Is she still working for Mrs. Conway?"

Sophie squeezed a necklace of opal stones against her throat and murmured, "This will do just fine, miss. I must be getting back now."

"Oh, I do so like the way it looks against your skin. Now mind, don't let Bridget be borrowing it when she's being an old meanie."

Lacey's hammering away had the desired effect, and the girl began to wail, "She'll not be setting eyes on me ever again! I feel it in the marrow of me bones."

"Sophie! You must tell me everything! And start at the very beginning."

It was the same nightmare; Court thrashed in his sleep, struggling to awaken before they were upon him. He smelled their breath, felt the heat from their fur as the hounds tore him to pieces. He bolted upright, nearly tossing Lacey from the foot of his bed.

"I'm still dreaming," he gasped, moist with perspiration and waved one hand at her. "When I wake up—you'll be gone."

"You are awake, silly," she said, rubbing her frosty cheek against his.

"Didn't this used to be mine? My dream and you're wearing my clothes. I wonder what that means?"

Lacey was wearing one of his old Aran ganseys and corduroy breeches. Tugging at his hair she asked, "Do you feel this?"

"Ouch! Let go, you vixen!"

"I couldn't sleep and I couldn't wait any longer." She offered this as a sufficient explanation.

Court held his watch to the low flame of the oil lamp. It was twenty past four. "Are you stark raving mad? Do you know you're in bed with a naked man?"

Lacey covered his mouth with both hands. "Devlin may be hard of hearing, but he's not deaf! Besides, I've seen you naked lots of times."

"When in blazes have you seen me naked?" he asked, twisting about to cover himself with the sheet.

"When you go swimming in Livvy's Pond—Padraic and I spy on you."

"You're evil through and through. It's a wonder you've lasted this long without someone driving a stake through your heart."

With robe in hand, Court gave her a menacing look, but Lacey refused to avert her gaze a fraction of an inch. She was enjoying the spectacle and how very handsome he looked with curls askew and gray eyes flashing.

"Do you suppose you could shut them all-seeing eyes long enough for me to make myself decent?"

"I can't see very well in here anyway."

Settled back on the bed, he was unnaturally at a loss for words. He stared at her, began to speak, paused a moment, and tried again. "Lacey, I know you wouldn't be here without a good reason."

When she started to speak, he stopped her with an ominous shake of his head. "I may treat you like a little girl more than I really should, but the truth is, you're well on your way to becoming a woman. You can't be acting on impulse. Do you understand what I'm saying?"

"Yes, Court."

"So tell me now, what's so important, it can't wait for another bloody minute?"

"I know Bridget is having a baby, and everyone thinks you're to blame!"

"What have you heard and from whom please?"

"Sophie said Bridget has gone to a cousin in Galway this very night. The baby's coming in the spring."

"I'm sorry you had to hear about it this way. I was intending to tell you before I leave."

Lacey's mouth slackened in astonishment; she wasn't sure if she heard correctly. "You're leaving?"

"This scandal must be put to rest. Even if Bridget goes on to the States, people won't let it be."

"But where will you go?" she asked in a pathetic whisper.

"Grandfather has arranged a commission in the army. I'll be stationed in India for three years, but it's the cavalry so it won't be so bad."

"Not India!" She startled him with her vehemence. "You could be killed!" She lunged at him. "No one is making you go. You want to go!"

Court took her in his arms as she wept and struck at his chest with tight fists.

"Lacey darlin', you mustn't think I want to leave, but this is how it must be! I've made arrangements for Bridget and the babe. I'm taking responsibility."

"It may not even be yours!" She had shown her duplicitous hand.

"What makes you say that?" he demanded, too well-acquainted with her shenanigans not to be suspicious.

"I was thinking maybe—you're not the only one. If there were others."

Court appeared lost in thought, so Lacey relaxed against him until he asked, "Is that what Sophie said? That girl has a tongue as long as a cow's tail, and I know for a fact, she's always wagging it around you!"

Lacey twisted the lapels of his cashmere robe. "I think I heard it somewhere else."

"Out with it."

"I may have heard it in passing."

"Exactly where might have you been passing?"

"Church—by the confessional. I may have heard one or two things—by accident."

"You violated the sanctity of the confessional? If I didn't know you were born to a Christian mother, I'd swear you were the devil's spawn! True as St. Peter denied Christ three times, you're going straight to hell!"

For all of Court's blustering, Lacey could see he was relieved to hear her ill-gotten information. Her stomach heaved with hunger; she would ask Aggie to have cook make a lovely mushroom soufflé.

"Do you suppose we could have some breakfast before my day of judgment comes?"

◆

Using the sleeve of his shirt, Court wiped the smudges from his parents' wedding daguerreotype and tucked it into the scarred portmanteau. Their pale, nervous faces shining with the hope of an uncertain future called out to him on this day of farewells. Lindsay's roguish grin, teeth bared to the world, contrasted with the demure set of Meghan's lips. They were just about his age when they eloped, defying both sets of parents in their passionate haste to be together.

Devlin liked to tell the story with bittersweet pride, harboring a secret admiration for his son's obstinacy while deploring his fundamental lack of horse sense.

"I was of a good mind to disinherit the reprobate on the spot and leave him to his fate." He would say of his brilliant bluff. "But I left it up to the self-righteous Squire Flynn to do all the carping and denouncing - a role he was born to play, and meself came out smelling like a newly blossomed rose of Sharon."

A less-than-contrite Lindsay returned to University College to complete his degree while Meghan was reclaimed by her parents. The recalcitrant couple's few nights of lovemaking had to sustain them until they could be together as man and wife. Court still was angry about the precious time they were deprived of, when two years after his birth, they perished in the Irish Sea, their ship torn asunder by a violent squall.

Devlin bore the guilt, as it was his gift of a belated honeymoon to Tuscany that resulted in their deaths. The intransigent Flynns denounced him as their daughter's murderer and punished both grandfather and grandson by excluding them from any claims to Meghan's inheritance.

Court finished dressing and realized that it would be a very long time before he would admire what a fine figure he cut in a hand-tailored suit. "A loss of vanity is the least of your problems," he reproached himself, wondering what his parents would think of this mess.

"What a foolish and woefully self-indulgent son you bore me, Meghan!" Lindsay might say, his mother keening as Irish women do for the dead.

"Somewhere, there's a randy farm hand or two larking about, as free as you please, while I'm being packed off to hell."

◆

An icy drizzle speckled the driveway with pools of slush as Devlin and Lacey waited in the carriage on this mournful January morning of 1912. Despite the weather, the entire household assembled on the front steps for Court's farewell. Each was the recipient of a waggish comment or affectionate observation; for some, there were last minute instructions.

"Lafferty, my good man, I'm leaving you in charge of Drummer. I don't want to return and find him flabby from too many oats and not enough exercise! Can I trust you to look after him?"

"Surely, sir," he bristled in his clipped Dublin accent. "Have I ever let you down before?"

"A time or two, John," was the soft rejoinder as he shook the groom's hand.

Aggie adjusted the bright shawl covering her head, drawing further attention to her reddened eyes and nose. This was the first of the difficult good-byes, and she could not resist making the first move, clasping his head between her calloused hands.

"I won't have you slinking off like a whipped puppy," she cried. "I've known you all your life and love you like you came from me own womb. It don't matter to me what's been said or done."

The years slipped away, and Court was ten years old again. "I'm not sure if I can go through with it," he had said, in the privacy of the pantry. "He's twice my size with fists as big as hams."

Aggie, shelling peas with graceful speed, said, "You can't be knowing such a thing till you try. You're fast and light. If I were a bettin' woman, my money would be on you, sweet."

He wavered under her assurances, rolling a pea on his tongue, considering those heavy fists on his slight frame.

She drew him close. "Even if that little barbarian knocks you down, bloodies you—get up so he knows you're no quitter. Stand tall with shoulders square, and people will know what you're made of."

Devlin called out with a peremptory reminder, "There's isn't much time."

"Pray for me," Court whispered to Aggie, unwilling to let her go.

Her resolve was fragile, but she pushed him from her and said, "Stand tall, shoulders square. Come back to me as handsome and brave as you are now." Wiping her eyes, she drew the shawl tighter. "Off you go now! Can't have you missing the train."

When Court climbed into the carriage, Devlin turned away, his face a mask, his ungloved hands folded in his lap. There was to be no conversation, or so it seemed to Lacey, as both men stared out the window, isolated in their own thoughts. She was unable to recall another time that passed in such excruciating silence. Even after a ferocious row, one would have the witless compulsion to ramble on while the other sat sulking. She wondered if it was up to her to break the standoff with some innocent remark. When she tried to catch Court's eye, he shifted in his seat, a not-so-subtle bit of body language indicating she was to leave him be.

The rain had faded to a numbing dampness as the carriage stopped by the stationmaster's bungalow.

"I'll see to your ticket," Devlin said, not waiting for Seamus's assistance.

Court finally turned his attention to Lacey and saw she was quite displeased with his slighting of her. She kicked the door open and with petticoats swirling, quickly stepped around people and puddles.

"Where the devil are you off to?" he shouted, lengthening his stride to reach her. "What about my good-bye?"

"So you've found your tongue and have the brass to ask such a question?" Before he could respond, she hastened over the bridge.

Court ran the distance between them, swept her under his arm like an unwieldy parcel, and toted her back. A slew of invectives and swinging legs attracted some attention, as he dumped her onto a corner of the loading platform.

"This is just the way I want to remember you! I may be every filthy thing you just called me, but I deserve a proper good-bye. If we botch this up— we'll both be miserable!"

Lacey's posture eased as the fight left her. He was horribly right, and these were precious moments not to be wasted.

"That's better. I've something I need you to look after for me, my lamb." His tone was businesslike as he hunted through his pockets and withdrew a burgundy velvet bag. "You must promise you'll take very good care of this and keep it safe."

"Oh, I will, I will! You know I can be trusted, Court."

He loosened the satin ribbon and revealed a gold oval-shaped locket, etched with an ornate floral design. She shivered as he slipped it around her neck.

"The important part is inside."

Their heads touched as he showed her its interior – on one side, a miniature daguerreotype of him as a baby – on the other, a more recent photograph. The same self-possessed expression was worn in both.

"Tis the only keepsake I have of my mother. You can imagine how dear it is to me." As he spoke, he undid her coat and the top buttons of her jumper. "If I take this with me, well, where I'm going, things are easily misplaced."

His fingers stole under her blouse and dropped the locket between her small breasts; its cold surface pricked her skin. "I thought if you kept it close to your heart, you could peek at it from time to time, if you forget what I look like."

"How could I forget?" she asked in a tremulous voice, seizing his face with her cold hands, her mouth fluttering over his with tiny kisses.

Court leaned into her, lost in the sensation, until a whistle shrieked, and he disengaged himself. "Mind what I said!" he warned with a flash of his domineering self. "We must find grandfather."

"No! Wait! I made something for you!"

"You made something for me?"

"Well, Aggie helped with the hard parts," she admitted, handing him a small package. It was a man's linen handkerchief, embroidered with the O'Rourke crest.

"I read it's beastly hot in India. I'm quite dreadful at needlepoint. Aggie did the crest but I did your initials."

"This is the best present I could have received! I can't think of another thing I'll get more use out of!"

The train steamed into the station, sending the waiting passengers to collect their belongings and say their farewells. "We haven't a moment to lose!" Court scooped her up and carried her at a fast trot toward the waiting train.

Devlin swung his cane testily, throwing daggers at them.

"It's about time." He handed the ticket and two envelopes to Court as she slid from his arms.

"We were having a little heart-to-heart, right Lacey?"

She stared at the ground and pressed the locket to her heart. The warning whistle shrieked again, and the swarm of passengers thickened around them.

"Here's a letter to Colonel Cullum and one to Humphrey Boyle, authorizing him to open accounts for you in London and Delhi. Cullum's a good sort for an Ulsterman. He'll see you're treated fairly. But my influence ends here! You'll have to make your own way."

The final whistle cut through them, and Devlin grasped Court's hand, his mouth twitching as he choked out, "May the good Lord keep you safe. Hurry back to us, dear boy."

"Thank you Grandfather—for everything."

Court knelt and drew Lacey into his embrace. "When next I see you, lamb, I expect to find this locket around your pretty neck. And in perfect condition!"

He kissed her palms and both cheeks as she clung to him in desperation. He freed himself and ran, not looking back until he leaped onto the steps of the last car. His mouth twisted in a lopsided grin as he waved the handkerchief once and disappeared inside.

For a long while, Devlin and Lacey watched as the smoke from the train spiraled into the thick clouds. It was as if the source of their energy had been sucked into the train and they were powerless to move. Seamus waited by the carriage, the horses chafing at their bits.

The dampness seeped into Devlin's bones, as his heart convulsed in despair, but he forced himself to brighten up for Lacey's sake. "Well now, the rake is off on his grand adventure!" He tucked her hand into his. "Such tears won't do at all, my dear. He'd not be wanting us to mope about. Our boy will return to us full of sass and swagger. I'll wager my very soul upon it."

Part II

"Discoveries Near and Far"
1912-1913

New York

The air had lost its sting and the waves flattened, as the roaring cadence of the ocean dulled to a purring drone. On this late August morning, Anthony pounded the ship's railing, calling out to his daughter, "Lacey! You must see how this little tug guides us into port!"

The voyage had bronzed his complexion, so his eyes gleamed with a more vivid shade of azure, and his handsome six-foot frame, dressed in a fitted navy blazer and linen trousers, distracted passengers from their first view of the Statue of Liberty.

"I've seen her do this a dozen times, yet it still amazes me. Isn't she magnificent?"

Anthony's enthusiasm was not contagious enough to stir Lacey from a deck chair. In contrast to his vivacity, she appeared aloof and somewhat frail, cocooned in a sea-green duster, with an oversized straw hat protecting her from unwelcome scrutiny. The only clue to her mood was decipherable from the grim set of her lips. There was a moment of mutual antagonism, and then an imperceptible shrug of defeat as he resumed his solitary watch.

Lacey's behavior after Court's departure confounded Anthony with its melodrama. She spent hours riding through field and meadow, an equestrian Ophelia, inciting gossip among the locals. He encouraged her to write to him, thinking this would lighten the pall of despair, but the long wait between letters stole her appetite and disrupted her sleep. On June 15, she vanished.

For a day and a half, a flurry of searchers trampled the grounds between Durbin House and Torrey Castle, attracted by the large reward posted by Anthony and matched by Devlin. The two men convened at the church to organize a more expansive search.

In the cool hush of the rectory, Devlin crumbled a biscuit into a glass of sherry, spooned up the sops, and said, "I blame meself for the poor child's disappearance. Aggie knew something was dreadfully amiss, but I thought it nothing more than her womanish imaginings. Had I but listened." He dropped another biscuit in the glass and stirred it.

"Must you do that?" Anthony asked, slouching against a wall. His unshaven face appeared even more haggard from the blue and green light streaming through the stained glass windows, and his last shred of patience had been sapped by the onset of Devlin's pitying brogue.

"Do what?"

"Play with your damn food!"

"'Tis surely a time stealing the strength from a body's soul. This bit of nourishment will sustain me for what lies ahead. You know I hold your darlin' girl close to me heart."

He refilled his glass and pushed the decanter toward Anthony, who ignored it and lit another cigarette.

"Speaking of those near and dear to you, Devlin, have you written to Courtland about this?"

"Not a word! I see no reason to alarm the boy at this time. He's struggling to fit in with the military way of doing things."

"I'm not surprised; he was never one to accept authority with any enthusiasm."

"To be sure. He's always been a thickheaded lad. But you'll see, Captain, my grandson will return a man, one we can all be proud of."

Anthony tossed the cigarette into a pot of well-tended ficus. "This is a new approach for you—the soft sell. Are you hoping I'll be impressed enough to consider him as a son-in-law?"

"I'm only hoping no harm comes to your daughter or my grandson." His heart contracted with the thought of what lay ahead. "Time to be turning the search in another direction. "Anthony's throat locked in a spasm of dread, so it was Devlin who uttered the awful words. "I'll take charge of the mail boat and gather up the

men for a search of the lough."

He clasped Anthony's arm in apology. "You know it must be done. God willing, nothing will be found. You see to the dragging of the ponds. There must be a goodly dozen in the district!"

The searches yielded no answers, and while Anthony felt some perverse comfort, the influx of opportunists crowding into Cloonsheelin enraged him. Some were harmlessly entrepreneurial, selling crude maps of the area, bottles of warm beer, and day-old sandwiches. All were eager to observe the spectacle of an upper-class family dealing with a potential tragedy. Lurid accounts of Lacey's demise circulated, fed by the servants and the arrival of muckraking reporters from Dublin and Cork.

One had the poor judgment to corner Anthony, as he returned to Durbin House for a change of clothes, on the third day. Distracted and exhausted, he was unprepared for a lurking blight of a man to spring at him from behind the lilac bushes.

"Captain de la Roche, there's much talk to be heard in these parts about your daughter…"

Before the question could be completed, Anthony's fist sent him backward into the shrubbery. As he stepped closer to deliver another blow, Padraic came running.

"Captain, sir, you must make haste to Torrey Castle. There's good news awaiting you there!"

"Have they found her?"

"Upon my word, Lacey is asleep in Master Court's bed—safe and sound as a newborn kitten. "

As the reporter flipped open his notebook and scribbled away, Anthony charged at him, raising his riding crop from on high. With one neat flourish, he walloped the man across the shoulders and sent the notebook sailing into the goldfish pond.

Devlin and Aggie were keeping watch over a slumbering Lacey when Anthony tripped in, too stunned to speak. She was wrapped in Court's cashmere robe, one hand clasping the locket, sleeping as solidly as Padraic described.

"Let her sleep—as long as she needs to," Anthony said. "Perhaps it's all we can do for her."

Dr. Seacord's diagnosis of melancholia, the old-fashioned term for depression, induced Anthony to book passage to New York. He was counting on a complete change of scenery and his mother's feminine wisdom to provide Lacey with the kind of nurturing that he no longer seemed capable of giving her.

Gramercy Park in the summer of 1912 was not unlike other aristocratic enclaves in London and Paris; a private Eden tucked away in a burgeoning city of social and economic polarities. The park existed as the verdant nexus of a prestigious square of row houses and mansions. An eight-foot iron fence and locked gate protected the outer perimeter from undesirables, while boxwood hedges concealed the interior from the wistfully envious. Each family possessed a key for their entry, and only they enjoyed the well-sanded pathways, dense plantings, and diverse array of shade trees. A demure water nymph presided over a gleaming marble fountain surrounded by flowering urns and thick waves of exotic grasses and ferns.

On this most oppressive day, the park offered its slight comfort to few creatures. All the prominent families spent the month of August in the country or by the seashore. This may explain why Margaret de la Roche stepped from her car with such visible irritation as she stiffened her small shoulders. It had been a vexing ordeal to leave Millbrook before the last important weekend of the season, and a greater nuisance to decline some serious social obligations, all because of the impending arrival of her son and granddaughter.

Margaret's meticulous eye inspected the window boxes planted with English ivy, white petunias, and red geraniums. When she purchased the Greek Revival row house more than twenty years ago, she wanted to distinguish it from the others on the western edge of the park and commissioned an iron verandah laced with hummingbirds and wisteria. The spidery ironwork softened the austere façade, complementing the slender symmetry of the floor-to-ceiling windows on the first two floors.

Before Margaret's foot touched the bottom step, William, her butler, somberly opened the door. Impressive in his black and gold livery, he extended a gloved hand, and wordlessly, she unburdened herself of parasol and reticule.

Scarcely had she removed her gloves when she said, "Tell Mrs. Parsons the windows are disgraceful and must be washed again! There are streaks and smudges on every single pane. I can't imagine where her commonsense has gone. Hasn't she eyes to see?"

The question was rhetorical as William awaited the rest of the tirade. "Remind her to use a clean cloth for each window and to dilute the vinegar with distilled water, not well water!"

She removed several hatpins, allowing them to drop one by one on the Spanish prayer bench and onto the floor of the vestibule. "How many times must I repeat myself before it's done correctly?"

"There's a cold lunch laid in the library, madam," William finally spoke while retrieving the hatpins. "I will inform Mrs. Parsons of your wishes."

Margaret patted a few tendrils of gray hair into place. "They are not wishes! See that she understands! I hope the rooms for my son and granddaughter have been prepared according to my precise instructions. I will not brook slipshod housekeeping, nor will I endure obstinacy from my servants. Please relay to the entire staff that they are on warning as of today! If I do not see immediate improvement—changes will be made."

Slivers of sunlight eased through the shutters, bouncing from the mirror and crossing her face at an unflattering angle. Although she had an unlined face at seventy-five, the coarse texture of her complexion, from a childhood bout with smallpox, distressed her. She had to rely on lotions and powders to disguise the marks. Her fine blue eyes, not as intense as Anthony's, were striking. But it was her wavy blonde hair that had always warranted admiration and remained her best feature, having turned a lustrous shade of silver. From her mother, she inherited a delicate bone structure and slight carriage, which apparently was what attracted her husband.

Tony had grunted in her ear on their wedding night, "So small—it's not possible I can fit inside you my dear."

He had, at least well enough to impregnate her, and she was relieved that once Anthony was born, her marital obligations concluded. Tony kept a litter of flamboyant mistresses; he even had the poor taste to expire in one's bed. His death liberated her from the scandal and gossip that tethered their ten-year marriage to the society pages, revealing the possibilities inherent in financial independence, and her own piercing intellect.

Anthony had inherited a few of his father's less appalling vices: a quick temper, restless nature, and competitive spirit. Several years after Tony's death, he was off to military school and then West Point, and upon graduation, dispatched to the cavalry, where he rose quickly through the ranks during the twilight years of the Indian Wars.

Margaret's vanity longed to flaunt how well she had fared despite Anthony's casual neglect of her. He was selfish and arrogant, qualities she attributed to all men, and now he had bullied her into an extended visit so that she might have the pleasure of becoming acquainted with her only grandchild!

She pulled herself up the stairs, ignoring the lunch, too fatigued from the long car ride and the incipient thrum of a migraine. She spied a fringe of a cobweb dangling from the rococo plasterwork, and rage sliced her brain in half.

"I'll fire every single one of them and replace them for half the cost and twice the labor!"

Delhi

For all its modern conveniences, India remained little more than a colonial outpost in a land of historical invasions. Its ancient and clashing religions invited interference from acquisitive neighbors, deluded into thinking that they alone could unravel the mystery and eradicate the chaos. During two centuries of occupation, the British arbitrarily moved the capital from Calcutta to Delhi, further antagonizing dissidents in the Bengal United Providences and the Punjab.

Where once regal cornfields swayed, the Amritsar rail station now dispensed crowds of all nationalities and denominations, taxing the city's frail infrastructure beyond saturation. Tramways failed to ease the congested avenues, as nothing deterred the daily fleet of motorcars, bicycles, gharries, and ekkas from careening in turbulent traffic patterns around—and at times, over—pedestrians. The King's Camp, with terra-cotta roads, unnaturally lush lawns, and rows of heirloom rose bushes, sprawled over eighty-five acres of arable land. Two enormous polo fields served as the primary outdoor diversion for the British military and civilian population.

A recent surge of sniper activity, followed by the attempted assassination of the viceroy of India, rustled through the city with the deadly chill of cholera. The suspects, leaders of several Muslim and Hindu factions, were interrogated, imprisoned, and in some instances, executed without a trial. These men were the subject of the turbaned ulema who gathered in the market place and in airless corners of cafes whispering of retaliation.

Into this world of sedition and secrecy, Court arrived in late February of 1912, unexpectedly invigorated by what he had seen of the East. Sailing through the Suez Canal, with the glare of the Egyptian desert searing the pyramids, he was enchanted by the spectacle of flying fish, humpback whales, and tiger sharks nosing through the Red Sea. Everywhere he looked, there was something startling and exotic to distract him from his brooding. The closer he came to his final destination, the lesser the pain and the dimmer the memory of so many sad faces.

By the time he disembarked in Bombay, Court's thoughts were directed to the immediate future and the best way to survive military life. Even in this cool season, the serge uniform stuck to him, its newness apparent to all who observed his tentative maneuverings. Small children, in shreds of cloth, flitted around him, their babble unintelligible, the desperation in their dark eyes reminders of their brethren in Dublin and London. He emptied his pockets of change, and when there was nothing left to give, he quickened his step so they could not keep up with him.

A whirl of colorful turbans, dhotis, and saris enveloped Court as he found himself already inured to the pummeling stench of urine and perspiration, the public intimacy of people bathing and children defecating, and the sheer indifference of the faithful kneeling on prayer mats. He was counting on all of it to distract him until it was time to return to Ireland and home. The two words coursed through him with a dull pang, but it wasn't Aggie or Devlin that tugged so fiercely at his heart; it was that last glimpse of Lacey, her face no bigger than the width of his hand and blurred with tears.

He berated himself for being so remiss in writing to her, and with her birthday only a few weeks away! The first thing he would do, after settling in, would be to write a lively account of all he had seen, making sure to describe the monkeys, camels, and elephants in staggering detail.

"Look here, this is of critical importance." Colonel Miles Cullum bent forward, his feathery sideburns brushing Court's cheek. "The pony's forelegs must be snugly bandaged from right below the hock down to the fetlock joint."

"Why?"

The Colonel straightened up with a wheeze and a grunt of exasperation. "Don't be a ninny boy! You've seen enough of this game to understand the kind of injury that can cripple a pony without this sort of protection." He sucked in his lower lip, peeved at Court's ignorance.

"Do you know why I requested you for my command, O'Rourke?"

"As a favor to my grandfather?"

"Damn the old pirate! I need a good number two man, and you're it!"

"Ah, I see now. Colonel, I've never played the game, and I've only been a spectator at a dozen or so matches."

"You ride like the devil and have a keen eye—that's all you really need." Cullum ran an appraising hand over the pony's withers and continued, "Davenport will show you the fine points, explain the rules. It's not all that different from hunting, except the prey is a ball."

It had been something of a shock that his commission was not the hardship he had envisioned. He was assigned to the first battalion of the Royal Munster Fusiliers, under the command of Lieutenant Colonel Miles Cullum. This portly and cantankerous career officer believed civilization could be manufactured, in the middle of nowhere, if one had the connections and resources.

There were occasional forays into the countryside to check on native unrest, daily briefings, diplomatic functions, and tea ceremonies with Indian leaders, but the rest of the time, Court was free to ride, explore, and study his surroundings with minimal supervision. He shared a bungalow with two officers and enjoyed the services of a domestic staff. Shrewd enough to know his value existed only in his horsemanship and talent as a polo player, he intended to avoid reassignment to a lesser post in a more volatile part of the country.

"If it's all right with you, Colonel, I'd like to try a few of the ponies before deciding on a regular mount."

"You have my permission to choose whichever suits you, but the albino belongs to Davenport." The two men admired the opalescent Arabian snuffling the hay. "He's a trifle showy but unbeatable on the field. Without him, Davenport doesn't have what it takes to be a pivot man. You may have noticed he's a man in need of expensive accessories—like a comely wife."

"I've yet to meet the much-talked-about Mrs. Sydney Davenport."

"Well, I've seen to that. I've offered your services to her as a riding instructor."

"Sir, I don't mean to question…"

"Look here, this is the army! When I say I've offered your services, it's a blasted euphemism for an order. You'll make yourself available to Mrs. Davenport at her damned convenience, or you'll be rousting insurgents in Calcutta!"

"I'll be more than happy to instruct the lady, but I do have a bit of a concern."

"Please illuminate me, Lieutenant, I'm mystified by your reticence."

"Davenport can't abide me. He's made it clear…"

"Can't abide you? You represent everything he loathes in a man! You're not military. You're not beholden to authority. You're not trained to do anything but sit a horse and entertain at tea time. And most lamentable of all—you're Irish!"

"So you understand."

"I not only understand, I don't give a bloody damn! If Davenport has a problem with this arrangement, let him come whining to me! Or better yet, let him take it out on you. It'll do you some good to learn how to deal with such unpleasantness, young man!"

"As the Colonel wishes," he conceded and turned his attention to a sorrel mare with a tapered muzzle. She gazed at him in mute sympathy as he caressed the delicate arch of her neck.

"This one has the look of a fine lady's horse. Think she'll do for Mrs. Davenport?"

Cullum had tired of the topic, longing for his tea and a plate of sesame and honey cookies. "Just see she doesn't break her fool neck. I'm sure after a few lessons in this beastly heat, she'll lose interest and be off pursuing another whim with the same unbearable intensity."

———◆———

Court awaited Mrs. Davenport with a degree of trepidation; her note included a desire to learn astride rather than sidesaddle. This was a relief, since he knew only one way of riding and had taught only one pupil, Lacey. He fingered the crescent-shaped scar on his upper lip and hoped Mrs. Davenport would inflict less aggravation and pain than the five-year-old Lacey.

How willful she had been that day with her imperious swagger and snooty attitude! Had it not been for her father's generous fee and his pitiful need for pocket money, he might have avoided considerable grief.

The introductions were made as Lacey sat on her father's shoulders, clasping the sides of his head with grimy hands, oblivious to Court's close scrutiny. He thought she was a very pretty child with a halo of coppery curls that brought out the bits of topaz in her brown eyes and the fresh pink in her cheeks.

"Lacey, this is Courtland O'Rourke, and he is to be your riding teacher."

Devlin, already enamored of her and oblivious to her wiles, exclaimed, "I think this will be an excellent match, Captain. There isn't another who can ride like my grandson the width and breath of the county. Taught him myself when he was not much older than Lacey."

Unaccustomed to such praise from his grandfather, the fifteen-year-old savored the moment and held out his hand.

"'Tis a pleasure to make your acquaintance, Lacey."

Wearing a fixed expression of stubbornness, she refused to acknowledge him.

"Lacey," her father warned.

"Don't want to touch the boy's hand."

Devlin's chuckle and her father's dismay did not lighten the rebuff for Court, as she slipped from her perch and was confronted by Anthony.

"Pet, you were the one who wanted to learn to ride. Courtland is doing this as a favor to me. Do you want to learn or return home in disgrace?"

She attended to his facial expressions, listening to every other word, then whispered in his ear, one arm draped possessively around his neck.

For Court, this was a telling moment, illustrating the balance of power in the relationship and what he could expect in the way of support and cooperation.

The adoration in her father's eyes deepened as he agreed to her request, and she lavishly kissed him, chanting, "Good-bye, good-bye."

"The darling, she wants us to leave so the lesson can begin," Anthony translated for them.

Assuming a brisk air, Court told her what she would be learning that morning. "If you want to ride properly, you must learn to use your hands and knees to control the pony."

Lacey interrupted him to issue her first of what was to be lifelong demands. "Boy, where's my pony?"

She barely reached his thigh, and yet, she exuded the haughty aplomb of seasoned royalty. Mastering his anger, he tried to remember she was only a child, if an ill-mannered one at that.

"Lacey, you may call me Court or Courtland, but you will not call me boy! I'll not tolerate rudeness from you!"

He eased into the role of disciplinarian. "Lesson one, don't vex me into losing my temper! When I ask you a question, you're to answer politely. Decide now or find another poor wretch to teach you."

She managed a nod and smile through clenched teeth. Feeling a small thrill of victory over her, Court naively thought he could accomplish what her own father, two nursemaids, five governesses, and three housekeepers had been unable to do — make her obey.

"Please, give me your hand, and I'll introduce you to Raffles. He's a lovely Welsh pony with a very kind heart."

He was indeed a lovely creature, gold and cream with velvet eyes and a soft muzzle. Encouraged by her gentle patting, Court gave her a small slice of apple for the pony.

"Go ahead, make friends with him. Open your hand and keep your palm perfectly flat. You don't want him nipping at your fingers."

Her rapturous glow commenced a thaw between them. In simple language, Court explained the different parts of the saddle and bridle and she followed attentively.

"I think you're ready to mount, which is always done from the left side of the pony."

"Why?"

"Ponies are trained that way. It makes it easier for them to stay still when you're getting on."

Lacey stretched to reach the saddle, wiggling her bottom. "Hold on," he laughed, "let me tidy you up."

As he knelt to retie her bootlaces and tuck in her shirt, she leaned against him, wrapping one of his curls around her finger and yawning noisily.

"You like being fussed over," he said, and she tightened her grip until he yelped. "And you like to play rough!" He handed her a riding crop and continued, "I want you to get used to the feel of the saddle and Raffles's gait, so we'll take a few turns around. Relax your ankles just a wee bit and keep your hands soft on the reins."

After the fifth go round, she asked, "Let me go by myself," and then added, "please?"

"Lacey, be patient, and in good time, you'll be trotting about all by yourself." What Court later would learn to read as a warning sign, a lifted brow of contempt, appeared on her face.

"Stupid boy!" she hissed and slashed him across the face with the crop, splitting his lip and rendering him semiconscious.

She urged Raffles forward, but he was too well-trained to react, so she turned and bit him on the rump. Minutes later, Anthony and Devlin converged on the scene to see Court bloodied and dazed, while Lacey triumphantly galloped around the paddock. When her father flagged down the irate pony, she was dragged from the saddle and escorted into the stables.

"I'm sparing you the humiliation of being spanked in public, young lady!" He towered over her in acute embarrassment. "How could you do something so vile to that poor boy?"

Anthony had never punished her, dreading the very idea of his hard and heavy hand on her fragile body. But she had drawn blood! God knows she deserved to suffer some consequence for her actions. He was torn between the harsh duty of a parent and the tender heart of a widowed father.

"Daddy," Lacey encouraged in a wispy voice, "I'm ready."

He lifted her onto his knee and shared his dilemma. "Lacey, this is very difficult for me. I can't bear the thought of raising a hand to you."

His desperation fed nicely into her manipulation of him. "Poor Daddy." She laid her cheek against his chest and wept. "I'm sorry. I'll give up the lessons—forever."

An agreement was reached. Lacey would apologize to Court, and it was up to him whether or not he wished to continue.

In truth, she would have preferred the spanking to an apology, but she dutifully recited the words. "I'm sorry I hit you. I'm very, very sorry I scared Raffles. I will never disobey you again."

It was painfully obvious to Court that she was sorrier about upsetting the pony than whacking him senseless. A hideous welt covered the right side of his face, and his lips were swelling into a purple mess. Lacey looked up to see the results of her handiwork, secretly pleased with his awful appearance.

This fleeting sadism was not lost on Anthony, who quickly issued a caveat to the agreement, freeing him from future dilemmas. "Courtland, you have my permission to spank my daughter, if she ever strikes you again!"

At the sound of Lacey's gasp and Court's grunt of surprise, Devlin protested, "Captain, there's no need to give the boy such license."

In a thickened voice, he said, "Who knows what she'll try the next time? If I'm to be around her for any reason, I need something to keep her in line!"

"So you'll go on with the lessons?" Anthony asked.

"Why yes, I'll teach the little lamb to ride."

"Lieutenant O'Rourke?"

"Good Lord, it's you!" Court uttered as Katherine Piers returned his look of astonishment.

Gramercy Park

Lacey welcomed the seclusion of the library, as she considered all the changes that she had been so cruelly subjected to in the last few months. There was a new vocabulary word she liked to repeat to herself—partly in anger, mostly in fascination—that described her grandmother: fastidious. Margaret de la Roche quested for absolute perfection in all things. She wondered how such a woman would survive for a single day in Ireland.

Over the stiff white blouse, the locket rested against her shattered heart. Just one letter from Court since August, and now the wait would be even longer, with another ocean to cross. There was a dignified knock, and Lacey wrenched herself from the brink of a crying spell. She hesitated, knowing William waited to announce her tutor, probably a woman as fastidious as her grandmother. How could she learn anything of real value from such a person? Another knock, and she hoped the butler would fade away, resigned to her defiant silence.

At Durbin House, but more so at Torrey Castle, servants, grooms, cooks, and gardeners blundered and blurted their way through their duties— oblivious to such formalities as knocking. Somewhat intimidated by William's decorous manner, she relented.

Anne Marie Wakefield hurried past the butler, more youthful than Lacey anticipated, and beamed at her from behind gold-rimmed spectacles. "You must be Lacey!" An armful of books cascaded onto the desk. "I'm so sorry to be late."

"I haven't been watching the time," she replied with weary disdain, "I've been thinking."

"A bit of daydreaming on a beautiful autumn morning? What were you dreaming of? Or should I ask, of whom?"

"If it matters to you, I was thinking of home and how different it is here."

Seated behind the desk, Anne Marie resembled a wary mouse, somewhat bewildered by her surroundings. Fumbling with a hatpin, she yanked off her hat and let it drop to the floor.

"Your grandmother tells me that this is your first trip to the United States."

"It's my first visit anywhere." Lacey's gaze soared over her tutor and through the window as she felt herself float away in a deliberate lie.

Besides traveling with her father through Ireland and Scotland, she had accompanied Devlin and Court to Dublin several times. For her ninth birthday, they had taken her to the Dublin Fair, where she nearly got Court killed.

The Dublin Fair offered something of interest even to the most particular of visitors. Devlin wanted to look over a brace of Irish wolfhounds for breeding purposes, Lacey intended to tour the stables for a glimpse of Emerald Fire, the recent winner of the Grand National, while Court schemed to meet up surreptitiously with Seamus Knox and his fighting gamecock, Corrigan. During breakfast at the Carrageen Hotel, the convivial trio sparked a lively conversation about their plans for the day.

"I, for one, must get round to Mulrowney's stall for a nice plate of cruibins," Devlin said, pouring a third cup of tea and dropping in a wedge of soda bread.*

Lacey shuddered, recalling the first time Mrs. McTeague served this version of pickled pig's feet at Durbin House. Being a sensitive child when it came to animals, she recoiled from the idea of sweet piglets being crippled for the sake of Irish cuisine and flung her plate out the window.

Seeing the revulsion on her face and knowing the oft told tale, Court solicitously spooned a quantity of moss jelly onto a slice of toast and said, "Here lamb, try a bit of this. It's a rare treat and one of grandfather's favorites."

His guileful sincerity, coupled with Devlin's benign nod, encouraged her to try the shimmering dark substance so reminiscent of Aggie's delicious mint jelly. But it lacked the familiar sweetness and texture of jelly and tasted like the smell of the sea. The horrid tasting muck slid down her throat and she grimaced with each swallow.

"You beast! It's seaweed!"

The mirthful light in Court's eyes betrayed him and turned to pain, as she kicked him twice in the knee with her booted foot.

"I do so want to get a good look at Emerald Fire! I think he must be the most beautiful horse in the world! Daddy says someday we could own one of his foals. Wouldn't that be grand?"

"You think your father will buy you anything you take a fancy to?" Court growled, nursing his injured knee.

"And why not?"

"It may well come to pass," Devlin said. "The captain and I are considering any number of ways to improve our breeding lines. There's talk Emerald Fire will be retired to stud the first of the year. So you see, my boy, Lacey will get what she wants!"

"Won't that be something new for this overindulged infant? You may waste the day as it suits you. I intend to see and do everything!"

"Before you go larking about, you'll come with me to Drummond's. The dogs will be your responsibility. You're old enough to learn how to choose good breeding stock, be it dogs, horses, or women!"

"Grandfather!" Court cocked his head at Lacey in genteel alarm.

"This darlin' child has more sense when it comes to choosing well than you could ever hope to have. Now finish up the both of you. I won't be waiting another minute."

◆

The arena reeked of tobacco and men. Its center burned with a garish glow, spotlighting a bald man in a capacious plaid suit wielding a megaphone and announcing the start of the dog show. Devlin studied the program, interested only in the sporting group and the magnificent Irish wolfhound, Germanicus.

A restless Court scanned the crowd, and Lacey followed his wandering gaze, spotting Seamus first. "Look over there! It's Padraic's Uncle Seamus! How nice. We should say hello."

Devlin, hard of hearing and focused on the proceedings, missed Court's indignant performance. "That good for nothing is taking advantage of our absence! I'm going to have a word with that freeloading idler."

She begged to tag along. There was something about his emoting that rang hollow to her inquisitive ear.

He hushed her with a kiss and a bribe. "I'll fetch you some of that ghastly cotton candy if you just stay put!"

She tried turning her attention to the parade of dogs but kept looking over at Seamus, drooping over the ring's fence, hat askew, chatting with a brawny fellow. When Court reached them, there was no exchange of angry words or arm waving but handshakes, guffaws, and a slap on the back.

Devlin finally noticed his grandson's absence and asked, "Where the devil did he wander off to? Germanicus is the next one up."

"He'll be back soon," Lacey said, slipping her hand into his pocket for warming. "He's fetching some cotton candy for me. If you like the way Germanicus looks, will you buy his puppies?"

The old man squeezed her hand in a conspiratorial gesture. "He's a splendid specimen, and the litter is worth a good deal more than his pitifully ignorant owner is asking."

"Devlin, you are a pirate! Just like Daddy says."

"I'll not deny I'm blessed with a keen business mind. Now would you like to be the one to name the wee ones?"

"Oh yes!"

He bristled at Court's panting reappearance with an enormous wad of pink fluff on a stick.

"Mind you don't get all sticky from this. I won't be toting you back to the hotel for a bath."

"'Tis a queer thing seeing you indulge her. You nearly missed what we came for."

"Why Grandfather, we brought Lacey here as a treat! What good is a treat without a bit of cotton candy?"

As the confection melted in her mouth, she realized that the truth according to Court was equally as vaporous.

For the next two hours, Lacey waited for Court to make his escape. She listened as they haggled over the price with Drummond, leaving the poor man bereft of his bargaining skills. She made the rounds of merchant stalls, enduring introductions to acquaintances and enemies with unusual grace and patience. At last, they stopped for dinner under a makeshift canopy, where the noise level was thunderous, the seats few, and the meals boxed. She was enthralled by the roughened faces, the pervasive smell of whiskey, and the crude banter that assailed her. Settled on Court's lap, she ate a chicken leg and a piece of apple, stealing sips from his beer when he wasn't looking.

"Grandfather, 'tis hardly the place for a child to be," Court shouted over the din. "Perhaps you should take her back to the hotel for a nap?"

"Pish! I'm not the least tired."

Devlin, swept up in the cacophony of greetings, was barely able to hear the question. "Fine, fine," he agreed, dismissing him to attend to a biting piece of gossip. "Go on with her and we'll meet for tea at O'Donohue's."

"What did you say?

"He said to go on and we'll meet you at O'Donohue's for tea," she said, preserving the misunderstanding.

His face creased in doubt. "I don't think you should be hanging about here."

"But Devlin promised to take me to see Emerald Fire," she persisted in a strident whine, knowing it would send him off without further ado.

"Give grandfather another five minutes then remind him of his promise." Court stood over her, awkwardly wiping her mouth with his pocket square. "What a sight you are, lamb! No lady's maid to tidy you up."

"Stop your fussing and be off!"

But he could not resist a parting admonition. "Mind you don't stray from grandfather's side. A pretty child like you is much too tempting for the gypsies!"

Lacey gave him a slight head start as she pushed her way through, bobbing around people for cover. A well-dressed, unaccompanied child attracted cursory interest, but no one cared enough to stop her. Court reentered the arena, and she hurried, anxious not to lose sight of him. He swerved to his left and picked his way carefully down a steep incline, sliding the last few feet into a saffron glow. Several *lanterns shed a weak light as the odor of damp earth grew more pungent; it was a familiar smell, fetid and moist. Trepidation mixed with nausea, as she thought of the poultry shack at Torrey Castle, where the slaughtering was done, the blood of dead birds mixing with straw and sawdust.*

In her dark skirt and jacket, Lacey blended into the shadows, unnoticed by the dozen or so men loitering around a sunken pit, about twenty feet in diameter. She recognized the brawny man as he castigated two handlers for the lackluster performance of their gamecocks.

"'Tis a crying shame," he bellowed with mocking sorrow. "These hardworking men have waged their money for the likes of them!" He tossed a purse of coins in the air for effect. "Why me blessed granny has brood hens who could put on a better show!"

The men, lathered up on adrenaline and poitín, flung bottles, hats, and clods of earth at the handlers, who scrambled to retrieve their property. Both gamecocks were impressive Irish grays, one fitted with a pair of metal spurs, the other with natural bony spires on his legs. Now hooded and chained, they were led away in disgrace.

Lacey searched for Court among the crowd, but he was nowhere to be seen. In desperation, she followed the handlers deeper into the darkening labyrinth and heard the unmistakable lisp of Seamus's brogue drifting over bales of hay.

"A gamecock needs time for building endurance, just like them boxers on the circuit. When Corrigan's in training, I rub up his skin to be toughening him. Look here." Seamus produced a valet's brush. "I trim them bristles just a wee bit, give it a coat of tallow, and work it right into his skin."

"What about his feathers and comb? Surely that gives the other something to hang onto?"

"Them must be kept short. Some of these pitters don't hold with the old ways, letting 'em fight dirty."

"Who's to be trusted? Every last one of them looks to be a cutthroat criminal. You said this would be easy money."

"Winning's as sure as rain on the roof. I know the ones to watch!"

"You're sure Corrigan is up to it?"

Seamus took affront at such a question. "This one's got a power of fight in him, if you'd be knowing how to coax it out. He'll take the best of them with fight to spare! It'll be the loveliest lump of money you ever made."

Lacey peered around at the dozens of caged birds, some torn and bleeding, others lifeless, and a good many untouched yet by the lash of battle. When Court and Seamus returned to the pit, she went from cage to cage, her chilled fingers easing the latches. The gamecocks strutted in circles, flexing their wings and pecking the ground. She stroked the breast of a bleary-eyed red quill, the weak thump of his heart fading to nothing under her caress. Dismayed to see that the uninjured ones were content to preen and socialize among themselves, she waved a burlap sack shepherding them into the passageway. They squawked in confusion, navigating through the dimness in clumsy twists and turns.

Soon they were in the brightened pit area where Corrigan was engaged, his screams echoing through the tunnel with frightening resonance. The clamor sent the gamecocks into a disorienting panic, some banged into the earthen walls with shrill cries, one knocked over a lantern, and several flew straight into the pit guided by instinct. When the drunken crowd grasped the true nature of the commotion, the hysteria escalated.

Lacey was in full view, a diminutive figure surrounded by surly, dumbstruck giants; their shouts bruised her with accusations and threats. There was no way out, so she closed her eyes in desperate prayer.

"This miserable brat's been mischief-making! Who does she belong to?" the brawny man asked. "If no one claims her, t'will be my pleasure to strap her."

"Leave her be. She's my affliction, not yours, McGloin." Court elbowed the others aside to confront the man.

"Who's to pay for the damage she's done here? It's on you to make it right."

"Shall we fetch the police to sort this out?" His levity belied his fear, as he edged close enough to feel Lacey's hand tremble in his.

"Don't be smart-mouthing me, O'Rourke! We'll settle this man-to-man. That's the way it's done in these parts."

She opened her eyes. How small and slight he looked in McGloin's menacing shadow—how dreadfully young and vulnerable.

"So it's your justice or no justice at all?"

The man's left hand curled into a mammoth fist and smashed into Court's chin, landing him against the wall of men who heaved him back at McGloin for another round.

Fearing a second blow would kill him, Lacey threw herself against the man's thigh and chomped down. His startled cry was followed by another's, as flames lashed at the barricade and spread to the matted straw. In the stampede, the two were forgotten.

"I feel bloody awful. What happened?"

"I thought you were dead!" she wailed, supporting him against her, tears streaming as the smoke enveloped them.

"Christ almighty, we're on fire!" he gasped and tried to stand but the effort overwhelmed him. "Get out of here now!"

"Not without you," she sobbed, dragging him a few feet and tumbling over.

"Hush, lamb. You go on and I'll follow."

"You can't do it alone!"

Seamus appeared with Corrigan in his cage. "We'd best be going," he said, as if the two had been basking in the summer sun. Handing the cage to Lacey, he slung Court over his shoulder.

"Tis a shortcut just beyond, leaving us far from McGloin and his thugs. I'll be needing to come up with something sly for the old gent. No one enjoys a well-told tale like himself."

"Miss Wakefield, shall we get on with it? My grandmother is paying you to teach me."

Anne Marie's face flamed from the rebuke. "Of course. I do need to see what grade level you're at, so I've prepared a general review."

Anthony's unlikely entrance with a tray of fruit and biscuits surprised his daughter and flustered Anne Marie. Having caught a glimpse of the young woman earlier, he was eager for a closer look.

"I thought you ladies could use a little break!"

When Anne Marie stood up, the chair tipped backward with a low crash, and this time when she blushed, it was a deep crimson. He shoved the tray at Lacey and in his haste, crushed the hat underfoot.

"What a clumsy oaf I am!" He handed over the smashed clump of black felt and satin to her with a roguish smile, taking in the deep amber of her eyes and waves of abundant honey-colored hair.

Anne Marie, in turn, stared up into the bluest eyes that she had ever seen in her twenty-three years of cloistered living.

Righting the chair, Anthony pushed it under her with such force, she fell back into it. "I do apologize for the destruction of such a lovely hat. I promise to replace it this very day."

"That won't be necessary. I have other hats," she demurred, as if she had the means to own more than one.

"I insist! It happens I promised to take Lacey shopping this afternoon, and now you can come along with us."

Lacey ate a russet pear, watchful of her father's genial badgering, surprised to hear of the shopping expedition.

Anne Marie stalwartly tried to evade the invitation. "I don't think Mrs. de la Roche would think it proper for me to accompany you. If you like, I can provide the bill of sale and you may reimburse me."

He was not to be put off, even when she stood to tidy the desk, signaling the matter was settled. He spun her around, her delicious reticence spurring him on. "It would mean a great deal to me if I could buy you a new hat." He liked the way her spectacles slid down her nose when she frowned. "I have something in mind that will bring out the curve of your cheekbone."

Standing back to squint at her in what he thought was a thoughtful manner, Anthony pictured her in a sable toque. Anne Marie interpreted this as his having fun at her expense. She was even more peeved that he had not had the courtesy to introduce himself, assuming in his arrogance, she would know.

"I've said how you may remedy this, sir!" She shook from the sound of the slamming door, keeping her eyes down, until Lacey spoke up.

"He's a captain."

"Really?"

"He left the army when he met my mother. She died. Women find him very charming. There's always so many of them about."

"It's not really any of my concern."

"I thought you should know."

The King's Camp

The gulmohar trees were in glorious bloom, casting a hazy warmth over the playing field, as Colonel Cullum presided over a practice chukkar. A trio of Indian musicians, perspiring in plaid kilts, clutched bagpipes and rehearsed another rendition of "God Save the King."

"You fellows sound absolutely abysmal. If there isn't a tremendous improvement by Saturday, I'll have the lot of you thrashed!"

He turned his attention to the field, heartened by the sight of Court, gracefully wielding a mallet with cheerful aggression. "Good show for a novice!"

Court, clad in tight white jodhpurs and a dark blue shirt, swooped in and around the seasoned players in a seamless display of expert horsemanship.

Suddenly, the Colonel's delight turned to anger. "This will not do at all!"

Practice was halted so that he could reprimand the newest recruit. "Lieutenant O'Rourke, must you always be the odd fellow out?" He pointed to the protective gear that the others wore. "You're of no earthly value to me injured."

"My apologies, Colonel. I'll return to the stables and suit up properly."

"And do find out what the dickens is keeping Davenport! I can't have a decent practice without my pivot man. There's another hour of daylight at best, and I've no desire to become bait for these infernal mosquitoes."

Muffled cries greeted Court as he entered the stables. The horses, in their freshly swept looseboxes, reacted with fearful snorts; he moved among them, quieting each with a murmur or touch. In the tack room, he discovered an Indian groom, curled in a defensive crouch, as Sydney Davenport whipped his naked back and legs.

"Stupid fool!" the man screamed, his arm flexing with each blow. "What good is he to me now?"

The groom whimpered an apology, but Sydney was intent on meting out punishment. Court sprang between them, ripping the belt away and shoving Sydney against the wall.

"This idiot fed Sultan a bucket of oats not more than ten minutes ago! He's useless to me!" He flung a hoof pick at the fleeing groom.

"Good Lord, there's a dozen fine horses for you to ride. It's only practice."

"No wonder you have such sympathy for these natives! You share the same lax attitude," he snarled, jerking the belt through the loops of his jodhpurs.

Court tensed in his search for a helmet, ignoring the disparaging remark for the moment. "I'll gladly help you choose another mount."

Sydney was absorbed with his toilet, combing his light hair in careful wisps across his head. Each time he looked in the mirror, it seemed his hairline had receded another fraction. As he added more wax to his moustache, he replied sulkily, "Don't expect a thank you."

"The bay will do the trick! Come and look him over. His withers are so snug, you won't need a saddle."

Katherine Davenport flitted among the players, a jasmine cloud of cooing compliments. "Colonel, the men look so darling in their outfits. But where is my Sydney?"

"He should be along my dear. Come and share my basket of refreshments." Next to food, he yearned for a sample of Katherine's abundant charms.

"Oh, you do think of every little nicety, but I must confess—I've been to tea at Mrs. Burleigh's. She serves the most exquisite sweets. Have you ever tasted her raspberry crisps?"

He groaned in remembrance. "The ones with the hazelnut centers and brandy glaze?"

"So you know how utterly divine they are! I've sinned at Mrs. Burleigh's table, and tomorrow, I'll atone by riding two hours instead of one!"

Even at thirty-six, she remained a chimera for men like Anthony, Sydney, and Cullum—white-blonde hair thick as a palomino's tail, agate green eyes, and a mouth painted the shape and color of a split strawberry. A newlywed for all of three months, she was indifferent to her husband's prowess on the field or anywhere else. After too many hardscrabble years as an actress and occasional mistress, marriage had provided an apt solution with its status and financial security.

Since that night in Dublin, Court had matured from a charming boy into a tantalizing young man. With his black cropped curls, his gray eyes burned bright with a brash sensuality. She had convinced herself that the cool professionalism he showed during the riding lessons was no more than a front for repressed ardor.

Practice had resumed, but now there was a commotion on the field, as Sydney froze and then returned the ball with a lethal smash.

Dismounting, he shouted, "This isn't a damn bit funny!" to the group of grinning officers. What had appeared to be the ball was a small skull, probably that of a monkey.

Court offered an historical aside. "I've been reading up on the game, and the proper way to play is with a skull, not a ball. I suppose you British are a touch too squeamish to do it the right way."

The skull whizzed by Court's head as he cantered away, laughter trailing behind him. Sydney remounted and tried to urge the bay over a cactus hedge in his pursuit of him. The horse knew he wasn't a show jumper or even a hunter but a solid polo pony trained for speed and quick turns; he pitched Sydney into the prickly shrub.

Court trotted over to Katherine, who favored him with a smile of mutual antipathy. "Mrs. Davenport, when your husband is finished impaling himself upon the vegetation, would you be so kind as to give him this message? Tell him, as any Irishman knows, you can't force a horse to go against his nature."

"The Shinwari are the best damn hunters in India! If you want to bag a rhino, get yourself a tribesman and prepare for three days of hell." Colonel Cullum shifted in his chair to admire an enormous ivory horn set above the fireplace. The effort made him wince as he placed his gouty foot on a low stool. "It was a bloody awful experience worth every blasted moment." He signaled for a servant to refill his glass.

"I prefer game somewhat more predatory," Sydney said. "The Bengal tiger is my idea of good sport."

An annoying trill of laughter interrupted him. "Must you be so serious about everything? I want to have fun on this expedition! I don't care if you kill anything. That's not the purpose."

"Katherine, don't be absurd! One doesn't hunt unless one intends to kill."

She looked to Court for consolation and asked, "Lieutenant, do you hunt for purpose or pleasure?"

With the whiskey warming his lips, he replied softly, "In Ireland, you never hunt anything more ferocious than a stag, lest it turns on you. Even then, the stag usually lives to a grand old age."

"That's because you come from a country of blighters! There isn't a one of you who understands the meaning of hard work and dedication to duty." Sydney's churlish attack was fostered, in part, by the lingering discomfort of microscopic cactus needles lodged in his posterior.

Before Court could deliver a witty retort, Katherine screeched and pointed to the rafters above them. A ten foot swathe of snake was devouring a rat with voluptuous ease.

With a dismissive wave, Cullum said, "That's a damon—rather colorful, don't you think? They're harmless to us, but do keep the vermin in check very nicely."

She could not contain her hysteria. "It's hateful! Everything about this country is senseless and cruel! The people have little regard for cleanliness, the animals feed off one another, the weather brutalizes you. Even my hairpins rust in this wretched humidity. And look at my gloves!" She clawed at the white kid gloves, moaning, "There's mold on them. Every time I want to wear them, I must scrape off this horrid green slime."

Court sympathized with her frustration; India was difficult to comprehend, even under the tolerable conditions of the King's Camp. The heat withered the spirit, insects plagued without pause, and the appetite suffered from a monotonous routine of tinned foods. The exotic allure of the East existed only in scattered moments. The rest of the time, one's senses were assaulted by a barrage of conflicting customs, tribal grudges, and primitive rites. He supposed it helped to be Irish, able to adapt to the punishing vagaries of life.

"What does happiness matter when we are all unhappy together?" he mused aloud.

"Spare me your Irish bromides. I've heard enough from you," Sydney growled.

"It's Urdu and rather apt for this moment."

Katherine had revived enough to agree with him. "I shall take comfort in those words Lieutenant. To know I'm not alone in my misery, that you too share my distress, will help me through my time here."

"My dear lady, I wish I could do more."

"Shut up, O'Rourke."

"Look here, Davenport," the Colonel chided, "you're throwing a pall over my little dinner party. I suggest we sit down before my cook vanishes for the evening. He's a most unpredictable chap."

Court was the last to leave, lingering to study the damon, wrapped in a languorous pose, one eye closed, a slight distention in its midsection. How Lacey would relish this spectacle, torn between the rat's fate and the snake's pleasure! He pressed the handkerchief to his lips to soften the wave of despair wafting over him. If he didn't steel himself against the likes of Davenport, he too would be devoured, inch by inch, with methodical malevolence.

A garrulous flock of peacocks roamed the grounds of the Maharajah Gurdatra's palace, the dominant male swaggering in contemptuous view of the hunting party. His jeweled plumage rippled in the steamy sunrise, while his belligerent gaze taunted the tethered hounds.

Katherine trailed after them, collecting fallen feathers, until her husband pounced on her. "Are you mad? These birds are sacred to them!"

"Oh pooh! What's a few old feathers? I'll have a fan made from these." She revealed the contents of a canvas bag.

Sydney seized her wrist in further warning. "Must I remind you, we're the guests of the Maharajah?" He set the stolen feathers adrift in the thick breeze. "He's being more than generous with his hospitality."

"You needn't remind me in such a brutish way." She rubbed her sore wrist and sought retaliation but had only words to inflict upon him. "Since when are you so considerate of the natives?"

"When the old swine is a friend of my commanding officer!"

"Damn you and your silly pig-sticking party!"

This wasn't the expedition she dreamed of; this little outing for wild boar would have to suffice. The maharajah had provided the hunting party with his best guide, a troupe of Indian stalkers, half a dozen horses, and his elite pack of boarhounds. At daybreak, he assured Sydney the boar had been tracked for several days and a kill was guaranteed.

Katherine thought the whole affair to be an exercise in male vanity. Wasn't the point to track the quarry yourself? The only bright spot would be the chance to spend time with Court and command his attention while Sydney chased after his prized pig.

Colonel Cullum limped toward her with a frantic wave. "My dear! The maharajah has been asking for you. It seems he had the delight of seeing you on the London stage, and is quite an admirer."

"How darling of him! But we must be off before the sun becomes too unbearable. Will you please tell the maharajah I'll see him for tea?"

He took her elbow and said, "That won't do at all, I'm afraid. I tell you this in confidence, I'm in a bit of a pickle with the old boy. Just a little misunderstanding over his son's tutor. We executed him along with some other upstarts a few months back. A beastly mistake—these things happen from time to time. If you stayed behind, it would smooth things over quite a bit."

She nearly screamed in refusal; it was too maddening for words! What did she care if the old bugger had his neck in the wringer? She cared even less for the fawning attention of some smelly native.

"These royals parcel out jewels like tea cookies. I'm sure the old boy will come up with some token of appreciation. Perhaps emeralds to match your eyes?"

She thrilled at the possibility, recalling the pearl choker that Mrs. Burleigh had received as a thank you from a regional prince after she sent his son a birthday present.

Clinging to the colonel's arm, she exclaimed, "I'll do it! If we play our cards right, each of us will make out quite royally!"

———◆———

Court tightened the cinch on the saddle for the third time, anxious about the hunt and how it was to unfold. It sounded barbaric if the colonel's description was accurate. The dogs would chase the boar to the point of exhaustion, and then the stalkers advanced with spears, tormenting the poor beast until the hunter put a bullet in it. It was grisly business, for which he had no stomach, but once again, Cullum had presented it as an order.

As he inspected his rifle, Sydney whispered from behind, "Do keep that close, O'Rourke, you'll be needing it."

"I'm coming along at the colonel's behest," he said, stroking the gelding's massive thigh, then checking the cinch for another adjustment. "I've no blood lust for the sorry devil."

"Don't have the stomach, eh? The boar's a clever beast. Just when you think he's done, doesn't have an ounce of fight left, he surprises you. You have to respect that in an animal."

The dogs tore through the light underbrush with shrill barks—the boar rousted in flight from their crazed pursuit. As the sun climbed above the Pradshipur Mountains, the black flies went to work, attracted by the lather of sweat on the horses, crawling into ears and noses, with stinging determination. Court's throat ached from the billowing red dust, and his head pounded from the sun's harsh glint. When he realized that Katherine was remaining at the palace, his unease deepened into dread. She was his best defense against Sydney's malice. Without her, he was no better off than the boar.

The guide disappeared into the brush, and Sydney said, "We may as well rest up a bit, until Ahmed returns. He'll see if the stalkers have moved in yet." He drank greedily from a canteen and watched as Court followed, sharing with his horse. "That's a bloody waste, there's no telling how much longer we'll be out here."

"Oh, I'm counting on you to finish him off with one shot and be done with it. Then it's back to the palace for a bath and dinner."

Perhaps, you'll fit my wife in between the two."

The water splashed over his fingers. "What the devil are you accusing me of, Davenport?"

"I know you're cuckolding me."

"Your wife means nothing to me! If she's led you to believe otherwise, it's pure fiction!"

Sydney's composure was more intimidating than his infantile rage. "You crawl out of a backwater country, reeking of the bog, and insinuate yourself into the affections of my wife! I'm putting an end to this here and now."

Fortuitously, Ahmed came running and announced, "Sahibs, it is time! The boar awaits you."

Following at a distance, Court wondered how Katherine could be so unthinking as to put him in jeopardy with her lunatic of a husband. There was not a shred of hope that he could convince the man that his suspicions were unfounded.

The first thing that Court noticed was the ominous silence. The dogs, leashed and at attention, were held far enough from the standing boar so as not to rile it further. Two spears pierced its side while several others littered the ground. Breathing in short heaves, its eyes flickered in wariness, blood oozing from a dozen gashes. Silvery vultures sailed in wide arcs above, observing the grim scene with high expectations.

Ahmed motioned for the stalkers to withdraw, telling the two men, "I will take your horses and leave you to your sport. Good luck, sahibs."

"See if you can catch his eye while I draw a bead on him," Sydney directed Court with chilly calm.

Court took a position a dozen yards away from the boar and waved his arm. The dying beast lifted its head in an agonized turn, snout thrusting in suspicion, and from deep within, found the strength to charge—straight at him. As the boar gained more ground, it became clear that Sydney was content to watch, relaxing his offensive crouch and laying his rifle across his arm.

"Try to get off one shot before he horns you, O'Rourke!"

Court had not mastered shooting with pistol or rifle, and fear cramped his fingers so that his aim was all the more suspect. He fired a shot that grazed the boar's head, causing it a moment of disorientation and then, an abrupt change in direction. With no time to react and regain his position, Sydney toppled backward as the boar gored him in the thigh.

With much regret, Court advanced and shot it between the eyes. The boar drove deeper into Sydney's leg and collapsed on the screaming man with a final grunt of surrender. Without a moment of consideration for his plight, the stalkers excised the boar and set upon it—knives slicing through the air with primitive expertise. The tusks were passed around with guttural approvals, and a fight ensued for ownership.

"It's always a treat to see you suffer, Davenport," Court whispered over the unconscious man, his eyes hard with contempt. "I'm sure you'd say the same about me."

The Claire Street Settlement House

Surreptitiously, Lacey curved a hand around Anthony's coffee cup, sliding it across the table and raising it to her lips.

"No coffee for you, young lady!" he said from behind his newspaper.

"I drink it at home."

Refolding the paper, he replied, "You know your grandmother doesn't approve. As long as we're her guests, we'll do as she dictates. How are you and Miss Wakefield getting on these days?"

"Fine." She hunched forward and sulkily ate her breakfast.

"Don't gobble your food. Are you that much in a hurry to leave me?"

"I can't help it if I'm hungry. I'm growing, you know."

"Yes, by the foot, every day according to your grandmother. She's insisting I spring for a new wardrobe because you haven't a stitch of wearable clothing." He refreshed his coffee and then, as an afterthought, poured some in her glass of milk and winked.

"You can't let her take me shopping! It will be too horrible! You know she'll find fault with every little thing. Please?" She grabbed his hand in desperation.

"Let's come to an agreement, shall we?" You be nicer to Miss Wakefield and I'll keep your grandmother at bay."

"I'm not as mean as I have been."

"Being not as mean is not the same as being as nice as you should be!" His relationship with Anne Marie had reached an amicable phase where she no longer scurried away at the sight of him. "I can't imagine why she's so skittish around me?" He looked to his daughter for some insight.

It was Lacey's turn to change the subject. "Where is grandmother this morning?"

Still preoccupied with thoughts of Anne Marie, Anthony muttered, "Has one of her headaches—had a tray in her room." The cloud lifted, and he said sternly, "It would be considerate of you to look in on her and see if she needs anything. Don't think I haven't noticed the way you do your damnest to avoid the woman!"

Lacey bridled at being confronted with yet another of her shortcomings. "She's always correcting me! I thought grandmothers were supposed to spoil their grandchildren?"

He laughed, "If you're looking for some petting, you'll have a long and chilly wait. She's not the type to bake cookies or knit sweaters. There are other ways for the two of you to get to know each other—that is the purpose of this visit."

"Pish! It's hard enough to sit still when she does talk to me. She makes me fidget. Even the servants are scared of her."

"She does have that effect on people," he agreed, then whispered, "I'm going to take advantage of her absence to enjoy a smoke! Promise not to tell?"

"I'll do it for you, Daddy!" she said, settling on his lap, a devoted accomplice, filling the pipe with his customized blend of Chinese and Indian tobacco.

"You do that so much better than me, pet."

"Do the rings, please!" Her command was a sweet purr to his ears, and he complied. "It smells so lovely. I like your pipe so much more than your cigarettes. Can I have a puff?"

Anthony wavered, not wanting to be caught in the act, but her winsome smile weakened him. "Just a tiny puff—it may give you a headache."

The acrid smoke moistened her eyes as she exhaled a wisp of smoke. "That was fun! Why don't women smoke pipes?"

"It's bad enough some of them smoke cigarettes! Smoking is something men do, the way women shop. It relaxes them."

He uttered this with such infallible male logic, Lacey paused before laughing derisively. "Daddy that doesn't make any sense! Even Miss Wakefield would say so. I hate to shop. Does that mean I can smoke a pipe when I grow up?" She beheld her father in a new and not very flattering light.

"I'm merely saying there are socially acceptable behaviors for women."

"Not according to Miss Wakefield, and she would know because she's a sufferer."

"A what?"

"You know, those women who march for poor people, and want to vote for somebody for something. I can't remember all of it."

"Our Miss Wakefield is a suffragette! One of those crazy women who makes spectacles of themselves?"

She sprang from his lap. "You should come with us tomorrow, to the place where she teaches poor children. We can find out about suffering together, and you won't think it's all such silliness."

"I think I'll do just that! Miss Wakefield should not be bringing you places without my permission."

"But Daddy, I gave you the note last week. Didn't you read it?"

In truth, Lacey had masterminded the outing.

"Where do all the poor people live in New York?" she had asked Anne Marie.

"They're all around us."

"How can that be? I haven't seen any about."

"It's understandable. I doubt your father or grandmother has any desire to venture into the poorer neighborhoods."

"Oh pish! Do you know where they are?"

"It wouldn't be safe for me to go unescorted to certain areas, but I do teach English two afternoons a week at the Claire Street Settlement House."

"In Ireland, we have poorhouses, which are frightful places—worse than prison!"

Anne Marie stacked some books and said, "We can skip ahead in your history book and read about the social reform movement if you like."

Lacey took the suggestion a giant leap forward. "I'd like you to take me there— to the settlement house, for a visit."

Dread colored her face. "How on earth will I convince your grandmother? She's certain to forbid it."

"You should ask my father! He's very progressive. Just write a little note and say it's educational."

Anthony tried to mask his absent-mindedness with a bit of blustering. "She should just come right out and ask, rather than have you slip me a piece of paper, and expect me to remember. Remind her I gave my permission and I'll accompany the two of you."

—♦—

Margaret's bedroom resembled the interior of an expensive box of chocolates, shades of pink and gold satin. The brocade-covered sofa and chairs hushed all sound, and Lacey felt like she was sitting in a luxurious confessional awaiting the priest. While her grandmother labored over the week's menus, she mentally composed a list of her sins. She had played marbles with the butcher's delivery boy twice, she had been disrespectful to Anne Marie many, many times, and she had frightened Mr. Wilcox, the iceman, with a dead mouse.

"Lacey."

"Yes Grandmother." She prepared herself for a recitation of her social blunders and lamentable transgressions.

"Please bring me that rosewood box on the dresser."

The octagonal-shaped box was carved with an elegant, geometric pattern and had a hinged lid with a brass lock. It was heavier than it looked, and when opened, the aroma of sandalwood mixed with the scent of the sterling roses filling several vases.

"You haven't worn a single piece of jewelry from all I have given you!" Margaret's reproach hinted at further interrogation, so Lacey leaped in with a hasty excuse.

"Daddy didn't want me to bring anything of great value. It's so easy to lose small things when you're traveling."

"I've never known my son to be attentive to such details," she said tartly, noting how both father and daughter were most accomplished at twisting the truth to serve their needs. "I have something very dear to me that I want to give you."

She held up a gold chain with a cameo pendant. "This belonged to my grandmother, and she gave it to me on my wedding day. I want you to have it now."

"But I'm not getting married!" Lacey panicked, hoping there was no groom lurking in a closet.

"Goodness child, such drama! I think I can say for certain, I'll not be in Ireland when that great event takes place."

Slipping it around her neck, she shrank from her grandmother's critical appraisal. "Lacey, it's not an albatross! Take that locket off so I can see how it looks."

"I'm sorry but I can't."

Margaret's headache returned with a surge between her eyes, nestling right in the center of her skull. "Are you defying me?"

"I can't take it off. I made a promise not to."

"A promise is an important responsibility. Your father has not been remiss in the development of your moral character. May I ask who warrants such a promise?"

For the first time in many weeks, the thought of Court engulfed Lacey in a telltale blush.

"Ah, I see. I know I spend a good deal of time pointing out your lesser qualities, trying to bring you up to my standard of deportment."

"That's very true," she agreed tactlessly.

"I'm giving you some advice for the first and last time. It took me many years to learn this, and my intention is to spare you unnecessary grief. Live each and every day as if you've achieved your heart's desire—everything else will fall into place. Keep the cameo as a reminder of me. In time, you'll make good use of it."

"Thank you, Grandmother." She waited, wanting to return the kindness. "Is your headache gone?"

"It comes and goes." Margaret smiled at this solicitous attempt. "Will you bring this to cook? If she has any questions, she may communicate them through William."

Lacey stooped to kiss her powdered cheek.

"Thank you, my dear."

"What for?" She was nearly out the door.

"For bringing the menus to cook."

"I'm glad to do it for you, Grandmother! I hope you feel better."

"And Lacey, please use the stairs and not the banister for your descent."

The Claire Street Settlement House sat on frozen haunches amid squalid tenements on the lower eastside of Manhattan watching as a glossy black Packard released a curious trio of visitors.

"Oh dear, we're so inexcusably late. Mrs. Broom does not like tardiness!" Anne Marie directed her annoyance at Anthony.

He had transformed a simple visit into an expedition. A taxi was a "foolish waste of time and not safe" while lunch at a small café was "too pedestrian when they could dine at Delmonico's and be damn sure of what they were eating," Even the drive down Fifth Avenue and a neck-wrenching glimpse of the library, with its richly detailed neoclassical facade and E.C. Potter's crouching lions, was more culture than Anthony could bear in one afternoon.

"Who are those people supposed to be?" he asked.

"The statues represent history, drama, philosophy—the humanities," Anne Marie said.

"That won't get you very far in this world."

"I like them," Lacey interjected. "I feel like I'm back in Dublin. What are humanities?" The adults ignored her, too preoccupied misreading each other.

"Must he be so opinionated and smug about every little thing?"

"She's listening to everything I say with such a look of amazement!"

The interior of the settlement house was unexpectedly cheery but Spartan. The long hallway acted as an art gallery for the whimsical watercolors of the children and the more sober oils of the adults. The front parlor served as a reception area and showroom, its whitewashed walls hung with textile displays of quilts, blankets, and shawls, its shelves brimming with an array of pottery.

A menagerie of ivory animals delighted Lacey and then surprised her when she saw they were carved from soap. The jumble of color and texture did more to warm the room than the sputtering glow in the fireplace.

"It's damn chilly in here," Anthony remarked, pulling close the collar of his mohair overcoat. "Where the hell is the coal scuttle?"

"Coal is a dear commodity," Mrs. Broom said, entering with an air of exasperation. "I expected you over an hour ago. I won't be able to give you more than thirty minutes of my time. I'm Lila Broom."

She shook Anthony's hand in a fierce grip and winked at Lacey. "You must be Captain de la Roche, and this, of course, is Lacey!"

"Yes I am, and she is," he replied, taking in the broad-shouldered woman with intense, dark eyes and scarred face.

"I had the misfortune to be a very curious child and play with a gas lamp," she explained, intuiting the unasked question. "I see your automobile is quite the center of attention." A swarm of people thronged the Packard. "We rarely attract such affluent visitors. Thank you Anne Marie!"

It was the first mention made of her embarrassed presence, which rose to mortification with the woman's indelicate remark.

Mrs. Broom resumed her monologue with gusto. "You can be certain, Captain, I'll not let you leave until I've charmed a sizeable check out of you. Maybe we'll be able to buy enough coal to get us through the rest of the winter! What would you like to see first? We have a fine carpentry workshop that may be of interest to you. Or perhaps, something more artistic in nature?"

"My rank is derived from fifteen years in the United States Army, which required my hands-on attention."

"Good for you, Captain! I like a man who can keep up with me. I was beginning to think you were painfully shy."

Lacey trailed the adults for more than ten minutes before taking off on her own. She was eager to meet some of the children whose artwork hung below, but the house was eerily quiet. On the third floor, she noticed a rusting spiral staircase leading to an attic room which ran the length of the house—an ideal setting for the making of rugs, tapestries, baskets, and laces.

While she knew nothing of weaving, she admired the shapes and sizes of the looms as they created spectral shadows. Two figures bent over a Jacquard loom with a bit of carpet on it. One woman's foot rocked the treadle of the spinner in syncopation with her right hand, twisting the thread as she spoke in a familiar brogue.

"Listen to me now. If I ain't discouraged, why should you be? Discouraging won't do for any pupil of mine for mistakes are how we learn."

She unreeled the broken thread, mended it, and set it right with a deft pat. "You will spin!

I'll see to it! 'Tis time to turn up the lamps. Me eyes are clouding over with this gloom."

The other woman moved slowly, both hands kneading the small of her back. "Rose, I don't know how you do this all day. 'Tis damn wicked on the back."

"'Tis this or standing on me feet like you, Bridey."

A cry erupted from a lump of blankets on the floor and Lacey reacted, catching Rose's attention. "And where did you come from, my wee one?"

Before she could answer, the baby began to suckle, and the wide yawn stretching Bridey's face ended in a harsh gasp; both Lacey and Bridget reared back from the surprise. The girl's bloom had faded in these months of privation. Gone was the robust, impetuous flirt. What remained was the bitterness and harsh tongue of a defeated woman.

"You! Come all this way to have a look at me in my pitiful state? Will you be reporting back to the others?"

Lacey was riveted to the woeful looking baby with tufts of red hair and a mottled face. "I had no idea you were here. No one does. Is it a boy?"

"Aye, Liam after my da."

She pressed on, "He looks very much like Corin Gallagher."

"And what does that matter to you? You were always one for putting your nose in other folks' business."

"You knew all along! And still, you let Court leave in disgrace? How could you, Bridget?"

"Should it matter to me his being disgraced when I'm the one shamed and sent away? He's off living the life of a gentleman soldier. Not much of a price to pay for his pleasure taking!"

"Bridey, settle yourself down. You'll sour your milk!" Rose warned.

"What does a tit full of milk matter to him? He'll not live long with the weakness in his lungs."

"I'm sorrier than I can say, Bridget. I'll speak to my father—he'll know what to do."

"A mighty poor thing t'would be having the likes of you and yours favoring me with charity!"

She dug through her coat pockets for the crisp one dollar bill Anthony had given her for spending money. She thrust it at her with faint hope. "Please take this for now."

She slapped it away and spat on Lacey's shoes. "Sod off, you little bitch."

"Bridey, don't be daft! Take it! 'Tis more than you have now. This one's not to blame for your poor luck."

"'Tis pity, nothing more," Bridget railed, as Lacey stepped backward. "I curse the day I first set eyes on you!"

Anne Marie admonished Lacey for wandering off and returned to fretting as they waited in the parlor.

"I do hope your father isn't bullying Mrs. Broom. It never occurred to me she might ask for a donation. But then, he wasn't supposed to come along in the first place."

"He has more than enough to give away. He's never had to go without."

Anthony walked in with an elated Mrs. Broom. "Shall we be off? We've stayed too long at the expense of this lady's valuable time."

Mrs. Broom whispered to Anne Marie, "Thank you for delivering such a magnificent benefactor! He's quite the shrewd businessman."

"So I hear, constantly."

"Straight away he demanded to see the books and did quite a bit of harrumphing, but wrote a handsome check. It will cover the coal bill and also the cost of wiring the house for electricity!"

Anne Marie was taken aback. "He did? He can be rather unpredictable at times."

"Not only that, he's pledged an annual contribution to be used for the upkeep of the house. What a marvelous man. You say he's a widower?"

"Yes, for a number of years."

"Well my dear, thank you again. Please bring him to visit anytime."

When the three were bundled in the car, Anthony delivered his opinion of Mrs. Broom. "She's a strange old bird, but for a woman, has quite a good head for business."

"You didn't feel coerced into making the donation?" Anne Marie asked with all the sarcasm her shy self could muster.

"Not at all; otherwise, I'd still be a hostage." He was quite pleased with his day of good deeds. "Lacey what did you think of the place?"

"I thought it was sad," she murmured, watching the ill-clad pedestrians skid along the icy streets.

"Sad? How's that?"

"Just sad." She wondered if she should write to Court about Bridget and the baby that was not his—the baby that would die soon. "So sad," she repeated and closed her eyes against the darkness.

The Jhanor Shrine

The Jhanor Shrine, carved into the sleek granite bluff of the Pradshipur Mountains, shared its shrouded mysticism with the Hindu, Moslem, Sikh, Parsi, and Jain in a rare display of communal accord among the fractious sects. Its massive bronze grill guarded a cavernous interior where every afternoon, pilgrims issued forth to pray and leave baskets of fruit and grain, loose bouquets of jasmine and camellias, or small offerings of silk, incense, and beads. Their blissful devotion reminded Court of his own Catholicism with its propensity for ritual and sacrifice, and the grim reality that faith and piety provide useless weapons against poverty and oppression.

While quiet contemplation was not possible among the riotous personalities of coppersmiths, robins, crows, and mourning doves, the shrine had become a refuge for him. It was a place to brood, hidden among the glossy casurina trees, under a sky streaked with ribbons of madras—the verdant shadows of the jungle deepening as the day grew to an end.

On this October afternoon, Court settled in his favorite spot and ruminated over the return of the Davenports from Cairo. Ahmed's medical intervention had been patchy, and the maharajah's personal physician only a shade more skillful in tending Sydney's wound. Within forty-eight hours, infection had turned the soft tissue into a putrid black mass, and he was whisked off to Bombay for emergency treatment, then on to Cairo for rehabilitation and rest.

Would Sydney persist in his vendetta? Would Cullum discover what happened that day? Would Katherine badger him with her unwanted flirtations? He sought relief in Lacey's first letter from New York, admiring her sweeping penmanship so unlike his twisted scrawl.

September 25, 1912

Dear Court,

I can hardly believe I crossed an entire ocean and did not see anything as grand as a flying fish or a shark! I must confess I was mean to Daddy for the whole trip, but he seems to have recovered from my despicable treatment. Grandmother's house is very beautiful but so much smaller than Durbin House. It could fit like a dollhouse inside one wing of Torrey Castle!

Grandmother doesn't approve of my curiosity and makes faces when I ask too many questions. She is appalled at my lack of propriety and thinks I am too forward with the servants. The nicest thing I can say about her, is that she's very fastidious. Most of the time, I hide from her.

Can you tell my vocabulary is improving? I'm using all the new words in this letter! Daddy wants me to have lessons in everything, even French (Mon Dieu!), so I can find a suitable husband. I don't want a husband who cares about such things. He must like horses and lots of questions, and let me smoke a pipe if I've a mind to! Please tell me what you think a wife should be in your next letter. It would be most illuminating.

This must be a short letter because we are going to the museum so I can become accomplished. I'm making Daddy come because I know he hates culture. Why should I have to suffer alone?

Every night I pray for you and ask God to keep you safe from harm. We will not return home until the end of next summer. It's a dreadfully long time to be away from Devlin, Aggie, and Padraic.

All my love,
Lacey

PS. Can you send me one of those little monkeys with the white faces? I promise to take good care of it and hide it from grandmother.

He read it through several times, laughing at her guileless notions about marriage and her valiant attempt to expand her vocabulary. This was the first letter that vibrated with her inquisitive nature and insouciant charm—a reassurance to him she was adjusting to his absence with resilience. The monkey was another matter; he would need to come up with something equally as exciting, not requiring care and feeding.

"Courtland, I must speak with you!" Katherine stepped into view with a tentative wave of her riding crop.

"You followed me?" he asked, stuffing the letter in his pocket and checking to see if they were alone.

"I had to see you. Please don't be cross with me. I've missed you."

Unmoved by her plea, he dragged her into the shrine and over to a dusty corner. She spun around in awe of the surroundings.

"What is this place? Are those bats up there?" she howled, covering her head.

"Quiet down, woman! This is a holy place, and the bats are fast asleep for now. We'll talk here or nowhere."

"Must you be so unkind? I've come to you with my heart in my hand."

"You've no heart to offer any man. Why the devil did you lie to Sydney?"

"Didn't you get my letters?"

"I tore them up!"

"I explained everything—laid bare my soul to you."

"Must I repeat the damn question?"

"It was all Sydney's imagination! I had no idea what he was up to," she sobbed. "When he thought he was dying, he told me he tried to kill you. I was devastated."

Court struck back. "Even if he acted purely out of his own delusions, I've no doubt you gave him good cause to suspect me! A word here or there. A calculated look. It's all bloody acting! It's what you do Katherine—what you get paid for."

"I swear on my soul, I never meant to put you in danger. How could I? I love you, Courtland!" She shoved the crop at him. "Beat me! Make me hurt the way I've hurt you." She dropped to her knees, eyes raised in supplication.

"What a performance! And with no one to applaud but me and these blessed blind creatures."

Her outburst seared the kernel of anger that had simmered within him for the last year. The temptation did not lie in the heat emanating from her body, sultry and intoxicating. It was the prospect of revenge against Anthony and Sydney. What if he yielded to the moist curve of her mouth, the pale flute of her throat? Her head swayed between his hands, and he responded with a hard thrust into her mouth.

"Show me Katherine. Show me how sorry you are."

December 31, 1912

My darling Lacey,

I am staggered by your generous present! There's a good deal of dressing up around here, and your gold cuff links will make me look even more dashing, if that's possible. I shall wear them this very night to a fancy dress ball and do my best to flash them about in your honor.

I don't have to wonder if you liked my present, for I know you so well. I can picture you thrilled to pieces with the scabbard and scimitar. But mind you don't go slicing up those who vex you! If your father thinks I'm a bloody fool, tell him the blade is rather dull and won't cause mortal harm. Go easy on old granny if she's as brittle as you say.

Grandfather and Aggie sent me an enormous hamper of lovely treats, which some of my fellow officers think they have a chance at. They've no idea just how greedy I can be...

Court paused; the only time he felt like his old self was in his letters to Lacey. He had become aloof, testy and, at times, downright surly. Addressing the envelope, he decided to return at midnight, finishing the letter as the year came to a close.

The officers' club overflowed with acres of Bokhara silk and dress uniforms. One had to look closely to see that the setting was not a ballroom on Eaton Place but a colonial imitation. The long damask-covered tables displayed buckets of champagne and Italian wine, platters laden with garnished hunks of boar, deer, and lamb, and intricately woven raffia baskets filled with mangoes, dates, and clusters of grapes.

Court found it depressing but submitted to endless dances and trivial exchanges with wives and daughters. Katherine swirled in and out of sight, pretending to ignore him and preening with pleasure at every compliment. She thought it wise to observe a social distance from him to protect their affair, when in truth, he inflicted this ruse upon her through callous indifference.

Seeking relief from the heat and music, he retreated into the shadows of the verandah. The moon burned with a white light that sent a shiver through him, and he thought he heard a snake stirring in the ferns, but it was the rustle of Katherine's glittering gown.

"Go away," he said heartlessly, wiping his brow. "I'm vexed enough by the heat and in no mood for your mindless chatter."

She snatched the handkerchief, bringing it to her lips, savoring his scent. "Do let me have this as a talisman. You bewitch me, Courtland." She tucked it between her breasts.

He had subjugated her sexually, in ways he would never use a flash house whore, disregarding any caress or gesture that might offer her a wisp of pleasure and still, she sought more.

"Give it back." His hand curled around her neck.

"But darling, you have others."

His thumb pressed the dimple on her throat. "Shall I leave you breathless, or will you do as I ask?"

"Take it! It's a small thing to ask of you!"

He secured Lacey's handkerchief in his breast pocket. "You've no idea how much you ask of me."

At 11:45 p.m., Court departed without the colonel's permission and found Katherine across his bed, reading the unfinished letter to Lacey.

"How dare you!" he shouted, tearing it from her grasp and striking her across the face. "Is there no scrap of decency left in your whoring soul?"

Undaunted, she lunged at him, grabbing one arm with both hands and revealing the cuff link. "Quite costly! So this is who is worthy of your tenderness—your affection? You make love to me but you're in love with Anthony's daughter! And you think me depraved?"

"We have sex because it gives me the satisfaction of cuckolding two men!"

He replaced the letter on the desk and covered it with a book. "I'm done with you."

"Do you want to do to her—what you do to me? Do you really think Anthony would let you plow his precious daughter?"

Katherine's words exploded in his head like bits of shrapnel—inflaming his brain with visuals so repugnant, so deeply carnal, there was no hope of restraining himself. His fist tensed, bruising her jaw with a solid jab, and when she fell, he kicked her in the side. Blood and saliva dripped from her mouth, she lay bent in half, barely conscious.

He yanked her up and twisted both arms behind her. "If I ever hear her name on your lips again, by Judas, I'll kill you. Go back to Sydney and attend to his pathetic desires."

After two quick shots of whiskey, Court settled himself at the desk, benumbed by his savagery, and smoothed out the letter. As the King's Camp reverberated with celebratory salutes to 1913, he wrote: *Thank you again for the cuff links, my dearest lamb. I'll treasure them as much as I do memories of you and home.*

◆

"Sorry to have roused you at this ghastly hour," Colonel Cullum said, dropping his sluggish girth into a chair. "But there's mischief afoot, and you're involved."

Court stood at attention, eyes weighted from sleep, confused by the summons. Were the Sikhs riled up again? Had the truce at Benzair been broken? Or had another arsenal been raided by Shinwari bandits?

"Something up with the natives, sir?"

The colonel made a motion toward the whiskey decanter, but he demurred and maintained his stance.

"Go on, take it, my boy. You're going to need it when I'm through with you. And do sit down. You're making me twitchy with your infernal propriety." Cullum waved a letter and said, "Katherine Davenport tried to kill herself tonight, and this identifies you as the reason! Read it before I destroy it. I daresay you'll need that drink now."

Court read the letter, losing color and stuttering, "These are all filthy lies Colonel. She's insane!"

"Of course she is! Did it with a six-spotted beetle trying to reenact Cleopatra's death scene. Next time, she ought to do it proper with a viper. That'll finish her off in a trice!"

"We were together, briefly. I ended it on New Year's."

"Well, no matter. She's accusing you of rape and blackmail—this little pregnancy claim seems to be what drove her to…"

"It's been more than two months since I touched her, and I never used her in that way."

"Do spare me the tawdry details of your coital proclivities. All this might have been avoided, had you come to me, when Davenport tried to feed you to that blasted boar."

"You knew?"

"It's my job to know every nasty and degenerate thing that goes on under my nose. Do you think only you Irish thrive on gossip? These natives glide about unnoticed, hearing all sorts of secrets. Eventually, it reaches me."

He tried to explain, but the colonel wasn't finished. "Why do you think I was so generous with Davenport's furlough? I wanted to put time and distance between the two of you. Then you muck up everything by getting into his wife's knickers as soon as they return!"

Court groaned, cradling his head. "I've been a fool—a bloody, vengeful fool."

"Listen to me, O'Rourke. I don't care what went on with you and the actress. But this bad blood between you and Davenport will destroy the both of you. I prefer it doesn't happen under my command."

"I understand, sir. Where am I to be reassigned?"

"Oh you'll be staying put! You're to be my new pivot man. Davenport hasn't been up to snuff since the boar got him."

"You would do that for me?"

"Don't get all sentimental, it suits my purposes. You'll never be a proper soldier. But as long as I have you, I'll exploit your other talents."

"What about Davenport?"

"I'll appeal to his insipid ego with a promotion and a new post. He's due back late tomorrow. I'm dispatching his wife to Calcutta, on the morning train, for medical attention. We're damn lucky her ayah sucked most of the poison out of her. She's bloated and rather bluish but fit to travel."

"Then what?"

"If Davenport wants to trek back from Hong Kong to have your hide— so be it! I doubt he'll care enough to make the effort."

"How can we be sure Katherine won't tell him everything once they're in Calcutta?"

"Look here, I didn't say it was a perfect plan." Cullum brought his hands together in a prayerful gesture. "I'll see to it she's kept sedated until they reach Hong Kong. I don't think he'll mind one bit. If it were up to me, all wives would be kept in a semiconscious state, less wear and tear on the nerves."

Part III

"Awakenings"
1914-1916

The Jalna Derby

The wind was up on the Liffy, ships slithering through the oily waters, docking at the stone quays and spilling their cargo. In February of 1914, Dublin was the Imperial City, defined by a reckless virility and powered by the economic hum of a strong British presence. Nowhere was their domination more keenly apparent than Dublin Castle, a Cyclops of politics and commerce, entrusted with preserving the colonial choke hold. A phalanx of government buildings, renowned schools and churches, exclusive shops, and hotels provided a luxurious lifestyle for the Ascendancy.

Beyond this circumference of comfort and prosperity lay the decimated east end, lacerated by rail tracks, freight yards, and antiquated factories. It was a dreary hellhole with aptly named neighborhoods like Misery Hill, Beggars Bush, and Agony Row. For thousands of families, this was their Imperial City, one of everlasting perdition.

Within a month of their return to Ireland, Anthony had enrolled Lacey in Saint Honoria on Camden Row. But not without a list of demands being negotiated.

"If you're sending me away, I must have Paladin so I may ride every day."

"Done! But you must not ride unaccompanied! Riding in St. Stephen's Green is not like riding in the country."

"Then you must make some kind of arrangement with the stables to hire Padraic!"

"What? Am I to have yet another member of the Knox family freeloading off me?"

"Pish! He needs to learn a trade, and I need someone I know, or I shall die of absolute loneliness."

"So it's all up to me, is it?"

"Well, this is your idea."

If Lacey leaned all the way out the window, she could see the lighthouse, by the river's mouth, inexorably peeping through the canopy of deepening mist. The narrow room was no more than a cell, furnished with the pious essentials, including a grimacing Christ, crucified above her bed. The nascent restlessness and arrogance of adolescence fueled Lacey's disdain for the twenty-nine girls of good breeding, for the sedate flock of Dominican nuns charged with their care, and for the ungodly expectation that she would yield to the yoke of obedience. She was primed for adventure and self-discovery in a city riven by centuries of oppressive rule and sectarian violence.

There was a light scratching at the door, and Lacey prepared for business. Every Monday and Thursday, starting at 9 p.m., a stealthy parade of girls crept in and out of her room to borrow, swap, and acquire any number of goods and services. The first two were upper level girls with all the qualities of a good customer: fashionable, greedy, and regrettably short of spending money. The deep bottom drawer of her armoire functioned as a showcase, and in seconds, a dozen lengths of grosgrain ribbons and shimmering swathes of lace trailed from extended arms.

"Do hush up, Elvira," Lacey said as their squeals escalated. "You'll have old Ambrose on us in a trice!"

"Where are the chocolates?" asked the other, Maeve. "You said you had a stash of dark nougats from Florens."

"So I do. But it will cost you." From beneath the bed, she pulled her travel trunk filled with more temptations. "I need two papers. One on early Greco-Roman architecture and an essay on Shakespeare's sonnets. Do we have a deal?"

Elvira and Maeve conferred as another customer tapped on the door. "When do you need them?" Elvira asked, twisting a red plaid ribbon through her fingers.

"By the end of the week. And do print nicely so they can be easily read and copied."

"What can we have on account today?"

"You may take two ribbons each and one chocolate." She carefully recorded the transactions in a notebook.

"Any chance you'll be getting some of those lovely macaroons again?" Maeve asked as they were leaving.

"If I get a few more requests, I'll put in an order. But mind, you need to take at least six, or it's not worth my trouble."

Lacey had been able to start this clandestine operation for two reasons: a father who dispatched money upon request and unwitting accomplices in Devlin, Aggie, and Padraic. It had taken but a day or two to figure out, that the best way to survive was to give people what they wanted. The girls were transparent in their needs, but the nuns required a bit more effort.

Cultivating a relationship with the youngest, Sister Placida, she barraged her with questions about religious life. It wasn't long before there were whispers about the wealthy girl with the indulgent father who may be blessed with a calling. Only that morning, Lacey had cast her net to gather in the big fish.

"What a pity the organ is in such shambles we must sing without it," she remarked to the mother superior.

"It is quite beyond repair, but there are so many other things to be attended to."

"When I write to my father, do you mind if I mention it? Perhaps, he can do something about it?"

"That would be a great kindness, but the captain has been so generous, I fear taking advantage of him."

"It can't hurt to ask."

◆

Ransom Longo was born to a consumptive mother in the privations of Misery Hill where even the vermin were cursed to exist. By the age of seven he was on his own, the soul of childhood snatched from him—sleeping where he could curl his slight body—stealing enough to keep his belly from cramping—drinking and bathing in fetid rain water. By ten, he had learned to keep moving and move fast, for lingering meant the poorhouse or jail. By twelve, he had the dubious fortune to be apprenticed to an exacting farrier who worked him punishing hours. In exchange, Ran had a warm place to sleep, a trade to master, and a handful of shillings to ward off starvation.

By the time he came to the Whiteoak Brothers Stable, at the worldly age of eighteen, he had gone from the heat of the forge to the spotlight of the winner's circle at Aintree. He still moved as though pursued by banshees, but his haste served ambition rather than survival. The good and bad of his nineteen years had nurtured a scholarly fascination with human nature, and this knowledge, the hints and foibles of character and behavior, equipped him with all he needed to manipulate his destiny.

Ran had observed Lacey for a few months now and liked the way she commanded those around her with a girlish but gritty charm. She flouted conventions with her language and dress and refused to be chaperoned when riding, despite Padraic's futile cajoling.

On a damp March afternoon, Lacey strutted in, dressed in a cream-colored wool suit with a saucy tricorne atop her robust curls. Her timing could not have been worse for Mazo Lonnigan, a new groom, who was baiting Padraic over some bit of nonsense.

Padraic was near tears as he tried to ready Paladin. "Leave me be! I've work to do!" he pleaded, dodging Mazo's jabs.

Just as when they were younger, Lacey descended upon the bully, striking him across the back with her riding crop. He whirled around, fists at the ready, only to behold his unlikely assailant.

"Huh?" he grunted, lowering his hands.

She was prepared to strike again, only to be lifted away by Ran. "Ease up, wild one! He's just having a bit of fun with the lad. No harm done."

Trying to wiggle free, she swore with such vehemence Paladin broke away in a fright. She was tossed aside in a careless heap, as Ran waved off the others, and approached the rearing horse.

Padraic, invigorated by the commotion, exclaimed, "Look at him, Lacey. Ain't he a sight to behold? See him blowing down his nose, speaking in a way only he and them be knowing. See how Paladin's cozying up to him—not a nervy bone in his body."

It was true the gelding was calmer, almost hypnotized by the murmurings of the lank-haired, unshaven groom. Padraic went on to describe Ran as a "whisperer," one of those touched by the fairy people, preternaturally gifted to understand a horse's delicate temperament.

Ran reminded Lacey of one of Seamus's fighting gamecocks, tough and wiry. She had seen him slouching around, watching her with furtive interest. It was this look that she was becoming accustomed to, even excited by, as it reinforced her sense of power over others.

He led Paladin into the yard and gestured for her to mount. "He's steady as a rocking horse now, no need to worry."

"I trust Paladin to keep his head when I have the reins."

"As you do with others, it seems."

Was he mocking her or flirting with her? She saw that his eyes were compelling, greenish blue with thick dark lashes—no doubt the source of his rapacious appeal to women.

"The reins, if you please. I don't have time to chat."

"'Tis my understanding, miss, you're not to be riding alone."

"Pish! Why does it matter to you?"

He shook his head as if the question was rhetorical, withdrawing a rolled cigarette from his shirt pocket. "Mind if I light up? I was about to, before you unleashed your bloomin' fury."

Lacey backed up a few paces, indicating she was through with him, but he caught hold of the bridle and continued with his desultory monologue. "I've been thinking about Paladin here, and what a shame…"

She raised the crop in warning. Unfazed, his grin widened. "This one was born to race. You can't deny that."

"What's this silliness about racing Paladin?

"I know a man. I can do some asking."

"Do that, and then you and I might have something interesting to talk about. "

Padraic was currying another horse when Ran strolled over and said, "She's a feisty bit of fluff that one."

"Aye, you surely don't want to be on the receiving end of that temper. There's no one quite like her."

"'Tis no reason for letting her make a fool of you! You need to be doing your own fighting, bucko, or there'll be no living with any of them. You're her pet, nothing more."

Padraic increased the rhythm of his strokes along the withers. "You've been a worthy friend since I came here, Ran, but you don't know what it's like having Lacey for a friend. We look out for each other."

"Well, it can't hurt to be learning you a few good moves."

There was something pathetic in the boy that both touched and repelled him; had he been younger, he too would take part in tormenting such a hapless lad.

"You mean boxing? You'd show me what to do?"

"I've been known to have a few slippery moves that'll keep you from being laid out."

Atticus Brady was a contrary hulk of a man, spewing foul oaths at a befuddled jockey and then, extending his hand and smile to Lacey. "So you're the little lady with the magnificent horse! Ran tells me we have a winner for the Jalna Derby."

"Nothing has been decided," she reminded the men, taking in the sights and smells of Phoenix Park, one of several racetracks in the suburbs of Dublin.

Atticus removed the gummy stub of a cigar and declared, "I have such faith in this boy's judgment, I need not see Paladin before making the deal!"

"Does your faith have anything to do with him being sired by Emerald Fire?"

"To be sure, pedigree speaks for itself."

"We'd best be getting down to business," Ran said. "It took quite a bit of doing getting her out here. We've not much time."

The office was tidy and efficiently set up, which surprised Lacey, given the man's inadequate hygiene. Atticus puttered about, brewing a pot of tea, cracking open a tin of shortbread, and laying out some cups. The tea was meant for her, as the men preferred whiskey. One wall was given over to sepia-tinted photographs of jockeys and their mounts in the winner's circle at several racetracks from Ireland and England to Australia and the Americas.

There were two of a very boyish looking Ran at fifteen. "Here you are!" she said.

"Fuck the past!" He sank into a lumpy leather chair, raising the cup to his mouth in rueful comfort.

"Pay him no mind. Come and look at this." Atticus opened a faded ledger book with dozens of newspaper clippings recording the span of Ran's brief racing career. "That goddamn lorry did him in. He'd still be riding but for that misfortune."

"Enough of the bloody reminiscing," he moaned, throwing a chunk of shortbread at his biographer. "Get on with it, man, before we all start tearing up."

"He's my horse. I'll ride him and split the purse with you."

Atticus vehemently protested while Lacey pointed out, "I weigh nothing and can easily pass for a boy. Paladin knows only me. I'm an excellent rider as Ran will swear to. Don't take it on faith, Mr. Brady, let me do a trial run."

"Not possible," he argued. "I'm already breaking the rules by pretending to be the owner of record. I do have a reputation to protect!"

"Only because I'm not of legal age."

"Underage, untrained, and female—have I made my point?"

Both turned to Ran for the final word. "Ain't no use," he said, emptying the cup.

"As I thought!" Atticus gloated.

"You've got it wrong, bucko. Once this was one sets her mind to how it's to be, that's it. By the way, your reputation don't have much left to it needing protecting."

"I don't like it! There are too many ifs!"

"Just leave them ifs to me," Ran said. "Won't be your head on the chopping block."

"Why did you do it? Why did you side with me and not Atticus? You could end up with nothing!" Lacey was flattered and suspicious of Ran's motives.

He kept his eyes on the darkening road, slapping the reins to hurry the horses. "I'm not nearly the fool I look. Atticus has always been true blue with me. Whatever happens, he'll see I get my share."

"You're taking a bigger risk than him."

"If you mean having you on my hands to train, you're damn right! But I'll enjoy bossing you around, and boss I will, if you're serious."

"You know I am." There was so much she could do with the money to help Padraic.

"I know what you're thinking. I know your thoughts without you telling me. We're alike that way, we're users."

"What a nasty thing to say! Just when we're getting along so nicely."

"Nice is it? Easy to be nice when you're not scraping to get by—when you don't have to grovel before your betters." His voice lowered to a resentful growl. "We poor don't have any rights. And the ones they say we do have change with the wind."

"You sound like a Fenian."

"And what would you be knowing about politics and the like? Them good sisters been filling your head about Home Rule and such?"

"I can see what's going on around me! I'm not blind to suffering, how unfair life can be." She resented having to defend herself when she was not the perpetrator.

"I'm touched." He put a cigarette to his lips, the flare from the match illuminating a small scar on his chin.

In that moment, Lacey saw him as a lost boy, discarded and deprived. This lost boy had insinuated himself into her life with his feral charm and thrilling proposition—fascinating her with his contempt for social convention.

"People can only take so much, and then they hit back," he went on with the whiskey-induced oration. "You'll see, there are changes afoot. About time, too."

———◆———

It had taken considerable plotting, but Lacey had orchestrated a series of lies, allowing her the freedom to prepare for the derby. Her afternoon rides became exercise and training periods. Exhausted by the intense routine, she bribed her customers to do her schoolwork. Since it was necessary for Paladin to acclimate to the rhythm of the racetrack, Saturdays were spent at Phoenix Park—early mornings for workouts and afternoons for watching the other jockeys and their horses compete before boisterous crowds.

Saturdays presented the greatest difficulty for getting away, so Lacey resurrected her dead, maternal grandmother, Lady Elizabeth Donovan. A poignant note and an expensive hamper from Florens convinced the sisters of Saint Honoria that the ailing woman wanted to spend her final days in the company of her only grandchild.

———◆———

"'Tis your weight keeping it secure," Padraic reminded Lacey as he adjusted the short leathers and forward seat favored by American jockeys.

"I just can't get used to it, it feels unnatural."

"Ran knows best about such things."

"Then let him ride this way," she grumbled and slipped from Paladin in disgust.

Through the stable doors, Lacey spied Atticus leading a group of men, only one of whom she recognized, Mazo Lonnigan.

"I wonder what brings Atticus out this way?"

"Oh, he's always about with some business for Ran to tend to."

"Why are we waiting on him? He has all day to talk to them."

"Lacey, them are Fenians with important work to do. Atticus is their leader. You can't begrudge Ran for helping the cause."

Just then, the trainer appeared with a wrathful expression and demanded, "Don't you two have work to do?"

"Who are those men with Atticus?" she asked, ignoring his question.

"You're wasting bloody precious time, wondering about what doesn't concern you! Get your high and mighty arse on that horse, or the deal's off."

"You're being vulgar! You needn't threaten to call things off every time I ask a question. It's really quite childish of you."

The hansom cab moved sluggishly along the narrow cobbled streets, rutted by the tracks of forlorn horses dragging carts of cheap wares, and the sagging wagons of the knife grinder, rag picker, and street sweeper. It was another suppertime flurry of cheerless people anxious to be home, unaware of the lengthening days and surfeit of sunlight. Lacey thought it glorious that April was nearly over, and in two weeks, she would be riding in the Jalna Derby.

She raised the locket to her lips and for the first time in many months, opened it. Court had been right; it was difficult to remember what he looked like. When she dreamed of him, he was more of a presence, and in place of the unbearable sadness that had eviscerated her heart was a lulling ache.

The cab was no longer crawling; it was stuck in some kind of traffic problem. There were fewer pedestrians, which is why it was so easy to spot Atticus and his associates heading toward Wellington Quay. Lacey might have shrugged this off, if Ran had not been following at a distance.

"Driver, pull over and wait for me."

"But miss, I dare not let you out. 'Tis no place for you to be walking about."

"Do as I ask, and I'll double that for your trouble," she said, tossing him two shillings.

Hastening to catch up, she had to quicken her pace when they turned into an alley. By the time she made the turn, the men were in sight, but not Ran. She stepped over garbage and bits of brick and broken glass; the crunching beneath her boots threatened to give her away. An arm shot out, pulling her into the hollow of a doorway, as the men retraced their steps.

A thumb to her lips, Ran turned her face away from the light and muttered, "That was a close one." His mouth felt moist against her ear, his perspiration mixing with the musk of tobacco and whiskey.

"Are they gone?" Lacey was all too aware of his body gouging into hers.

"Just another minute and we'll be off." His cheek grazed hers, and her shoulders stiffened from the sudden surge in her loins.

"Steady, wild one. Never been this close to a man with a hard on?" He covered her mouth with his, stifling her resistance with deft thrusts of his tongue, until he tasted her surrender. "That needed doing."

He dragged her out to the street. "Suppose you tell me what you're up to?"

"You kissed me!" she shouted, rubbing away the traces of his saliva.

"So I did."

"Why?"

"You're the first lass who's ever asked me that. You're a smart one, you'll figure it out."

She swung at him, but he was expecting it and swiftly pinned one arm behind her. "I've no interest in deflowering you. There's no sport in that. I like my women to know what needs to be done."

Her free hand smashed the side of his face and he laughed, twisting her arm a little higher. "I'll not repeat myself. Why were you following me?"

"You beast, you're hurting me!" I'll yell if you don't let go."

Several people drifted closer to observe the row. Ran did not want to attract a police officer, so he stepped away, hands swinging in the misty breeze.

"If we're to go on with this partnership, you need to stay on the up and up with me. I'll not be drawn into your schoolgirl games. Now, put a smile on that pretty face and walk away with me so these nice folks will leave us be."

"I was curious, that's all."

"You've no cause to be prying into my affairs. Another stunt like this, and the deal's off."

"There you go again! I thought it rather queer, you were trailing after Atticus."

"Not that you need to know, but I was doing him a favor, by looking out for him."

"Why? Are those men dangerous?"

"I'm putting you back in the goddamn cab and have done with you!"

"Pish! In two weeks, you'll have me off your hands for good."

"Can't be bloody soon enough for me."

The Jalna Derby commenced with keening bagpipes and a crescendo of fiddles and flutes, welcoming the crowd on this, its fiftieth anniversary. There was a significant showing from the British to honor the syndicate of retired officers who financed the purse. The wave of scarlet and gold braid uniforms, ensconced in the first five rows of the viewing stand, dampened the festivities for the scattered bands of Fenians, who gathered at these events for socializing and unfettered discussions.

The course had been sealed overnight due to the heavy downpour and harrowed twice before the race. There was a sturdy northwest wind, shuffling passels of clouds across the sun, keeping it cool for the jockeys and their mounts. Paladin was among sixteen entries, with only one horse scratched for pulling a muscle. The odds were on the favorite, Damsel of the Nile, who had not run a bad race since her maiden effort as a two-year-old.

Locked away in Atticus's office, Lacey, Ran, and Padraic nervously prepared for what lay ahead.

"Fuck! Did you sprout tits overnight?" Ran fumed, the indelible swells of her breasts obvious beneath the silk shirt.

Lacey was mortified as he continued, "We'll have to bind you up. Paddy, fetch me some of those flannel bandages."

He reached for the top button, but she slapped his hand away. "Don't be going shy on me now! Take the shirt off and keep the damn vest on if you like. There's little enough of them to stiffen me." He turned her around and began to wrap her chest.

"I can't breathe!"

"It must be tight, or you'll be found out before you have one foot in the stirrup. Take a deep breath now."

"I can't imagine women allow themselves to be corseted," she wheezed. "It's madness."

"Take this charm off. Paddy will mind it for you."

She covered her neck in protest. "No, I never take it off, I can't."

"I've no patience today for your sentimental notions. 'Tis the top and bottom of it!" He finished with an angry tug.

"I'll tuck it into my vest."

"Wear the fuckin charm! If you lose it, don't expect us to roll around in the muck looking for it."

Lacey stood before a small mirror to adjust the jabot. The racing silks were a brilliant shade of aquamarine like Lough Phair.

"Right then, onto the breeches." Ran held them out to her.

"You must turn around. I can manage on my own."

Padraic helped with the boots, but it was the snug-fitting hat that left them bewildered. She had worn a soft wool cap as part of her disguise when training.

"What the hell was I thinking? Ran exclaimed. "You'll never be able to pull this off—not with that mane!"

"We've come too far." She grabbed a pair of scissors. "I've always fancied being a boy!"

"Don't do it," Padraic implored. "Tisn't worth it."

"Leave her be! She's up for the game and willing to go the distance."

Lacey yanked lengths of hair through her fingers and cut. "You'll have to do the back," she said calmly to Ran.

"What will you say to the sisters?" Padraic asked.

There was a startled silence among them. "I'll say I did it as an act of contrition! They'll think I'm moving closer to a calling."

Ran's incredulous snort reduced the tension with a round of desperate laughter. "Paddy, fetch the saddle and meet us at the weigh in." He handed Lacey the crop. "Keep this between your teeth once you make the final turn. Remember what I told you about my last race at Baldoyle?"

"You thought you were pacing fine and then you ran out of horse."

"Pick your moment to prod Paladin. 'Tis a speed-favoring track, and you'll have the wind at your back. Don't get cocky and let him loose on the lead. Once you open up too much ground on them, you're done for."

"Let's go," she urged, ready to bolt out the door and onto the saddle.

"One more thing, wild one." He kissed her hard and fast. "Just for luck, nothing more."

Astride Paladin, Lacey had a monumental view of all that lay before them. She understood now why Ran had drummed into her head the need to isolate and focus on the horse.

"Treat him with kindness," he had repeated again and again to her. "For without that, there's no reason for him to please you, and he does want to please you. He wants to fly with his heart and soul in your hands."

Lacey felt the quiver of Ran's lips against hers, his words about kindness and the need to please. Which was she to him? The horse or the rider?

She put her mouth to Paladin's ear. "Sweet, sweet darlin', show me what you can do."

They were off! Early on, the gelding had to steady himself several times before angling out and stalking the pacesetter. By midstretch, they were being crowded with no place to go. Then a hole opened along the rail, and alertly, Paladin broke for it, leading for nearly a length until they dropped back and settled in for a ground-saving gallop. At the top of the stretch, she used the crop for the first and only time, a gentle reminder that they needed to regain the lead from Damsel of the Nile. They won by half a length.

Now Lacey became aware of her surroundings and the throbbing hysteria of the crowd, the wall of flaming uniforms. Standing in the stirrups, she realized only then, they were soldiers, and there among them, Court.

Transfixed by the sight of him, she gasped, "Oh my God … oh my …" and pitched forward in a dead faint, caught by Ran's lunging grab.

He tried to stand her up and shake her into consciousness as the race officials presented Atticus with the trophy and purse. Court barreled through the knot of spectators and descended upon Lacey, Ran, and Padraic.

"She's not a sack of potatoes," he said contemptuously, lifting her in his arms.

Ran stood back, sullenly deferential. "You can bring her round to the office. She's just in need of some breathing room."

Padraic awaited instructions, terrified that somehow Court would blame him. Ran saw his discomfort and this added to his curiosity as he diverted the boy with orders.

"See to Paladin. Make sure he's cooled down proper before you let him drink."

Ran wielded the scissors and said, "This will do the trick," to a mystified Court. Lacey was laid out on the desk, and he pulled open her shirt, neatly snipping through the binding.

"You lunatic! You could have killed her with this stunt! Bring me some water." Court ran his fingers through what was left of her hair, aghast at the pile of curls on the floor.

Raising her to a sitting position, he forced some water into her mouth. She stirred and swallowed before opening her eyes; this was more unreal than the race. How could this man be Court?

"It's me, lamb, in the flesh." He drew her hand to his cheek. "See, I'm the same, just a wee bit older."

Lacey recoiled from him, distraught that the boy she remembered was no more. Instead, there was this muscular, rougher version with a hideous moustache.

"How did you know about the race?"

"I've been reassigned to Cork. You can imagine my surprise when I came to fetch you for the derby, only to learn you were at the bedside of your sweet, long dead, granny. When I saw Paladin was entered, I knew there was some mischief brewing."

"I can explain."

"Explain this?" He waved his arms in astonishment. "It would take more time than I have the patience for. How you were able to pull this off without breaking your idiotic neck…"

"See here, bucko," Ran spoke up. "Give her a chance to make this right; bullying her won't work. Believe me."

"And who would this be, making so free with you, miss?"

"Ran, please let Padraic know I'm all right."

Court pounced. "Do you have the least notion what a spectacle you've made of yourself? Does your father know what you've been up to?"

"I can explain," she repeated tearfully "It's not as horrible as you make it seem. Daddy doesn't have to know."

"Have you completely lost your wits? Look at you! You've disfigured yourself for some foolish prank, and you think no one will notice?"

"Promise you won't go running off and tell!"

"I promise nothing! I've just enough time to put you in a cab before I make my train."

"What?"

"You heard me. I've better things to do. Heap those tears upon the sisters and your father!"

Lacey leaped off the desk and struck him across the face, her small hand leaving a fiery mark. He caught her by the belt of her breeches, braced his foot on a tack trunk, and heaved her across his knee.

"If you recall, your father has given me permission to do this. How about one for each year?"

She squirmed frantically, but he held her fast with one hand while bringing the other down hard, the thin fabric of the silks offering no protection against the sting.

"One … two … three. This isn't the welcome I had in mind, but it will do!"

"You bastard, you've no right to do this!"

"Ha! I've more than earned the right … nine … ten." He paused. "How old are you now?"

"I'm only fourteen!"

"Then one to grow on!" He delivered the final smack with reluctance. "Well, I must be off."

"I hate you!" Lacey tore the locket from her neck and threw it at him.

Unable to endure the fracas any longer, Ran charged in. "What the bloody hell is going on?"

"So be it," Court said as he retrieved the locket. "There must be a beginning and an end to everything."

Cross Currents

"I'm in somewhat of a bind and need to ask a great a favor of you," Anthony said to Devlin as they stood by the ravine separating their two estates.

Long before either man existed, a stonemason had built a fanciful footbridge of limestone and mortar over the cleft. Beneath its picturesque decay, pools of stagnant water blazed with activity on this August morning.

"You need only to ask," Devlin encouraged with a wink, easing himself onto the cool stone. "I've just the thing to keep these pests away while we chat." He withdrew two cigars from his vest pocket.

Anthony took a long succulent pull, explaining, "After I settle Lacey at school, I must sail to New York. My mother's affairs are too complicated for me to handle from here."

"Sad business indeed. A most gracious lady she was, though we met but once."

"And with this damn war making such a ruckus, I've no idea how long it will be before I can return!"

"We were wise to rid ourselves of the South African holdings—let them thieving Huns have what's left of the mines and be done with it!"

"So you see, I'm in a bit of a quandary. I need you to look after Lacey."

"That's it? Such a trifle. Aggie and I will be delighted to have someone to fuss over. Lacey can come for the holidays and any time she has a mind to. Tis been a great sadness having Court so close by with nary a moment to spare for a visit."

"Don't you find that somewhat odd? After being away for so long, you'd think he would spend all his leave time at home?"

"These are troubled times, dear Captain, and my grandson has important responsibilities. His time is not his own."

"I've not seen Lacey and Courtland in the same room for more than a minute or two. There's a coldness between them that's unnatural." He loomed over Devlin with a quizzical squint. "And you don't seem to be the least bit concerned about it. Why is that?"

"Think of how much they've changed! Neither is the same as when they parted. They need a wee bit of time to get reacquainted. After what she endured at that abominable convent, I'd pay it no mind at all."

Anthony had been artfully misled by Lacey, and certainly her appearance assisted in the deception. With shorn locks, haunted eyes, and a listless demeanor, she made it inevitable for him to blame the sisters of Saint Honoria for what he thought was religious exploitation.

"Those blasted nuns! Can you imagine anything more ludicrous than my daughter taking the veil?"

"To be sure." Devlin smiled and grasped his arm. "I'll be needing my sherry and biscuits. Won't you join me? How grand it will be having Lacey flitting about the place again!"

"You're not to spoil her and let her do as she pleases! I've done quite enough of that as it is."

"You can depend on us to be firm with the child. Why, she's always been a perfect angel for Aggie and me."

The Charlotte Wooster Academy sprawled over a cul-de-sac on Thistle Lane. With half the enrollment of Saint Honoria, it was an intimate and luxurious setting for young ladies devoted to their social, rather than educational, development.

Lacey's bedroom delighted Anthony with its feminine finery and aesthetic views as he sat on a window seat, admiring the sculpture garden below.

"Well pet, what do you think?"

"It's nice, I suppose," she answered in a flat voice and collapsed in his lap. "Why must you leave? I can't bear the thought of not seeing you for months and months. Are you going to fight in the war?"

His raucous laugh ruffled the filmy curtains. "They'll not have me! I'm much too old and rusty. Besides, this isn't America's fight, or for that matter, Ireland's."

"But won't you be terribly lonely in New York with grandmother gone?" She burrowed closer, wishing to slip into his pocket where it was safe and warm.

"Oh, I'll look up some old friends and maybe make some new ones. I expect you to do so as well!"

"Pish! They're just silly girls. Will you be looking up Miss Wakefield by any chance?"

"Perhaps, just for old time's sake."

"She's probably married to some dull teacher or minister—someone just as dull as her!"

"I doubt it. You know those suffragettes are a troublesome lot. No sane man, not even a dullard, wants that sort of headache."

"You can't put me off. I know you like her, so don't pretend!"

"Now remember," he admonished, dismissing her observation. "This is the kind of school where you can learn and still have fun. I'm told there are lots of teas and parties, and all sorts of social outings. Mrs. Wooster has a list of the shops on Grafton Street where I have accounts, so you need not go without a new hat or dress, or anything that takes your fancy. Lacey, you must promise to spend my money!"

"Yes Daddy. I may ride every day as before?"

"Certainly, the same arrangement but without Padraic." He paused and looked at her with probing curiosity. "According to the rumormongers, your playmate has been blessed with some good fortune. What do you make of such a thing?"

She was not about to confess the reason why. Wisely, and with the help of Atticus, the money was put in a trust, and Padraic received a weekly allowance. His room and board were paid from the trust, leaving him free to decide what he wanted to do with his life. Lacey's plan was for him to learn a trade or start a business. But it was not to be.

"There's something I've been wanting to do," Padraic said with a trace of childish reticence.

"Go on," Lacey encouraged with Ran by her side.

"I'd like to box, go on the circuit."

She turned on Ran. "I blame you for this! You're the one putting such things in his head!"

"Me? I just taught the lad a few moves to keep him from getting pulverized."

"What kind of life is that for you? Boxing is nothing more than two idiots brutalizing each other. You could be beaten senseless or killed!"

"Oh no, not the waterworks," Ran snickered. "She'll have you running a tea room and knitting your own cozies before the tears have dried on them downy cheeks."

"Lacey, 'tis truly what I want to do! I'll be able to take care of meself—get some respect."

It was the look in his eyes that convinced her. Gone was the cloud of fear and trepidation.

He seemed happy and purposeful for the first time in his young, tormented life.

"There's a groom Paladin adores and he won't mind riding with me. I'll need to give him something for his time."

"I'll see that Mrs. Wooster takes care of him." Anthony grabbed her hands and held them tightly to his chest. "Promise me you'll try your best to be happy here?"

"I'll try, Daddy. I'll write every week, and mind Devlin and Aggie, so you'll not have a moment's worry."

"I know you will, pet."

◆

"Why are you vexing me over this?" Lacey asked as Ran led Paladin from his stall.

"I've been pinning for the sight of you all these months, and now, I'm being paid to be in your glorious presence!"

"Pish! Must you be so thickheaded? I don't need a nursemaid to ride with me!"

He finished saddling the gelding and lightly whisked the reins against her thigh. "Like it or not, wild one, I'm being paid to do just that. So what's it to be? Ride with me or not at all?"

"Fine! But don't think for a moment it'll be a pleasant experience for you."

"When has it ever been?"

St. Stephen's Green had ripened in the warmth of the late September haze, a wash of autumn brushing the foliage, as Lacey's petulant canter escalated to an angry gallop. Ran made no attempt to catch up with her; he was savoring the secret pleasure of her return to him. The June morning, when he was instructed to prepare Paladin for transport to Kingsbridge Station, he experienced the searing panic that comes with emotional loss. His stomach churned, his mouth went dry, and his body warmed from the heat of despair.

Ran despised himself for being vulnerable to such feelings, and after steadying himself with a bottle and a whore, convinced himself he cared little that she was gone. But that first glimpse of her tore through his denial and reclaimed his desire. Even her childish stubbornness excited him.

Catching up with her at the duck pond, he said, "You and me have been through enough ups and downs to let this fussing come between us."

"I suppose."

"If you like, one of these afternoons, I can take you round to Corbett's gym. We can look in on Paddy. See how he's doing."

"I'll not step one foot in that place! I'm heartsick he's using the money for such a horrid thing."

"When you give a gift, you can't be holding on with one hand," he chided as they trotted in companionable accord. "Have you and that soldier boy kissed and made up?"

"What?" A slow blush flooded her face and she resumed a hasty canter.

"So he's the one."

"I've no idea what you're going on about."

"That little charm you wore, the one you gave me bloody hell over. He gave that to you."

"And what if he did?"

"Makes sense, that's all.

"We'd best get back." Lacey said. "Mrs. Wooster insists we dress for supper. You're damn lucky to be a man."

"Aye, so far it has agreed with me."

Christmas in Cloonsheelin

Torrey Castle was in a sublime state of holiday bedlam. Aggie had assembled an earthly choir of angels to cook, clean, and decorate, in celebration of Court's first Christmas at home in three years. Devlin became more Scrooge-like as expenses mounted, bemoaning the waste of money during these "uncertain times." Lacey was left to contemplate Court's arrival and reconcile so many feelings with so little insight.

Lafferty set down a massive Scotch pine in the drawing room for inspection and approval.

"We should have chosen a blue spruce, much more majestic," Aggie frowned in disappointment.

"Will the king be stopping by for high tea, woman? This will do nicely. I'm partial to the smell of pine. Move it a wee bit closer to the mantel."

"Are you daft, old man? Move it by the window if you don't want it to be tinder before the goose is plucked clean!"

Lacey offered a compromise. "If you put it in the middle of the room, we can move the furniture around so no matter where you sit—you have a lovely view."

"The lass is a genius!" Devlin said, ignoring Lafferty's pained expression.

"I must be getting back to the kitchen. John, gather up some of the boys to help you move things about. And you!" Aggie raised a finger of admonition at Devlin. "Are to stay out of their way!"

The kitchen simmered with the aroma of nutmeg, cinnamon, and clove as a dozen women measured, sifted, kneaded, and iced a trove of baked goods.

"So many new faces," Lacey said as they looked up from their tasks with ready smiles.

"I've hired two day cooks. What a misery finding decent help! All the big houses are wanting for extra hands. Your Mrs. McTeague skittered back to Morvern the moment your father closed up Durbin House. This war has 'em all spooked."

"I hope she stays there! I'll not miss her sneering down on me for every little thing."

"Help me finish packing the hamper for Sophie and you can be off."

Sophie had married Lacey's old nemesis, Sholto Gallagher, and given birth to a daughter, Fiona. He had been among the first of the local boys to join up with the seventeenth brigade in Fermoy.

Aggie wiped a vintage bottle of her blackberry brandy and instructed Lacey, "Tell her, when a coughing spell comes on, to take no more than half a glass. The babe will do fine with a tablespoon or so. She can keep the custard in the hamper and leave it on the porch to stay cool. Where did I put the soda bread?"

"What about some of your crab apple jelly?"

"Where's me head? I set it aside with the soup."

At last, the dogcart was packed, and Lacey fidgeted to be off.

"Are you sure you can manage by yourself, my angel? I can send little Kevin along if you like."

"Stop fretting! I'll do just fine."

"Remember, there's no more shortcut! You'll need to follow the lane right up to Assolas and turn left."

"Aggie darlin', I know the way like the back of my hand."

◆

Badger's Hut was so quaintly named for its origins as a hunting lodge in the 1880s, but its rustic charm belied its primitive amenities. When Anthony needed more living quarters for his expanding staff, he made a few improvements and gave it to his new groundskeeper, Sholto.

A wan plume of smoke misted around one of the chimneys, and in the front yard, a cantankerous goat foraged through heaps of scraps. Lacey had to step carefully to avoid the missing planks on the porch as she balanced the hamper and knocked. With no response, she entered and called out to Sophie. The room was dark and frightfully cold with no fire in the hearth.

"We're in here, Miss Lacey."

The bedroom was brighter, if only for the meager glow of the fire and a single candle by the bed. Not that it was much of a bed, to Lacey's way of thinking, just a straw pallet on a wooden frame with a few blankets. A heavy shawl enveloped Sophie, the baby nuzzling at her breast.

"How nice of you to come all this way just for us."

"Sophie! I had no idea this place was so awful!"

"Sholto's a bit of a lump when it comes to being handy, so there's a few things that might need doing."

"It must be hard for you without him."

"Ha! He couldn't wait to leave us. Here's where he's needed, not parading around like a trussed up rooster, waiting on the carving knife." She began to weep, the tears spilling onto the baby.

"I'm here now, tell me what needs to be done."

"Oh no! Uncle Seamus has been looking in on us from time to time. But you know what a tipsy excuse of a man he is. I thank you for the hamper."

"What a goose I am, standing here when you've not eaten! Let me get busy in the kitchen."

With no fire in the hearth and no idea how to make one, she returned to the bedroom with a stoic expression and suggested, "Why don't I build up the fire in here and heat the soup?"

"We've only a smattering of turf in the creel and not much coal. It needs to last for two more days."

"We must get it nice and toasty. I'll see to getting more tomorrow."

Lacey labored to make Sophie and Fiona cozier. She was relieved to see some semblance of indoor plumbing, if only for a hand pump and a tin sink in the main room, and a crude toilet in an attached shed. Under Sophie's direction, she warmed the soup, learned to change a diaper, swept the floors, plugged the drafty niches, and bundled soiled laundry to be washed at Torrey Castle. At last, mother and daughter slumbered warmly as Lacey departed with a plan of action.

On the afternoon of December 20, with a light snow icing the ground, Court stepped from a chauffeured car, an impressive accessory since his promotion to captain. Aggie and Devlin crowded through the door, but it was her arms that snared him first.

"Is it true we have you all to ourselves for the next two weeks?" Devlin pulled him close in a clumsy embrace.

"So you do! But the high command is known to be somewhat capricious in these matters."

"Of course, you have serious obligations. We'll make the most of every moment! Aggie's been an absolute harridan."

"I'm standing right next to you, old man! Do you think I'm deaf like you? Pay him no mind, I'm only doing what I get paid so pitifully for."

"Well, it looks like a picture postcard from where I'm standing. No one can pretty up this old place like you, my darlin'!"

"You're looking so handsome in your new uniform! I can't take me eyes off you. Can you believe he's really here?" she asked, poking Devlin in the side.

"Why don't you pinch the boy? He's real enough, so is this chill aching my bones." He hobbled back inside.

Clinging to him with motherly adoration, she explained, "Tonight, 'tis just us, but tomorrow, there'll be a big to-do!"

"Oh, I don't want any fussing over me. I'm content to putter around and look things over."

"You can't come home and not expect us to show you off!" she argued, green eyes dilating with pride. "Why, there isn't a one among them who won't be swooning over the sight of you!"

"Speaking of showing off, where's our little mischief maker?"

"You won't be seeing Lacey till supper. I want your promise, you'll be patient with her. You've given her quite a fright."

"So now I'm to blame?" he asked, slamming the door behind them. "I'm the big bad wolf?"

"I'm just saying, you're old enough to know better. Girls her age are moody creatures. You can start by getting reacquainted with your razor."

When Court bounded into the dining room, clean-shaven and dressed in his old gray flannels, he was rebuffed by Lacey's impassive expression. Devlin looked to Aggie for divine intervention.

"Enough," she scolded with a thump of her spoon. "I won't endure two weeks of this!" She directed her ire first to Court. "You need to apologize for your churlish behavior! And you, miss, are to ask for his forgiveness! Now, do as I say, there's a lovely veal roast waiting on us."

The two exchanged murmured apologies without making eye contact. Perfunctory as it was, it helped to diffuse tension and allow for the possibility of polite conversation.

"Tell me, Lacey, is Sophie on the mend?" Devlin thought this to be neutral ground.

"Scarcely," she replied, frowning as she tried to avoid the potatoes in the chowder. "She still has a wicked sore throat and a bone rattling cough."

"I'll make up some camphor poultices for her and add them to the hamper." Aggie rang for the next course. "And the wee one?"

"Oh, Fiona is such a trouper!"

Her sudden effervescence illuminated the dark corner in Court's heart where he had banished her. While her hair had grown into a charming froth of ringlets, he thought that she was too pale, and the blue smudges under her eyes were worrisome.

"Though she's not feeling at all well, she still has the most beautiful smile. Just like Padraic."

"Lord, there's a curse to get out from under," Court said, not intending to provoke but failing miserably.

"What's that supposed to mean?"

Squirming between the reproving looks of his elders, he hastened to backtrack. "I meant the thought of a babe resembling such a lad is rather, disconcerting."

The rest of the meal proceeded uneventfully, studded with nuggets of gossip and innuendo, the cornerstones of Irish society. By the time dessert was brought out, there was a palatable air of conviviality among them, until Lacey asked to be excused.

"What? No sweet for you, lamb?" Court asked, sounding as natural as ever. He was unprepared for the bewildering cascade of tears that followed.

"My precious! Whatever is wrong?" Aggie cried. But Lacey was beyond explanation or consolation. "Let's get you to bed. Sleep is what you're needing. You've worn yourself out."

"That was damn queer," Court remarked to Devlin when they were in the library. "Don't you think she's looking a little off?"

"Not in the least. 'Tis one of those womanish mysteries; we men are not meant to understand. Fetch the brandy and the cigars before we're found out. You came with presents for her, I hope? A sure way of having her come round."

"I've some trifles from abroad I never got to give her. Though I'm not of a mind to indulge her."

"You may be right. It's probably best to go about this slowly."

He was wary of his grandfather's unexpected consensus. "What mischief are you up to, old man?"

"We find ourselves in agreement, for one of the few times I can recall, and you suspect my intentions?"

"Let's just say, I have reason for suspicion when it comes to your intentions."

"Tell me now, what's the latest on the war?"

"Pretty bleak, I'm afraid."

"And what of their plans for you, dear boy?"

"Please don't let on to the others, but after the first of the year, I'm off to the western front. They've been schooling me in all kinds of warfare: history, strategy, weaponry. Gruesome stuff."

"Are you scared?"

"I'd be a bloody fool if I wasn't. In all my time in India, I never saw more than a handful of skirmishes, and we always had the upper hand. But this will be different. The Germans are a fierce bunch and well equipped."

"If you like, I can have Humphrey Boyle come out, and you can update your affairs."

"Already done! See what a responsible lad I've become, Grandfather?"

"You're the man I always knew you would be. Here's to you!"

"Thank you, you've been exceedingly patient with me. I wonder how delighted the captain will be when he hears we share the same rank? Isn't that a delicious bit of irony?"

The morning before Christmas Eve day, Devlin fled to the conservatory, lest Aggie find another reason to vex him. For most of his adult life, this place had been a refuge for him, sheltering him from the devastation of loss, with the solace of making things grow under his nurturing manipulations.

"Must you tease me with your prodigious budding and no blooming?" he asked an assortment of African gardenias.

He had wanted to surprise Aggie with a showy offering of their lustrous flowers and potent fragrance, but he might have to make do with a reliable rosemary tree. Settling himself on a bench, wreathed in sunlight, he enjoyed the moist warmth easing the stiffness in his body. He would sit for a while and then steal into the library for some sherry and biscuits. There should be time for a quick nap before dinner. He was pleased with his plan for the first half of the day, until Court strode in, arms in the air, his voice a discrete roar.

"Grandfather! Do you know Lacey has been looting Durbin House, in some idiotic quest, to furnish Badger's Hut more to her liking?"

"Dear me. How did you hear about it?"

"Lafferty got wind of some strange doings over there and had the good sense to come to me."

"How did the little minx manage it?"

"She's up to her neck in wheeling and dealing with old Seamus. What possessed the captain to make him the caretaker? 'Tis a bloody wonder he hasn't turned it into a rooming house!"

"Oh my, I'm afraid that was my doing. I thought it best to keep it in the family, so to speak."

"And naturally, you chose the most untrustworthy, poitin-swilling reprobate!"

Court had gone to Durbin House to confront Seamus and found him overseeing a delivery of coal to Badger's Hut; the man's temerity when caught red-handed was astonishing.

"What the devil do you think you're doing?" he demanded.

"I have me instructions from her ladyship. Off you go, Dilly."

Court tried intimidating the driver. "By Judas, you're not going anywhere. That's an order!"

"Sorry sir," said the unfazed Dilly. "Her ladyship's the one I'll be answering to, not you."

"This is lunacy!"

"Now Master Court, why be carrying on so?" Seamus asked, as if reasoning with a skittish horse. "Her ladyship has every right to…"

"Stop calling her that. It sounds absurd coming from the likes of you!"

"… she being born to the title."

"She's a child, you imbecile!" He switched tactics. "Tell me, how does Miss Lacey pay you?"

"Ah, the saints preserve your innocence, with a bottle of course. We each get a bottle of something stimulating for every chore, we sign up for."

"There's a bloody list?"

"To be sure. Her ladyship is most organized."

"She's gone through eight cases of French wine, and now she's dipping into her father's stock of brandy and whiskey," Court raged.

"Has all the makings for a very merry holiday."

"You find this amusing, old man? Are you not responsible for her?"

"Settle down, boy. I'll wait to hear Lacey's explanation, if you please."

"That's just grand! I'll ride over now and fetch her. Then we can all have a little sit down."

Lacey halted in front of Badger's Hut, reveling in the changes she had wrought with her resourcefulness and inherited leadership skills. The yard was raked clean of debris and animals; the front door and shutters had been mended and painted an audacious red; the porch boards were replaced, and the roof was rethatched. She had no difficulty securing willing hands. Everyone had been exceedingly accommodating, she assumed, in the spirit of the season.

Before she reached the door, Sholto opened it.

"So you've returned!"

"Aye, just three days leave for Christmas."

"How nice you decided to spend it with your wife and child!"

"I'm most beholden to you for all of this," he said, opening his arms as if to embrace the new furnishings.

Both rooms had been transformed; rugs covered the floors, Sophie's day bed from her old room at Durbin House sat by the hearth along with a rocking chair. A small fir tree stood in the corner awaiting its ornaments. In the bedroom, Mrs. McTeague's large brass bed with its feather-down mattress and fine bed linens kept Sophie snug. Fiona had her own cradle and a trunk of Lacey's baby clothes. Every other day, Assolas farm delivered fresh milk, eggs, butter, and cheese. There was enough coal for two winters.

"I did it for Sophie, not you!"

"So be it. We've never got on. You should know…" He was interrupted by a wrenching wail.

Sophie emerged from the bedroom, eyes wild with fear. "She hasn't touched a drop of me milk since last night. I fear she's dying!"

"I've sent for Father Ryan," Sholto whispered to Lacey.

"You would have done better sending for the doctor!"

"As if he'd take the time from his paying customers."

"I'll see he comes! Unpack the cart."

Fiona burned to the touch, and a flaming rash covered her from the neck down; her blue eyes held the haunted stare of one too weak to cry.

A day that had beckoned with brilliant sunshine and so much promise turned ominous, skies darkening and rain pouring down in torrents. When Lacey reached Dr. Seacord's home, she was told that he had been called away to the other side of Lough Phair to Pembrooke Manor. She would lose another hour of precious time; drenched and shivering, she drove on.

Undaunted by the young maid in an immaculate, starched uniform, a wringing wet Lacey demanded to see the doctor. She wondered what could be so urgent in a family with two gorilla-sized sons and a wife beyond childbearing. It took the doctor a full ten minutes to pull himself away from Lord Pembrooke's neuralgia.

"What's this about?" Dr. Seacord asked. "Something amiss with Devlin?"

"I need you to come at once to Badger's Hut! There's a dreadfully sick infant with a high fever and rash."

He grimaced in annoyance. "Mrs. Conway can see to it. She's well versed in such things. Babies get sick like this all the time."

"It must be you!"

He looked at his watch and deliberated. "I've two more calls to make before…"

"You'll come now!"

"Mind your tongue, young lady. I'll come when I can."

"Don't try to put me off with excuses! Leave with me now or I'll see your reputation suffers mightily. "

By the time they reached Badger's Hut, Father Ryan's carriage and Drummer stood in the pelting rain. A cloud of despair seemed to hug the small cottage, and then, a shrill keening rent the air.

Sophie clutched Fiona and moaned by the fire while Sholto squatted over the empty cradle, lips moving silently along with Father Ryan's prayer for the dead. Court stood to one side, dazed and helpless.

"She can't be dead." Lacey knelt in disbelief. "She's sleeping, I'll show you." Sophie allowed her to take the infant, nodding in hopeful desperation. "Open those pretty blue eyes," she crooned, "give us a smile, precious." She looked at Court and cried, "I can feel her breathing in my arms. She's alive!"

"Can I hold her? Is that all right, lamb?"

"Mind her head."

He laid Fiona in her cradle and tenderly tucked the blanket around her. "Let's give the doctor some time with her and Sophie."

Wrapped in a quilt, Lacey refused to look away from the closed bedroom door. When Court tried to speak to her, she heard nothing but the steady creak of the rocking chair. Dr. Seacord emerged, signaling for the priest and Sholto to enter.

When she tried to follow them, the doctor turned her away, saying to Court, "From what I can tell, Sophie had a bad case of strep throat and infected the infant. It turned into scarlet fever."

"Good Lord, isn't that highly contagious?"

"The younger you are, the more vulnerable. I need to examine Lacey."

"Take your filthy hands off me!"

Court raked his fingers through his hair, trying to reason with her. "Just let him have a little look, so we know you're all right. Will you do it for me?"

After a cursory examination, Dr. Seacord said, "As I suspected, she has an infected throat and fever. This could be the beginning of it. Get her to bed, and I'll come by first thing in the morning."

It seemed the only time Aggie wasn't crying were those moments when she tended to Lacey. A pall had fallen over the castle, and all the extravagant decorations served as mocking reminders of a holiday gone awry. Lacey was in the third day of high fever and delirium with a hideous rash covering her torso.

Dr. Seacord was insisting that Anthony be informed. "He must know how grave it is! If the fever doesn't break soon, her organs will be at risk, and death will soon follow."

It fell to Court to send the cable. Devlin was too distraught to do anything more than stay by her bedside, a worn rosary his companion and comfort. Father Ryan came every afternoon to say mass in the family chapel, and it was he who raised the question of the last rites.

"No Father. You don't know how strong her will to live is. No one fights with more passion, more determination than Lacey," Court said defiantly. "She and I…" his voice trailed off, consumed with the fear of losing her, while bearing the weight of the others' anguish. "Well, I'll know when."

At night, he took over the vigil, stroking her hair and soothing her with his words. He told stories of India, and when this repertoire was used up, he spun new adventures to quiet her whimpering and shuddering. As dawn approached, she grew calmer, and only then would he curl up at the foot of her bed for a few hours' sleep.

On that fourth morning, when Aggie found him in his usual contortion of exhaustion, she emitted a harsh cry of panic that wrenched him awake.

"I don't think she's breathing!"

"Hush!" He pressed his ear close to Lacey's mouth and a hand against her heart, and then brushed her forehead with his lips. "Thank God! The fever broke. She's in a deep sleep."

Dr. Seacord announced that Lacey was on her way to a full recovery. When she woke later that afternoon, her thoughts were muddled, and she wasn't sure if she dreamed the nightmare of Fiona's death. Court was reading the *Last of the Mohicans* to her, but his words made no sense.

"No more reading for now. How long have I been like this?"

"Almost a week. You've been through quite a struggle, but you're on the mend."

"I'm not sure if I dreamed… Sophie's baby… is she?"

"I'm sorry to say, it wasn't a dream, Lacey. The babe died of scarlet fever."

"Court, Fiona should have a headstone."

"I've seen to that."

"She shouldn't have died."

"You'll come to learn these things happen. Even in your own family."

"It's because they're poor. Sophie never thought to ask for the doctor, not even for herself. Just like Bridget and her baby."

"What?"

"I didn't know how to tell you," she whispered with effort. "I saw Bridget in New York. The baby was so sick. By now, he's gone."

"A boy?"

"I'm sure by the look of him, he was no part of you. More like one of the Gallagher boys. I tried to help. She didn't want my money—what could I do?"

"There's too much talk going on. You need to rest, my lamb."

"Can you stay till I'm better? Must you go back soon?"

"I've received permission to extend my leave for a wee bit. It may not be Christmas on the calendar, but as soon as you're up to it, we'll have a splendid celebration!"

Lacey emitted a deep sigh of contentment and closed her eyes. Court was his old self again, she was safe, and everything would be all right from now on.

On the afternoon of New Year's Eve, Court shared a cable from Anthony with Devlin and Aggie as they took tea in the drawing room.

"I am most grateful for the good news! Thank you for your extraordinary care and devotion. Please give Lacey my love. Keep me abreast of her recovery. All my best wishes in the New Year.

Aggie and Devlin trilled with pleasure over his magnanimous words. "As if we would do anything less for our precious angel," she said, slicing into a thick chocolate layer cake.

"To be sure," Devlin chimed in, putting a drop of whiskey in his tea, under her supervision. "The captain knows she's in good hands."

"And what if he knew the truth?" Court asked pointedly, pacing in front of the Christmas tree. "How is it I can oversee the comings and goings of an entire company of men, but the two of you cannot supervise one child?"

"Mind your tongue, young man!" Aggie knew where this was leading and hoped to derail him.

"Never have I seen such a flagrant lack of judgment and commonsense. If you were under my command, you'd be charged with dereliction of duty!"

"I suppose with all the fuss over Christmas, I was a bit remiss," she said in defense.

"Aye," Devlin joined in with the mea culpas. "I may have been distracted by all the excitement over your homecoming."

Court warmed to the challenge of decimating their excuses. "Remiss, Aggie? Remiss is when you forget to put nutmeg in the eggnog. And you, Grandfather, distracted is when you misplace your spectacles. You knew about her shenanigans in Dublin. Lord knows, you've seen enough of her mischief making over the years! And yet, what happens when she comes to stay with you? You put on bloody blinders and the child nearly dies!"

"You know, my boy, Lacey's only a child when it suits your purposes. You need to make up your mind. Aggie and I think of her as a young lady; she can't be tied to our apron strings. But we do promise to be more diligent about her activities, if only, for your peace of mind."

For the first time in over a week, Lacey was out of bed, stretching with languid grace in the pale morning light. The wool dressing gown did little to conceal the rounded contours of her hips and breasts.

"You must be feeling better," Court declared as he balanced a tray in one hand, somewhat unsettled by this womanly apparition.

She pirouetted in an ambitious attempt to show off her improved condition, but the sudden movement left her weak, and she slumped against the windowsill. "I'm a bit light-headed from lying about for so long."

He lifted her up, saying, "Your temperature may be rising again! You must take care or you'll have a relapse."

"Silly, I'm not feverish in the least." She rubbed her cheek against his. "Perfectly cool."

How provocative she could be, without the slightest notion, he thought, mesmerized by the inviting pucker of her lower lip. One little kiss, what could it hurt? He used to kiss her all the time.

"Court?"

When she said his name in that caressing exhale, it unnerved him. "Yes, lamb?"

"What did you bring me for breakfast? I'm famished."

"Famished?" he repeated, forgetting the tray.

"Yes. Has cook made something special for me?"

"Indeed, she has."

Lacey returned his scrutiny with an impulsive kiss on the mouth. It lasted only a second yet lingered long enough to rattle him. Could she read his mind?

"What was that for?" he asked, dumping her on the bed and shoving the tray at her.

"You haven't kissed me once since you've been home. Don't you want to kiss me anymore?"

"What I want you to do—is to eat your damn breakfast!"

"Oh lovely, a salmon omelet." Despite his scowl, she continued to prod him. "Haven't you noticed?"

Court stirred her tea. "'Tis a strange topic of conversation for an invalid. But to refresh your fever-addled memory, there was an incident between us that created a less than affectionate atmosphere."

"Oh that."

"Yes that! I have some grim holiday tidings for you, miss! You're going to write your father a detailed account, starting with the derby, right up to your plundering of Durbin House."

"Pish! You should know better than to badger me when I'm ailing. I am an invalid, you know."

"None of your excuses! I had hoped some pangs of a conscience would lead to a confession"

"I'll do it," Lacey blithely agreed. "Better to tell him now, when he's too far away to make a fuss. I'm sure Daddy will be so relieved I didn't die, he'll not hold any of it against me!"

The Western Front

Spring trudged forward; puddles of flowering snowdrops marking the blasted earth where a strategically cursed hamlet had been obliterated by a stunning German offensive. Dozens of handmade crosses shuddered against the rasp of the March wind, sepulchral reminders to the British troops of their tenuous existence. Within the subterranean penumbras of the trenches, the men coexisted with the scuttle of vermin, streams of muck, and clouds of miasmic air.

Under the cloak of nightfall, the bombardment would erupt with a sizzling hiss, followed by the sky brightening with incendiary ribbons of light. A deluge of shells burst from camouflaged nests, protected by rows of howitzers, impenetrable to defensive tactics. The words "hold the line" became a loathed refrain as the soldiers awaited air support.

Time became meaningless after weeks of such torment, and Court's spirit grasped for some small pleasure to sustain him. He sat on a damp cot, dressed in the same wool uniform from his arrival a month earlier. It had become his practice, during the lull in the shellings, to write letters to the next of kin. This morbid duty no longer violated his senses, since he had mastered a cryptic paragraph, suitable for all. He had no illusions that soon, another would perform the task for him.

Dear Mr. O'Rourke,

It is my sad duty to inform you that your grandson, Captain

Courtland O'Rourke, died on March 19, 1915, during an encounter with the enemy. He died bravely, defending the honor of king and country. I will see that his personal possessions are dispatched to you immediately.

The canvas drape stirred, and Corporal Charles Devereaux inched his way in, hugging a sizeable box. Fluent in French and German, with the powerful upper body of an English bull terrier, he had a proclivity for transforming the inedible into the appetizing.

"Look here, sir! Aren't you the lucky dog to be so favored on this dreary day."

"Open the bloody thing!"

The first layer served as a cushion with several pairs of socks, gloves, and mufflers. Four square rattan baskets came next, each holding coveted treasures: tins of tea and fruit, bottles of sauces and spices, bouillon and lemonade tabs, crackers and chocolate—even a box of expensive cigars.

"You won't recognize the bully beef tonight, sir," Charles promised, opening a bottle of curry and inhaling it's fragrance with closed eyes.

"I won't care what it tastes like after we down a bit of this," he chuckled, carefully unwrapping two bottles of Irish whiskey.

"Bloody better than the watered down rum they've been forcing on us!"

"Hush! Or we'll have to share."

"Righto, I do believe it's tea time."

———◆———

April 20, 1915

Dear Grandfather,

We are stuck in this sewer of death. I can barely bring myself to write of what I have done in the name of patriotism. I choke as I write the blasted word. I am an Irishman fighting for a British cause, for an army that despises who I am but needs me. I pray for every life I've taken and weep for those to come. There is no cause that can justify such evil indifference to life.

I dread speaking to my men, brave and worthy fellows, for all they can see in my eyes. This insufferable waiting has sucked every last bit of morale from them. Seldom do they see any true results for all their heroic patience and effort. More than half are dead, many are sick or grievously wounded. We have begun to envy the dead.

I use to think the flamethrowers were the most fearsome of weapons, but they do their scorching deviltry in a flash, and you're gone. It is the gas that is the most insidious of all. It settles in the lungs and throat, feeding on the membranes. We've been cursed with mustard gas with its pernicious blisters and stabbing pain. Men drown as their lungs fill up, thrashing about in blind terror, as sight is the first to fail. We can do nothing for them but pray for a quick death.

I beg you not to share these letters with anyone. I cannot bear the thought of Aggie and Lacey suffering over my suffering. Lie if you must and tell them I'll be back. If this is the last you hear from me, know that I remain your loving and devoted grandson.

Court

◆

Deadening cold had given way to drought and unremitting thirst. Water was so painfully rationed that urine was used to moisten the respirators of makeshift gas masks. Only the carrier pigeons were able to get through, returning with the despised plea, "hold the line." By May 5, the men were in dire need of supplies, and Court instructed them to scavenge the food kits of the dead.

The noonday sun seared the treeless plain with such intensity that the rats burrowed deeper into the walls. As the sick and wounded perished faster and faster, a shallow ditch beyond the perimeter served as a convenient graveyard. There was no time to cover the bodies with more than bits of canvas, so nature's predators set to work, returning bodies to the earth. Shifting winds raised the stench of decay—yet another noxious intrusion upon the men.

Across the barbed wire barricades designated as no man's land, the German troops appeared immune to hardship and deprivation. There were fewer lulls between mortar attacks, and for the first time, behemoth tanks began an onslaught of sunrise attacks.

"The men have nothing left to give," Charles confided to Court on the afternoon of May 9. "You may have a revolt on your hands if you don't nip this in the bud, sir!"

"What would you have me say to them, Corporal? No one in the high command seems to give a bloody fuck about us? Or shall I give them one of my dress shirts to use as a flag of surrender?" He had known for the last forty-eight hours that the air reconnaissance report indicated the Germans were poised for a final, all-out attack.

Charles blinked hard, unaccustomed to such bitterness from his commanding officer. He depended on his wry wit and steady spirit to pull him through another forsaken day.

"We need to placate them a bit longer," Court scribbled a message. "This will buy us some time."

"I'll not ask much more of you. You've given me your absolute best, and for that, you have my admiration and appreciation." Court addressed what was left of his command, observing the flicker of rage tightening their faces. "I'm sending off this message to headquarters. They have until sundown to provide us with relief. Or we surrender to the enemy."

There were grunts and sighs but no protests, as Charles appeared, bearing the basket that housed his beloved carrier pigeon.

"Listen up, lads! Matilda is eager to be off, so let's give her a proper farewell."

A handful trailed after Court and Charles, perversely giddy at the prospect of an end to their hell. The corporal clambered up to the parapet, Matilda strapped to his back. He had done this dozens of times, perfecting a crawl and release method that provided him with sufficient cover. The dry packed earth beneath him pulled at his sticky uniform, the dust filling his nose and throat.

Matilda fussed over the delay. "Settle down, little one. You'll be aloft soon enough."

Wanting no harm to come to her, Charles went a few more yards to ensure her safe release. As he reached to undo the latch, her breast caressed his fingertips, and for a fraction of a second, he felt her heartbeat pulse through him.

"Off you go, my brave beauty!"

Matilda soared straight up and then veered to the east, a fragile puff of gray against the blue sky. As Charles maneuvered to turn himself around, he saw Court and the others peeking anxiously over the sandbags, and he boldly gave them a thumbs up salute. He dragged himself with arduous care but strayed an inch or two from the path his body had etched, detonating a mine. The explosion hurled him through the air and tossed him by the ditch of corpses.

Court cleared the parapet and raced toward him; he was alive, but partially severed from his lower body.

"I'm begging you. Finish me off. You'd not let a dog suffer like this."

Wordlessly … tenderly … he pressed Charles against his chest, until he lay still. Court and the departing soul cherished this interlude, for less than a minute, when a familiar hiss swept both into an eddy of nothingness.

The harsh smell of antiseptic sent Devlin sneezing again, which this time woke Court from a morphine slumber. On the very morning his grandson had been transferred from a Paris hospital, Devlin arrived in London. As detailed as the correspondence had been with the French surgeons, he was unprepared for the sight of Court so grossly disfigured. Head shaved and patched in several places where shrapnel had been removed, eyes vacant and hungering in a face thinned to a skeletal shadow, the cynosure of his youth had vanished.

"'Tis me, dear boy, come to see you through this," Devlin said, "I've brought along Lafferty to help me manage. He's never been to London before, completely agog!"

There was no reaction from Court, as he asked in a detached whisper, "Where am I?"

"You've been ferried across the Channel to this hospital. The doctors say you're progressing quite well! This bit of nuisance will be coming off next week." He pointed to the cast on Court's left leg.

"What day is it?"

"The seventh of June and a beauty of a day! Right outside these windows are the most ravishing cabbage roses, the likes of which I've not seen. Do you know who I am, dear boy?"

"You're Grandfather."

"Nothing wrong with this." He gently tapped the ridge of plaster over Court's right eye. "Sharp as a harpy's tooth!"

"Don't leave me alone!"

"I won't be leaving your side."

"Never alone… not even in my uniform. There was always something crawling about… making itself at home." He struggled to sit up.

"Put such things from you mind! All your thoughts must be about getting well, getting home." Devlin pressed him back against the pillow.

"I won't go back! They can shoot me. I'll never go back."

◆

June 25, 1915

My dearest Aggie,

You would not recognize our beautiful boy after all he has endured so bravely. While his body is on the mend, I fear for his mind and spirit, so crushed by destruction and death. Between the nurses I've hired and myself, we tend to all his needs. He seems unable to muster the strength to do anything more than sleep and brood.

This morning, I coaxed him into sitting on the balcony that overlooks a very pretty courtyard. It may sound like a trifling thing, but he has not been out of bed for more than a few minutes since I brought him to the Hadley over a week ago. So distressing is his state of mind, I have sought out one of those psychiatrists, a fellow named Trimble, who is well thought of. He has this horrid expression for what Court is suffering from, "shell shock," There are times when he is so dreadfully out of sorts, it takes both Lafferty and myself to settle him down. Trimble gave me a vial of morphine, but I fear it to be addictive, so I slip the boy a few nips of brandy instead.

All these years, you have been the one to do the petting. Now, it is my turn. In the queerest way, this war, which has taken so much from our dear boy, has given him back to me.

I'm sure by the time you read this, Court will be much improved. It looks as though we'll be staying on through the summer. We need to be close to his doctors.

Keep us in your prayers and close to your heart.

Affectionately,
Devlin

The full wrath of summer's heat descended upon London, and the temperamental snatches of rain only exacerbated the humidity. Devlin's routine revolved around the weather and Court's state of mind. On a good day, he arose early and searched the market stalls for the delicacies that would inspire the chef's imagination and tempt his grandson's appetite. A bad day had no beginning or end. These were the days of restlessness and despair, anger and recrimination, compelling him to use the morphine as a balm for Court's ranting.

It seemed to Devlin that his grandson would be ensnared for eternity in this tug of war between the mind and the spirit. He wondered how many others were shut away in hospitals and sanitariums, battling the invisible enemy of poisonous memories and wrenching trauma.

"Ah! Another letter from Lacey!" Devlin adjusted his spectacles. "Shall I read it to you?"

"Put it with the others. Must you move my things about? Can't find my cane, no good without it."

"Over there, on the doorknob."

He waved off further assistance. "I think you enjoy seeing me hobble about like a cripple."

"You're hardly a cripple, my boy. That leg is healing nicely according to the doctor."

"As if that bloody bastard knows the first thing about my pain! I can feel bits of shrapnel cutting into the bone. You try and live in such agony!"

Lacey had persevered and written twice a week without a direct response from Court. Devlin answered each one, encouraging her to write, hoping that eventually, one would make a breakthrough.

"Grandfather! There's not a drop of whiskey! Send Lafferty to fetch more."

Devlin had begun a most unusual practice for an O'Rourke, curtailing the amount of spirits available and diluting what was.

"You have a perfectly good burgundy sitting right there for our dinner."

"I've no stomach for that piss. What I need is whiskey!"

Such belligerence could escalate or dissipate; there was no rule of thumb. Devlin set up the gramophone and put on a Vivaldi recording with its sprightly violins. Music was one of the few things that had a subduing effect on Court. But not today, the notorious empty decanter flew passed Devlin's head, crashing on the balcony.

"Do you know why I need to drink, old man?" Court screamed. "I need to be stinking drunk so I can't see the blood on my hands!" He raised the cane and smashed it down on the record. "Do you know what Trimble and I talk about, over and over again, day after fuckin' day? I killed one of my own men! He begged me to do it. I smothered him…"

He collapsed, weeping, "Will you do the same for me, Grandfather? Take the pillow… go on… I won't fight you. Do it now!" he implored.

Dragging his wounded sparrow of a grandson onto the bed, Devlin held him in a rocking embrace. "Don't be blaming yourself for any of it! No one will sit in judgment of what you had to do. Our Lord knows what's in your heart. You need time to heal." He broke into sobs. "You have your whole blessed life ahead of you—but you must fight for it!"

By late September, there were signs of solid progress but no miracles. Court had gained some weight and slept with less disruptions, but he was unsure of himself and needy of Devlin's attention. Trimble came by less often, assigning small tasks to prepare him for reentry into everyday life. Devlin was thrilled with each tiny step and looked forward to their evening strolls, with linked arms and walking sticks.

On this night, a raucous crowd spilled from a small stone church. The two men watched, as the groom enthusiastically bussed his new bride. She curled into his shoulder, seeking relief, from the chants of "more, more."

"Time to go back," Court said, riveted to the sight of such boundless joy.

"Of course, if you're tiring."

"No. Time to go home."

◆

"Lacey will be meeting us in style," Devlin said, nestled in the folds of his overcoat, as they sailed across the Irish Sea. "With a motorcar and driver."

"A bit much," Court drowsed, gray eyes dim with fatigue from the long train ride to Liverpool. The overnight stay did little to restore his spirits, and much to cause him despondency over his decision.

"Not at all. It was idling away at Durbin House, so the captain had it brought up to school. She's quite the envy of the other girls."

A slight smile creased Court's face. "I'm sure she's lording it over them, with all the pomp of a dowager queen. Risky for her to meet us at the quay, be dark by then."

"Nothing could keep her away! The captain pays this lad to drive her about. I understand he's most capable."

Appearing to doze, he murmured, "Poor beggar, she must have him sadly beguiled by now."

"Let's stay here until we see her," Court urged. "I'm not up to shoving my way through. Do you think she'll be frightened by the sight of me?"

He was remembering their reunion at Phoenix Park. Then at least, he had been healthy; now he felt pitiful and alien. While his hair had begun to grow back, the scars on his scalp were still visible.

"You're looking every bit like your old self!" Devlin assured him with a quick embrace. "I promise you, Lacey knows what to expect."

The quay was so well lit, it was only another minute before he saw her.

Dressed in a pale blue suit of the latest fashion, with a smart fox stole and matching muff, she stood out from the less elegantly attired throng. For the very first time, he saw her hair swept up, under a rather amusing hat with a drooping peacock feather. It was he, who was startled, by her appearance.

"Ready, my boy?"

"I don't think I can do this, Grandfather."

"We'll take our time, no hurry."

Lacey waited patiently, ready to fly at him, at the first sign. When they reached the dock, he acknowledged her with a relieved grin.

She was crushing him to her, her full weight forcing him against Devlin, who returned him to her arms. There was no escaping her robust hold, so he fell into it, dazzled by the scent of lavender and roses. He had forgotten how wonderful it felt to be hugged like this.

"Not put off by the sight of me, lamb?"

Lacey gazed at him with ferocious tenderness, and seeing the fresh scar over his eye, lightly traced one finger over it. Standing on tiptoe, she pressed her lips to it, exhaling his name like a sweet caress.

The Easter Rising

It was a leaden Sunday afternoon in February of 1916, and all eyes, except Lacey's, were on the swooning chameleon before them. Madame Ravevsky had transformed into Lady Teazle, but not before channeling Cassandra and the Honorable Gwendolen Fairfax, in an amateurish homage to dramatic female characters through the centuries. The actress's balding, acerbic husband had vanished halfway through Cassandra's spooky monologue, to wander the grounds of the Wooster Academy. Through the French doors, Lacey saw him sharing a relaxed smoke with Ran, slumped against the Silver Ghost.

Lacey was feeling proudly proprietary toward Ran these days, having outfitted him in a well-cut navy suit with impressive brass buttons and custom-made riding boots. With regular trips to the barber and bathhouse, he had become the unlikely object of fervent crushes among the girls. She wondered how their girlish notions of romance, all wooing and cooing, would survive the rough and tumble reality of copulation as she had observed it among horses and dogs.

Though he had kissed her but twice, she liked to relive those moments, hungering for what came next. Her daydreams no longer consisted of fuzzy, wishful thinking but graphic "what if?" scenarios. What if Court kissed her the way Ran did? What did men look like when aroused? What did it feel like to be penetrated? She savored the pleasurable sensations rippling down her spine and fluttering between her legs.

Juliet expired at last, and the girls squealed, clapping in appreciation for a performance that satisfied their provincial expectations. Lacey galloped to the front of the reception line, eager to get her social obligations out of the way. If she inhaled her tea, she might have an entire thirty minutes for a driving lesson before dusk. The actress extended a pudgy hand, as if expecting a kiss of gratitude upon it.

"Mrs. Davenport, this is Lacey de la Roche. I believe the two of you have something in common," Mrs. Wooster said. "She often entertains us with dramatic recitations and has a compelling, emotive quality, I think you would appreciate."

"How very charming," Katherine replied, as Lacey stepped back and let the wave of gushing girls surround her.

Before she could finish her tea, Katherine sought her out. "My dear, are you the daughter of Captain Anthony de la Roche?"

"You know my father?"

From nowhere, an oversized feathered fan appeared, accompanied by an unattractive shriek. "A lifetime ago! My stage name was Katherine Piers then, and your father was one of my most attentive admirers."

Having no patience for this goose of a woman, she asked bluntly, "Were you his mistress?"

"You have the same American-bred audacity as your father. How is the darling man?"

"He's in New York for business."

Katherine waved her fan in a whoosh of reminiscing. "I do believe, the very last time I saw him, was right here in Dublin. We were dining with an old family friend of his—a rather witty fellow. My memory is no better than a leaky chamber pot! I think his name was Courtland, his last name escapes me."

"It's O'Rourke. He's the grandson of my father's business partner."

"Such a handsome rogue. Do you see much of him?"

Jealousy speared Lacey, as there was no disguising the desperation in her voice, and the veiled longing in her eyes. Her heart heaved in violent comprehension; Katherine had been the lover of both men! It was a struggle not to spit in her face and say, "Court's mine! He belongs to me!"

During the long weeks of his recovery, it seemed the most natural of role reversals, for Lacey to take charge—planning every detail of his day, fussing over his meals, conferring with his physicians by cable and reassuring Aggie and Devlin. This possessiveness had led to a passionate awakening of her need and desire to protect him, make him whole again.

Lacey discovered that you can learn much from watching a loved one sleep; it's what you must do when they are in pain, physical or psychic. You watch them sleep, so you know when the nightmare has lessened its grip on their subconscious and healing has begun. She studied Court when he napped in the drowsy warmth of the library and at night, when he thrashed and moaned in his bed. She waited patiently, in a voyeuristic vigil, for the first inkling of dreaming's return—the slow yield of the fists, the rhythmic deep breathing, the reappearance of the Mona Lisa smile.

"He was wounded at the front some months ago and is convalescing in London," she lied with easy conviction.

"The poor boy! How serious are his wounds?"

"It's hard to say. I've been so busy with school and parties. I suppose, you think it's awful of me, to sound so uncaring?"

"Not at all, my dear. You're young and somewhat pretty. I won't scold you for having other things on your mind. But I would like to dash off a note to him."

"You can send it in care of his grandfather, Devlin O'Rourke, Torrey Castle, in the town of Cloonsheelin.

"Thank you! This will be my modest contribution to the war, comforting one of its wounded heroes."

"What about your husband, Captain Davenport—what about his contributions?"

"Oh pooh! The closest Sydney has come to the war is sitting at the breakfast table, reading the newspaper."

In response to the burgeoning resentment against the oppressive rule of Great Britain, Court had been promoted to the rank of major and reassigned to

Dublin, as a diplomatic liaison. The advent of the war had derailed the newly enacted Home Rule Bill and prompted stringent government regulation of agricultural production, leaving the Irish farmer with little profit for his labor. While recent legislation had exempted Ireland from military conscription, recruitment numbers were dwindling, and the British could never be trusted to honor a promise. Intelligence dispatches, scurrying between London and Dublin, tracked the activities of the Irish Republican Brotherhood, Sinn Fein, and several splinter groups, as the specter of rebellion simmered.

This was familiar terrain for Court after his experience in Delhi. His political naiveté led him to believe that he could protect his countrymen from within, wearing the despised uniform for another year until he could resign his commission. He was given plush accommodations in Portobello Barracks and the services of a frenetic lieutenant, as an aide-de-camp. The two men were driving rather precariously to the Whiteoak Brothers Stable where Court was to meet Lacey for a ride and lunch.

"Lieutenant Yates, why don't you slow down just a wee bit?

"Yes sir! But we mustn't keep the young lady waiting."

"I can assure you, she is most resourceful when it comes to keeping herself amused."

Within minutes of saying this, he was confronted with the sight of Lacey, sauntering among several men, two of whom were Ran and Padraic. She was dressed in a forest green riding habit with satin collar and cuffs; with every self-possessed toss of her head, the tartan bow on the back of her velvet beret shook in syncopation.

"I thought we were dining at the Carrageen Hotel?"

"So we are!" she concurred, aglow at the sight of him.

"Then you should be wearing a riding skirt, miss! They won't let us into the dining room otherwise."

"Pish! It's a silly old rule. They know us! I'm sure you'll find a way to convince them."

It had become harder for him to be strict with her over such improprieties, when his bruised spirit cherished her winsome defiance. It was this sheer life force that had turned him from Devlin's pragmatic and task-oriented nursing to her distinctly feminine and intuitive nurturing. She alone had been able to coax him into more physical activities and reward him with lavish affection. When she returned to school, he felt adrift without her.

Court brusquely acknowledged the other men with a nod, ignoring Ran and saying to Padraic, "Hullo, lad. What are you up to these days?"

"Ran and me are off on an errand," he said, without a trace of his customary stammer. Boxing had loosened its hold on him, but not before strengthening his self-confidence. "The captain has sent Lacey a birthday present, and it'll take the two of us, to fetch it from the quay!"

"How impressive."

"And mysterious," she added.

"Now then, Paddy, let's be off," Ran said and then, in passing to Lacey, "You've got a fine day all to yourselves."

"So we do," she agreed, tugging on Court's arm. "Wait till you see Paladin. He's in such splendid form! Ran takes wonderful care of him."

"I would imagine no less from him."

"Well lamb, you've gotten your way, again." Court sighed, perusing the menu.

"Look at that old biddy! She's positively aghast. As if I give a bloody hell!" Lacey bridled, pulling off the beret, auburn curls spilling past her shoulders.

"This isn't the stables! Mind your tongue and sit up properly."

Yet how could he look disapproving, when he was transfixed by this flagrant show of her beauty? Most of the men had paused in their eating to take in her antics with delighted grins.

"I see you're back to form, ragging me like I'm a child," she sniffed.

"You think turning sixteen makes you anything more? Your behavior has not improved one whit, after all the money your father has spent on your education. I saw you making free with those ruffians at the stables!"

She threw down her napkin. "That's just your way! Making judgments out of pigheaded ignorance! Daddy thinks enough of Ran to employ him."

"How cunning have you been, deciding what you want him to know? Did you happen to tell him about Longo's part in the derby fiasco?"

She returned to her menu with a stubborn jerk of her chin.

"I thought as much. Lacey darlin', I've no mind to go head-to-head with you today. What shall we start with? How about some nice oysters and a bit of soup?"

By dessert, they were smitten again, as she thrust more shortcake at him, saying, "Aggie didn't fatten you up very well after I left."

"She did her best, lamb. Now it's up to you."

"I still don't understand, what it is you're doing these days?"

"I attend meetings, write reports, read dispatches—that kind of nonsense. Sometimes, I chat up government officials at social functions. It can be pitifully boring."

"Is it about the war?"

"My work is confidential. I can't discuss it, not even with you."

"Oh pish! It's politics. You can't go more than thirty paces in Dublin without tripping over someone spouting off about something. People fear we'll never be free of the Crown."

"And where is this coming from?" he asked, stunned by her rhetoric.

"I've listened to some speeches by MacNeill and Pearse, read a few newspaper articles by Arthur Griffith. Oh! Ran and I saw a labor protest, led by James Connolly, in Parnell Square!"

"Lacey, you must promise to keep away from such doings! All it takes is one troublemaker, and all hell breaks loose. Look what happened at Bachelor's Walk! You could be caught up in it and harmed."

"I promise, Court, I'll not be reckless." She raised her hand to stroke his cheek in acquiescence.

He relaxed and turned her hand over to kiss it. "That's my darlin' lamb."

Ran and Padraic caressed the satiny contours of a late-model Rolls Royce Silver Ghost with Mrs. Wooster looking on in astonishment at yet another display of paternal excess. It was well-suited to be a town car with its enclosed passenger cab, improved horsepower, and luxurious trappings.

"But what is she to do with two motorcars?" asked Mrs. Wooster.

"Not to worry, ma'am. I've a letter from the captain which I'm sure will see to it." Already, Ran was picturing himself, resplendent behind the wheel.

As Court and Lacey turned into the driveway, she began to shriek with excitement. "That must be it! How pretty!"

"Good Lord! Your father's outdone himself this time.

As she frolicked around it, Ran and Court exchanged grimaces while Padraic urged her to open the letter.

My darling Lacey,

Happy Birthday pet! This is a very special birthday. I wish with all my heart that I could share it with you. To make up for it, I've sent along this little beauty.

Please tell Mrs. Wooster that I'm donating the old one to the school. You must remember this is not a toy! It's a very expensive and powerful machine. I expect Mr. Longo to take the utmost care in maintaining it.

Lots of love and kisses,
Daddy

"How sweet of him!"

"And idiotic," Court snickered.

"How generous of the dear man. But how am I to thank him?" Mrs. Wooster wondered, still wearing a look of astonishment.

Lacey was quick to offer her a crafty solution. "I know the very thing! You can hire Padraic to be your driver. Daddy won't mind paying him a modest salary, he's like family."

"Are you up to it, Paddy?" Ran asked.

"I've got some free time on me hands when I'm not doing for Atticus."

"Lovely, it's settled. I'll write Daddy this very minute!"

"Young lady, where are your manners? Major O'Rourke, will you stay for tea?"

"Certainly, ma'am."

This left poor Padraic as the only buffer between Ran and Court's animosity. For the first time since the derby, Ran felt equal to Court in position and rank.

"Right then Paddy, drive the other one round to the back and cover it up proper with a tarp. It's your job now." He turned his back on Court, thumbing through the maintenance pamphlet.

"I'm impressed you can decipher that," Court remarked, wondering how long the small talk must endure before he could excuse himself.

"Impressed I can read?"

"I'm not trying to insult you man—only making polite conversation! It's what civilized people do."

"That's right, lay it on. Make yourself feel superior."

"Oh what's the use? You like feeling persecuted, always the underdog."

"I must be a fuckin' marvel to you! Me, with the stink of the poorhouse. Able to read and write. Hold a job. Move onto your turf."

"I've noticed how quickly, you slithered your way into Lacey's affections; made a cozy niche for yourself."

"You'd be wanting her all for yourself when you haven't the least notion what she needs from a man."

"What would she be needing from the likes of you?"

"I know what she tastes like."

Court's fist collided with Ran's eye, and the two pummeled each other until Padraic and Lieutenant Yates descended upon them. As they tried to break free, their words twisted into garbled threats.

"I've gone easy on you, soldier boy! You being a wounded war hero and all."

"Filthy gutter trash! If you've taken liberties with her, I'll break you in two!"

"Hold on to your flippin' temper! Our little rose is still a bud—waiting for your manly prick to make her bloom."

It was Padraic who spun Ran around, pounding his face into the ground, and only stopping because of Lacey's bewildered cries.

"Are you all mad?" Her gaze roved over the bloodied trio. "Tell me, what is this about!"

Lieutenant Yates spoke up while the others stood in sullen silence. "Just a disagreement, miss, nothing more."

"Let them speak for themselves, Lieutenant."

Each mumbled an incoherent version of the events, further taxing her patience.

"If you don't have the brass to explain yourselves—you can all go to bloody hell! I'll be having tea by myself!"

"So you see, Mrs. Wooster, it was a most unfortunate misunderstanding that got out of hand," Court explained the next day. "I take complete responsibility for creating such a disturbance."

"Major O'Rourke, before Miss de la Roche came to us—there was a certain air of tranquility and decorum blessing our daily existence. I was hoping, in the captain's absence, your influence would have a moderating affect. She's the only student with an entourage, and to some of our young ladies, it's rather unseemly."

"She's never been one to stand quietly in the shadows, not with her high spirits. But the lad Padraic is like a brother, and a trustworthy soul."

"And Mr. Longo?"

He pondered his next move; here was an opportunity to remove Ran from Lacey's life. "I've only met him a few times before this little altercation. I find him to be an ambitious sort with suspect influence over her. If he were gone, surely some of your tranquility would be restored?"

"He was engaged by the captain. I've not the authority to dismiss him, unless he's guilty of some flagrant misconduct."

"I could write to the captain of my concerns. Would that be of some help?"

"Just between you and me, it would be a great relief. Now, I know Lacey would like to see you before you leave.

He felt successful in his strategizing, but for the first time in his life, took no pleasure in scheming behind her back.

"I suppose you've come to make amends?" Lacey asked, still displeased with him.

"So I have, lamb. Mrs. Wooster was most gracious in accepting my apology."

"And I'm next on your list?"

"Are you in a forgiving mood?" he jested. "I've not much time. I'm off to London, for at least a fortnight."

"But you can't go away now!" she cried, snapping out of her pique.

"I've no say in the matter. I must follow orders, you know that."

"But it's my birthday next week and you'll not be here!"

"By Judas, you're worried about your present! Well, it can't compete with the likes of your father's."

She responded with a coy smile, "I know exactly what I want, and it won't cost you a penny. I want a kiss."

He held up his hand in disbelief. "Nothing more?"

"Yes, but I want it now!"

Her plaintive tone reminded him of her childish greed for immediate satisfaction. She stood before him, a young woman, but he saw the loose braids and smudged cheeks of the nine-year-old Lacey. With this image in mind, he pulled her into an easy embrace and kissed her on the forehead.

"No, no! I want a real kiss! She pushed up against him and wrapped her arms around his neck.

Court experienced a wave of delirium; all the misery and suffering, loneliness, and loss of the last year drained away. In its place was the delicious shock of her tongue touching his, the sweet sucking away of his resistance. His mouth captured hers and she moaned, snaking her fingers through his thick curls. When the friction of her body…womanly…divine…stoked his desire, he panicked and broke away.

"This must never happen again—it's wrong. Never again!" he rasped, gathering his things and fleeing while she preened in triumph.

———◆———

On Easter Sunday, April 23, 1916, the viceroy of Ireland removed the high alert that had been in place for the army and local constabulary during a calamitous week filled with the rhetoric of independence. The National

Volunteers had united with several political groups, including the Citizens Army and Sinn Fein, to mount a protest. Unknown to the leaders of the Volunteers, a radical faction planned to take it to the next level—insurrection. Then on Good Friday, a high ranking British consul, Roger Casement, was arrested for smuggling German arms intended for the rebels. Messages were hastily dispatched all over Ireland, saying that the parade was canceled while newspapers ran bannered announcements warning people to stay away.

By Easter Monday, April 24, the army's senior command felt so confident that violence had been averted, a contingent attended the Irish Grand National at Fairyhouse Racecourse. Among this group were a subdued Court and ebullient Lacey.

"I wish Padraic could be here to see all of this!" she said, squeezing closer to Court. "Did you miss me?"

"What kind of question is that? I barely had time to breathe. It was one bloody meeting after another."

It was a self-serving half-truth, for his nights had been roiled with castigation over his body's betrayal. Katherine had accused him of harboring these feelings, and then, there was Longo's vicious taunting. How could he be so transparent to others and yet so horribly deluded?

"Pish! I'll not feel sorry for you. I'm the one who's been neglected."

"I'm trying my best to atone, lamb. Am I doing such a miserable job of it?"

"It might be fun to lay a wager or two."

"I forgot, you're well versed in the ways of the racetrack. A wager would not be a bad thing, but I'll pick the mount since it's my money we're risking!"

As they made their way through the crowd, Lacey became the object of considerable male attention, dressed in a pale pink afternoon dress with lilac stripes and matching wide-brimmed straw hat.

"You do have a way of getting looks."

"And what's wrong with that?" she asked, a little too boldly for his liking.

"A proper lady does not solicit attention!" he began to scold, then tried to steer her in another direction. It was too late. Katherine and Sydney Davenport halted in front of them.

"O'Rourke!" Sydney exclaimed, as Katherine looked from Court to Lacey in dismal bewilderment.

"Miss de la Roche told me of your ordeal. You're looking quite fit. Isn't he, Sydney?"

"So you caught a bit of shrapnel and got a promotion? You Irish always get off easy."

Would any more of his dark secrets materialize to torment him? "You must pardon us, we've only a few minutes to place a wager." Court whisked Lacey away and asked with some chagrin, "Do you mind telling me how you crossed paths with that abominable woman?"

"Mrs. Wooster invited her to perform a few months ago. Katherine made a point of telling me she was an old friend of daddy's and asked about you." She watched him squirm then asked, "Did you bed her as well?"

"Christ! Where do you get such notions? I had the ghastly misfortune to be stuck with them in Delhi!"

Lacey was pleased with his discomfort and decided he had been tortured enough for one afternoon. "Let's not think about them. You should wager on Knight's Down; he shares the same bloodlines as Paladin."

After the race, everyone gathered in an open tent, but before the first cup of tea had been poured, a disquieting ripple washed over the officers. By the time Lieutenant Yates had whispered in Court's ear, most were conferring over an alarming report.

"Take Miss de la Roche back to school at once," Court instructed, thrusting her at the lieutenant. "Tell Mrs. Wooster to keep the girls locked in. You're to stay with them until you hear otherwise."

Lacey stood her ground. "You might at least tell me what's going on!"

"It seems there was a parade after all. And thanks to some of your unsavory acquaintances, it's well on its way to becoming a riot!"

By the time that Lieutenant Yates and Lacey were in full view of Trinity College, a fog of thick smoke crested over the Grand Canal. On Harcourt

Street, looters paused in their thievery, pounding on the motorcar and jeering at the occupants. Women flaunted armloads of finery, and men, many inebriated from the flow of free spirits, wrestled to acquire the most expensive goods. Gleeful children, with candy-filled mouths, thought it must be some kind of holiday, and pursued their elders into the chaos.

Lacey thought of Paladin and called out from the back seat, "We must stop by the stables. It's just one more block down and to the left!"

"Sorry miss, I have my orders," the lieutenant explained stoically, trying to navigate through the frenzy.

"We must get Paladin. There's no telling what will happen to him!"

"The major will have me court-martialed if any harm comes to you."

Lacey resolved the dilemma by jumping out and skittering down the street, leaving him no choice but to follow her. A few minutes later, she barged in on Atticus, Padraic, Ran, and Mazo loading rifles into canvas bags. Their surprise compounded when the lieutenant tripped in after her. Before Yates could fumble for his revolver, Mazo had him pinned to the ground.

"See if there's anyone else," Ran said to Padraic, then turned to Lacey. "What the bloody fuck are you doing here?"

"I was afraid for Paladin so I came to fetch him."

"All the horses have been moved to Phoenix Park. I wouldn't let anything happen to them, my dear," Atticus assured her.

"You've put a noose around our necks, wild one," Ran lamented.

Mazo cut in, "Seems her little ladyship has done us a favor! Paddy, bring in that motorcar—we're going to load it up!"

"I'll be doing the ordering around, not you!"

"Are you sure you're up to it, Longo? Surely, by now, they've set up check points. Your little darlin' is our pass through them."

"And what about this fellow?" Atticus asked, nodding at Lieutenant Yates.

"Truss him up and toss him in a stall," Mazo said. "I'm just about his size, I'll wear his uniform and drive. Longo can lie on the floor with the guns. This one will be sitting pretty with a blanket over her lap."

Atticus disagreed. "What if you're stopped and searched? They'll execute all of you on the spot and not care one bloody bit if she's innocent!"

"Not if we tie her hands," Ran said. "They'll think she's been kidnapped."

"I am being kidnapped, you idiots! Or do I have a say in this?" she cried, banging the table in frustration.

"Sorry, wild one, there's no other way."

"Where are you dragging me off to?"

"To Marsh's Library," Mazo revealed, reaching for the banded boxes of ammunition.

"We've already men in position."

"And once I've served my purpose?"

"You'll be tucked away for a bit." Ran grabbed her hand and pulled her close. "Till we can get you back to school."

By the time they had passed through two checkpoints and made it unscathed to Upper Kevin Street, it was dark. The ominous crackle of martial law heightened Ran and Mazo's skittish nerves. When he realized that only a half dozen rebels held the building, Ran exploded in a tirade. He had been promised two dozen well-equipped men. What he got was a band of boys, untested and drunk on rum and adrenalin.

Lacey was "tucked away" in the attic of the library, free to move about the stuffy room but still a hostage to the whims of the rebels. It was a tower room, with small windows rimming the perimeter, and served as an ossuary for the remains of abandoned texts and crumbling manuscripts. Dusty and bleak, it exacerbated her anxiety with a dose of claustrophobia.

The bells of Christ Church Cathedral thudded twelve times against the shrill volley of machine gun fire, offering Lacey a scant measure of normalcy. The trap door lifted, and Ran carefully juggled a stack of supplies, intended to make her stay less primitive.

"Sorry about the wait, but I've been ransacking this place to provide you with all the comforts of home!"

"That would be impossible."

"You've got a jug of water for drinking and washing up. This old bucket is the best I can do for indoor plumbing, but I can make you up a cozy bed."

"I doubt I'll be doing much sleeping."

"Aye, but you do need to eat."

"What's going to happen to me?

"Lacey, I'll not let anything happen to you! Haven't I always been true to my word?"

"It's not you I worry about! It's Mazo and the others. I'm nothing to them. They've no use for me, now."

"I'm in charge of this operation. In a day or two, it'll be over, and you'll be back at school."

"You've no way of knowing that. I'm as good as dead!"

"Settle down now." He guided her to the makeshift bed. "Comfy?"

"It'll do."

He unwrapped some black bread and cheese, holding it out to her with an encouraging nod. "For breakfast, I can promise there'll be tea and a boiled egg. Mind if I join you?"

Lacey relaxed against him, picking at the bread. "Ran, I'm really scared."

"I know, wild one. Bloody awful timing to show up when you did." He filled a mug with water. "But you handled it like the wonder you are."

"That's me, always up for the game. Why didn't you let me know what you were up to?"

"So you'd go blabbering to your soldier boy?"

"You know Padraic has gone to Court."

"That was a sure thing. But it's bought us some time."

"So you can kill more people?"

"You've got to trust me on this!"

He grinned like they were larking about the stables, squeezed her thigh and leaned in to kiss her. She wanted him to, needed to be reassured by his touch. The rough of his lips caressed her cheek, then her mouth and she yielded, wanting more from him. In a flash, he was on his feet, waving over his shoulder, and disappearing into the gloom.

"You think you can get me in there without tipping your hand?" Court asked Padraic, as Lieutenant Yates spread a large map on the desk.

"A bit of a dare, but if you look the part—they'll be none the wiser. They'll be needing supplies by now."

It was the beginning of the third day of the Rising, and the rebels gripped Dublin in a vise of strategically held points. Eamon de Valera stood fast at Boland's Mill and Padraic Pearse controlled the General Post Office. Both the Four Courts and the College of Surgeons had fallen to the rebels while St. Stephen's Green, torn up into crude trenches, provided cover for the machine gunners.

The British did not tarry in their response, anchoring the massive gunboat, Helga, in the Grand Canal quay. It cruised along the periphery of the rebel strongholds, bombarding them with artillery. The Irish bourgeoisie, angered by the complicity of the Germans and offended by extremist attempts to undermine the moderate John Redmond, supported the British in their murderous restoration of order.

Court studied the map of the city, now divided into sectors, under the command of a designated officer and his platoon. "Here's the library. Yates, who's in charge of the fifth sector?"

"Captain Davenport, sir."

"That's a bit of bad luck."

"Shall I inform him of the situation?"

"He'll not be of any assistance, I can assure you. We'll proceed without his blessing."

"But sir, if I may remind you, such unilateral action might be seen as…"

"I'll risk it, but you've no stake in this. Give Padraic your coat and hat. He'll be my driver."

The disconcerted lieutenant protested, "I'll not shirk my responsibility! I'm the one who allowed the young lady to be put in peril!"

"You're not to blame! Believe me, you're not the first to be compromised by Lacey's recklessness." Court smiled knowingly at Padraic. "Or the last. You can serve me best by staying put and coming up with excuses for my absence."

As the car crawled through the ravaged heart of Dublin, Court and Padraic beheld the smoldering detritus of corpses, animal and human. Cannons and howitzers loomed everywhere, manned by British soldiers who appeared rapturous over this opportunity to wreak havoc upon the Irish. Marksmen crouched on dismembered walls and rooftops, peppering the street with gunfire whenever a civilian strayed into sight.

"Easy lad," Court said, his stomach clenching from the familiar swathe of carnage. The weapons of war were decimating his countrymen.

They abandoned the car two blocks from the library and walked past a patrol that saluted Court, oblivious to Padraic lugging an overstuffed duffel bag. Waiting for a quiet moment, the two men disappeared into a thicket of shrubs and prepared for their mission.

"You'll need to do all the talking." Court checked his revolver. What have you in the way of a weapon, if it comes to that?"

"Just these." He held up his fists.

"So you do. Listen lad, I've known you all your life, and not always have I been kind to you. For that, I'm sorry. You're a brave man, and I thank God you've stuck by Lacey. She's much to be grateful for."

"You've got it all wrong, Master Court. She's the only one, the only sweet soul, in my entire life who's believed in me. Treated me like we came from the same blood."

He doubted if Padraic had uttered so many words, in a single breath, in all the time he had known him.

"Do I look like a rebel?" Court asked. With his unshaven face, black watchman's cap and coat, he appeared properly forbidding.

"Sure enough, but you don't smell like one." He opened a bottle of rum and offered it to Court, who took a quick swallow then splashed some on himself. "That's the finishing touch!"

The two men had to cut across an alley and over three rooftops, vaulting over two fences before reaching the back of the library. Padraic signaled the lone sentry with a white rag and approached the cellar door.

"Thought you lads could use some supplies, Eoin. This one has a message for Ran."

"We'll be needing a might more than that," the boy said morosely. "Them guns was tinkered with. We've no ammunition. The bloody boxes were filled with fuckin' gravel!"

"But I was there when we packed up everything. I sealed them meself!"

"So swears Longo. He's been on a bloody rant for the last hour. I'm glad to be down here away from the fireworks."

When they reached the first floor, Court whispered, "Start from the top and we'll meet up on the third floor. If you find her, stay put and out of sight till I can get to you."

Minutes after they separated, the building rumbled from the impact of a cannon blast goring the front door. Court took cover in a screened reading niche, at the far end of the main room, and had a poignant view of the frightened boys, scrambling into position with their unwieldy rifles and precious handfuls of ammunition. The soldiers would overpower them in a trice.

Ran had not been to the attic since the first night, assigning one of the boys to see to Lacey, ensuring she got the best of what was edible. The wearying whip of gunfire had kept her from sleeping, and the faint light penetrating the filthy windows left her disoriented. When the cathedral bells tolled, she no longer could distinguish between night and day. It had been six hours since her last meal of a roasted potato, and pathetically, she waited for the boy who mumbled.

When the trap door swung open, it was Mazo. "Expecting someone else?" he asked, relishing the desperation on her face.

"I thought you were bringing me something to eat."

"I've brought meself for your nibbling pleasure."

If she screamed would anyone care? "What do you want?" she asked, willing herself to be calm.

Every pore of him exuded the menacing scent of lust. "Why don't you and me have a little tumble? It don't matter to me Longo was first—I'll be your last."

He came up behind her, a glint of silver swishing through the air and stroking her throat. "Need some persuading? I call this my lady killer."

Faint and terrified, her legs gave way and he followed her down, pressing his full weight on her chest. He raked through her underclothes, tearing through the fabric until he found the cleft between her legs.

"Oh, you're a ripe one all right." The attic shuddered from the sudden onslaught of the cannon. "Don't you be getting off first."

Lacey wept in tremulous silence as he positioned himself above her, grazing her inner thigh with his penis. "Please, don't…"

"That's right! Beg. I like the sound of it. It makes me…"

The word "hard" stuck in his throat as he was bent backward and lifted up by Padraic. Their struggling movements folded into a balletic embrace, making it difficult to see who had the advantage. They whirled around the small room, their grunts muffled by the staccato of gunfire from below. Finally, Padraic subdued him in a headlock, wrenching his jaw from side to side. The neck cracked, the head flopped forward, and it was over. Padraic dropped to his knees, Mazo's knife wedged below his heart.

"Oh God no!" Lacey screamed, dragging herself across the floor.

Her hands circled the knife, trying to stanch the bleeding, but he writhed away, pleading with her to stop. "Let it be! Did he hurt you?"

"Nothing happened, thanks to you. You mustn't speak, Padraic. Just rest for a bit and we'll find Ran. He'll know what to do."

A fresh torrent of her tears washed over him and mixed with the blood filling his mouth. "You're safe now. Master Court is here." He nodded off and relaxed in her arms.

She shook him back into consciousness. "I need you to hold on, dearest."

"It don't hurt much now." He gazed at her with his crooked smile and whispered, "I'm not so scared, Lacey, you're with me." His breathing gave way with a final gurgle.

The humble-hearted boy who had followed her faithfully… heedlessly… no matter the risk or consequence, lay dead in her arms. She wiped her tears from his face and kissed his eyes closed. Her lips swept the length of his nose and settled on his sweet, softened mouth. The taste of his blood kindled a primitive need to mark herself with his essence. She rubbed the wetness onto her cheeks, then covered him with her body, her heart just above his, commanding his soul to pass through her.

"Take a part of me with you," she begged. "Take whatever you need. I won't let you be alone for all eternity."

◆

The bedlam had ceased and a boy lumbered into the reading room, scarlet-stained hands pushed into the cavity of his abdomen. Court sprang from his hiding place, just as he cried out, "I'm dying" and crumpled to the floor. Then Eoin followed, hands on head, stifling a sob of terror as Sydney Davenport prodded him forward.

"On your knees, mongrel!"

Seconds later, he too was dead. Sydney realized that he had an audience when Court smothered a gasp of agony.

"Giving aid to the enemy, O'Rourke? That's treason you know." He waved the revolver in scoffing dismay then cocked it at Court.

"It's not what it looks like, Davenport."

"Is that a reason not to kill you?"

"I see reason has little to do with it! You've gone from slaughtering natives to butchering boys. That's quite a step up for you."

Ran darted into the room, gun drawn and asked, "What's this?"

"Personal business!" Sydney brayed. "But you may watch if you like."

"Ain't much of a watcher, Captain." He grinned and shot Sydney in the head. "Never did like that pompous bastard. Lacey's in the attic, shall we fetch her?"

"What a cold-blooded cur you are, Longo, playing both sides of this mess!"

"Unlike you, who's so sure where your loyalties lie? I'll not be judged by you, Major."

"I suppose you expect me to thank you for this?" Court gestured at the deceased Sydney.

"Not necessary, but I'll enjoy you owing me."

Marsh's Library had been reclaimed by the British, and only one of the rebels survived. A platoon sergeant stood over him, pelting him with cigarette ash and describing his immediate future.

"You'll soon be feeling the snug bite of the noose. Ever seen a man hanged? What a miserable way to enjoy your last hard on."

"Enough, Sergeant," Court said. "I expect fair treatment of this prisoner, or you'll answer to me."

"Sod off!"

"He's one of yours, bucko," Ran laughed. "Show him your identification, Major, before he takes a bite out of you."

"I'm taking command. Your Captain's dead." Best see to him than be wasting your time tormenting this lad."

The attic seemed deceptively serene, a halo of faint light obscuring the gruesome tableau; every object, each body remained composed in the surreal intimacy of death.

"Lacey!" Her name flew from Court's lips in an anguished wail as she peered up at them. "Where are you hurt?" he asked, his hands clutching at her.

Blood crusted under her nails, matted her hair and soaked her dress. "Look what he did to Padraic. Get that thing out of him!"

Ran tore the shirt from Mazo and deftly twisted the knife out and bound the gash.

"He must have the sacrament. We can't let his soul be condemned. Padraic must be in heaven," she wept, clinging to Court.

"I'll see he does, lamb. Please, let me look you over."

While she was distracted, Ran rolled Mazo's body to the trap door and kicked him down to the floor below. "Good riddance to you maggot."

Using the little water that was left, Court tried to clean her face and hands, but she resisted, in a renewed bout of hysteria.

"Don't touch me! Leave me as I am. This is all I have left of him."

She drew both hands down her breast to pat the dark stains with reverence. Using her fingertips, she repainted her face and returned to her stupor—the mask of mourning intact.

◆

The Easter Rising of 1916 lasted less than a week, the proclamation for an independent Ireland dying with its leaders. Pearse, Connolly, Clarke, Plunkett, and McDonah felled by firing squads and the hangman's noose; de Valera and others given life sentences, while Collins escaped to England. There was a profound shift in public perception when Sir John Maxwell systematically executed all the signatories of the proclamation. These men, so conspicuous in their bravery and determination, ascended to the rank of martyr, ensuring the inevitability of further rebellion.

Part IV

"New Beginnings"
1916-1918

Here and There

Number fifty-seven on Upper Pembrooke Street possessed little to engage the eye: three stories with a limestone façade, lacking ornamentation or imagination. A tufted mourning wreath was nailed to the green door, and the lion's head knocker had not been polished in weeks. It took a series of rapid bangs and several minutes, before a shuffling woman in a frayed apron and house slippers opened the door.

"I'm not dressed to receive callers." Katherine Davenport adjusted the lace cap covering her blonde hair. "These last weeks have been quite a trial, as you can imagine."

Court touched her hand and raised it to his lips. "I'm a thoughtless fool for not calling sooner. I doubt you could look any lovelier, had I given proper notice."

He surprised himself with the sincerity of his words. Though age had rounded her face and figure, widowhood had erased some of the artifice and revealed a girlish softness. She wilted under his flattery, inviting him to enter with a coy swish of her hips. The front parlor was stacked with boxes and trunks; every surface held a pile of something, to be packed away.

"I'm being booted out! Once the eulogy has been given and the coffin sealed, a widow becomes superfluous to the army."

"What are your plans?"

"I've little choice but to live with Sydney's mouse of an old maid sister in

Kensington." She pressed two fingers to the worry spot between her brows. "I can't picture myself in London. It's been so long. Dublin has been more of a home to me than anywhere else. Do you remember the night we met?"

He could not allow the conversation to wander and gracelessly interrupted, "Katherine, I'm returning this letter to you."

She remembered kissing the back of the envelope after sealing it, the day after her performance, at the Wooster Academy.

"I never opened it. I thought it best not to."

"Rebuffed, yet again." Katherine held it to her breast and moved to the window seat with languid purpose. She arranged herself in profile, aware the light at this time of the afternoon was kindest to her. Gazing upon the quiet street, she sighed, loosening the strings of the cap and shaking out her long hair.

"The insufferable conceit of men!" she exclaimed to her audience of one. "I've quite a history of being desired and discarded. You weren't the first, you know. When I was young, younger than your precious Lacey, I thought suffering for love was romantic. Oh my! I've dared to say her name."

Court flinched, knowing there could be no atonement for his willful debasement, his unconscionable abuse of her. She never would relinquish this power to remind and humiliate him.

"I'll not intrude any longer. My condolences to you."

"Oh pooh! Must you be so painfully sensitive? I've forgiven you! Had you read the letter…"

"Katherine, I don't know what to say. I'm not worthy of your forgiveness."

"So few are. Shall we celebrate with some of this divine Madeira?" She roused herself for Act II, pulling apart a packed box and wiping two crystal glasses.

"We must have a farewell toast. Do think of something clever and Irish! Did you know my mother was a Dubliner? Sydney could never know of course; he thought me common enough as an actress."

"May your heart be warm and happy, with the lilt of Irish laughter. Every day, in every way, forever and ever after!" he recited, quickly refilling the glasses and welcoming the warm liquid release from guilt.

"To Sydney! May his time in hell last as long as his days on earth, multiplied by a hundred!"

"'Tis Irish enough for me!"

"I think you despised him more than me." She poured another round, impulsively stroking his arm.

"It's damn impossible not to despise a man who wants you dead. Preferably by his hand. But the good Lord was looking out for me, and Davenport got his just reward."

"You don't still blame me for that?"

The wine had muddied his thoughts, as he frowned and muttered, "What? You mean that nasty business with the boar? No, no—the day he died."

"You were there?" Her voice lost its cheer.

"You should have seen him! He was on a bloody rampage. Shooting helpless boys, like they were no better than sewer rats! It came down to the two of us. The gun may have been held by another, but it was my heart and soul pulling the trigger!"

The glass tipped from her hand and shattered, the dregs of wine casting a rusty pool at her feet. "I don't understand. They told me he was killed by the rebels. If you were there…"

"Christ! He had a gun pointed at me! Someone got to him—it doesn't matter who."

"It matters to me! All this time, you knew, yet said nothing. Did you intend to tell me, or is it the wine?"

Court knelt to gather the slivers of glass. "Had I kept my wits intact, you'd be spared this needless suffering."

"Leave it!" she screamed, raising a slippered foot and knocking his hand away, scattering the glass.

When he looked up with a surprised jerk of his head, she sent him reeling with a second kick to the chin.

"What does my suffering matter to you? When did it ever matter? This is what I loathe about you—this show of compassion, masking your heartlessness."

Katherine threw the half-filled decanter at him, but he dodged the impact with a wave of his arm. A path of broken glass stretched between them.

He leaned on one elbow, shouting, "I swear on the graves of my parents, I had nothing to do with his death!"

"Your oath means nothing to me!" Eyes closed, her arms fanned out in the sweep of a curtsy and she sank to the floor. "Courtland," she whimpered. It was the first time that she had said his name. "Courtland," she repeated, savoring the sweetness of it, lurching forward, the palms of her hands grinding into the glass.

She reared up between his legs, holding them apart with her hips, pillowing her face against his groin.

The absurdity of her passion provoked a snort of laughter, breaking the trance of the deranged supplicant mouthing his genitals.

"So this is how we shall say good-bye." Court pushed her away, bloodied hands scraping at him in desperation.

"Don't go. You're all I have left."

"Then you have nothing, Katherine. You and I, it was never a fair exchange. You got the worst of it."

"Yes, yes, the worst of it! Still, I love you! I loved you when you spurned my womb. I loved you when you filled my mouth with blood, and cast me out. No one could love you more than…" She lay inert and began to moan, lacerated hands crossed on her chest.

Her words grew stronger and clearer. "And I, of ladies most deject and wretched, that sucketh the honey of his music vows… now see the noble and most sovereign reason…"

He recognized it as something from Shakespeare, unaware that it was Ophelia's soliloquy from Hamlet.

"…that unmatched form and feature of blown youth blasted with ecstasy. O, woe is me… that I've seen what I have seen, see what I see…"

There was no applause, only the muffled thump of the front door closing. Katherine's audience of one had departed before the final curtain.

Lacey placed a sheaf of autumn leaves and purple asters on Padraic's grave, and a nosegay of burnt orange chrysanthemums on Fiona's, while in the farthest corner of the cemetery, under the arching wings of an angel, reposed her neglected mother and brother. Padraic's marble headstone, reflected the fleeting measure of his life, as dictated by Lacey:

Padraic Harris Knox
Devoted Son of Liam and Kathleen
Beloved of Lacey
May 5, 1898 – April 27, 1916
All alone you are not
Though your body is dead
And your soul is on a journey.
All alone you are not
For you are with us always
Remembered dearly in our hearts.

It was six months to that terrible day, and little of Lacey's grieving had abated. Time crawled, infected by her own enervation, offering no respite, no numbing of the stark and violent memories. The morning light nudged her into waking, with the unspoken reminder, "Padraic is dead." As before, sleep became the anodyne pushing her through each day, bringing her to this season of sumptuous decline.

The war had accelerated, luring the United States closer to the conflict. Court spent most of his time in Dublin negotiating his discharge, and Anthony was forced to take the long way home.

"Such splendid news!" Devlin thrusted a letter from Anthony between Court's and his breakfasts. "The captain has left Caracas and is sailing to Rio. When he finishes up there, he promises to book passage on the first available steamship to Lisbon. If all goes well, he'll be home by early May. Lacey will be so pleased."

Court ignored the letter and resumed his attack on a plate of blood sausage and eggs.

"Must the man be taking the scenic route when his daughter is needing him?"

"Have you forgotten the grim fate of the Lusitania? He would not risk making her an orphan!"

"She may as well be a godforsaken orphan for all the time he's been away! You and he make a charming pair of schemers—weaving opportunism with paternal caution, and coming up with a cozy blanket of half-truths. How much profiteering have the two of you been up to, this last year?"

He began to count on one hand, wiggling his fingers at Devlin. "There's that bit of speculating in copper and uranium—them lovely shares in the tin mine. And what about the oil drilling?"

"War's good for business, I'll not deny it! But every penny lining my pocket will end up in yours!"

Lacey drifted into the room, putting an end to their sniping.

"Good morning, lamb!" Court greeted her with beckoning arms.

"Aggie made me get up to help with the Christmas baskets for the parish tea," she complained. "I'm not at all hungry."

"Try a bit of this," he coaxed, settling her on his knee and offering her a bite of sausage.

She grimaced and mumbled into his shoulder. "Maybe some toast with marmalade."

Devlin watched in dismay as his grandson hand-fed her, holding up a cup of tea for reluctant sips. His glare of disapproval lost on Court, he announced "I've the most wonderful news from your father, my dear."

"He's coming home?"

"He's on his way! You know, this war has made a frightful mess of sea travel. He's sailing to Rio…"

"I thought he was in Havana!" She broke loose from Court.

"That was Caracas. I fear you've lost track of time somewhat."

"It's my fault I can't keep up with his comings and goings?"

"Not at all child! Considering all you've been through. But now, you must begin to prepare."

"For what?" she cried, in further exasperation.

"What grandfather is trying to say, my lamb, is this: Durbin House needs some attention. There's much to be done to make it habitable again."

"Thank you for translating the King's English!" Devlin barked and then switched to a more consoling tone. "You can see to it, right after the New Year. There's no haste."

"I barely have the strength to dress myself, and you want me to take that on? I won't do it!"

As predictable as Pavlov's dog from years of emotional conditioning, Court made a speedy one-hundred-and-eighty-degree turn. "She's absolutely right!" he assailed his grandfather, with a rap of his fist, sending the china askew.

"It seems I'm caught between the devil and the deed! Don't fret another moment, my dear. You need not lift a finger!"

Homecomings

Badger's Hut sighed with the whispers of the dead. It remained well-furnished and had become a ghostly refuge for Lacey. She sought its isolation and troubled memories, like an acolyte drawn to the Eucharist, keeping the cupboards stocked and the kettle steaming. Here were the chalky traces of Sholto's scribbling upon the stone hearth, his crude way of marking time. Poor, dead Sholto stricken with the pox in far-off Belgium. She had given what was left of Padraic's trust to Sophie, who used it to pay off her husband's gambling debts and move to Galway.

Lacey sat in the rocking chair, hands warmed by a mug of tea, and immersed herself in the past. Ten had been a good year. In this game, she picked a year in her life and recalled moments with Padraic. That was the spring they had made kites and flew them along the blustery shore of Lough Phair. The mighty March wind billowed under the kites, turning them into sails. They had wrestled with the kites, trying to avoid the waves, dancing on tiptoe. How she had wished that they could sail over the foamy crests to a new land where there were no grownups, no lessons, no rules.

"So this is where you come to brood your life away! At least Paladin gets to feel the sunshine and smell this sweet country air. Bit of a balmy day for February."

"Ran!"

He held a crude walking stick in one hand and a cracked leather satchel in the other, grinning at her in merry expectation. "You might at least invite me in for a cup of something, to clear these lungs of London's bloody soot."

Lacey fell on him in rapturous delight as he kissed her with boisterous enthusiasm. "You disappeared without a word," she gasped, her chin scraped by the stubble of his beard. "How could you!"

"Missed me, wild one?"

She was overwhelmed by the physical yearning his question provoked. They had been alone like this only once before, in the attic of Marsh's Library. She stepped back in wariness, only to be swept back into his arms, the force of his kisses trumpeting his intentions. Ran's hands, strong and deliberate, clasped her bottom, and she felt the push of his erection. When she offered no resistance, he lifted her legs to grasp his waist, and they stumbled toward the day bed.

Intoxicated by his show of desire and her body's willingness to respond to his caresses, Lacey yielded to his hands sliding under her clothes. His fingertips stroked her breasts, wringing exquisite sensations that shimmered through her, like rays of sunshine. It was a daydream brought to life that slowly, inexorably, turned threatening.

"Don't hurt me!"

He rolled off her in confusion and snapped, "I thought you were wanting me?"

"It's not you! I was remembering being in the attic—with Mazo."

"How could I forget?" He fumbled for a cigarette, castigating himself. It was all his fault. Padraic's death, the slaughter of the rebel boys, and now, this moment of near splendor, snatched away. "Can you look at me without blaming me?"

"I don't blame you for any of it."

Ran was not surprised that Court had revealed nothing of his duplicity. It was obvious that denial and avoidance were his way of protecting Lacey from life's unpleasant complications.

"Want a taste of this?" It was all he could think of to comfort her.

She moved closer and he put the cigarette between her lips. "Easy now."

"Pish! You sound like my father when he lets me try his pipe."

"Do I now? That'll put a damper on a man's wanting. Listen here, men like Lonnigan are cowardly brutes." Many would say the same about him. The irony amused him. "He was a pig bastard who got what was coming to him."

Lacey wanted to believe him, needed to let go of the fear and shame, but it was too fresh, too painfully woven into the raw spectacle of Padraic's death.

"Is there anything to eat?" he asked with customary deflection.

Refusing to linger in the gloom, Ran drew her to the porch, where they devoured soup and several sandwiches. "'Tis the finest meal I've had in many a day," he said, layering cheddar between slices of Aggie's black bread.

"Do you need money?"

"I don't go without, but I do miss good company."

"What were you doing in London?"

"Conditions in Dublin were not favorable to my well-being, so I took off and bunked with some old racing mates."

"You were hiding out," she said, paring an apple and offering it to him.

"Aye. This from your orchards?"

"It's the last of the pippins. Are you running away from anyone now?"

He shook the crumbs from his jacket and relit the stub of the cigarette. "Not away from. I guess, I'm running to you."

She felt another clutch of desire and blushed. All her daydreaming had not prepared her for this moment of truth, made all the more real, by their reckless behavior.

"I was hoping, you might have some work for me, or know someone in need of my services." His sly inference was lost on her naiveté.

"Must it be with horses?" The germ of a brilliant idea percolated in her lust-saturated brain.

"I'll put my hand to anything that keeps me in whiskey and tobacco."

"Good! You can work for me! Durbin House needs lots of fixing up, and you can oversee the men."

"Won't that soldier boy of yours get all twitchy with me around?"

"Who is it Durbin House belongs to? By the time Court returns, we'll be nearly done."

———◆———

"It's too dreadfully Victorian," Lacey said, in answer to Devlin's perturbed question as to why Durbin House was under siege by an army of day laborers.

"But my dear child, all it needed was a spot of paint and a good scrubbing." He winced at the wedge of bills set before him.

"Everything must be perfect for daddy's homecoming."

"I quite agree. But it might be best to wait for Court. Such an undertaking requires a man's oversight."

"Pish! I've already engaged Ransom Longo for that." She must make short work of Devlin's protests; there were fabric swatches to decide upon. "It makes me happy to be doing this. I've been sad for so long." A strategically mustered tear splashed down her cheek.

Devlin's backbone sagged in proportion to her manipulations, and he quickly rationalized, "Well, 'tis your father's money and he has made quite a bit of it lately."

———◆———

Lacey's time in New York and Dublin had introduced her eye to the more graceful curvilinear style of Art Nouveau. It was her intention to banish the lumbering oppressiveness of the past and bring in the light palette, elegant textiles, and small-scaled furniture of modern design. She was ruthless in disposing of that which conflicted with or offended her vision, but sentimental enough to retain those objects that had made Durbin House a home. Devlin was impressed enough to compliment her on her cagey business transactions. Most of the more ornate pieces were appraised and lent to several museums, others auctioned off, while the lesser quality ones found their way to the servants' quarters.

The kitchen and bathrooms were updated with the latest appliances, fixtures, and plumbing. Their stone floors and white-washed walls were covered with Italian tiles. The house was wired for electricity and became the first in the town to have a telephone. No room was overlooked or shortchanged because of status or function.

Mrs. Wooster had recommended an interior decorator from Paris. His gleeful anticipation of a large fee from a novice client was soon replaced by a cringing acquiescence to an exacting mistress with a demand for speed and craftsmanship. Men came from as far away as Belfast when word spread that there were good wages and accommodations to be had.

The fine April afternoon could not suit Court's mood any better than if he had the power of the Almighty to command nature. He had made the trip from Dublin stripped of his penitent's garb. Since the Easter Rising, the viscous feel of the wool uniform against his skin had returned him to the claustrophobia of the trenches and the sensation of his pores being invaded by parasites.

He was burdened further, with a measure of paranoia, by the increased scrutiny of his superiors and the appalling randomness of interrogations directed at Irish officers. The British continued to punish all suspects for their temerity in seeking independence, and pursued the flimsiest of intelligence with vengeance and cursory justice. Court had no idea of Ran's whereabouts and had lost sleep wondering if he would materialize spinning some tale of treason.

Squirming in the hamper that he carried along the path to Durbin House was a three-month-old Parson Jack Russell terrier—a belated birthday gift for Lacey. Devlin's frequent and frantic correspondence, regarding her latest whim, had provided the only levity during the interminable wait for his discharge. Little of the house could be discerned from its shroud of scaffolding. The squadron of workmen were being beleaguered by the threats of a disturbingly familiar voice.

"Listen up, buckos. You've less than a fortnight to finish up! If there's a man among you who can't give me your back and hands for a solid twelve hour day—stand aside! There's another waiting to take your place."

"Longo! What the bloody hell are you doing here?"

"Good afternoon, Major. Didn't old granddad make mention of me?"

"Do I not look unpleasantly surprised?" Court set the hamper on the grass. "I suppose you've come to collect. How much is this going to cost me?" If he could be rid of Ran forever, it would be worth all he had.

"I've no desire to disappear with a wad of your money in my pocket."

"Isn't that what you do? Stir up trouble for a price, then vanish?"

He had less than fifteen seconds to recalibrate his expression from glowering to glowing as Lacey threw herself at him. To see her happy after months of heartache and despair, to feel her mouth soft against his, froze his brain long enough to respond without inhibition.

"Are you all done with the army?" she asked, rosy from the kiss.

"All done, my lamb, and at your disposal."

He could not bear to let her go and held her in a loose hug.

She noticed the rocking hamper. "Is that for me?"

"Who else would I be owing a birthday present to?"

"What an angel," she cooed, the terrier rolling in her arms. "Look how sweet his markings are! You know, I've never had a dog of my very own. I've much to learn."

Unfazed by Court's menacing squint, Ran said, "I've a knack for training all kinds of animals. This one should be a good bit of fun."

"He's relentless!" Court seethed to himself. "He cares nothing about the danger that follows him."

Ran rubbed the puppy's belly and leaned in close to Lacey with one of his predatory smiles. "This breed is known for its intelligence and loyalty, but they're a right handful. He'll need proper training."

A carbonized fury took root in Court; yet he managed a steady voice. "Can you find him a bit of water, lamb? We don't want him getting overheated from all the excitement."

When she was out of hearing range, he confronted Ran. "Are you forgetting, there's a boy rotting in the graveyard, just down the road? A boy you put there!"

"Don't be throwing a fuckin' moody with me, O'Rourke! You owe me. I find this soft air congenial to my good health."

"You're a marked man and think I can save you from a bullet to the head? I've no influence in such matters."

The smirk on Ran's face vanished into a solemn seam of foreboding. "You may have picked your side of the fence, but me, I'm a man in need of opportunities." He opened his tobacco pouch and methodically rolled a cigarette. "Tell you what, Major. I won't be having tea in Dublin Castle, and you won't go blabbering to Lacey that Paddy's death was of my doing. Not on purpose of course, but dead is dead."

"I agree to nothing unless you stay away from her!"

Ran's shoulders rippled with silent laughter. "Can I help it if our lamb finds me irresistible?"

Court gripped the front of his shirt and twisted him close. "By Judas, I could kill you on this very spot! I'll not let you cause her another moment's grief. You're tainted by greed and lust. And your soul, if you have one…"

"Don't be concerning yourself about my soul." His hand rested lightly over Court's fist. "Let's keep to our devil's pact—for now."

◆

A pale wash of yellow brightened Durbin House, so recently roused from its slumber. Ropes of orange roses tumbled from the railings, and on the sides of every granite step, dark green ceramic urns displayed white tulips and cascades of ivy.

"What's got you to pondering, Lacey?" Court asked, after several minutes of critical contemplation.

They had paused on horseback, at the foot of the avenue, flanked by swaying golden poplars.

"I wonder if daddy will be pleased with all I've done? He can be just as stubborn as Devlin when it comes to change." She smoothed Paladin's mane. "Why are men like that?"

She looked to him for an immediate explanation of his gender's idiosyncrasies. But he was absorbed in his own contemplation. What if he was a stranger, seeing her for the first time? This stunning young woman wearing a cropped, black velvet jacket and white shirt. Would he be drawn to the gleaming expanse of her throat and the undulating dip of her décolletage?

"Court! Are you listening to me?"

"So sorry." He fingered the silk cuff of her shirt, remarking, "I like the way this feels."

"It's silk. You never notice what I'm wearing, unless it happens to be your castoffs. You seem so far away."

She grabbed his chin to see what lurked in his eyes, but they were bright with affection and surprise. "You'd tell me if you were having nightmares again—from before?"

"Lacey, you're not to fret about such things!" His fingers fluttered along her arm in a nervous staccato. "I'll admit to a rough patch, every now and then, but I muddle through."

She leaned in to kiss him, but Paladin and Drummer drew them apart, restless for their meal.

"It seems our chaperones disapprove of such a spectacle. Come now, there's much to be done before your father arrives this afternoon. I'm yours to order about."

"I can't wait to have daddy all to myself again! It's been an eternity."

"The man does have a queer knack for losing track of time."

◆

"Lafferty's spotted the motorcar! The captain's but a whisker away, your ladyship!" Seamus clutched his chest, wheezing dramatically, as befitted the delirium of the moment. "By the good grace of St. Peter himself, there won't be a precious breath left in me body to say welcome home."

He fell back onto a settee, next to an agitated Devlin, who grimaced and waved at Court. "Get me up on me feet, boy! We can't be gawking about like a gaggle of clucks. We must make a proper show of it. Lacey, gather the servants!"

All heads swiveled in her direction, poised to mobilize at her behest. They had been well-trained from months of her benevolent, and often despotic, command. She swayed beneath the portrait of her mother, a kaleidoscope of emotions flickering across her face. Three years —more than a thousand days missing her father. The staggering number lodged in her brain, and she receded from the clamor of the present.

Since that afternoon when she had wished to hide away in Anthony's pocket, in a bedroom of fluff and flounces, Lacey had freed herself from the thinning bonds of childhood. All that had come before, would never be again, not even her relationship with him. He had existed in a dream dimension of wistful memories and childish sentiments; the same place where Court had resided, until he found his way back to her.

Court saw her paralyzing bewilderment and abruptly let go of Devlin's elbow, sending him flapping onto Seamus's lap. "Out! The lot of you! On the steps and smiling is what I want to see—now!"

The room cleared in a clatter of haste, and they were alone. ""What is it, lamb?"

She shrugged and turned her back to him, tapping the newly refurbished marble mantel. "It's been so long, too long. I can't…"

His arms encircled her from behind and he rested his cheek against hers, the sweet vibrato of his voice echoing through her. "'Tis natural to be feeling anxious. But surely, it can't compare to our reunion? He nudged her into turning around. "I can promise you, the man will be no better than a crow, pecking away at a gleaming new penny—dazzled by the woman you've become."

The Silver Ghost inched along the driveway, with Ran narrating a litany of all the changes, and Anthony savoring every detail of Lacey's meticulous renovation.

"I'd forgotten how lush it is here. I could be in South America again."

"Just a hint of what's to come Captain, sir. The inside's a treat! Your daughter has the eye of an artist and the heart of a craftsman."

"Where is she?" Anthony was half out the door, one foot on the running board of the moving motorcar.

Lacey stepped over the threshold into a spot of sunshine, startling him with her resemblance to Caitlin. Regret squeezed the air from his lungs, and he vowed never to leave her again. Voices shouted all kinds of greetings, but what mattered was the sweet peal of "Daddy! Daddy!"

The crowd parted in biblical accord as father and daughter collided in an embrace that vaporized time and distance. Lacey was swept up and secured in Anthony's arms.

Ran assisted the second passenger, who shrank from the spectacle.
"Suppose this will take a bit of getting used to, ma'am."
"If only it were as simple as that," Anne Marie Wakefield sighed.

Harbingers

August 28, 1917

I am jealous of his love for her. He makes love to me but always—always— she will be first in his heart! Even if I am able to bear him a child, it will be so. I hate her! She would like to see me dead and buried alongside her mother. She, who has never known the grasp of loneliness or hunger of wanting…

A splash of tears smeared the ink and the heat of emotion roiling within Anne Marie raised the temperature in the stifling bedroom. This was the only place that she felt safe from the withering scorn of her stepdaughter. She removed her spectacles, blotting her eyes with one of the dozen of lace handkerchiefs purchased in the ancient lace-making town of Peniche. They had cost more than she could earn in a month of teaching but were mere trifles compared to the staggering trousseau insisted upon by Anthony. During the eighteen months that they had spent touring Central and South America, he had been nothing less than devoted and solicitous—surprising her with small gestures of consideration. There was Annunciata, the motherly lady's maid, who shepherded her through that first night of marital anxiety and then, through that awful morning in Caracas when she suffered a miscarriage.

Like the creep of the tide, every day swept away another remnant of her other life—of what once was her. Who was she before falling in love? Someone who knew only of books and hardship, thrift and modesty? She was a minister's daughter, cursed with an Alice in Wonderland ability to shrink to the size of the Mad Hatter's teacup when confronted by life's challenges.

Now, she was immersed in luxury with domestic responsibilities that surprised her with the daunting obstinacy of the house staff. Unlike those employed by Mrs. de la Roche and her ilk, Irish servants seemed possessed of a single, infuriating mindset: "We hear what you're

saying, but we'll do as we think best." Just that morning, she had engaged Bernadette Howser, widowed sister of Padraic's mother Kathleen, in a duel of wits.

"Ma'am, that Saint Tochmura would strike me stone-dead, nothing t'would be a better choice on a day such as this, but a nice bit of cold cucumber soup with a poached salmon! Light as a fairy's wing upon the stomach."

"But Mrs. Howser…"

"Please, ma'am, 'tis Birdy to you and the captain."

"Birdy, I thought we agreed to start with the chilled beet soup? And then, the terrine with the rabbits the captain brought back from his…"

"Aye, t'was so at the time. But her ladyship sent round old Cubby Muldoon early this morning, whilst you were still abed, with a leapin' fresh salmon. Hardly bruised at all from its thrashing about!"

"What does that matter?"

"Well, you know, he ain't been right since he took that terrible tumble from Sully's beer wagon last Hallowtide. And him, with only one bright eye left in his head, so he's no good for hunting no more. Why his old ma needs to be tucking him in at night so he don't go rolling …"

"Mrs. Howser! What does any of that have to do with the rabbits?"

"Ah, her ladyship had me trade the rabbits for the salmon."

Lacey. Always Lacey.

"Here you are, dearest." Anthony surprised her with a stealthy entrance, two fingers brushing the nape of her neck. "It's hotter than hell in here!"

Anne Marie closed the diary and stoically composed herself. Of late, he had no patience with tears.

"There's a slight breeze, but it hasn't helped my headache. I wasn't feeling well enough for a lesson. Court doesn't mind. He's visiting with Lacey on the terrace."

"You must learn to ride well enough to keep up! This is Ireland after all. Almost all socializing is done on a horse, around a horse, or about a horse!"

"Court thinks I'm doing well, and he would know best."

"About some things."

She saw his attention stray beyond her and the room, past the listless curtains, down to the terrace, alighting on Lacey. Always Lacey.

"You know, it's only a matter of time."

"What's that?" He turned the full azure gleam of his eyes upon her in flustered perplexity.

"Anthony, they're in love!"

"Is that what you call it? I call it a damn shame. But I'll not come between them, if that's what you're all fired up about. If it were up to me…"

"Well it isn't, and I'm glad!" Defiance did not come easily. "All the time you were gone, it was Court who watched over her. It's only natural."

"It's nothing more than goddamn proximity! She's not seen enough of life to settle for him. But he's worked his wastrel charm on her."

"Wastrel? After all he's been through—after all he's done for you and her?" I'm ashamed of you, Anthony! Can't you see beyond your smothering possessiveness and appreciate what a good man he is!"

"So, he's turned your head as well? You wouldn't be the first." He remained uncontrite and aroused by her scolding schoolmarm routine. "It's much cooler in my room. We could have a little lie down before lunch."

Anne Marie's new life revolved around this imperative of desire, and the yearning to draw him in, to drown in his vitality. His fingertips grazed her throat in a beckoning caress, and an invisible leash drew her up and out of her timidity.

◆

Flurry sat on his hind legs, enraptured by the round, squishy object held out to him.

"Listen to me, you scruffy little beast! I throw the ball, and you fetch it back to me. 'Tis what you do. You're a dog."

The puppy watched the high trajectory of the ball as it flew into a mass of blue hydrangeas. He tipped over, tongue lolling, delighted with Court's performance.

"Another one of Longo's miracles, I see."

"You know he listens only to me." Lacey raised one hand to her chest, and Flurry settled in her lap for a nice petting.

"Aren't you tired of doing nothing but cater to that one?"

"It's too hot to do anything but sit here. Don't you have a lesson with *her*?" The "her" came out in a huff of bitterness.

"Not this morning; plagued by a headache. If you were of a mind to rouse yourself from this petulant stupor—you'd see for yourself just how nicely she's coming along. Not a natural, her being a twitchy little thing, but she's trying damn hard."

"If she broke her neck, we'd be rid of her!"

"What a ghastly thing to say! All I'm asking is you give her a wisp of a chance. You carry on like she's a succubus sent to devour your father."

"Pish! What need does he have for a wife after all this time? And one not much older than you!"

"By Judas, a man has the right to bring home a wife and not have his daughter torment the bloody piss out of her!"

One pair of brown eyes bore into one of gray in a hostile stare-off. The same passion that aligned them, held the power to polarize them. He made a conciliatory gesture, sitting next to her, tickling Flurry's neck.

"See here, why don't you come along with me when I go to Cork next week? It's years since you've been there and will be a nice treat for you."

"I'm not ten anymore!" she snapped and wiggled away from him, but he shifted forward, resting his hands on the arms of the chaise.

"My business won't take up all that much time. We can stay at the Imperial."

"Why is it you've been spending so much time there? What kind of business are you talking about?"

"Just some loose ends in need of tidying up for grandfather. You know what a fierce finagler he is, making one deal after another. He may be getting on in years, but his mind is as sharp as the devil's pitchfork."

When the palavering commenced, she knew he was being avoidant. "I can pick and choose what we do?"

"Of course, lamb. Whatever your heart desires."

His choice of words echoed those of her grandmother from several years ago. She thought of the locket with a nip of remorse, wondering what he had done with it. Her petulance vanished.

"Court?" She pushed Flurry away so she could snuggle closer to him.

"Yes, Lacey."

It may have been the heat, but she thought she detected a sudden flush of desire warming his cheeks. "It would be lovely to go away, together."

"Indeed, it would." He laid her hand on his palm and stroked it with shy tenderness. "What's old Birdy concocting for lunch?"

"Poached salmon."

———◆———

"You don't like Anthony. I didn't, not at first. Yet, here I am."

"And having a devil of a time!" Court exclaimed, tearing at a spray of shiny vines trailing across the stone. "See how these spread? They're relentless, nothing can stop them. Even a good tug won't kill the root. In a few days, they'll be pushing out and starting all over. Just like Lacey."

Anne Marie winced at the sound of her name intruding upon the serene spot. Drummer and one of Anthony's mares, Juno, grazed contentedly by the stone footbridge.

"What am I to do?"

"Well, there's no stopping her, but I've learned how to distract her. You could say, it's been my life's work."

She wondered how such a thoughtful and kind man could be in love with such a spoiled and spiteful girl. Then she remembered a remark by Anthony, when he learned of their planned trip to Cork. "He's been mooning over her from the first moment! She knocked him out with one crack of her riding crop, and when he came to, it was love!"

"You can't go at her head on. She's not one to let go of what she thinks belongs only to her. Not without some blood being spilt."

"I don't have the strength to take her on. It took all I had to come to Ireland. I had to let go of so many things… teaching… friends…what's left of my family." She looked up from her clenched hands and cried, "If you could have seen how happy we were! Just the two of us. It didn't matter I was in one strange country after another. I was with Anthony!"

Court pushed his handkerchief into her hand. She was a weepy creature with an austere kind of beauty—not the sort to bewitch a man upon first glance. He could see what had attracted Anthony: the tawny shimmer of hair, the eyes reminiscent of the amber veins of granite running through the Pradshipur Mountains, and her smile, radiant though fleeting. Anthony would want a wife as different from Caitlin as the sun is from the moon.

"Please forgive me, Anne Marie. I've been going on about Lacey and her beastly ways when you…"

"You've been nothing but wonderful to me! Do you remember when we first met? You took my hand and said "'Tis grand to meet you, Mrs. de la Roche. Welcome to Durbin House, your new home." Lacey just stood there with hate in her eyes!"

The weeping resumed, and both horses looked up in reproach. Court was beginning to tire of her fragility and neediness. Lacey was a Hussar in comparison, and he was thankful for it.

"'Tis no good wearing yourself out over her shenanigans. I'm thinking, if you take to ignoring every little spite, every little poke to your sweet nature— soon enough, the shameless vixen will give up! There won't be much sport in it, and she'll go on to something else."

"You really think that would work?" Anne Marie asked with a dazed appreciation for Court's keen understanding of Lacey's perversity.

"If I know my lamb, 'tis a sure strategy."

Ran heard Lacey ride up on Paladin but remained with his back to her, on the porch of Badger's Hut, shirtless, suspenders hanging from the waist, sponging himself from a bucket.

"You were going to slink off without so much as a good-bye?" Still mounted, her anger bridged the distance between them.

"Mind your caterwaulin', I've a thumpin' headache. I did it proper. Gave notice to your father."

"Are you forgetting who hired you?"

"So now, you're the mistress of me?" He swung around, wet and tensile, the top two buttons of his trousers undone. "Where the bloody hell has that gotten me, I'd like to know? Languishing away the summer—you flitting between him and me!"

She was riveted to the dark furrow stretching from his navel to the swell of his groin. A spasmodic stirring warmed within her.

"I'm done feeding your girlish fantasies. I'm off to Kildare! There's a job waiting for me at the Curragh, thanks to Atticus."

"Why now? Is it because I'm going away with Court?"

"He'll have you wedded and bedded by Eastertide. I'll not hang around waiting on such a thing."

"Don't I have a say in any of this?" she asked, following him inside.

If the interior was a reflection of Ran's state of mind, Lacey was in for a hellish time. The plank table was cluttered with odds and ends, including the reason for his headache. Every cupboard had been ransacked; the floor carpeted with dried leaves and anything else that had stuck to his boots. It smelled of him: tobacco, whiskey, and animal sweat. His satchel sat half packed on the daybed, along with a hamper that he was stocking with tins and bottles.

She knew that she had been playing a risky game "flitting" between the two men. But in her naive thinking, she had been fair, even virtuous, faithfully attentive to the one at hand. Why must she have to choose?

"I want you both." There she said it! The shock of saying the words out loud had no effect on him. *"I know your secrets without you telling me."*

"It don't work that way, wild one, well, not for your sort." He was banging around in the sink, a cigarette stuck between his lips.

"Look at me!" She grazed his shoulder with a flick of the riding crop and he spun around, seizing her wrist.

"Prove it then! Words don't mean a fuckin' thing to me!" He dragged her to the table, scattering the mess with one sweep, and freed his penis.

It was thick and pulsing, arrogant in its upright stance. If she sheathed him in her hands, caressed him to climax, would it be enough to make him stay? She touched it and he slapped her hand away; the rebuff bewildered her.

"That I can get from a gutter tart for a half shilling. I want what you're saving for him!" He plunged his hand between her legs and raised her on tiptoe to ravage her mouth.

His kisses had never been gentle, but these were harsh and bruising. Impaled on his hand, the primal lick of desire became a despairing urge to be invaded, to be rid of virginal inhibitions. Suddenly, he wrenched himself away, leaving her gasping—suffocating in mortification.

Ran fussed over Paladin, stroking the slope of his nose. "I'll write as soon as I'm settled." He kept his gaze on the stirrup in his hand as she mounted. "Maybe you and the soldier boy will come by for a race or two."

"Why are you punishing me? Have I been so awful?"

His hand rested on her thigh. "Just selfish, 'tis your nature. Life's a queer thing if you let go and see where it takes you. That's what I'm doing; you best do the same."

Lacey touched his hand, warm and familiar against hers. "Promise, you'll not let Atticus involve you in any of his political doings?"

"Oh, I'm done with that kind of intriguing. One whiff of rebellion is more than enough to keep me from an early grave."

"Ran, you'll always be welcome here."

"I'm much obliged, wild one."

There was nothing more to say, so he kissed her hand and with hunched shoulders, held one arm aloft in a final salute. Lacey gave Paladin free rein, trusting him to lead her back to Durbin House, and the decision that had been made for her.

◆

The city of Cork, emerging from the briny tangle of reclaimed salt marshes, resembled Venice with its web of canals and fanciful architecture. It bristled with a lively tempo, which Court had found most agreeable during his reassignment from Delhi. Here he had come of age, establishing an identity, apart from being the grandson of Devlin O'Rourke. Here there was less of a British presence, no looming Dublin Castle to chastise the effervescent Corkonians. Here Irish culture and politics flourished in symbiotic syncopation with the written and spoken word.

Here playwrights, poets, journalists, and republicans commanded the same respect as the prosperous businessmen of the mercantile class.

Court and Lacey had settled into a domestic routine by the third day of their stay. Each morning, they ate breakfast in the dining room of the Imperial, mimicking the gender specific roles of the married couples around them. He perused and muttered his way through the early edition of the Cork Examiner, and she composed lists, crossed off items, and began anew.

"There's a special performance tomorrow evening at the Sheridan with that dancer Duncan—the American girl who's quite the sensation. Proceeds will go to a war widows' fund. What say we go?" He shared a tantalizing photograph of Isadora Duncan cavorting barefoot.

She was unimpressed but consulted her calendar. "It means we can't stay for tea after the Field recital."

"Is that tomorrow?" He was rueful about being reminded. Listening to music without anything to stimulate his senses, like the scandalous Isadora, would be quite a chore. "What if we forget about the recital and do something else? We could go to Cash's. May as well get that out of the way."

"You want to go shopping with me? I've been to Chesselwaites for a bolt of green velvet for Aggie, and you've seen to Devlin's present."

"Have I now?"

"The crystal decanter."

"Well, Grandfather will be needing a few more trifles, as will Aggie. There's still the wedding present."

"Remember that damn tray you made me pay for out of my allowance? It's being engraved!"

"'Tis only fair you loosen them purse strings for something, my lamb."

"If you're loathe to go to the recital, just admit to it! You needn't pretend a keen interest in shopping."

The waiter appeared, as he had every morning thus far, with a letter for Court.

"Shall I wait for a response, sir?"

"No need, lad." He frowned and tucked the letter into his breast pocket, saying with one of his disarming smiles,

"Lacey darlin', I must get to the notary at once. Shall we meet at the Madrigal Gardens by noon? 'Tis a lovely day to dine by the river."

He had perfected the deft exit. Allow no time for discussion or argument while collecting one's belongings and depositing a hasty kiss on a sulking countenance.

"Here we are. What do you think?"

Court was curiously giddy. It had nothing to do with the half bottle of wine at lunch, or the leisurely drive around the rim of the Lee where they admired the late Victorian houses. They had stopped in front of a cluster of bright brick homes, carefully terraced into the side of a hill.

"Are we calling on someone?" Lacey asked with sedate enthusiasm.

She had not expected him to be so well-known in the city. Wherever they went, he was recognized and greeted with cheer and conversation. It was a reminder to her, how much of the last five years he had lived a life unknown and apart from her. The fact that the same could be said of her held no irony.

"Remember this address, 22 Adelaide Lane, my new home!"

"You bought it? But why? You have a home!"

"I find it tiresome to stay in a hotel for days at a time. This will be much more to my liking. And will pay for itself, if I rent it out, now and then." He guided her up three steps to a handsomely carved door. "Look at the detail on this. Thick as a Minotaur's skull! You can help me decide what to do with it. 'Tis rather musty from being shut up for so long. Let's get some of these windows opened and the river breezes blowing through."

The main floor had a spacious parlor and compact dining room, with stained glass casement windows facing the river. The kitchen took up the entire basement and was quite a sorry mess but opened onto a scrap of a garden, with a headless faun reclining atop a crumbling fountain.

"I could manage with a day cook/housekeeper type, don't you think?" he asked leading her up a narrow staircase.

The top floor housed two bedrooms and a bathroom in disturbing decay.

"Tell me now, and don't be kind! I want your expert opinion."

As the tour unfolded, her doubts gave way to the irresistible possibilities of design and domesticity.

"I think it's wonderful! There's so much you can do with it. You must find a good architect I can work with, someone young and clever. You'll want a modern look." This time she would dispense with the French interior decorator and apply her own talents.

Court, humming with delight, swept her up in a little jig. "You do love spending my money. But mind, spend it well."

◆

"They'll be holding the curtain till Terence arrives," Court explained to a fidgeting Lacey, clasping her hand to his chest and scanning the program.

It was 7:55 p.m., and the Sheridan Theater was the scene of contained hysteria. The performance was sold-out, including the rows close to the rafters. There, a welter of what she recognized as Fenians jostled one another in well-lubricated excitement. She longed for Ran to be among them. And if he was, what good would come of it?

"Tell me more about this MacSwiney," she asked, needing Court to scratch the errant tickle of wanting.

"Well, he's a great man, a playwright and poet. The kind who will work to the death to see Ireland free. There aren't many who can compare with him."

The house lights twinkled several times, but not for Isadora Duncan. A spotlight flashed upon the balcony, to the right of the stage. What began as a mewl of anticipation swelled into a howl of welcome. Terence MacSwiney waved in blushing embarrassment, but the woman beside him lifted her arms high above her head, offering him up for their voracious adulation. He tried to muffle their enthusiasm by pointing to the stage with an elegant twist of his wrist but it was futile. The roaring continued, abetted by the shouts and whistles of the Fenians.

"Miss de la Roche, at last you are flesh and blood to me! For too long, you have frolicked through my imagination as the most whimsical of characters in the story of this pup's life."

Terence MacSwiney was taller than Court and easily a head above the animated clusters of patrons in evening dress. He bent over her hand with an awkward courtliness that she found charming; a persistent thatch of dark hair covered one blue-gray eye, making him appear more boyish than his years.

"Aren't we the most blessed men in the room?" he asked, cosseting his wife in an embrace. "My Muriel is a treasure of a girl. She keeps me tethered to the almighty truth when I begin to flounder and fuss."

"I think you do a rather splendid job all by yourself. Terence, my love, we could do with some champagne."

"That is a task suited to our talents!"

Lacey noticed the woman's eyes on her husband as he threaded his way through the room, pausing to accept an embrace or clasp a hand. It was slow-going, and often, he looked over to meet her gaze with a shrug of resignation. Lacey understood this kind of vigilance only too well.

"Has he been ill?

"Oh, they tried to grind him down! Beat the very heart and soul, right out of him, but he's on the mend," Muriel said with steely pride.

Her accent was boarding school British, and she exuded the regal confidence that comes with wealth and a formal education. She wore a beautifully cut black lace dress that made her pale blue eyes seem depthless. Her powdered complexion reflected the brittle luminescence of winter light, casting her as the perfect subject for a Sargent portrait. Lacey found her oddly beautiful and peculiar. She supposed that if ever she had need of a female friend, it would be someone like Muriel.

"I see I may as well be speaking in tongues. I assumed… when I shouldn't… you knew. My husband has been a guest of our British occupiers since the Rising. We married in Bromyard, a dreary place, this June past. My family is quite appalled."

The men returned with four glasses on a tray and some pretty petit fours and marzipan.

"This is to be sipped slowly," Court admonished Lacey, winking at the couple. "She's spirited enough without the likes of this."

"Pish! You'd think I was raised among the temperate and virtuous."

Terence erupted in a deep and merry laugh. "I can't remember the last time, I've felt this joyful!" He kissed Muriel's cheek and murmured, "Well, not since our first night together."

She was not embarrassed by the intimate remark, and raised her glass and voice in such a forthright manner, the room stilled to listen. "A toast to Ireland and God himself! No sacrifice shall be too great for the sake of liberty! No suffering, too unbearable, if it delivers us from the devil's dominion!"

The crowd surged around them, enthralled by Muriel's exhortation. The words struck Lacey through the heart, piercing that still tender spot of grief and remembrance. So many had died, and many more were sure to follow. The swarm pulled the couples apart, spinning her in a whirl of foreboding. She saw Court mesmerized by the moment and the man. She saw Terence, a head above everyone, propelled forward as the bell sounded and the lights dimmed—fading into the shadows.

Haste To The Wedding

"Are we lost? We seem to be lost. Anthony, we're miles away from the others." Anne Marie's voice, lofting over the veil of mist and web of brush, revealed her anxiety, just enough for him to turn around in exasperation.

"No need to fret," Court called out from the head of the line. "We seem to be swept up in the eighth circle of hell! He's toying with us, for sure."

"Anne Marie." Anthony paused as he caught the sneer on his daughter's face. "Dearest," he resumed with an extra dollop of sweetness. "While it may seem as though we're going nowhere, the point is to follow the prey, where it goes. And right now, the blasted thing is going in circles!"

They were riding single file through a dense stretch of woods between Durbin House and Assolas, following the lead of one tenacious beagle who had picked up the scent.

"So we're not lost?" she persisted, not satisfied with his explanation.

The mist had become distinct drops of rain, and the cool October morning was turning cold, as was her enthusiasm. Anthony had taken her through a longer route to avoid the jumps. But she saw that the detours taxed his competitive spirit, and soon, she was left behind. It had been two hours of a marathon game of hide-and-seek, stop-and-go. When the pace quickened, Anne Marie feared she would lose her grip and fall off. When the hounds slowed down, the steady trot threatened to wrench her neck from her spine.

"Unless I've suddenly become a dithering idiot, I doubt I could be lost in my own backyard!"

Anthony's barbed response deflated her. She had felt confident in her navy blue riding habit with its beautiful fur trim. But that was before the horn blew. Wedged between a demanding husband and a sullen stepdaughter, she was stuck in her own circle of hell.

"It's bloody hopeless!" Court exclaimed as the beagle laid down in defeat. "This rain will wash the scent away; we may as well call it a day."

"Pish! I'm not giving up," Lacey insisted and muscled her way to the front, bending back a heavy branch and letting it go.

It whacked Anne Marie across the chest; she gasped and toppled from Juno. Lacey flew past the men without a mortal care as Anthony dismounted in a stuttering panic and Court, head swiveling, decided what to do.

"Lacey!" He turned Drummer in pursuit, but they were no match for Paladin's speed. Taking a shortcut through the freshly harvested barley fields of Assolas, he was betting on her wily sense of self-preservation.

As the drooping apple trees of Durbin House appeared, so did Paladin, nosing through the fallen fruit. Lacey had fled on foot to the shelter of a cold cellar, concealed within a rise of earth, deep in the orchards. This was a childhood lair shared only with Padraic but well-known to

Court. The splintered door could not withstand a furious kick from him as he stooped to enter.

She was pink with excitement and utterly without remorse, welcoming his fury as some kind of challenge. The wind had whipped her hair into loose curls and a moist sheen covered her face. She seemed as luminous and ethereal as Botticelli's Venus until that perfect rosebud of a mouth spoke.

"If you've come to drag me back for an apology, you can bloody well go to hell!"

"Christ! You could have killed her! Are you so riddled with hate, you'd take the very life from her?"

"Wait till she leaves him dead and steals the coins from his eyes! Then you'll see…"

"Enough! I cannot stomach another moment of this madness. You'll marry me and have done with it!"

"You call that a proposal?"

"'Tis a damn sight more than you deserve, you miserable, vindictive brat!"

"So you think insulting me is the way to my heart? Why, you haven't even said you're in love with me!"

"Haven't I now? What else would possess a fool like me to want the likes of you for a wife?"

The spontaneity of the proposal colluded with the sweet bite of apples and the scent of lavender and roses, her scent, casting an aromatic spell. In this dank hole, reduced to atavistic longing, desire trumped denial. He: pragmatic, brooding, and skeptical; and she: vivacious, impetuous, and mercurial were two lambent bodies spinning within the same orbit. He deflected the heat from her volatility, and she burnished the rough from his reticence.

He crossed both arms behind her so there could be no escape and kissed her with ravenous need. His harsh groan of retreat left her weak and wanting.

"Say yes!" The weight of her filled his arms.

"I suppose it was always meant to be."

"No truer words were ever spoken, my lamb." Court's lips returned to that perfect rosebud, made all the sweeter by surrender.

"I do so like toile," Lacey remarked, stroking the blue and white counterpane on what was to be their bed.

"You do say the queerest things, wife to be."

"Don't make fun. I've spent a good deal of time making everything just perfect for us."

Court joined her on the bed, arms drawing her close. "So you have! The house in Cork, this ramshackle suite of rooms, and let's not forget the wonders you worked on Durbin House."

Where had this mysterious talent sprung from he had asked himself of late. He thought he knew every little quirk and talent contained within her contrary being, but this was beyond the best guessing that he could muster.

"Once the "I dos" are said and done, you'll have an entire castle to transform!"

"I doubt Devlin will let me stray any further. He needs his memories; I'll not touch them."

"Then you and I will create a lovely batch of new ones for him, and if I…"

His words were smothered by a kiss. She had taken to kissing with feline curiosity and dexterity, always wanting more than he could give without losing control. This was the somewhat scandalous reason they were to be married five months after the proposal, rather than the customary one year. He had let her loose on the family to share their decision.

"We'll be wanting a spring wedding," Lacey said, her eyes locked on Court, who was passing the tea as Aggie poured.

"Just what Aggie and I were thinking on this very morning!" Devlin's smile was wide enough to swallow a Christmas goose whole. "It will give us lots of time to plan a grand wedding."

"No, this spring, May 5. On Padraic's birthday."

"Heavens!" Aggie gasped, sloshing the tea. "Wed in May, rue the day!"

Before the crush of protests could be sorted out, Anthony removed himself to the liquor cabinet, bracing himself for her next words.

"We can't wait that long to be husband and wife; it will kill us!"

He located what he needed and raised his glass. "The sooner the better, I say. Haste to the wedding!"

He nuzzled her ear and whispered, "I do love you, my lamb."

"You can't call me that anymore!" she cried, pulling away.

"What the devil are you talking about?"

"Court, you can't make love to me and call me that! It's too damn peculiar."

"But I've always called you that… and only you." His astonishment turned to wounded dismay. "Lacey, you're being ridiculous."

"My feelings are ridiculous to you?" One eyebrow arched, indicating it was a matter of seconds before some object took flight.

"Nothing has changed because we're getting married! It was meant to be. You said so yourself."

He lunged to his right, avoiding a doomed porcelain figurine. His burst of nervous laughter from behind a heavy pillow worsened the onslaught.

"Everything has changed, you idiot! I'm not your lamb…your little sister." A silver candlestick crashed against the headboard. "…your bloody affliction…" A perfume atomizer whizzed by his ear. "I'm to be your wife!"

An ebony hairbrush ricocheted off the pillow; her aim was improving, so he grabbed it in defense. "Are you done assaulting me, you little vixen? I'll not think twice about using this!"

A more reckless man might have succumbed to the provoking heat of her tantrum and wrestled her onto the bed. It was an excruciating effort to channel his arousal elsewhere.

"Is this how it's to be?" she sobbed, arms thrashing the air.

It was then that he realized just how little he understood women. A titanic shift had occurred in their relationship and escaped his notice.

"Lacey darlin'." He was careful to avoid the forbidden term of endearment. "Please forgive my obtuseness."

"Are you humoring me or do you really understand?" she asked, reluctantly sitting on the edge of the bed.

"I'll admit, you always seem a league or two beyond me when it comes to us. Let me see if I have this sorted out." He slid closer and warily held her hand to his lips, nodding in thought. "If we're to be husband and wife, I need to let go of the past."

"Not all of the past. Without it, we have no future. When you call me lamb, it pulls us back to a time when I was a child… vulnerable… helpless."

"Lacey, you were never either. You always found a way around me. It was a game we played."

"That's what I mean! No more games, Court. I want us to be equals. I want to be all you need, all you want."

"That you are, my sweet," he murmured, lips brushing the pale crest of her brow, lingering to kiss both damp eyelids, and then hurriedly feeding on her mouth. "You are my life."

——◆——

"It's an embarrassment on your finger! My mother is spinning in her grave." Anthony scowled as he held Lacey's hand. "I don't know which is worse, this fossilized nonsense or that puny piece of metal, he calls a wedding band."

Court had given her Colleen's engagement ring, a cushion cut moss agate in rose gold. The matching band, a filigreed wishbone style, was modest and well-worn.

"It was all Devlin could afford at the time. I think it's sweet. Look, it's like having a drop of the sea on my finger." She held the ring up to the morning light, wisps of green and brown floated through the clear prism.

"I gave your mother a star sapphire and a platinum band with diamonds! They're waiting if you…"

"Daddy! You can't expect Court to give me something you gave to my mother."

"I know for a goddamn certainty there's a treasure trove buried in that castle, and this is the best he comes up with?"

"Why can't you say Court's name? You must try harder!" She grabbed his face with both hands, as when she was a child in need of his attention. "We'll be one family. You can't hold onto old grudges. I love him."

He shifted her to his other knee and pressed his forehead to hers. "If we're negotiating, what do I get in return, pet? Don't say grandchildren! The very thought of it, at your age, turns my blood to ice water."

"I'll try harder with Anne Marie. How's that for a trade?"

"Don't promise something you can't deliver."

"If we remember why we're doing it—it won't be so bad."

"Am I intruding?" Anne Marie's voice shook from yet another wave of nausea. The sight of Lacey so robust in her riding clothes, cuddling with her father, made it all the more worse.

"Certainly not! I'll ring for a fresh pot of tea. Can you manage some toast? You look like hell."

"Aggie sent over some peppermint tea. She said it will help with the queasiness." Lacey was enjoying her stepmother's suffering.

Anthony looked at Anne Marie as if to say, "You see, she does care about you."

"Court and I will understand if you can't attend the wedding. We wouldn't want you to overdo for our sake."

Now that she had made it to the second trimester, such insincerity no longer fazed her. She would allow nothing to penetrate the cocoon, so carefully spun, to protect her baby. Each difficult day that she made it through, meant that he was holding on, getting stronger. There was an unexpected advantage to her condition that she was feeling less guilty about exploiting.

"Anthony, forgive me. I need to lie down again."

"Dearest!" He upended Lacey and gathered Anne Marie in his arms. "Those stairs are too damn much for you! Lacey, see that a tray is brought up at once."

◆

"Well my angel, you showed all of us," Aggie sighed, stepping back to admire the results of her fussing as Lacey stood in her wedding dress.

It was of her own creation, much to her father's consternation. The expectation that she would wear her mother's Doucet-designed dress had been dismissed, rather ruthlessly, when Aggie and Anne Marie unwrapped it from its tomb of tissue.

"It belongs in a museum under glass. I won't wear it!"

"Try it on, get a feel for it."

Aggie's plea was lost on Anne Marie, who was transfixed by the mounds of ruffles and lace—the demure bodice edged with intricate satin roses—the delicate handwork on the veil. It was so unlike the tailored suit that she had insisted upon wearing to City Hall on her wedding day.

"So beautiful," she murmured, daring to touch it. "It would be a sin not to wear it."

"Pish! There's a war going on, men are dying. How would it look if I indulged in this kind of extravagance?"

"Not a one would say boo!" Aggie argued. "Why, everyone's pining for a real show of a wedding. Lacey, you must consider your social standing."

"I don't want a spectacle. Everyone's invited to the garden reception. That will have to do."

She had lost interest in the discussion and was fingering the veil with its tiny shamrocks. "This I can use. I've decided to design my dress."

Callot Soeurs took her sketches and created what Lacey saw herself as, a modern bride. The dress had an underlay of pale peach silk charmeuse and a candle-white chiffon overlay, embroidered with metallic silver thread and exquisite crystal beading. It had a high bodice, V-shaped neckline, satin cummerbund, and cap sleeves. The front of the dress was a daring two inches shorter than the mid-calf back. There was no train, only Caitlin's shortened veil, pinned to the back of her upswept hair with a pearl comb.

She had incensed Anthony further by choosing to wear only a pair of tiny pearl cluster earrings from her grandmother's collection. "What? Am I supposed to escort my daughter half-naked down the aisle?"

Aggie heaved another sigh. "'Tis been many a time I've dreamt of this moment. Now, it's upon me, and I can't think what to say to you! You've never been a shy one, but if you had a worry or two... about certain things... you'd speak up?"

"Oh Aggie, you dear, dear woman. I think I know what to expect. But thank you. Thank you for taking such good care of me all these years! You've been so much more than a mother to me."

"Don't be stirring me up again! I'll be a weeping mess for the church. Where's me head? Our boy gave me something for you." She fumbled through her apron pockets. "This wee one first and then the box. I must go down and see if Birdy has ruined the soufflé. She's a one that could do with a good thrashing."

Lacey pulled apart the tissue packet, and there was the handkerchief that she had given Court at the train station. It was threadbare from laundering, and the dark blue initials and crest had faded to a watery blue. The note said: "Something borrowed and blue for you to wear today." While she was not observing this tradition, she was touched that he had kept it all these years. It was another reminder of all the little ways they had found to stay connected.

The black velvet box was enticing. Had her father's badgering unlocked the treasure chest? It was the gold locket, the one she had thrown at him in a fit of furious retaliation. He had it refashioned into a brooch. The note said: "I'm returning this to you...somewhat changed, as we are now. Peek inside."

There was a photograph of them, cheek to cheek, taken when they were in Cork.

Tonight, they would make love and sleep in each other's arms—as they would every night—for the rest of their lives. Lacey was ready to be married.

◆

"Just poking my head in to see how your nerves are, my boy." Devlin had invested in a new suit and was looking quite youthful for his seventy-eight years.

"Not a care Grandfather! And nary, a drop to fortify me."

"They'll be time for that soon enough. I don't want to keep you from dressing, but I do want to say this. Your father and mother are looking down on you. And your darlin' grandmother as well. There's not a soul in heaven, happier than they are now." His composure was wavering as

Court wrapped him in his arms.

"Grandfather, if it wasn't for you, I'd be dead! You saved my life… brought me back to Lacey. When I think of the hell I put you through in London and not once…"

"All that misery is behind us! Remember what I said to you then?"

"I have my whole blessed life ahead of me, but I must fight for it!"

"The fighting is over and now, the living begins. You'll have children and grow old with Lacey. I'm hoping to share a wee bit of that before I die." He wiped his tears with one of his yellowed handkerchiefs. "Ah, I've been so addled of late, I forgot to give you this. It came in yesterday's post. I must be off to rescue poor Lafferty. Aggie's been hounding him about the carriage. She wants him to pretty it up a bit! He's sure to be sparring with her."

It pained Court to recognize the handwriting with its childlike penmanship, each word crafted in perfect cursive.

Major,

Forgive me for intruding upon your nuptials, but our investment requires additional financing…

The letter sailed to the floor. What a clever bastard he was! Building upon what he had laid out in the first letter, the one delivered on that September morning to the Imperial Hotel:

> *As agreed, I am investing with the Curragh Breeders Association's stud nursery. I will require a bank draft of one hundred pounds immediately.*

From now on, he would have Humphrey Boyle respond to all requests. Let Longo take the hard way to get his filthy hands on the money.

His wedding suit had been laid on the bed, a sprig of Lily of the Valley already pinned to the lapel. *"Now the living begins…"* It was time. Lacey was waiting for him.

The night sky had descended upon the bedroom; the silvery blue tips of dozens of candles dazzled like a meadow of fallen stars. The heat from the fireplace coaxed forth the voluptuous scent of jasmine scattered around the room. But the most profound jolt to Court's senses, was the groin thumping sight of Lacey, draped across the bed, wearing his paisley robe.

"I was wondering where that went to! You wear it well, my sweet."

It was all she wore, loosely belted to reveal the sinuous shadow of her legs, the iridescent shimmer of her throat and breasts. Her hair, tumbling carelessly around her shoulders, tightened the coil of his desire. He doubted he could kiss her without exploding like a schoolboy, and looked to the chilling bottle of champagne for distraction.

"Shall we have a sip of this?"

"Let's share a glass. My head's still a flutter from all the toasting. Devlin was quite eloquent when he wasn't crying."

"Well, you know grandfather… loquacious and sentimental. Quite taxing on one's sobriety."

Except for a few sips, he had abstained, not wanting anything to compromise his self-control. He could not be reckless with her.

"Let me help you, husband."

She knelt before him, and the belt came undone, exposing more of her womanly charms. Her eyes held no shyness as she looked up at him, nimbly undoing the remaining buttons on his dress shirt. He held the glass to her lips and she drank deeply, coloring from the rush of blood to her cheeks.

"Lacey, I can't remember a time when some part of me didn't love you, even when you were a child. There seemed to be this unspoken thing binding us to one another. I know you think it's all fate and such. But it's more than that…" Christ! He was babbling like an imbecile!

"Court, I've always loved you, and I meant every word of my vows. Not the obeying, of course. You don't really want a wife who is obedient, do you? Where's the fun in that?"

"I want you to be just as you are now… bewitching… beautiful… mine."

He abandoned all effort to proceed with restraint. The robe fell away, mouths fused, hands roamed. They toppled back, her lips clinging to his until he broke away to kiss the pulse of her throat and the dip between her breasts. When his teeth grazed her nipple, she bucked, and he held her wrists above her head, returning to the stiffened peaks.

His exploration continued downward, searching the dark delta between her thighs, brushing the folds with heated flicks of his tongue, probing the tender bud until it quivered and swelled. He listened closely to her little gasps as she softened, her acquiescence an aphrodisiac. He wanted her awash in pleasure when he penetrated her, making quick work of her maidenhead. Feeling the tremor of her orgasm, he raised her legs over his shoulders, the tip of his penis pressed against her sex; she was snug but welcoming.

"Oh yes! This is what I've wanted!" Barely a moment later, her cooing dissolved into pleading. "It hurts! No more, Court!"

"Stay with me, Lacey." The membrane gave way and he relaxed inside of her. "Look at me, my darlin'. The worst is over."

The taste of her tears spurred him on, and ignoring her fitful mewling, he plunged deeper. She was radiant in the throes of pain and ecstasy, her body blushing with arousal, her breasts rosy and taut. His release surged through him, fierce and exquisite but left him wanting more of her.

He turned her over and lavished attention on the slope between her shoulders, whispering kisses along her spine.

"You are perfection."

She was mute, drugged into oblivion by his caresses. His hands fondled her buttocks with unruly regard, and she felt the nip of his teeth again. Her body was primed to respond; the simmering warmth in her sex sent her writhing again.

"I want you on your hands and knees, wife!" His tone compelled her to obey. But when he stretched her wide, she squirmed away in embarrassment.

"Hardly the time for maidenly modesty. Before this night turns to day, every inch of you will be revealed for my pleasure!"

Keeping her firmly in place and with less care than before, he bore into her with one quick stab. She reared up in surprise but he laughed, grasping her elbows, easing her back into position. "I'll be holding the reins."

Court was pleased when she pushed back to meet his thrusts, contracting her muscles to squeeze him—an apt pupil for lovemaking. He played more roughly with her breasts, listening to the rise and fall of her moans, letting them be his guide as to what she could tolerate. He drew her fingers to her cleft, showing her how to tease the bud, worrying it with circular strokes.

"Come now, don't be shy. Give it a good rubbing and we'll come as one…"

Lacey's reflection assured her that she was the same, though her body felt otherworldly. The wet sponge between her legs gave a stinging reminder of how devoted her husband had been, as did the aching swells of her breasts. He had promised that no part of her would be overlooked, in the divine madness of lovemaking, and he had been true to his word.

How different would it have been with Ran? *"I like my women to know what needs to be done."* Had he walked away out of kindness or contempt? Would he think her more desirable now? She knew that such musings were wanton, even sinful, for a married woman yet she could not deny the inequity. Court had made love to many women with the same lavish and intimate touches—pouring his seed into their bellies with casual arrogance.

Discontent drew her back to the slumbering sprawl of her husband. There was an insouciant beauty about his body in its nakedness, and a vulnerability in the repose of his manhood. The muscular ripples in his arms and legs tweaked her desire, and she relived the power of his movements within her, the strength and skill of his caresses. It was thrilling to be subdued by his passion for her. They were wedded in body and soul. How far they had come to get to this moment! How much she loved him! There was the crescent scar above his lip; the souvenir of their first meeting. Lacey leaned over to kiss it, Court stirred. It would be her turn to hold the reins.

Part V

"Destiny's Embrace"
1918-1920

The Marriage Game

On November 11, 1918, the armistice was signed and the ghastly war was over. For the first time since 1910, the United Kingdom held a general election that was dominated by a new electorate: men no longer required to own property. In Ireland, this majority of young men, many of whom survived the Great War, exuberantly gave control of seventy-three constituencies to Sinn Fein. The elected refused to take their seats in Westminster and defiantly set up a provisional parliament, the Dail Eireann, in Dublin.

Along with political upheaval came the first surge of the Spanish influenza, and unlike previous strains, this one preyed on the young and robust. In Cloonsheelin, there were few doors without a mourning wreath or scrap of black cloth flapping in the breeze. The remaining Gallagher boys, Corin and Malahide, returned with high hopes amid whoops of cheering, only to be struck down a month later. Mrs. Fitzgerald's twin daughters succumbed within hours of each other, and that same day, Mrs. Conway, who had nursed a dozen or so of the ailing, slumped over her tea tray with a quiet gurgle. Padraic and Sophie's eldest sister, Katie, and her infant son died on Christmas Eve, and their mother Kathleen, soon after. For a country so accustomed to loss, the pandemic was yet another punishment to be endured and embraced as God's divine will.

Court and Lacey had drifted through a sultry honeymoon in Mallorca with little thought of their families. They reluctantly arrived home in July for the birth of Anne Marie and Anthony's son. William Wakefield de la Roche was premature in his delivery but hardy in his squalling and insatiable in his suckling. Now it was the New Year and the weather so delightfully temperate, the green shoots of spring's crocuses poked through the earth.

While Shakespeare's Kate may have proclaimed "Thy husband is thy lord, thy life, thy keeper" who asks only for "… love, fair looks and true obediency," Lacey was of a different opinion. Instead of fair looks, she was glaring at Court with one of her rapier sneers. Marriage seemed to be an endless joust for control. She was leaning forward on Paladin in a crouch of fury, and had she mace in hand, would have swung it at her beloved's head.

"'Tis senseless for you to come with me! Terence and I leave for Dublin the next day, and I know damn well, you won't step foot there!" Court maneuvered Drummer into an ever tightening circle around her.

"I'm perfectly content to stay in Cork and amuse myself! I can look in on Muriel and the baby."

"Ah, she'll be coming with us. Terence depends on her so."

"Will she now? How nice it must be for her to be part of her husband's life! Sharing his work and interests!"

"Lacey, be reasonable. You're safe here, away from the crowds and contagion."

"And does not Terence MacSwiney have the same concerns for his wife?"

"Are you forgetting you had scarlet fever? You're more susceptible than most. Dr. Seacord said as much."

"Pish! I've been stuck here for months while you've been wandering about electioneering. You can't keep me wrapped in eiderdown and tucked away. I'm suffocating!"

He grabbed her arm, pushing against Paladin's flank; the horse shied away. Court's grip slipped to her hand, then her fingertips, and then, she was free of him.

"How many new graves have been dug since Christmas Day? Losing more of Padraic's family should be all you need…"

"All I need to behave? To do as you dictate? I thank God every day our family hasn't been touched by the scourge of it!"

"Yet you're willing to put yourself at risk just to have your way? You're deluded by selfishness and disregard for all who love you!"

"Don't! Don't be flinging guilt at me! You're free to do just as you damn well please."

"I'll not deny it. But you, madam, will do as I say! And don't be thinking you'll get a whisper of sympathy from Aggie or grandfather. They agree with me!"

With a jerk of her chin and a twist of the reins, Lacey headed home—to Durbin House.

◆

The domestic staff of Durbin House observed a fraction more formality than those of Torrey Castle. When Court appeared, the housemaid merely stepped aside when he proclaimed, "I've come to fetch my wife!"

"Court! Say hello to baby! See how much he's grown." Blocking his ascent to Lacey's bedroom, Anne Marie descended with an armful of baby William.

"What a charming babe, and look at those ruddy cheeks!"

William frowned at the interloper with his pungent smack of the stables. It was familiar and unwelcome, reminding him of the loud man who bounced him too roughly, blowing smoke in his face just to see him sneeze. He burrowed into his mother for protection.

"Do forgive him. He's going through a shy phase; they say it's quite normal. It's a shame we don't see more of you. I do so want you to be great friends."

"In time, it will be so. I've come to take Lacey off your hands. She's had long enough to sulk."

"But she's not here! They left before I woke. Baby had such an awful night."

"Where the devil did they go off to? Did the captain say?" His temper had been set to simmer for her sake, but her news turned up the heat.

"All I know is he took the car and asked Birdy to pack a lunch for them. I'm so sorry."

"I know I'm being a bit of a brute, but I can't have her running here after every tiff!"

"Oh, I agree! It's just what I said to Anthony. But you know when it comes to Lacey.… he just can't say no. I suppose it's only natural he wants to protect her. But from you?" She added with her quicksilver smile, "It's really quite tiresome for the rest of us."

Court frowned, twisting one of William's platinum curls as he dozed against her shoulder. "Lacey had hair like this but auburn, of course. The very first time I saw her—she had these small ringlets like a crown of fire on her head."

His sadness drew her in. They were both of the same nature, hostages to the ones they loved above all others.

"Why don't you stay for tea and we'll catch up! I'm sure they'll be back soon. I'll meet you in the library."

Court watched from the library as Seamus attacked a dead birch tree with an axe as old as him and probably, of the same weight. "What's the old fool thinking? Surely, he'll cut off some part of him with all that mad swinging!"

He felt compelled to intervene, if only to spare Aggie from burying another family member. Unlatching the French doors, he hurried over, shouting, "Seamus Knox! Are you bound and determined to meet your maker today?"

"Ah, Master Court, I didn't see you slip over here. Come to reclaim your bride?"

"Indeed. I imagine we're the talk of the locals, thanks to you and your blabbering kinfolk. Hand over the bloody axe! I'll take a few whacks at it and you can finish it off."

Once he established a rhythm, he found the exertion a tonic for his anger and frustration.

"Keep at it!" Seamus exhorted, waving Court's jacket, pleased with the spray of flying wood chips. "T'will make a grand mass of kindling for the hearth!"

With one final chop, the tree keeled over. Only then, did it occur to him that he may be an accomplice to some petty thievery.

"Did the Captain ask you to do this?"

"He was of a mind it needed doing."

"What exactly did he say to you?"

"Let me think on it. T'was summer and the tree was naked of leaves, being dead and all. And the good Captain said something, about a day coming, when it might blow down and do harm."

"So he never told you to…"

"Why be fretting over the particulars? I'll snip off them boughs and have the rest cleared away before…"

"You're a wicked, scheming old man! If I planted your head on a pike in this very spot, it would be no more than you deserve!"

Returning to the library, he was startled to see Anthony settled in a wing chair, drink in hand, thoroughly amused by the arboreal debacle.

"I see our Mr. Knox is up to his usual antics."

"In his defense, I think he was a wee bit presumptuous in his initiative."

"My wife tells me we need to talk. About Lacey, I assume."

"Yes, we do." He slouched in a chair, tossing aside the rumpled jacket and gathering this thoughts.

"Help yourself to a drink or some tea."

"No thank you, Captain. I won't be taking too much of your time."

"Have it your way. But we are one… big… happy family now. As Lacey, so painfully insists."

"Except when she has a mind to split between us! I'm hoping as a husband yourself, you can understand why I can't have her running to you every time we spar. She's my wife and her home is Torrey Castle."

"She's my daughter and I say her home is wherever she damn well chooses! If she's being mistreated.

"Mistreated? Christ, what nonsense has she been spouting? I've never raised more than my voice to her. You know very well what a vexing creature she can be."

Anthony shrugged and went to refill his glass, pouring a whiskey for Court. "Go on," he encouraged with a wink. "You know you want it."

"Your daughter has a queer knack for shattering my peace of mind."

"You'll be soothed with some very nice trout for your supper. We caught a mess of them, this morning at Shreelane Falls."

"You drove all the way to Skibbereen?"

"Why not? Lacey and I haven't gone fishing in years. I'd forgotten what good fun it is."

"And she's home?"

"I dropped her off about thirty minutes ago."

"Captain, you've lifted a brick off my mind. But I must extract a promise from you. I'm asking you not to come between us in these matters. Leave us be to sort through our troubles."

"Then I expect something in return. If you want me to leave you be, as you so quaintly put it, then you must be honest with her about your political involvement."

"I haven't an inkling as to what you're referring to?"

"Can I freshen that for you?" he asked, looming over Court with an intimidating squint. "You haven't been very discrete. And you're damn lucky she isn't one to read the newspapers with any devotion."

"Lacey knows I've commitments to some of the local officials in Cork."

"She knows only what you pick and choose to let her know!"

"Captain, I've tamed my reckless nature. The war taught me that all too well. My political commitments consist of nothing more than helping Terence MacSwiney with some strategizing on raising money and getting votes. As you know, he was elected to represent Mid-Cork in the Dail."

"You make it sound so benign. But you and I know, the British will not stomach a provisional parliament of any kind! You and your friends have riled the lion. How long before Dublin Castle starts cracking down on your MacSwiney … your Collins … your de Valera? How long before both sides reach for a gun?

As easily as water slips off a duck, Court dropped the pretense. "As an American, you know all too well any struggle of this magnitude will come down to that. There can be no independence for Ireland without great sacrifice. Without blood spilt, as it's been spilt for hundreds of years, trying to break this vise of oppression."

"I've heard the rhetoric."

"Let me finish. I can only speak for Terence, for I know what's in his heart. I trust him to lead us with reason and diplomacy as long as…"

"You're a fool, Courtland! Do you think Lincoln ever thought his presidency would be steeped in the blood of so many of his countrymen? No matter how just the cause … how decent the men who lead … there will be unspeakable violence. I've no quarrel with your beliefs or what you must do. But you can't hide how deeply you're involved from Lacey! You can't protect her from what's to come."

"I've no quarrel with you calling me out. But realize this! It was I who rescued her from the attic of Marsh's Library. It was I who carried the body of Padraic Knox to the undertaker. It was I who lived through every awful moment of her grieving. So you must forgive me, if I've acquired the habit of sparing your daughter from the worst of what life heaps upon us!"

Lacey paced the landing on the lookout for Court, Flurry nipping back and forth, expecting a game of catch. This was to be a new game: whoever apologizes first, loses. It was dusk and a storm had broken minutes earlier, crashing against the casement windows with restless disregard.

Anthony had listened with bemused patience to her indignant tirade and then, rather oddly, asked if she cared to go fishing the next morning. It wasn't until they were having lunch on the banks of Shreelane Falls, marveling at their impressive catch, that he offered his point of view.

"To this day, I bear the burden of your mother's death. She sweet-talked the doctor and I into letting her give birth at home, as she did with you. She should have been in a damn hospital! That last month when she was confined to bed, I could see she was losing strength every day. But she laughed away the fatigue …

playing games with you on her bed … distracting me with flirtatious nonsense. I loved her so much, I bought into her denial. Hell, I was swimming in it! She had no appetite … her sleep was off.

Lacey, you must understand something! A man wants to … needs to … keep his wife and children safe. Even if it's out of our hands, we'll keep at it like a blind mule, till we're battered and bleeding. You may think we're thickheaded, pathetically foolish, but it's our curse. So for the first, and I hope to God last time, I stand with Courtland."

She heard the thump of his boots on the stairs and scurried to the bedroom, arranging herself on the sofa. Flurry was all atwitter with this new game, watching as she artfully draped her dressing gown, and shook out her hair. With magazine in hand, she glanced up at Court and turned the page. Flurry, the incorrigible traitor, flew to him and pawed at his knees.

"What a monstrous downpour! I got the worst of it." He dripped water with every step and disappeared into the bathroom.

Flurry beseeched her with a plaintive bark for the next move in this curious game. She shifted her strategy; she would meet Court's blithe nonchalance with regal indifference.

Stripped to the waist with a towel around his neck, he returned, asking, "Are we dressing for dinner?"

"If you want. It's just us."

He stood over her. "How cozy, just us and the trout."

Now, she knew where he had been. Her father's words poked at her stubbornness.

"Let me do that for you."

He knelt and shook his head, grinning with insolence and smelling of the rain and earth. She was losing ground fast.

Grabbing the towel, she yanked him to her. "You don't play fair."

"Something I learned from you, my sweet." His hands clasped her waist, keeping a few inches between them. "What's a man to think? Coming home and finding his wayward bride laid out in such a tempting fashion? Are you trying to make up with me? If so, I'm waiting for a few words of heartfelt remorse."

"Beast!"

"Vixen!"

Both savored the exquisite torment of wanting while each was loathe to relent.

"I won't be bullied." Her lips were a soft whisper against his ear.

"I won't be faulted for loving you." His fingertips parted the dressing gown and teased her breasts.

Flurry whined and thrust his head between them. Was the game over? Court grabbed him by the scruff, heaving him out the door, then hoisted Lacey up and over his shoulder.

"You've won this round of the tormenting game, madam!"

What Is The Good Of Praying?

March 1, 1919

I am dead. Dead to life. I have no life. My baby is dead. My baby is dead. My baby is dead.

If Anne Marie wrote the words over and over, would they loosen their grip on her? The words had wrapped themselves around her throat three days ago. Then, their ominous chant had been: my baby could die … my baby could die. Earlier that morning, William gave a little shudder in her arms and drifted away.

"I must take her somewhere. She can't go on like this! What else can I do?" Anthony demanded of Court and Lacey.

"Of course you must, Daddy." She kissed his hand and led him to the sofa, wedging herself next to him. "We'll stay at the house and look after things." She looked at Court with an expectant lift of her eyebrow.

"No trouble at all. You won't have to fuss about closing it up. Grandfather has contacts in Tuscany. Do you think Anne Marie might fancy going there?"

"Italy? That would do. Lots of art and other things to distract her. It'll take a good deal of convincing, though. I may need your help."

Again, she looked to Court, unrepentantly aware she had no influence. While she had come to love her half-brother, her feelings toward Anne Marie remained chilly and critical.

"Lacey and I will do all we can," he promised, refusing to let her off. "I'd be glad to see to the arrangements, if you like?"

Anthony nodded, morosely staring out the bay window where Drummer and two mares nibbled their way through the last green morsels of Aggie's herb garden.

"I tried calling Seacord, but what's the use? He's running up and down the district like the headless horseman."

Spring emerged with unyielding cold, the wind raw to the cheek and bitter in the mouth. It did not deter Anne Marie from her daily visits to William's grave, nestled under the archangel statue next to Caitlin. She had begged Anthony to let him lie there so Caitlin might keep watch. His headstone was a small marker set into the ground.

"This blasted wind will tear the hair off your head by the very roots!" Court exclaimed, coming upon her with a deliberately noisy step.

She invited him to kneel beside her. "It's not so bad down here."

"'Tis a bit better but not much."

He hadn't seen her for more than a month and only then for the funeral. An IRA ambush in Soloheadbeg, on January 21, had led to British reprisals, which had Court running between Cork and Dublin, at MacSwiney's behest.

"If I had the time, I'd like to go someplace warm with Lacey. Just till spring takes hold, gets going with its bloomin'."

"I don't care about the weather." She smoothed away some leaves from the marker, her gloved hand tracing the etched letters over and over.

Anthony was right; she was fading away into her own world of mourning. He wondered how he could break through.

"I've been shamelessly remiss in telling you this. But I know it was you who saw there were flowers on Caitlin's grave on our wedding day."

After the vows had been said and there was a lull in the kissing and congratulating, Lacey swept through the cemetery and planted her bridal bouquet on Padraic's grave. Anthony's embarrassment was mitigated somewhat by the lush blanket of roses and lilies covering Caitlin's grave.

"Oh that."

"A lovely and thoughtful gesture. One I should have seen to myself … knowing my wife."

"I'm quite fond of Caitlin. I feel a special kinship with her. Anthony wanted to take down her portrait, but I insisted it stay," she sighed and stood up, the wind lashing at her clothes and hair. "I use to think a cemetery should be beautiful, ornamental. Now, I think it should be a bleak, forsaken place, a reminder of loss. No flowers for my baby … ever."

She said this calmly with tears gathering, then flowing, as she bent over in a wail of agony. He bundled her in his arms, guiding her into the Lady Chapel where he had been married. The stone walls magnified the din of her sobs. She struggled for a breath and went limp in his arms.

"Anne Marie, can you hear me? You're shivering. I must warm you up." He wrapped her tightly in his coat and kept her close, rubbing her hands.

"I want to crawl into his coffin and hold him…keep the maggots away. He grew inside me and he was perfect. He was perfect and now he's dead. How can that be?"

"I don't know."

"But you do! I know you do. You saw men—strong, healthy men. They were perfect and then, they were dead."

"Whether sickness or war, we're miserably mortal. Death comes to us all sooner or later."

"Yes, later! Much later! Babies shouldn't die. Why does God kill babies?"

"I'm not sure it's any of his doing. Blaming him is like blaming yourself."

"Anthony wants to have another baby! I can't fill this hole with another baby. I want my baby!"

"Of course, you do. You'll be wanting him for a long time… maybe forever. When you do have another, that emptiness will still be there. Our hearts are made of little nooks. Each nook is filled by a loved one. When they're gone, no one can fill that space. There are memories to be sure, bittersweet in their comforting, but transparent like our souls, nothing solid to hold onto."

"It would be a relief to die."

"Hush! Do you think the good Lord wants to hear such talk? I wanted to die—many times—at the front, in that ghastly hospital. The worst yearning was in London when poor grandfather was trying to get me well. The thought of living was so unbearable, I asked him to finish me off."

"How terrible for you!"

"Indeed. But here I am, comforting you. Though I confess, I don't know how you have the strength to leave your bed."

"You're always so caring, so sweet to me," she murmured, relaxing with the warmth of his body.

"Will you do one thing for me?" he asked, lifting her chin to meet his eyes. "Will you go away, as Anthony wants? Will you do it, not for me, but for yourself? You've been a good and loving friend to me, Anne Marie. I need you in my life."

"If you think it would help…" She wavered in surprise and confusion. "Yes, yes. It will be good for me to be away from here."

◆

"Hullo folks!" Court bounded into the breakfast room of Torrey Castle on a fresh morning in late June. "Grandfather, your roses are spectacular! I could smell them on the breeze a mile away."

"My sweet boy, have you eaten?" Aggie rang for another pot of tea, stroking his cheek as he kissed her.

"Birdy fed me her blue plate special, fried eggs and bacon, but I could do with a nibble."

"I must say, with all true modesty of course, my Tuscany Superb will outshine Moira Feeney's pathetically pedestrian Louise Odier at the Fermoy Exhibition next week. The old dragon will be spitting sulfur from both nostrils when I walk away with the ribbon." Devlin's smugness was immune to Aggie's contemptuous snort.

"See how well marriage suits him! Such a light in his eyes and bloom in his cheeks. Has he ever looked more handsome?" she asked Devlin.

"And so content!"

Whenever they spoke of him, as if he was framed and hung on the wall for their reminiscing pleasure, Court knew there was mischief afoot.

"What have you two been conspiring about now?"

"'Tis hard to believe your first anniversary has come and gone," Devlin noted dolefully, casting a prompting glance at Aggie.

"Without a smattering of a celebration," she added, plucking crumbs from the cloth. "We've had so little to be happy about."

"You know damn well why we chose not to make a fuss! The graveyard has been replenished with the bones of our families and friends. Now is not the time for merrymaking."

"We're of the same mind, my boy," his grandfather reassured him. But as we get older, there are less and less occasions for celebrating." Then, as if it was a thought out of the blue, he wondered, "Perhaps, we'll be having a celebration of another kind? It will be Lacey's time soon enough."

"Time for what, Grandfather?" Court knew the answer but wanted it slapped on the table and swept away by his hand.

It had been heavenly to escape to Durbin House and recapture some of the privacy that they had enjoyed on their honeymoon. Lacey was more relaxed and forgiving of his time away, and he was more inclined to indulge her moods and whims.

"Why, a babe of course!"

"Listen to me! Don't think I'm not onto this one," he jabbed a finger at Aggie, "tracking my wife's cycle with unseemly curiosity, and you, taking an unnatural interest in her appetite, weight, and coloring! We may never come back here, if you don't keep them inquiring snouts out of our bedroom!"

"You can hardly blame us for being a bit anxious. 'Tis more than a year." His grandfather tried to placate him with a twinkle in his eye and pat on the arm.

"It will happen, when it happens, and not a bloody minute sooner!"

Aggie poured another cup of tea and sniffed, "As if it's something you can command like a dog. "

As Court bristled for the next round, Devlin switched the topic. "Has Lacey told you of the captain's change in plans?"

"Of course. The little vixen is more than happy to have him dragging Anne

Marie off to Geneva, so she can play her highness of Durbin House a while longer. I doubted from the start he could stay put for his wife's sake."

"There's a magnificent spot on the lake she's sure to find most enchanting." Devlin lowered his voice, as if there were others lurking to hear what came next. "Then, it's Zurich! The Swiss are converting their entire railway system to electricity and are desperate for investors. The captain believes we should act without hesitation. What a grand investment!"

"Just like the man, to mix in some business dealing with his wife's recovery."

"Must you always be running him down? I thought some of this confounding animosity would lessen with the marriage."

"Settle down, Grandfather. We've reached a compromise, more or less." He remembered why he had come. "Before I forget, Lacey is having a formal dinner party on Saturday, and your attendance is requested. The MacSwineys will be there. I'm most anxious for you to be acquainted."

"Not me," Aggie declared obstinately. "I'm not one for them kinds of gatherings. Too much talk of politics and the like. I hardly have a good enough dress."

Court stood and bent down to kiss her, saying brusquely, "Out of your hands, my darlin'. Lacey had a dozen dresses from Chesselwaites delivered for you to salivate over. You're coming back with me, so finish up what you need to do and be ready in fifteen minutes!"

"The very idea! Me prancing around with the likes of them."

Devlin squeezed her hand. "Get on with you. It would be my honor to show you off."

◆

Thumbing through the packet of mail he had brought from Torrey Castle, Court froze over a familiar handwriting, anxiety twisting his gut. Correspondence from Ran was infrequent, the amounts nominal, and the oversight delegated to his solicitor, Humphrey Boyle.

The last letter had arrived around the New Year with a Londonderry postmark. While he thought it curious at the time, he quickly forgot about it.

The one in hand was from Belfast, and after opening it, he immediately placed a long distance call to London.

"Humphrey! Thank God you're there."

"Courtland, this is either a rare treat or a calamity."

"The latter, I'm afraid. Another letter from Longo."

"What exactly does it say?"

"Send two hundred pounds. Nothing more. And it's postmarked from Belfast."

There was a disquieting pause before Humphrey responded. "As I recall, the last one came from Londonderry around the holidays?"

"Aye. He seems to be moving around."

"In your enemy's backyard."

"What a damn queer way of putting it!" He was impatient, knowing Lacey might interrupt at any moment.

"This fellow is a master blackmailer, tiring of the game. He may be looking to tighten the screws. I daresay … the time is ripe for it."

"What are you saying?"

"Courtland, you must understand what happened in Tipperary is the beginning of what many here are calling a prelude to war."

"Christ! We're far from that. We're advocating civil disobedience. MacSwiney believes we can be more effective ignoring the British rather than…"

"And what does Collins believe? He turned a blind eye to the IRA, his own men, because he wants to provoke a war. If Churchill had his way, you'd be under martial law right now! He wants to mobilize an auxiliary police force to be sent over there. I doubt they'll be keeping the peace. Longo may be thinking, now is the time, to make you a sacrificial lamb."

"You're not being very comforting."

"It's not what you pay me for. I advise you to ignore the letter. Destroy it! This is the only one where he's not using the pretext of being your agent for some fictitious business transaction. I can use the others to make a damn solid case, if need be, that was the extent of your relationship."

Lacey and Aggie's laughter sailed through the hallway, curtailing the conversation.

"Look here, Humphrey, I must get off. I'll think over what you said and let you know. We'll speak soon."

There were too many terrifying possibilities ricocheting around in his head as he stumbled out of the library.

"I thought we'd have lunch on the terrace." Lacey and Aggie stood arm in arm at the foot of the staircase, smothering another fit of the giggles.

"What's that, sweet?" He tried to appear calm, but his long curls were askew, and his mouth was tight with distress.

"Whatever is the matter? You look like you've had awful news. Is everything…"

"Going through the accounts, madam! Always good for a fright or two."

"I'm going to the kitchen to see about our lunch," Aggie announced. "I don't trust that one with fish or fowl."

"She wants to put the fear of God in poor Birdy," Lacey whispered to him. "Just for the fun of it!"

"Tell me now. What's the damage to my bank account?"

Wearing the mien of a reluctant penitent, she pushed him to sit on the stairs so she could perch on his knee. "Aggie had a very hard time of it. So I thought it best to relieve her of the fussing and keep the three she liked best. You don't really mind, do you? She needs to indulge herself more."

"As usual, your thinking defies all laws of logic."

"So you agree?"

This time when she laughed, it rumbled through him, stirring his heart to embrace her vivacity. He had done as Anthony asked, and laid out for her what to expect with the creation of the Dail and the British counter tactics. She was distraught, reliving the Easter Rising and all she had lost. When he was honest about the role that he was playing, she became further upset, and he hated Anthony for forcing his hand. But her natural resilience came through, and she promised to be more like Muriel MacSwiney—steadfast in her support. There was a caveat though, he had to be forthcoming at all times, and not spare her from the truth.

"Where are you?" Lacey pressed fluttery pecks across his forehead. "So far away from me." Her fingers massaged his temples. "I need your absolute attention when I make love to you."

Her mouth took hold of his and the kiss obliterated any thought of sharing the bad news. He had not made any promises about Longo. What he needed was to slide into the beckoning warmth of her, where solace awaited.

A Parliament of Felons

Dublin Castle would have no more: no more obstinacy, no more talk of independence, no more guerrilla skirmishes and no more Dail. Newspaper censorship returned. The legal status of political prisoners was revoked. Again, the city was divided into sectors, patrolled by troops and armored vehicles. Traffic was disrupted by inexplicable road blocks and searches. Pedestrians were stopped at gunpoint for questioning and proof of identity. Any reluctance to cooperate quickly led to arrest. Across from Liberty Hall, a machine gun post was erected as a reminder to the Irish citizenry that even their most prosaic movements were controlled by the unyielding fist of the Crown.

In Cork city, the small house on Adelaide Lane hummed with the comings and goings of visitors, some who stayed for an afternoon or a week. Lacey was willing to play hostess and exist in a self-induced state of denial, even as it became disturbingly apparent that her home was part of a safe house network.

The renovation suited these needs. The large kitchen had been reduced to half its size and while modern and efficient, not much cooking was done. A bedroom and bath took up the rest of the basement, providing discrete accommodations for clandestine guests. The diminutive garden was paved with bluestone; its narrow borders planted with flowering shrubs, and anything willing to climb up its walls. Now in late autumn, the Virginia creeper had thinned and turned the same rusty hue as the brickwork. Lacey was deciding what should take the place of the leggy pansies in the terracotta urns when Court came looking for her.

"Lacey darlin', I'm expecting a visitor any moment who'll be staying for a day or two. Is Ella about?"

"She's at the market. The room is ready, if that's what you're asking."

"Lovely. He'll be most anxious to rest up before our meeting."

"Another meeting? You promised we'd have the evening to ourselves! You even asked me to make a reservation!"

She was growing tired of running a hotel for strangers who rarely spoke more than a few words to her, as if she was some ghostly presence, and even more tired of endless meetings behind closed doors, where testosterone levels were spiked by tobacco and whiskey.

"Indeed, we shall. I only need to look over some papers."

"What is that?" She was pointing to a trail of muddy footprints, on her immaculate bluestone, leading to the back wall. There were no return prints and the Virginia creeper had been torn in several places.

"Just a security precaution."

In fact, it was a door, hardly visible, embedded in the brickwork. He showed her how one brick protruded ever so slightly, and when pressed, the door creaked open, leading to a cluttered alley.

"Takes you to a path by the river," he explained a little too spritely.

"Was it always there?"

"No, no. I had it done a few weeks ago. Tis nothing to wonder about."

"Why didn't you tell me?"

"It just slipped my mind."

"Why do we need it?" she persisted, closing the door.

"You're really making too much of this. Suppose there was a fire, or some kind of an emergency. Doesn't it give you some peace of mind to know there's another way out?"

"Pish! How could I have any peace of mind when you forgot to tell me about it? And what was the emergency that caused these footprints?"

"Christ! You know I've barely had time to take a piss! Yet you're hounding me over this bit of nonsense."

"There you are! Your housekeeper sent me down. Dear me, am I intruding?"

"Atticus!" She turned to her wincing husband. "You couldn't tell me it was him? Must everything be such a bloody secret?"

"Please forgive me, madam, if I can't remember all your acquaintances, past and present!"

"Why don't I wait in the parlor?" Atticus resembled himself, only grayer and more rumpled, still chewing on the stub of an unlit cigar, still impeccably polite.

"Please stay. Don't mind our sparring, were done for the time being," she assured him.

"What a wonderful surprise, my dear." He took her hand for a quick kiss and a stiff bow. "I knew you had married this young man but didn't think I'd find you here."

"Lacey likes to come from time to time, just to make sure all her hard work hasn't been undone by my slovenly ways." Court tried putting a possessive arm around her, but she eluded him.

"I'll show you the room. I think you'll be quite comfortable. Ella will make you some tea and sandwiches. You look exhausted!"

Atticus inspected the room closely, saying, "I've not been in a hotel room as fine as this! The bed looks very tempting to a tired old man."

"If you brought a change of clothes, Ella can launder your things."

"No need. I'll make do."

Though she could see how fatigued he was that would not spare him from an inquisition.

"What have you heard from Ran?"

"Very little since he left the Curragh. But I myself have not been in one place for very long. I did get a post card with a few scribbles. Do you mind if I sit down?" He kept the satchel on his lap.

"I'll turn down the bed for you."

"He's partnered with a Spaniard from Andalusia, quite wealthy and in need of good breeding stock. The name's Zambrano, and his family has raced for several generations. Years ago, Ran rode for him in Argentina."

"You've no way of contacting him?"

"I've a few connections, but it would take some time. My dear, you seem rather distressed."

"I do worry about him. We were so close and now, he's gone." She drew the curtains and laid a robe on the bed.

"Oh you know him, doesn't stay put for very long. Was never one for getting too attached. He's happiest roaming about with a few coins in his pocket."

"I suppose so."

"How is Paladin?"

"Quite splendid, though slowing down a bit."

"Aren't we all," he yawned, scrubbing at his face. "I remember what a pretty child you were but so very headstrong! You've bloomed into a beautiful woman. Your husband's a very blessed man."

"I doubt he feels that way most of the time. I can be quite beastly when I'm crossed."

He pulled himself up in a lumbering stretch, finally letting the satchel slip to the floor. "A small price for a man to pay; you're well worth the fuss."

"Atticus? Please don't say anything to Court about Ran. They don't get on."

"He'll not hear a peep from me."

"Things are quite tense. Every day, more troops arrive. The quays are choked with them and their provisions. It means only one thing." Atticus accepted a cigar and large glass of whiskey from Court, admiring both before indulging.

"They'll be spreading those little marauders throughout the countryside, stirring up trouble if there's none to be found."

"Mick has a plan for that. You must get this to MacSwiney right away." Atticus removed a bible from the satchel and tore out the flyleaf. "It's in code. He'll know what to do with it."

"What is it?"

"The less you know, the safer you are."

"I'll be meeting a courier tonight at the restaurant. It should go like a charm."

"Lacey thinks I'm staying over, but I'll be gone by the time you return. There's a house in Kilkenny where I can take the time to rest."

"Are you sure? You look half-dead to me."

"If Ella can pack me something to eat, I'll be fine."

"Of course. I must ask you, in confidence, about Longo. Do you know of his whereabouts?"

Atticus hesitated, not wanting to be caught between a husband and wife, with their separate reasons for inquiring.

"Doing the auction circuit, purchasing breeding stock for a wealthy Spaniard."

"How do you know this?"

"He left the Curragh to go into partnership with this fellow. He sent me a postcard from Galway some months ago."

"I know you consider him a friend, but he's not to be trusted."

"What are you saying?" Atticus set down the glass and pointed the cigar at him. "That boy is like a son to me!"

"This will be brutal for you to hear. Longo's an informer. It was he, who switched the boxes of ammunition meant for Marsh's Library. He has the blood of all those boys on his hands…including Padraic Knox!"

"I don't believe you! Not for one bloody minute!"

"How do you think I was able to get Lacey out of there when I was in disguise? The soldiers were well acquainted with him. Longo vouched for me when I took command."

"Why have you kept quiet all this time?"

"I've my reasons which I can't share with you. Part of it is to protect Lacey."

Atticus rummaged through his pockets for a handkerchief, eyes filling, hands and mouth trembling.

"What a fuckin' day this has been!" Court thought. "I've infuriated my wife and now, I've broken an old man's heart! If hell exists… surely its portal is through my front door."

"BATONS & BAYONETS FOR RESISTERS" "ENGLAND'S IDEAL: AN IRELAND WITHOUT IRISHMEN" "DUBLIN CASTLE TURNS PROSPEROUS PLOUGHSHARES INTO SWORDS" "BY ORDER OF DUBLIN CASTLE: SUSPECTS SHOULD BE ROUGHLY HANDLED"

"OFFICIAL PROVOCATION & DRASTIC REPRESSION – NO FOLLY LEFT UNDONE"

Devlin called them a necessary evil; Aggie was less forgiving and considered them to be instruments of the devil. All three were ringing and ringing until Court sprinted from the dining room to the library, followed by the heat of Aggie's wrath.

"Would it be possible to get through one meal without that hideous shrieking disrupting my digestion?" Devlin fussed.

Taking out her watch, Aggie said, "I'll give him one minute and then, his soup will be taken away! Don't these people have families to go home to?"

"Only bad news comes at this hour," Lacey said with wifely fortitude. "I'll see what's keeping him."

"Don't you be wandering off now! Makes no sense for the both of you to go starving. Poor Annie can't be running up and down them stairs keeping your food warm."

"Bad news?"

Court's hands were braced against the desk, steadying him for what he had to say. "Very bad indeed. Dear Atticus is dead. Floating in the Tralee Canal—a bullet in his head."

"Murdered?" Lacey cried, tamping down a sob.

"Most likely executed."

He suspected the old Fenian had made a sentimental and fatal mistake—confronting Longo.

"It's a mystery why he was there. He was expected in Limerick yesterday morning, to pick up some documents for Terence. You don't take a short cut through Tralee when you're coming from Cork! We're of the mind he was lured there."

"Who could be so ruthless? He was a harmless old man!"

"Not to some. You must understand, there are those motivated by greed alone. Spies and informers of all kinds are looking to profit. Men and even women, with smiling faces and a ready finger on the trigger."

"It doesn't matter who killed him. He's dead. You could be next!"

"I can't think about that! I can only be with you in this moment. You must learn to do the same. Savor the present and let the future be."

"I did that when you were at the front! Forcing myself not to wonder if you were dead. I can't do it again."

"You must! You found a way then."

"Do you know what you're asking? Do you know how I worry when you're away from me? I wait for the telephone or a cable, telling me you're dead. These moments, you're so keen for us to live for, it takes only one for you to die."

"Our sacrifices may not be recorded in the history books. But we'll be two of the good souls who did the right thing. Our children will live free! What is that worth to you?"

"Nothing! Nothing is worth losing you! Not even a free Ireland! I love you more than any cause … more than any child I'll bear you! You may think me selfish, but it's who I am!"

Court realized that he was asking too much of her. She was almost twenty. In comparison, he had been a feckless and self-indulgent boy, with little interest in anything, but sporting with the local girls and gambling away his pocket money. He had not allowed her the time to mature into his world where adults played dangerous games of politics and power.

That night, for the first time since their wedding night, she wept, as they made love.

"Am I hurting you, my darlin'?"

"I'm heartsick. Here is where you belong. In this moment… this is all that matters."

"How pretty the white lace will look against the hydrangeas," Anne Marie remarked to Lacey, helping her into the dress.

A few months ago, such a polite conversation would have been unimaginable. Whether it was pity or performance on her stepdaughter's part, she no longer cared. They were hidden behind a screen in the drawing room of Durbin House while the portrait artist's assistant rearranged the furniture.

"It's more bridal looking than my wedding dress."

"Maybe that's why your father couldn't resist it when he saw it in Milan. I think it was his subconscious desire to see you in your mother's wedding dress."

Of late, Anne Marie had done quite a bit of reading on psychoanalytic theory, much to Anthony's scoffing amusement. He had been more accommodating of her other interests—dabbling in Mediterranean cuisine and landscape drawing. He was eager for her to submerge herself in anything that would distract her from mourning their son.

"I doubt my father's subconscious is so complex." Lacey yawned and turned around to be buttoned up.

"It's a perfect fit but snug across the bust."

"Leave those undone, I want to be comfortable; it won't matter to Monsieur DuParc. Why didn't you want your portrait done?" She reached for her grandmother's pearl choker as the finishing touch.

"I despise having my photograph taken! A painting staring down on me, would be unendurable. Your father is holding out hope I'll relent. He should know better by now."

"The light is perfect! Now! Now!" Monsieur DuParc bellowed, and the assistant guided Lacey to the sofa, arranging her according to his master's precise directions.

"Too, too pale! Where is the rouge?"

The assistant handed a small pot to Anne Marie, too shy to be so bold. "In

Paris, all the women wear rouge on the lips and cheeks, very modern," he whispered, then scampered away to fetch a pad and charcoal.

Lacey was surrounded by large porcelain vases of blue hydrangeas as she reclined on the sofa and fought off another yawn. Anne Marie wondered why she was being so uncommonly docile these days, suffering without so much as a snarl through the arduous process of preliminary sketching while moving between Torrey Castle and Durbin House. Or wherever Monsieur DuParc's inspiration sought the ideal setting.

The lighting was perfect, as was the subject. Anne Marie looked from Caitlin's portrait to Lacey, noting how their facial features were nearly identical. The essence of mother and daughter merged, then diverged, in their distinct personalities. She liked to think that she and Caitlin had similar temperaments, and that is what attracted the same man to them.

Lacey's eyes closed, though she held the pose without relaxing. It was as if some narcotic had been slipped into her morning tea. Anne Marie stopped breathing, her heart held a beat, then resumed pulsing with a familiar ache. Lacey was pregnant.

"Why the devil is the captain coming over?" Court asked Devlin, slamming shut the ledger books.

"I'm just as curious as you, my boy. Should I tell Aggie he'll be staying for lunch?"

"What did he say when he called?"

"That he was taking advantage of Lacey being there for the sketching because he had an important matter to discuss."

"You didn't think to ask?"

"The less time spent handling that thing, the better."

"Grandfather, it's a telephone, not a hand grenade."

"Don't be mocking me! I'm an old man with old-fashioned ways! I'll pour the sherry, fetch the cigars."

"I doubt this is a social call."

The deafening clang of the front door reverberated through them. "There he is. Dear me, 'tis only a few biscuits in the tin."

"Good day, gentlemen. I see your foals are out and about—helping themselves to the front lawn."

"They're a pesky lot! Grazing wherever they please." Devlin offered him a glass.

"You do know that's what fences are for?"

"Confining them would be an inhuman thing. A free horse is a happy horse and worth more at auction."

"Courtland, I must commend you, on finally outmaneuvering my daughter."

He had not moved from the desk, not even to retrieve the cigars, giving Anthony a wide-eyed look of ignorance. "How's that?"

"You've got her nicely distracted with this portrait business."

"I thought it would be a fitting birthday gift, seeing as Caitlin was the same age when you commissioned her portrait."

"Why do I get the feeling this is more than a competition between you and I?"

""Would you like to stay for lunch?" Devlin interjected, swishing a biscuit in his sherry.

"No thank you. I promised Anne Marie I'd be home to experience Birdy's first attempt, at risotto alla Milanese. My wife has become fascinated with all things Italian, especially the food. We trucked back sacks of pasta and rice, and several cases of olive oil."

"Birdy Howser may have met her Waterloo!" Court hooted. "Captain, please don't breath a word of this to Aggie. She takes great pleasure in Birdy's suffering."

"I've more pressing things on my mind than domestic rivalries. I've hired six men to patrol my property. I suggest, you do the same."

Both O'Rourkes reacted with surprise. "It's come to this! You must do as you think best." Devlin finished off the last soggy biscuit with a sigh.

"I think it's best, we realize how bad things are!" He pulled open his jacket to reveal his army holster with a .45 caliber gun. It was silver plated with an ivory grip and engraved with his initials.

"Most impressive. Almost too pretty for causing mayhem."

"Don't you think having armed guards prowling about might raise anxiety just a wee bit?" Court asked with a smirk, fiddling with a letter opener.

"They won't be showing themselves or socializing. They're bunking in Badger's Hut and sleeping in shifts."

"You know the word will get out that Durbin House is under guard?"

"Better under guard, than under siege!"

"Well now," Devlin said gently with raised hands. "I think we can agree, this is a necessary measure. If they're so brazen as to murder the lord mayor in his bed."

"Tomas MacCurtain was assassinated! It was an act of terrorism!" Court shouted, stabbing the desk with the letter opener.

"And MacSwiney has taken his place!" Anthony's voice matched his in volume. "By the next full moon, they'll be hunting him… then you."

"I'm not visible. I work in the shadows."

"You can't be so stupid and naive, as to think your name isn't on some list… on somebody's desk in Dublin Castle!"

"You've made your point. Get out!"

It was Devlin's turn to roar as he struck the floor with his cane several times. "I won't have this behavior in me own home, from either of you!"

When Court stood up, still armed with the letter opener, Anthony took a few steps closer to him and warned, "When the time comes, and it will. I'll not leave without my daughter! Even if I have to put a bullet in you, to get to her."

"You're a fuckin' wonder, Captain. She's half Irish… the half that counts for something… believes in something!"

Anthony was done; if he stayed, he would put a bullet in Court

"Devlin, I thought we could come to an amicable understanding. You know, I won't back down. Consider what you must do."

◆

"I'm most grateful you could get away," Court greeted Anne Marie, reining in Drummer to dismount by the stone footbridge.

"I did tell a little white lie," she confessed, puckering her brow. "I said I wanted to look for morels for a new recipe."

He helped her down and squeezed her hand. "You're in luck! There's a spot farther down the ravine where you can have your fill. Drummer is quite partial to them. Have you succeeded in transforming Birdy into a five-star chef?"

"I suppose it would be less of a chore if she wasn't so, opinionated." Despite his playful air, she knew he was worried these days. "Any news about Mr. MacSwiney?"

"Alas, 'tis grim. He's been tried, found guilty, and sent off to Brixton." His voice wavered, and his shoulders rounded in sorrow.

"Oh no. His poor family."

"He's vowing to go on a hunger strike. If he does…he'll die there." Court's sadness was as palatable as the thick air engulfing them amid the rattle of the cicadas.

"And poor you," she whispered, resting her cheek against his shoulder.

They stayed like this for a few minutes, letting nature absorb their melancholy. Anne Marie never had known a man so inclined toward a woman's comforting. He liked to be around women, he liked to be petted and fussed over by them. Their feminine energy seemed to invigorate and inspire him.

"What will you do now?"

"Wait for instructions from Cathal Brugha. The Dail is in a bit of a shambles with this feuding between Collins and de Valera. It will take some time." Court blotted his face with his shirt sleeve. "Tell me now, how's the pretending going?"

"The what?" she gasped, squirming just enough for it to be true.

"Pretending to be interested in this and that just to placate your husband. You've been putting on quite a show since you got back from abroad. I can see behind them smiles of yours! I see the longing. I know it can't be easy seeing Lacey with child, remembering what you've lost."

"There are moments when I can't stand it! But I'm not jealous. I'm joyful for the both of you! This baby is the future you're fighting for."

"Ah, an apt choice of words. 'Tis the fighting we need to talk about. I'm guessing Anthony told you about the row we had a while back?"

"Not right away. He was out of sorts for days before he said anything. I made it worse by taking your side. Just saying your name stokes his blood pressure."

"I don't want you fighting with him over me! His dislike won't harm our friendship. He and I can be bloody intractable. That will never change."

"Does Lacey know about the quarrel?"

"I gave her a somewhat tamer version of it. More of a "what if" discussion. I said it would be worth considering with the baby coming."

"And she's willing to leave, if things get worse?"

"My lamb would have none of it! Which brings me to the favor I must ask."

"Court, you know you need only to ask. Anything I can do."

"Aye, that's of goodly comfort to me. But I need you to be honest. I rely on you, to sort me out, when I'm hopelessly befuddled. Until Terence was arrested, I'd been deluding myself into thinking we weren't at war. Your husband was right in calling me stupid and naive. I'm seesawing on a precipice and can't have Lacey following me into hell. You must promise to get her out of here when Anthony makes his move. You must tell her anything to convince her. If she refuses, take whatever drastic measures you must!"

"Do you want me to tell him that you've had a change of heart?"

"No, let him go on thinking I'm an idiot. He'll choose his time when I'm unable to interfere. If he sees you're on his side, it will be best for all."

"What about Devlin and Aggie? Surely, they'll resist us?"

"Not at all. They'll do as I've asked."

"In my heart, I doubt it will come to this! I'm promising only to ease some of your worrying."

"As I knew you would, my darlin' Anne Marie."

"I don't want to be pregnant," Lacey said to Dr. Sykes as he finished his examination. She straightened her dressing gown and resumed the sullen air that had greeted him.

"Few women find this time to be enjoyable. In the end, you'll see it was worth it."

"Pish! Why do men think they know what this feels like? Have you had something growing in you?"

Drying his hands, he said "I recall having roundworm as a child."

Though she never could abide Dr. Seacord, she had taken an immediate liking to the very young Ethan Sykes, with his endearing Yorkshire accent and cottony cloud of orange hair. While Devlin and Aggie complained that he couldn't possibly be a "real" doctor, it was this youthful brashness and mocking humor that appealed to her.

"My life is ruled by shoulds and should nots! Everyone has a bloody opinion about what is best for the baby. The baby is all they care about! You'd think it was the Second Coming of the Messiah."

Ethan sat back down, daring to pat her clenched fist. "Nothing makes a family dottier than a baby on the way. To make it even more of a circus, this is the first grandchild. So yes, they'll behave as if you're carrying the baby Jesus. Fortunately, you're more than halfway through. You've not been incapacitated by morning sickness as many women are. True, you need to gain more weight to keep up with his growing, but you're in splendid health. You should manage very well during labor."

"Oh yes, labor. I'll be torn asunder so he can escape. It's supposed to be excruciating. Something, I'm sure the Virgin Mary was spared."

"I'll not lie to you. It will probably be the worst pain you'll ever experience. There are things you can do to make it less so. We can talk more at our next appointment. I want you in my office in two weeks. Can Court come with you?"

"We don't know from day to day where he'll be needed." She thought of Terence and Muriel, and the little girl who would never know her father.

He saw a shadow sweep over her. "What are you not saying?"

"I don't want my child to be fatherless! I don't want to hold him over a grave. I don't want that to be how he knows his father—a headstone in the ground."

"Have you spoken to Court of this?"

Lacey turned her face toward the pillow. "I can't. He promised to tell me the truth about what's happening, but the baby has changed all that. I don't have the strength to make him tell me. Nothing is the way I thought it would be! I thought we'd have more time… for us. I never thought another war was lurking in the shadows…"

Court was on the run, galloping through the front door and up the stairs, colliding with Aggie.

"Has she arrived?" He swung her around in a dizzying pirouette.

"Put me down, young man!" she shrieked. "She's unpacking."

"Does Lacey have a clue?"

"Not a one. Dr. Sykes is with her. I'm sure he'll be wanting a few words with you." Aggie composed herself and fretted, "Are you sure now she shouldn't be seeing someone a wee bit more familiar with childbearing? A few whiskers and some gray hair would put me mind at ease. That one looks like he was weaned from his ma's breast not more than a minute ago."

"Aggie, she likes him. That's…"

"Mr. O'Rourke! Do you have a few minutes for me, sir?"

"Of course, Doctor." He shot a mischievous grin at Aggie. "We were saying, what a comfort it is knowing our lamb is in your capable hands."

"I do find it rather delightful how she expresses herself. And what a unique disposition!"

"Ah, so you've had a glimpse of the vixen within?"

"Pregnant women are entitled to their moods. It's more efficacious to sympathize and support."

"We could use a man of such discriminating diplomacy in the Dail!"

"I hear things are quite tense and unpredictable these days." Ethan stowed his bag in the motorcar.

"We're being squeezed from within and without."

"Are you sharing your concerns with Lacey… keeping her apprised?

Court shrugged and drummed his fingers on the windshield. "I don't want her to fret. It will all work out, one way or another. I'd much rather talk about how she's doing."

"She's in perfect health! More than midway through her second trimester. This is a critical time for her to be gaining weight—keeping pace with the growing baby. Her appetite is lackluster, at best. Besides three regular meals, there must be several smaller ones, of protein and calcium. I've written down some recommendations."

"I'll see to it. In a month, she'll be as plump as a Christmas goose!"

"And what if you're called away? She needs someone willing to coax her. I doubt your grandfather or Miss Knox has the time."

"Not to worry. I've seen to it." He was eager to say good-bye.

"In two weeks, I want to see the both of you in my office."

"Not a problem. We'll be there." He gripped Ethan's hand and nearly shoved him into the front seat.

"You may call me with any concerns," the doctor shouted after the fleeing Court.

Back up the stairs he dashed, sprinting to the bedroom and charging in. Lacey was dozing and awoke with a start as he threw himself across the bed.

"You seem strangely exuberant," she remarked, her hand caressing his head as it rested on her belly.

"I'm feeling strangely exuberant, my sweet." He raised his head to kiss her. "And strangely frisky." His kisses multiplied and intensified.

"What's so strange about that?" she laughed, holding him back from his amorous quest. "You must wait till tomorrow. I'm sore from being poked and probed."

"Am I not to be rewarded for my good deed?"

"What have you been up to? You've been gone all morning."

"Seeing to your happiness! Down the hall, in the room with the green brocade drapes and that four poster bed with the medieval canopy you want to rip to shreds—is a most special surprise."

"Court, that's not where the nursery will be! I thought we agreed on the room next to ours? They've taken the measurements and the work begins next week."

"I'm not interfering with any of that. I've learned to stay out of your way with such doings. You must guess."

"Don't make me guess. It's mean."

"Very well. Sophie is settling in."

"Sophie? Sophie is here? You fetched her home, just for me?"

"Just for you, my lamb." He had used the banished endearment!

"You called me lamb!" She dissolved in tears, slumping against the pillow, pounding the bed with both fists.

"Lacey, you are not to be believed!" He was astonished by her melodramatic response. "Haven't I avoided it all this bloody time?"

"You called me lamb," she repeated and took a deep breath. "I've missed you calling me that."

"Have you indeed?" he erupted with prickly indignation. "It would serve you right if I never called you that again!"

"Pish! We're well past the point of you needing to see me as a woman and not a child. This is proof enough." She cradled her belly for emphasis. "If it makes me happy to be called…"

"So this was some kind of lesson I needed to learn? You have the brass of a hundred church bells and the balls of Goliath!"

Lacey had not seen him in such a rage for quite some time. He needed to be calm when he was told that Sophie's room must be completely redone, lest she be forced to live with hideous furnishings.

"Court," she whispered with that sweet exhale. Her hand wandered… his anger waned… desire hardened. "I do love you."

Part VI

"In the Eye of the Tempest"
1920-1922

Suffering and Sacrifice

"I have decided the terms of my detention ... whatever your government may do. I shall be free, alive or dead, in a month." Terence MacSwiney, August 16, 1920

MacSwiney persevered for seventy-four days without food, wielding the only weapon left to him. Despite international pleas for mercy, the British would not release him. They were not humbled by his death on October 25 but instead, aggrieved by what promised to be a political spectacle of funerals in London, Dublin, and Cork.

"I'll put these shawls aside for the motorcar, but a blanket would be best," Sophie advised Lacey as she sorted through what needed to be packed.

"I'll not be needing a blanket, take one for yourself. I'm feeling so warm these days! Ethan said I'm pumping more blood to keep up with the baby." She straightened, rubbing the small of her back. "I can feel him pushing right up against my lungs. I'm winded already."

"Them little darlin's do that. 'Tis worst when they hug your bladder. You're peeing all the day long."

The Sophie who returned was in some ways, just like the old Sophie, cherishing gossip and scandal, and speaking with careless familiarity. The other Sophie was the woman pushed into maturity by grief and loneliness, accustomed to making her own way. Being a servant was all she knew, so upon arriving in Galway, she signed with a domestics' placement agency, specializing in short-term assignments. She wanted impermanence not enslavement to one family with their quirks and ceaseless demands. If she was unhappy, there was an end in sight. Sophie had learned to suffer with grace.

Living this way for several years enlarged her world, gave her a perspective on how much there was to savor and learn from people and their differences. She would have gone on this way until a bitter reality smacked her into awareness. She still was no better off than an indentured servant. When her mother and sister died, she could not leave for even two days, because that would void the contract and she would lose half her accrued wages.

Court's letter, wooing her back, came when she was considering her next step. It didn't matter that her Aunt Aggie resented her return; such a thing would dissipate to a grudging level of tolerance. What mattered was Lacey's ecstatic embrace with its flood of sweet memories.

Both women were shaken by a rude pounding on the door and a hoarse exclamation. "Lacey! We need to talk, young lady!"

Flurry leaped to protect them from the intruder, barking with the ferocity of the larger dog that he thought he was.

"Shall I leave you to do battle?" Sophie pulled a dress from the closet. "This needs steaming."

"No need for you to suffer through his ranting," Lacey sighed, hushing the dog.

"Good morning to you, captain. 'Tis a fine day to be out and about." She slid past him, showing none of her former wariness.

Anthony scooped up Flurry, who made quite a show of not resisting him. "At least, the damn dog is happy to see me!"

"You can't expect me to kiss you after he does! I am pregnant."

Her father took a moment to assess how she looked and how ready she was to do the dance of wills. "You cannot be serious about attending MacSwiney's funeral by yourself!"

"I won't be alone. Sophie will be with me."

"And where is your husband?"

"Daddy, you know Court is in Dublin helping with the arrangements. He can't be in two places at once!"

"So he'll leave you in Cork, without a care for your well-being?"

She sat at her dressing table, organizing a collection of Lalique perfume bottles. "We haven't discussed it. It's my decision."

Unlike Anne Marie, she could not be cowed by hulking intimidation; she had too many years of supple manipulation over him.

He dragged over a diminutive slipper chair and straddled it. "Just driving there will be hellish. They've set up roadblocks manned by those goddamn thugs! Every car is searched. Every person is questioned. They don't need an excuse to shoot you. They answer to no one!"

"I hardly think two women, one of whom is quite pregnant, will set them off."

"What about that pregnant woman in Balbriggan a month ago? The one who fell on a bayonet?"

"I can't allow myself to think about such things! One day, it could be me walking in a funeral procession. This is what my life has become."

"Only because you choose to live this way! You say Courtland has no idea. Do you think he wants you to be in harm's way?"

"A man I love and admire is dead. I simply want to pay my respects. If you can't understand then leave me alone!"

How did he lose her so completely to Ireland? Was she ever truly his? Anthony prowled the room, his size and temper making it feel like a cage with two well-matched combatants seeking the other's weak spot.

"I vowed when I came back… I'd never leave you again! I'll not leave you alone now. If you must do this… I'll go with you."

"You will, Daddy?" she cried, flinging her arms around him in relief. "It won't be more than a day or two."

After a well-orchestrated display of politics and martyrdom, when more than thirty thousand mourners immobilized London, the British made the tactical decision to divert the funeral procession to Cork, leaving Dubliners cruelly forsaken. The authorities, shrinking from the world's disdain, wanted Terence MacSwiney buried and forgotten.

◆

The city of Cork wore the veil of mourning for its native son with somber pageantry and a good dose of rancor toward the occupying troops. Anthony and Lacey attended the lying in state at City Hall and now were settled in a plodding cab back to Adelaide Lane. Through three hours of prayer, song, keening, and condolences, Lacey had fretted over the deceitfulness of the British.

"Court will be devastated if he can't be a pall bearer! It means so much to him. What time is the train due?" Her eyes wandered to the churning crowds and the black arm bands. Some held or wore signs speaking of their sorrow: "Soldier of the Republic," "He Shall Be Remembered Forever," "Unbeaten. Unbroken. Unrepentant."

"Another thirty minutes. He'll have a hell of a time with this traffic. He should go straight to St. Finbarr's." Anthony tucked her closer. "Now pet, you must lie down as soon as we get back. Let Sophie see to things. You want to be well rested when he sees you, or I'll never hear the end of it!"

"You should have woke me when he called," she mumbled through another wave of fatigue.

"He told me not to! Don't put me in the middle of this. Each of you does just as you please! Expecting the other to bend to it." There was no response; she had nodded off.

This was not the Ireland of twenty-five years ago. That Ireland embraced him with its picaresque charm and vividly verdant countryside; that Ireland blessed him with Caitlin and Lacey. Had affluence and privilege isolated him from her true nature? Today, he had seen a country polarized and brutalized yet unvanquished. From the smug clusters of soldiers smoking and laughing, to the stoic IRA members gripping rifles, to the Irish everyman in well-worn black with bleak faces and despairing hearts, this was no longer the Ireland of his youthful recollections.

"Thank the Lord you're back!" Sophie exclaimed, bolting the door and hurrying them into the parlor. "This here was stuffed through the mail slot soon after you left." She handed Anthony a ragged sheet of paper. "Them peelers out there showed up about an hour ago."

He discreetly parted the curtains for a look. There were two black motorcars idling down the street.

"I doubt they're the police. The two I see are wearing trench coats. There could be several more." He read the single sentence aloud. "You are in danger."

"They're after Court! Daddy, how can we warn him?"

He turned on the lights so the men would think they were settling in for the evening and checked his revolver. "They'll need a battering ram to get through that front door. It will buy us some time. Where does the door in the garden lead to?"

"A footpath and bridge to St. Patrick's Street. But it will leave us far from the garage."

"I'm sure they're watching that as well. Ladies, we must move quickly. Take nothing. We may have to walk for quite a bit before we find a cab."

"I'm not leaving." Lacey said with a predictable thrust of her chin.

He did not have the patience to coax her. "Whoever warned us knows Courtland never left Dublin. He's probably been arrested. They'll use you to break him! That's how they do it. I promise to find out what happened but we must leave now!"

By the time they secured a cab, it was dark and the streets had taken on a menacing mood. The Glanmere Road train station was thick with people, which suited Anthony's need for cover. He sent Lacey and Sophie to the women's wash room to exchange coats and hats. Sophie was given the money for a first class ticket to Cloonsheelin and a note for Anne Marie. After she departed, he purchased first class tickets to Mallow.

"Who do we know in Mallow?" she asked as he escorted her into the dining car.

"I cabled the Sheppertons. We visited them when Paladin was foaled."

"Of course, Ravensmount. I remember the secret passageways. Their daughter and I got lost for hours, wandering through them."

"The manhunt for the two of you disrupted Lady Shepperton's very elegant dinner party! There must have been ten of us, dressed in our Sunday best, crawling through two centuries of cobwebs, mouse skeletons, and withering odds and ends. Let's hope she's forgotten all about that little fiasco."

"Why them?"

"Lord Shepperton does some work for the British consulate from time to time. We can use his connections, and I can lean on the American ambassador as well."

"Can they be trusted?"

"We'll be quite safe, and you can rest up. Now, do you think that bartender looks like he can be trusted to make a decent Singapore Sling?"

It had been ten days since Court was confronted at Kingsbridge Station by a swarm of trench-coated auxiliaries from the Royal Irish Constabulary and knocked to the ground with fists and kicks while six members of the Dail grappled with the attackers. Anthony had wheedled, cajoled, and coerced his diplomatic connections, but all that could be extracted from Dublin Castle was the acknowledgment that Court was somewhere in its bowels, facing serious charges. Then a telephone call from Lord Shepperton cast a sinister light on the nature of the charges, and Anthony gathered the family at Torrey Castle, along with Dr. Sykes who might be needed to reason with Lacey.

"I don't have absolute confirmation, but it seems Courtland has been accused of conspiracy and murder. There are no details." As expected, disbelief and horror rippled across faces and unleashed an eddy of emotion.

"'Tis nothing but vile falsehoods! I expect no less from the filthy swine!" Devlin put a comforting arm around Aggie who sobbed into her apron.

"I must see him! Daddy you must find a way."

"I can't allow that," Ethan protested. "Lacey, traveling so far at this late stage may do great harm to the both of you."

"Pish! My husband needs me. He could be dead as we speak! I'll not sit here and do nothing!"

"There must be some way to negotiate with them." Anne Marie cried, a moment away from tears. 'Why can't he be transferred to Cork so we can be close by? He needs to feel our love and support."

"Indeed! We need to make a fuss. Shame them into showing a bit of compassion." Devlin was fired up to do battle with an enemy beyond his comprehension.

"The idea that my sweet boy could do such things!" Aggie added with maternal ferocity. "The more stirring up we do, the better t'will be for him."

Anthony was not surprised by the outpouring of unrealistic and unhelpful demands. But he was miffed that his own wife was so emotionally aligned with the others. What must it be like to be the very sun, warming their hearts and sparking their emotions? If it had been him, could he expect the same?

"Before you start plotting a prison break, you need to listen to me."

He found his way to the liquor cabinet and swiftly fortified himself. When each was resettled with a comforting glass of sherry and for Devlin, his precious biscuits, he issued his edict.

"Tomorrow, a British attaché is meeting me in Cork. With him as my official escort, I won't be pestered by the likes of the RIC or MI5. I promised both the US and UK ambassadors, it would only be me dealing with the authorities. No one else!" He eyed his daughter with sufficient steeliness to quell her. "The best way to get Courtland out of this mess is through diplomacy and a generous helping of bribery. The Crown will not respond to public pressure. They've had enough of that. Now, if you don't agree, you're welcome to figure this out by yourselves!"

"Captain, when have I not felt mercifully blessed to be in your good hands? I'll not be the one to bring the hammer down on such delicate maneuverings." Devlin nudged Aggie who unpursed her lips and nodded.

"Daughter?"

"Can you take him a letter?"

"I'll do my best, pet."

"Oh Anthony, you darling!" Anne Marie cried, hugging him in a bold display of public affection. "You are my hero!"

He accepted their gratitude, knowing all too well, his was a light no brighter or more lasting than a shooting star.

"This won't do at all! You'll be dead of pneumonia before the trial starts. Guard! Inform your lieutenant that I'm most displeased about the condition of this cell. I expect the prisoner to be moved to an upper floor with a window and the amenities befitting his former rank! And it's to be done before I leave so I may personally inspect the accommodations."

Colonel Miles Cullum's imposing physical presence sucked the air from the claustrophobic cell. Court stood at attention as a reflex, then relaxed in an unexpected bear hug.

"We'll get you a hot shower and a good meal as well. There's no excuse for this hellish treatment."

"Whatever you can do, I'm forever in your debt, Colonel."

"You know, O'Rourke, I don't like many people. But I do like you. You always want to do the honorable thing and damn the consequences! Even when you've made a botch of it, you won't stand down."

As always with the Colonel, it was difficult to distinguish between a dialogue and diatribe. Court stayed silent.

"Making yourself another martyr for the cause won't bring back MacCurtain or MacSwiney. These accusations are damn serious. But it's the murder charge that will fit you for a noose! Well, what do you have to say for yourself?"

"I didn't kill Davenport. What happened in Marsh's Library may have saved my life but set me up for blackmail. I gave in to fear and stupidity."

"I'm going to do you an enormous favor and pull a nice, fluffy rabbit out of my bottom." His voice softened and if possible, sweetened, as he called out, "Kitty my dear, you may join us now."

A stout woman shrouded in veil and fur entered, infusing the rank space with a burst of tuberose.

"I hope, you haven't been too uncomfortable, puss?"

"Not at all, Miles. The chaplain was telling me a most amusing story."

"Katherine!"

"I must be the very last person on earth you expected to see." She laughed in her notoriously shrill way, oblivious to the surroundings. "It's heartbreaking to see you so thin and mauled over. My husband has convinced me that I'm to be your salvation."

"Let's not overwhelm him with hyperbole. I must hunt down that ninny of a lieutenant and a cup of tea as well…some biscuits would be nice."

They were left to dwell in an awkward silence until Court corralled his racing thoughts and asked, "You married the Colonel?"

"If you recall, I was a destitute widow with few prospects and forced to live under my sister-in-law's roof!" She shivered in recollection, despite being wrapped in sable. "Can you imagine how I suffered? Perhaps you can… now." She had become aware of the dampness and extreme wretchedness of his cell. "The rats aren't about during the day, are they?"

"No, they keep to themselves till midnight and then come out with fiddle and pipe to dance a jig or two with me."

"I see your wit has not deserted you."

"Forgive me. I'm truly happy for you, for the both of you."

"You're like all the rest with their smug assumptions. Miles is kind and exceedingly generous. And in return, I'm dutiful and wifely. My future is secure. That's all I ever really wanted from a man."

"Again, please forgive my skepticism, Katherine. I've no right to begrudge you this happiness."

"To think, I may be the only one standing between you and the hangman. Why, it's just too perfectly ironic!"

"Indeed, it is."

"I cannot make it all go away. I'm just a woman after all. But I do have some credibility as the victim's widow and now, as the colonel's wife."

"You do like to fiddle away while Rome burns."

"Very well. I must start at the beginning and don't interrupt me! About a week after I arrived in London, who should appear on the doorstep, looking like a half-drowned tomcat, but Ransom Longo. I knew him only in passing. Sydney paid him to slink and snoop around."

"Thank you for seeing me, Mrs. Davenport. 'Tis a dirty bit of weather we're having. Not an auspicious welcome for you."

"Mr. Longo, my sister-in-law will return shortly. She will not think it proper

I invited you into her home."

"Of course, ma'am. I'll get right to it. If your late husband was standing here, he'd be the first to tell you, I'm a man blessed with a sensitive conscience. 'Tis how I came to work for him.*"

"As an informer?*"

"A harsh way of putting it. But I did keep him aware of certain treasonous doings.*"

"Whatever you and Sydney were involved with is your business! And nasty business at that!*"

"All politics is nasty business ma'am. Picking a side means surviving, nothing more. Captain Davenport chose his and died for it. Courtland O'Rourke saw to that!*"

"If ever a man deserved to roast in hell."

"Will you please be quiet? It's hard enough for me to keep my remembering in proper order. Sydney must have run his mouth many times over for Longo to know all he did. He was quite clever in his performance, knowing just how to prey on my emotions."

"I can see you're embarrassed your husband shared such intimacies. But I can tell you his soul was being devoured by the humiliation! I'm not blaming you, O'Rourke seduced you. I wouldn't waste a heartbeat on the likes of him.*"

"What is this all leading to?*"

"I'd be willing to go to the authorities and say, I saw O'Rourke shoot the captain. Your husband's death will be avenged.*"

"You would do that for me?*"

"Katherine! How could you?"

"Oh pooh! I was still upset over your loutish disregard—leaving me bleeding on my parlor floor!"

"By Judas, you never fail to leave me speechless…and afraid."

"Mr. Longo, you would make an inferior playwright. You rush to a climax without building up to it! There must be a sequence of actions and reactions. Why were you there? Why did you wait to come forward? Who can verify what you saw?*"

"Fair enough. I was posing as a rebel, as was O'Rourke. For different reasons but that *don't matter. I had to stay in place until the soldiers took control. By then, the captain was dead. I know some lads who will back me up, if we make it attractive for them."*

"Ah yes, the money."

"I'm only asking for enough to tide me over for a bit. And then, some for persuading purposes. Fifty pounds should do it."

"My head is spinning with all of this! I need time to think. Return next Friday at 10 a.m. My sister-in-law has a regular outing with her church group, bestowing their good deeds upon the less fortunate."

"Then what happened?"

"It all fell apart. He did show up as expected but raving that I had betrayed him."

"How?"

"He had someone watching the house. Miles came to see how I was getting on. It was really quite sweet of him. He bought me the biggest box of French chocolates, three pounds! And an armful of pink lilies..."

"Katherine, please."

"Be patient with me. After all, I'm here for your sake!"

"I apologize." He sat on his hands to resist strangling her.

"Longo leapt to the assumption I had confided in Miles. He was rabid in his accusation I had marked him for death. I don't see how. "

"An informer's life is worthless if anyone within his circle has reason to suspect him. He was desperate to get back to Ireland and now, I know why. I played right into his filthy hands."

"I've nothing in writing...no witnesses to prove any of this...only my sworn testimony. Which I'll gladly give."

"If you do, some of the tawdry aspects of our affair will be revealed." He sagged deeper into the mattress, wondering if any of this would save his life.

"There will be nothing Miles doesn't already know. I don't care about anyone else." She reached down to touch his matted curls. "You always had such beautiful hair," she murmured, aching to touch more of him.

Court brought her hand down to his unshaven cheek and nuzzled it. The rough caress stirred the yearning of long ago. Miles was wrong. It was not hyperbole...she would be his salvation.

Blood and Tears

Autumn Sundays in Ireland were devoted to the worship of two religions: Catholicism and football. For many Dubliners, it was Mass followed by a match. This was a precious outing, a spot of leisure that endured during the worst of times. Sunday, November 21, 1920, began with the same predictable rituals and ended as the turning point for the Irish War of Independence. It would become known as Bloody Sunday.

The Crown had recruited a small but lethal coven of intelligence officers who had served in the Far East during the Great War. This "Cairo Gang" was charged with an execution order aimed at Sinn Fein and the IRA. Michael Collins responded with a tried and true remedy, political assassination. He was a meticulous planner of all guerrilla operations, and for this, he implemented intense surveillance, relying on an extensive information network. The scope of the plan covered thirty-five agents, including the Cairo Gang, most of whom were living in secrecy in a middle-class area of south Dublin. Surprise was critical; the ambush ripped through the early morning hours with stunning savagery before the first Mass was said. The fatalities included eleven agents and two auxiliaries.

After a breakfast of watery porridge and tea, Court was assailed by the violin whine of sirens coming through the high window of his new cell. He had room to stretch and a table with chairs. The mattress was no better except for fresh straw; the vermin remained abundant.

Down the corridor, a chorus of muttering voices swelled, and one rose over the others. "…like a fuckin' slaughterhouse! Bits of 'em splattered about. Their faces were gone." He recognized it was Desmond, the youngest guard, a drooping lick of a boy with a blushing birthmark on his left cheek.

There was no lunch, and some of the prisoners made a fuss, calling out and banging away. The dinner hour came and went; they became rambunctious. The lights in the corridor turned off, and darkness drew them into silence and foreboding. Sounds emanated from far below, from the pit where Court had been. Where ungodly things happened. Where every wail, every gut-churning shriek left you to fear if you would be the next to be taken away.

He set the chairs side by side, about two feet from the cell door, stumbling to feel his way. He dragged the mattress under the window and used the table as a barricade. If they came for him, he would have a minute or two to react. It was absurd but gave him comfort. At the front, he expected each day to be his last. There was no preparation, only inevitability. The sounds became more soul crushing; he covered his ears. The only thing left to do was cry.

——◆——

Dublin Castle lifted the prohibition on visitors after two long days of trepidation and sleeplessness. Court hoped that finally, he could make sense of the fragmented conversations among the guards. He also was desperate for a letter from Lacey, and for this, Anthony served as the messenger. Letters to him were permitted only after they had been reviewed and censored. He was allowed neither paper nor pen.

Devlin had the inspiration to send along the letters that she had written to him while he was recuperating in London. These letters, which he had rebuffed so petulantly, were filled with affection and amusing chatter. While they returned him to one of the most despairing times in his life, they spoke to his present state of mind, giving him bittersweet consolation. They were a tender reminder of the girl she had been and what he missed, then and now, her vivacity.

"You've got visitors," Desmond announced glumly. "The lieutenant says no more than fifteen minutes, so don't be clamoring for more."

"Thank you. I'll watch the time."

Anthony and Major Aubrey Yates appeared a minute later and from their faces, he knew that the news must be dreadful. Anthony stayed by the door, watching the corridor, while Aubrey huddled close to him.

"You're looking seedy but unharmed. There's been a massacre; and I say that without exaggeration. A squad of the RIC showed up at Croke Park Sunday afternoon and opened fire on the crowd! Thousands tried to get away…trampling women and children. I can't believe the fatalities weren't in the hundreds!"

"Why…why?"

"Reprisals!" Anthony hissed. "Collins and his men went on a shooting spree. They gunned down a dozen or more intelligence agents."

"He was determined to wipe out the Cairo Gang," Aubrey explained, "…had the Bulletin publish proof of Wilson's plan to exterminate members of Sinn Fein and the IRA. Somehow, he got his hands on the very document, printed on official letter head, and decoded it! It's been a war of denial and self-serving finger pointing since."

"I told you it would come to this! Matching one atrocity for another, like some biblical eye for an eye."

"Captain, we all know too well…there are no clean hands in war," Aubrey said with undisguised exasperation.

Court's former aide-de-camp had enjoyed a well-paced rise through the ranks after studying military law. There was still a breathless energy and cheerful earnestness about him that helped to neutralize the most hostile of circumstances. Of late, he found himself, more and more, playing mediator between the two men. Neither of whom could make it through a conversation without an exchange of lacerating jabs.

"I was staying at the Gresham," Anthony continued, accenting the "was" as he rolled an unlit cigarette between his fingers. "And was rudely awakened by an artillery blast in the next room! Suppose they had the wrong room number? It could have been me strewn about the place! Is my daughter to be both widowed and orphaned?"

"You blame me for that? Sitting here in this hellhole? By all means, Captain, put it on me, if it makes you feel vindicated! All you've predicted is coming to pass. I've no defense to offer and I damn well won't apologize!"

"Gentlemen! We've just a matter of minutes to discuss the only fortunate thing that's come out of this nightmare."

Anthony resumed his post and lit the cigarette as Court turned to his counsel.

"It seems Longo has vanished. We've suspected he was working for the Cairo Gang. Could be dead or gone to ground. Without him, the murder charge has no muscle and should be voided. But it will take some time."

"Christ, 'tis good news! Does it mean we won't need Katherine's testimony? If she can be spared that."

"You're unbelievable!" Anthony snapped. "Always the considerate opportunist… even of the woman you couldn't wait to bed just to show me up!"

"You were long out of her bed when she came to me. Quite willingly!"

"And married to the man you're accused of murdering! I've watched, for most of your life, how you take what you please. Without thought or consideration. How you beguile and manipulate those around you!"

"What a disappointing son-in-law I must be. So far below your holy standards. Why, Aubrey here would be much more to your liking. Hell! He even looks like you!"

It seemed that Aubrey's bright blue eyes, fair hair and ramrod posture were the genetic components propelling him into another squabble. He wondered just how jolly Christmas could be when these two families gathered under the mistletoe, hands wrapped around throats, whilst singing carols of vitriol.

Desmond appeared with a warning jangle of keys and Aubrey never felt more relieved. "Gentlemen, we're done."

What Are We Without Our Secrets?

"Sophie! Your uncle won't be waiting on you one more precious minute! Enough of your dawdling, girl." Aggie returned to fretting over the menus.

The war's migration to Cork and the surrounding area meant shuttered warehouses and erratic deliveries of the specialty items needed to make this Christmas the grandest ever. She already had pleaded with St. Joseph to speed up Court's release in time for the holiday and the birth of the baby; she could not go whining for more.

"She'll be needing her tray no later than nine," Sophie said, stepping from the pantry with the ingredients for Lacey's bedtime snack. "And don't forget a good shake of nutmeg in the cocoa!"

It was this tone of insufferable solicitousness that never failed to needle Aggie where she was the most vulnerable. "As if I don't know what my angel fancies? Have I not been indulging her from the very moment I saw her in the arms of her dearest mother?"

"The lot of you've done a mighty fine job of that! What sort of mother are you supposing she'll be? She'll drop it like a cat and leave it to us! Mark me words." She set her hat at a fashionable angle and wrapped a muffler around her neck.

"Mind your tongue! She's loving and kind. Are you forgetting the way she looked after your brother? Nature will see her through."

Sophie ignored her aunt's blazing expression and further provoked.

"Don't you regret giving your life over to them, not having your own family? I remember all them moonie-eyed lads panting after you. And you turned up your nose, like this here was your calling. Won't be me! I'll see her through this and then come spring… I'm off."

"Good riddance! You were always one for discontent. You only married that half-wit because you thought he was making his way to Dublin. When he stayed put, you were stuck with him and a swelling belly."

The blade cut both ways, yet Sophie could not resist a final twist. "At least, I've had the pleasure of being seeded and bearing fruit. You've a womb of dust and ashes, not fit for ploughing."

Seamus stumbled in, testy from waiting. "Sweet Jesus, we're all frozen to the marrow waiting on you! Didn't the good Father say half past seven for the rehearsal? He'll be in a fine snit all right, and it won't be me doing." He saw Aggie seething and Sophie preening. "What's this fussing about? You never used to go at it like this."

"Just a little truth-telling, Uncle. 'Tis all."

"I had a peek at the nursery. Quite charming and so very cozy, my dear," Devlin said, eyes closed, immersed in Mozart on the gramophone.

Lacey was puzzling over the blanket she was knitting. Why did her stitches look so woeful compared to the ones that Aggie had done to start her off?

"It will look perfect once the furniture's in place. Anne Marie will lend us what we need if the baby comes before."

"You still have some time. The first one likes to keep you waiting and waiting. You know Lindsay was our third, and he came shooting out like a comet! How my poor darlin' suffered with the others, all for nothing."

She had done her best not to think about labor, shutting her ears to every female, eager to share heroic tales of endurance and suffering.

"We agreed not to talk about that," she reminded him, confronted with yet another knot in the yarn.

"So we did. I'll be content just to have my grandson home."

"Or that! I know daddy said it could be any day, but I don't trust them to act with any urgency. Remember how long it took for his discharge?"

"'Tis the conspiracy nonsense mucking things up. But this Yates fellow seems right on top of it. And your father does have a few arms left to twist."

"Don't you have another room to haunt, old man?" Aggie bustled in with Lacey's tray. Flurry roused himself; he smelled molasses cookies.

She didn't begrudge Devlin this little routine that he had begun and often, took her sewing and joined them. Lacey would bring his spirits up when he started to slide into hopelessness, and he, in turn, distracted her with some amusing recollection when she grew despondent.

"Aggie, what am I doing wrong?"

"Let me see, my angel. You've dropped a stitch here and there and another one here, making it all loosey-goosey."

"Have you been crying? Your eyes are red."

"Nothing but a cloud of smoke coming at me from that damn oven!" She leveled a purposeful scowl at Devlin. "'Tis another cross I bear with all its belching and heaving."

"Quite a relic," he agreed. "The kitchen needs to be modernized. As nice as the one at Durbin House…no…nicer."

Who or what had taken over the body of Devlin O'Rourke? "To be sure, there's a good amount of work to be done everywhere. We'll be wanting all the modern conveniences for the baby. We can't be raising the wee one in such antiquated surroundings."

"'Tis a Christmas miracle!" Aggie exclaimed. 'And I've a witness, so you're bound to it."

"Oh, I'll be true to my word. Please excuse me, ladies. I must be seeing to my gardenias, whispering a bit of encouragement to them."

"Mind you don't sneak a cigar. You're sounding raspy, and you know what that means!"

"Leave me be, woman! I'm just past eighty and have the constitution of a sixty-year-old!"

"A dead sixty-year-old."

She pursued him out the door. "If you think I'm nursing you with all I have to do…"

Torrey Castle was silent, too silent for Devlin as he puttered around the conservatory. Such silence was meant for the graveyard. It would be a late night for the servants with the pageant rehearsal and a well-stewed Seamus certain to land them all in a ditch. When the hall clock chimed ten, it stirred the silence, but the somber echoes chilled him. Suddenly, a sweep of bright light enveloped the conservatory and he found himself trapped by several enormous headlights. The glare was frightful as he raised his arm to fend it off.

"What nonsense is this?" He hobbled into the entry hallway. He'd give them a good whack of his cane and send them on their way.

A slurring voice barked out an incomprehensible command. "Attention papist-loving cock suckers. Get out now or burn!"

Why had he not done as Anthony warned? They were utterly defenseless! How could he get to Lacey and still warn Aggie? The dilemma induced a petrifying inertia as more frenzied voices joined in, bellowing drunken threats.

"Good evening Granddad! Best do as they say. Them Auxies are in a foul mood and won't look kindly on your dithering." The intruder emerged from the library with a smile and wink.

"I know you!" Devlin stuttered. "You're Longo!"

"So I am. Where's Lacey?"

"What do they want? Why are they here?"

"Who can say for sure what pisses them off? Half a Cork is burning."

"I must speak with them!"

"If you walk out that door to conversate… you'll get a bullet between the eyes! Where is she?"

"Third door, left of the second landing. Hurry!"

Without Court beside her, Lacey could not bear the darkness. It drove her to such suffocating despair that drawing a breath became a willed effort. She kept a small lamp burning through the night; its shadows wavering along to the comforting rasp of Flurry's snoring. But tonight, there was no position, no well-placed pillow that allowed her more than a few minutes respite. Soon after dinner, she became aware of a vague twinge in her lower back, but it was nothing compared to the gripping cramps of the past few weeks.

"He's headed south," Ethan had explained. "Pointing his little head towards the exit. It will come and go. No worries."

The twinges had sharpened into pulsing bites, making her restless and anxious. Flurry abandoned her with a reproachful snort to lie by the fire. She must keep her eyes closed; she must not think of all that was left to do. Without decent sleep, she would be useless, compelling Devlin and Aggie to take on the burden. They were not as energetic as they liked to think. Anne Marie would insist on helping, and that would lead to certain drama.

Flurry, in some kind of nocturnal madness, shuddered awake to sprint between the door and the bed. He chewed at the bedding, begging for her attention. When she leaned over to quiet him, a spasm seized her, leaving her gasping. The dog scooted back to the door, wailing and leaping.

"Sod off, you little bugger!"

She knew the voice but could not quite place it, for that would be more than her exhausted brain could muster.

From the drawing room came the distressing crash of glass followed by a rocking explosion. It threw Devlin against the wall, the back of his head absorbing the impact. Dazed but still on his feet, he stumbled to the dining room, grabbing onto whatever he could. The heavy door leading down to the kitchen resisted him; he had so little strength left. As he shoved his shoulder against it, it gave way and he clung to it, crying out, "Aggie! Aggie" Where are you my darlin'?"

"Holy shit! Look at you!" Ran materialized out of the shadows, yanking off his cap and looking thoroughly annoyed. "I wasn't expecting this." For all of his maniacal plotting, it had not occurred to him that she might be pregnant and repulsively so.

"Where did you come from? Is someone after you?" Lacey was trying to reconcile the reality of Ran, standing in her bedroom, with her furtive longings for him.

"No time for idle chat, wild one. A squad of Auxies is on your doorstep itching to torch this place."

The first explosion shot tremors through the foundation. It sounded like Marsh's Library all over again.

"I asked 'em for a fuckin' ten minutes! Them bastards got no bloody sense of time." He boldly searched through her closet, pulling out a fur cape. "Bundle yourself up good. Time's run out."

"They can't be doing this! They can't drive us out of our home!" she screamed as Flurry cowered in her arms.

He tussled with her. "Let go of the damn dog! He'll follow for sure."

"We must find Devlin and Aggie!"

"I reckon they're halfway to Durbin House by now."

"I need time to think. Let me be!"

"Are you fuckin' crazy? Another blast and we're done for!"

Smoke was spiraling up from the landing; he had no doubt that they were moments away from another explosion. "The back stairs will get us clear into the kitchen and out to the garden."

In the harrowing darkness of the stairwell, she feared that with every lurching step, she might fall and harm the baby. Her throat constricted as she struggled for a shallow breath.

"We'll die here if you can't keep up! Hold still. You're going over my shoulder."

Devlin wondered if Aggie may have gone up the back stairs to the conservatory looking for him. In the two minutes that he had been behind the door, the dining room had ignited. Flames skittered up the walls, licking at the drapes and snaking across the plasterwork. Dense smoke swirled around him, and he dropped to his knees. The tinkling of the crystal pendants in the chandelier grew into a dreadful clatter. When it broke away, he felt the biting spray of glass on his face and hands.

Making his way to the hallway, the heat was fierce, and each breath scalded his lungs. Behind him, the drawing room, library, and dining room had merged into a single, undulating wall of fire. The conservatory would be a refuge if only he could get to it. A second explosion flattened him, scrambling his senses. He could not figure out which direction it came from, all he could do was keep crawling. The headlights of the armored lorry guided him back to the conservatory. There was Aggie, sprawled face down under the broken potting table. This blast had blown out most of the windows and as the cold air rushed in, it created a vortex of wreckage.

"Lacey…Lacey," she moaned as Devlin gently turned her face to his.

Her belly slapping against Ran's back, Lacey nearly vomited as he thumped his way down. The kitchen was a spot of surreal tidiness, everything polished and in its place. The hearth's smoldering embers, so soft and benign, were a bitter contrast to the burning chaos above them.

She leaned against the table and whispered. "I need water. Let me sit; we're safe enough for now." Flurry stared up at them with trembling confusion as she poured some water into her hand for him to lap up.

"Are we done refreshing ourselves now? Can we get the fuck out of here?"

"You only curse like that when you know something I don't! When you're hiding something from me!"

The second explosion hurled them to the stone floor. Whatever had been attached to the walls flew off, crashing into shattered piles. Smoke washed over them, the haze too thick to see through.

"Let it rise, then head for the door!" he yelled. "Stay low…keep moving!"

The fur cape felt like a smothering beast as she dragged herself over the rough floor, knees and hands scraping with every inch. She followed the sound of Flurry's barking as he scratched at the door. Once outside, she was grateful for the frosty air, taking it in deep gulps.

"Where can we hide?" Lacey refused to look back at the inferno consuming Torrey Castle. One look and she would surely perish from grief.

"With them bare feet, I'll have to carry you. The stables will have to do."

"Promise not to leave me! Those men have killed women…pregnant women!"

All he had to do was walk away. What he had come to collect was not to be his—not this night or any other. He saw the headlights of the armored lorry bending toward the road.

"Looks like they've had their fun and won't be lingering. We should be safe enough."

She collapsed against him, a searing contraction radiating from deep within her womb. "It's too soon!"

"Babies come when they damn well want to!"

"Lacey's safe so don't be fretting anymore." Devlin assumed that Ran had got her out. "Are you in pain?"

"Bleeding somewhere. I can feel it. Me leg is paining me something awful."

"Listen to me, my darlin'. We must lie quietly. All that clamoring outside is the bucket brigade. In no time at all, the fire will be out and we'll be rescued."

"What happened? There was a terrible roar. It shook me up!"

He coughed into his handkerchief, his lungs raw from the smoke.

"Save yourself, you old fool!"

"Once I'm down, there's no getting up on me own. You know that." He pressed his cheek against hers.

"'Tis where I wanted to be you know," she whispered, clutching his collar. "All them years ago. I knew you were the one."

His mouth warmed hers; the kiss was long and tremulous.

"No regrets," Aggie sighed.

The stables gave Lacey the reassurance that within their walls, all was as it should be. The horses, agitated by the ruckus, quieted down when Flurry danced over to greet them. Paladin swelled with frantic joy as she caressed him.

"Nothing to be frightened of my sweet, sweet boy," she cooed, oblivious to her bleeding hands and knees.

Ran was busy in the tack room, piling wood in the stove and setting a pot of water on it. "Fetch me some blankets and flannel," he shouted. When she did not appear, he accosted her. "If you think you can tear yourself away, I'd appreciate a helping hand! You'll be wailing like a banshee when the next one comes and good for shit!"

"You're doing it again."

"Don't be questioning me! If you don't want me around, I'll be off."

She returned with the supplies, sluggish and subdued until the next contraction pulled her down to her knees.

He looked at his watch. "Less than fifteen minutes since the last one. You're leaking." He pointed to the puddle that she was standing in. "You'll be needing a cup of something to take the edge off. Take this and time the next one."

Soon she was gripping the watch, cringing from another contraction.

"How many minutes?" he asked, pouring whiskey from his flask into a cup of tea.

"I…I can't…keep time. The pain is too…awful."

"Give it back then! Must I do everything? Drink this down quick. You need to be good and scuttered." He took a long sip from the flask, watching her with a resentful curl of his lip.

"Why are you mad at me?"

Not inclined to answer with any haste, he lit a cigarette and doused a rag with antiseptic. If he kept his eyes above her breasts, she was the same desirable creature of his twisted fantasies.

"Is this how you pictured it? He knelt before her and refilled the cup, taking another swig for himself.

"Pictured what?"

Again, he was in no hurry to respond, gently turning over each hand to wipe the blood. He pushed the torn satin nightgown above her abraded knees and swabbed each one, resting his palms on her thighs.

"Being his wife."

The whiskey was warming her as quickly as a fever and she struggled to rid herself of the cape. "Help me!" she snapped, trapped in the plush folds.

Surely by now, he thought, she must know about the blackmail and his role in the arrest? But no. Her husband seemed religiously obsessed with preserving her ignorance. The green flint of his irises hardened and he began to unwrap her until she was revealed. He smoothed away the knotted curls from her shoulders, leaning close to blow a few breaths across her face.

"Cooling down?"

His insinuating nearness frightened her. "Ran, I am Court's wife."

"Who is it, risking his life for you? Who's with you, right now, when his spawn is clawing its way out of your belly?"

"It's not his fault! He'll be home soon!"

"Drink up."

"I can't. I have to urinate."

"Get yourself out to the bloody shed and piss. I can't be doing that for you!"

"You're being cruel! Hideously cruel!" She rose to push him away but he dodged her and she landed on the matted straw.

"Ain't that a pretty invitation," he remarked, as she struggled on her hands and knees, "…so very tempting."

He crouched over her, tucking himself into the crevice of her splayed buttocks. She made no protest, only whimpered, as he enjoyed the friction of his sheathed erection rubbing against her.

"You'll always be mine for the taking… remember that."

He pulled her up, feeling the vibration of the next contraction, as it soared through her. She wet herself and began to cry.

"My, my…you're making quite a mess."

Her humiliation seemed to appease some essence of his sadism. "Let's get you cleaned up and settled down for the birthing. It shouldn't be much longer."

The work table was cleared off and a blanket and saddle laid upon it. Without a murmur of resistance, Lacey stepped out of the night gown and allowed him to wrap a blanket around her. He positioned her so that she was resting against the saddle with her knees bent.

"I'll be taking a look to see how close you are," he explained, washing his hands. "Let me know if you feel a contraction coming on. Don't want to be losing my fingers up there."

"How long since the last one?" she asked meekly, resigned to the intrusive intimacy.

"About three minutes, so you're due for another but mind…no pushing. Hear me?"

"Yes, Ran."

"Lie back. This will hurt."

His fingers felt like two heated knives slicing through her. "It's starting," she warned. The pressure was horrific and she could not stop from pushing.

"Fuckin' Christ on the cross! Don't be pushing!"

"I can't help it. He's tearing me apart!"

His fingers resumed their exploration. "I can feel his head. No breech. When the next one comes, try panting through it."

"Is that what you say to one of your broodmares?"

"Them's a lot less fussing than you are! They keep their mouths shut."

"Where's Flurry?"

"Tied up. He'll be chiming in soon, I'm sure."

"You do know what to do when he comes?" She grabbed his hand. "You need to make sure he's breathing!"

"You're so sure it's a boy."

"It feels like a boy to me."

"As if, you would know how one feels, over the other." He smirked and sponged her face. "You always have some bloomin' answer for everything."

"A woman knows these…" The rest of the sentence ended in a keening howl, accompanied by Flurry's own. "Let me push!"

"Hold on. Let me take another look. Be ready with the next one. Bear down hard and long. That should get him past the shoulders."

The head cleared, and she felt like a pair of giant hands had split her, and she would be forever rent. Her bowels exploded but she was beyond mortification. He grabbed some rags and wiped the slime from the emerging newborn.

"On the next one, push harder!"

"I can't! Don't make me. Pull him out!"

"His neck will break. Push now or he'll die!"

A last remnant of adrenaline surged within her and she braced herself, gripping her knees, bearing down with one final, mighty push.

The silence returned to bless those in repose. Devlin's white hair, darkened by smoke and ash, recalled the peppery vigor of forty years ago. Aggie's green eyes remained open in an immortal stare of defiance. Joy and sorrow were no more for them.

◆

The full moon weighed sharp and luminous against the winter sky, and with each sweep of a breeze, the acrid air pinched the nose. From the darkness of the paddock, Ran watched pensively as more men surrounded Torrey Castle, pathetically ill-equipped to best the fire. He finished his last cigarette and drained the flask. How easy it would have been to smother the newborn or snap its neck, with Lacey suspecting nothing more than one of nature's heartless whims. Didn't he deserve some kind of satisfaction after being thwarted at every turn?

He would console himself with raiding Badger's Hut. Anthony's guards were distracted, and he required a few necessities to see him through to his next opportunity. There always would be one, somewhere, for Ransom Longo. He was that kind of man.

Beyond the Tempest

Anne Marie beheld the newborn in his tiny splendor. Wiped clean, diapered, and swaddled in a soft blanket, he in turn, beheld her with a seeking grimace.

"What a time you've had, my sweet one!"

He made a familiar sucking sound and she offered her finger, provoking him into a shrieking fit. Where was Sophie? She had dispatched her to Assolas for the services of a wet nurse. Lacey was half-dead from her ordeal and unable to breastfeed. Easing into the rocking chair, she coaxed him into taking her finger. He accepted it with the same peevish reluctance of the maternal grandfather that he resembled. In the nursery, where she had cuddled and played with William, they rocked in the mystical stillness that comes with dawn. Those moments before the trees sing and dreams float away into consciousness.

"How did I get here? Too much light… hurts my eyes."

Anne Marie drew the drapes and returned to the foot of the bed with her brightest smile. She feared answering any questions until Dr. Sykes arrived. "Would you like tea or some broth?

"How did I get here?"

"Seamus Knox brought you. Mr. Longo told him where you were."

"And Ran?"

"I've no idea. There was such chaos with the fire…so many tried…"

"The pain came on so quickly. I thought it would kill me. He knew what to do." Lacey felt herself falling backward into oblivion. "Have they seen the baby? Where's Aggie? I want Aggie."

When Lacey awoke hours later, Sophie was huddled in a heavy black shawl with only her pale profile visible. Woven tightly through her fingers was Aggie's silver rosary, notched with Lacey's teeth marks, from when she was a baby.

"Dear Sophie, you needn't be praying over me. I'm not sick, just very tired. She felt her hand raised and kissed, the rosary pressed into her palm. "Do turn on the lamp. I can hardly see you."

"If you was to look upon me, you'd know what I know."

"What is there to know?"

"I'm wicked… cursed… doomed!"

"I want to see Aggie!"

The shawl slipped away and Sophie's doleful expression was the same as on that December morning when Fiona died. "Gone."

There it was, the pure clarity death casts upon consciousness no matter the choice of verb. Its stunning wallop, its brutal randomness, elicited the same crushing collapse.

"You should have told me."

"I didn't have the words. And you were in no condition to hear them, if I did!" Anne Marie hated this—hated having to go it alone—hated having to be the one responsible. Anthony was meant for this.

Lacey had cried until she passed out, only to be revived and to do it again. She had screamed and vomited, wrestling with Sophie and Anne Marie. Dr. Sykes had sedated her and now, ten hours later—after tea, toast, and another sedative —-she wanted the details.

"How did they find them?"

"In the conservatory. It was the smoke. The fire never touched them. You must believe me when I say they looked peaceful! John Lafferty carried them out. He can tell you himself."

"You must promise me…you must never tell Court it was Ran who helped me! He must believe that Seamus brought me here in time, and it was you. Promise me that! She gripped Anne Marie's hand. "Do it for Court… not me. It would destroy him to know the truth."

"Lacey, the truth is best. He has the right to know."

"Hasn't he suffered enough for a hundred lifetimes? He'll blame himself for all of this. It will be worse than when he came back from the war."

"Am I to lie to your father as well?"

"You know how it is between them! Daddy will use it against him. Who is left to say otherwise? Ran is gone. You were barricaded in here. Everyone ran off to Torrey Castle. Sophie didn't get here till hours later."

"What about poor Seamus?"

"If the stroke doesn't finish him off, a broken heart will." She was fading away to that lovely place of blissful quiescence. "Court has no one but us now. We must be…everything to him. Promise me. I'm begging you."

"I promise, Lacey." Anne Marie would not have her one, true friend suffering more than what was his to bear. Did the truth matter all that much when they were drowning in loss and heartache?

Anne Marie's feet swung ungracefully in the air as Anthony impressed upon her how much he had missed her. Spectacles askew, she gasped, "We mustn't, not here!"

"Who the hell's around to be scandalized?"

She tensed and he dropped her with a deliberate thump as the teasing glimmer in his eyes vanished. They had been apart for weeks, the first separation of their marriage, and all she cared about was propriety.

"Would you like a drink?"

Sprawled in his favorite armchair, he accepted the peace offering, allowing her to smooth his hair and straighten his collar.

"What a relief to have you home after all you've been through!"

With surprising finesse, he swung her around and onto his lap. "I was out of my mind with worry. You, here all alone, surrounded by that murderous scum."

"Not alone. Your men were most capable. I felt quite safe." She snatched the glass and leaped up.

"You're deluding yourself! Were they safe in Torrey Castle? Thank God for old Seamus. Thank God you were here for Lacey."

"I did what I had to do."

"How is Seamus? I must look in on him."

"Dr. Sykes won't allow it! Even Birdy hasn't seen him." She kissed his cheek, handed him the glass, and stepped beyond his long reach.

"Why are you being so damn skittish?" Instantly, he regretted the question. She had a right to be. "Dearest, I want you close to me." He beckoned to her.

"Anthony, you mustn't worry about me! I'm made of strong stuff. Please tell me all the news. None of your letters have gotten through."

"The writing's on the wall…in blood. The British are pitting Collins against de Valera with a treaty proposal. The first to take it, will be denounced by the other. A civil war will surely follow."

"Isn't some kind of compromise better than more fighting… more dying?"

A disgusted grunt was his response, followed by a huff of dismay with her sudden interest in a bowl of roses.

Anthony's wincing scrutiny was making her susceptible to revealing what he must never know. She caressed the fallen petals, laying them one on top of the other in her hand, recalling when Devlin presented her with the silver bowl as a wedding present.

"'Tis an old and dear thing I'm bestowing upon you. My darlin' wife always kept it overflowing with roses…only roses. I grew them and she enjoyed them."

Dear Devlin, dear Aggie. How could they be dead? The crimson petals drifted to the floor. "Why? Why did they have to die? It's all so senseless! So cruel!"

This time when Anthony embraced her, she clung to him."He's lost so much. How will he go on?"

"Anne Marie, his past life is buried under a foot of ash and rubble! What he can hold in his arms…Lacey… his son… should be all he needs! We'll bury the dead and get the hell out of here."

"What are you talking about?" The bitter nonchalance of his words restored her composure.

"None of this matters anymore! Courtland must leave. That was part of the agreement. They must leave, and soon. We'll follow in the spring."

"I won't leave my baby!" She wrenched herself away and when he tried to hold on, struck his arm with both fists.

"I anticipated that. William will be reinterred in our family cemetery in Millbrook."

"You decided, all by yourself, how it's to be?"

"Do you prefer living here under a state of siege? For God knows how long?"

"I'm your wife! Not a child to be led around. You always think you know what's best for me!"

"I do know! That's why you married me."

Anthony descended upon her like a bird of prey—swooping her up, smothering her outrage with kisses and extracting at last, what he had waited impatiently for—absolute surrender.

Lacey had been dreaming of this for so long—the heat of his cheek against her breast —the weight of him, so fretfully slight, wrapped in her arms. Hours had passed, and he remained asleep as the room took on dusk's misty serenity.

"Sleep, my darlin'. Sleep it all away."

The beauty of the moment could not be preserved, not when there was a fervent adherent to the feeding schedule, looming in the doorway.

"Time for baby to nurse."

"Is he fussing?"

"Not quite. Your father is amusing him but you know what's on his mind."

This elicited a rather unmotherly response. "Wait till he cries for a bit then bring him in." She didn't like being tethered this way.

Court jerked awake. "Lacey! Are you real?"

"Quite real." She kissed him several times and resettled him against her.

"We have a son," he murmured.

She needed him strong again and would do as before. This would be the last time that he would be subjected to torment and persecution, no matter how noble the cause.

"A fine and healthy son…Devlin Padraic O'Rourke."

The unrelenting February wind thrashed through the charred womb of Torrey Castle. One turret, scourged by smoke and flame, slumped against the pewter sky. The swath of fire had consumed the west wing and rear parks, tunneling well into the orchards.

All had been arranged. A caretaker hired to oversee the property and collect the rents. The iron gates wrapped with two sets of chains to repel the scavenger and the morbid. Twenty thoroughbreds auctioned off, except for Drummer and Paladin, who retired with John Lafferty to a farm in Skibbereen. The town house in Gramercy Park and the farm in Millbrook made ready for the exiles, who would have a choice between city and country or both, if they so desired. Passage booked to Mallorca via Galway. Lacey thought that a return to a happy place was what Court needed to regain his strength and prepare for their new life.

Flurry, the disgraceful scamp, whirled through the graveyard as Sophie pursued with leash and invective. While the headstones still waited to be engraved, the inscriptions had been composed and the dead buried.

"This is how it ends," Court said with angry resignation. "How many stories, whether of love or hate, remain unfinished and lost under six feet of earth?"

These words exacerbated the stealthy gloom of mourning that followed Lacey from waking to sleeping. She stretched her imagination to think of something positive, even joyous. "How sweet that Devlin lies between them. I think Colleen understands."

"Ah well, 'tis only fitting. Though I'm sure, many a one is speculating." He glanced over at Sophie kneeling between Padraic and Fiona's graves.

"Thanks to our holy mother of the wagging tongue!"

"Father Ryan promised to plant bulbs in the spring and fall, and dear Birdy will see there's always something blooming."

"Bless them both. Grandfather will be pleased."

"And when we come back, we can plant some rose bushes and a few…"

"Lacey, there's no coming back! Not ever!"

Though there was very little that she could be certain of these days, there was one constant: nothing stays the same. And because of this, she had renewed her belief in the light of the soul—the light of possibility warming from within. If this didn't exist, on some metaphysical level, then she wouldn't exist. So it followed that there would be a time when Ireland would be free of British rule and they would return.

"Wherever we are, as long as we're together, we'll be home."

She slipped her arm through his, peeking at the sleeping infant sheltered in his coat and drew Court's gaze back to her. When had it not been just the two of them? Two lambent bodies spinning in the same orbit.

"I love you, my lamb." He pulled her tight against him, fortifying himself with the heat of a kiss. The intensity of it startled baby Dev, who emitted one of his signature howls.

"'Tis best the lad gets accustomed to such amorous displays." He dropped a quick kiss on his son's wrinkled brow. "Christ! Will you look at him glowering away at me? The very image of your father!"

Alas, as each day passed, Devlin Padraic O'Rourke, looked more and more like Anthony. "Is this some kind of divine irony? A throwback for a son? Have I not suffered enough?"

Here was a flicker of the old Court. A reminder of his swift indignation and sarcasm. It was hers to coax back.

"Pish! What if he does look like daddy? I'll wager he'll grow to match you in mood and temper! Then, who will be doing all the suffering? When I think of how unbearably pompous you were as a boy, I shudder, picturing what my life will be like!"

"And what about you, madam? Was there ever a child more prone to mischief and mayhem? He could very well take after you!"

Their sparring intensified along with the mauve shadows sweeping the graveyard. This unseemly bickering among the dead may seem rather odd to some, but after all, this was Ireland.

About The Author

Elizabeth J. Sparrow is a native New Yorker and a graduate of Hunter College and New York University. She is working diligently on the sequel to *The Irish Tempest*. She can be contacted at elizjsparrow@gmail.com. Please visit her at www.elizajsparrow.com for the latest updates.

www.ingramcontent.com/pod-product-compliance
Lightning Source LLC
Chambersburg PA
CBHW020957120726
47905CB00009B/2737